The Space Between Dreaming

ALSO BY CHERIE BURBACH

Nonfiction

Painting the Psalms
Art and Faith: Mixed Media Art With a Faith-Filled
Message
…and more

Poetry

Belonging
Poiema
Angel Toughness
My Soul Is From a Different Place
Father's Eyes
The Difference Now
A New Dish
New and Selected Poems
Yes, You

The Space Between Dreaming

A novel

CHERIE BURBACH

CONTENTS

PROLOGUE

What I felt was peace, like a child sitting snugly in her mother's arms. The feeling of safety. Of careful handling. The brushstrokes eased over me, flowing back and forth, until my eyes were opened. And suddenly, with varnish and paint smell all around, I felt very much aware. Awake.

It was only then that I saw him, my painter. He stepped back from his easel, the brush poised to add another piece, another line, reaching out to me like a father sweetly kissing good night on the cheek of his daughter as she drifted off to sleep.

He wanted to add more color, the bright blues in contrast to the dark room and stuffy wooden dressers that flanked the girl he painted. I became her, every inch of the bed where she slept, every hair painted on her head, and the look of confusion and anguish as she reached out into the darkness.

I felt his grief, the ache that tore his heart apart, the sadness that pulled him from one moment to the next, not wanting to give in to the depths of despair and yet not able to acknowledge his future. He wanted to move forward but couldn't bring himself to tell her that his heart had healed, that he was ready to accept their life as it was. His paintbrush told me everything that he couldn't say to another soul.

I'd seen him pace for days before me, my blank canvas an invitation to create, to be wild, to think beyond the moment, and make up a new story. I'd felt his shame, his confusion, and finally, the resolve that he must face the truth. It was then that he stopped pacing and looking at me for answers and, finally, created answers of his own.

The light from the window shone on me, warming my surface and making me the one thing in the room that the painter could not ignore. He'd slept there in the past; after each heartache he'd spend days pacing and crying and shouting out to God, while she did the same in another room.

But this time, it was different. He didn't ask God why but just released his anger to him instead.

I tried to whisper to him, comfort him, but I wasn't finished yet. I needed him to find his soul before I could come alive. We needed each other, and so it is with a creator and the object that forms from his hands.

He stayed up all night working on me until sleep took the paintbrush from his hand and gently set him down on the couch in his studio. He dreamed darkly, tossing angrily until finally, he relaxed, allowing his dreams to take him where they may. I could see his mouth release the frown that held his smile captive and witnessed his mind go to happy places filled with possibilities.

He had fought against the bright dreams that could bring him joy, not just this night but for the years they had continued trying. The two of them a special kind of army that simply wanted to share their love with another little person. Twenty years later, goodness had worn him down, and when he awoke, he looked relieved that I was still there waiting for him. I could read his thoughts, of what he had planned to add, layer by layer, to move me from blank canvas to masterpiece. Even then, I knew what it was I would become.

He moved the small table where he kept his paints nearer to where I stood, alone on his easel, and looked over my canvas with a new vision. He added the base, a mix of dark brown with shades of orange. Darkness that hinted at the light. The bed came next, a lighter wood that stood out against the night colors with a brilliant blue cover, shocking in its vibrancy, to protect the girl against her own dreams, the dark spirits that threatened to pull her out of this world.

Her red-gold hair and flowing curls softened the hard look of her face. She was sitting up, under the covers, looking out into her room, past the dressers that flanked the bed to the window outside. Was she seeing a nighttime visitor who had come into her room? A ghost that haunted her from the past? The painter asked these questions as he worked, dipping his brush into the mineral spirits and wiping it down with the old rag that had once been a pillowcase they'd bought for an unnamed, unformed soul they expected to share their life with in the years to come. He tore it into pieces the night before last, angry and desperate for answers. The pillow inside remained bare, stuffed in the corner of the room where he punched it each time he sat down to rest, a break from pouring his emotions out onto the canvas.

In six hours, he had the background completed, the bed where the girl sat upright under the blue cover, and the beginning of the darkness that would be her undoing. He took a break then, filling a cup with water and drinking it down without stopping, then doing the same with a second cup. He was thirsty for relief and answers, and he needed a clear head before continuing.

The painter left me to dry, opening the small window so a gentle breeze would help with the fumes and drying, solidifying my colors and the outline that would become his greatest work. With a last glance at me, he left. I knew he was walking down the hall to comfort his wife, to hold her close, and try and ease her grief.

But this time, he would stand again and walk back to his painting room a different man. The path to healing had begun, slowly but gently, and now he would return with a new sense of purpose.

He worked on me for three days, waiting for layers to dry, pacing before me slowly this time, not with desperation but with patience. He knew he was doing something that was now bigger than himself, something that would reach into his heart and steal the dark memories away. He knew I was part of his healing. There were times when he painted with hurried assurance and other times when he tentatively stepped back, allowing the universe to move his brush where it needed to go. He had calmed enough to listen to what God was telling him and in doing so accepted the gift of his greatest work.

He called me The Space Between Dreaming.

CHAPTER 1 - GRACE

Grace sat on the bed with her laptop open in front of her. She was editing a children's book about overcoming disappointment. It was cheerful, and light, and she wondered how the illustrator would convey these elements through the imagery. It was fascinating to her how kids' books came together. First, a writer with an idea, then, an artist brings that idea visually to a page. What a wonderful combination.

She'd grown to adore children's books now, much more, she thought, than she ever had as a child. She loved the vibrant colors and the way even the heaviest of subjects could somehow be dealt with in a way that addressed them with hope and not defeatism. Although she supposed, the heaviest of subjects were perhaps saved for adulthood. Maybe that was why.

But no, she realized, her childhood hadn't exactly been light. She hated the sweet stories that kids' books offered her as a child. They were different then and had made her feel left out somehow, reminding her that she had been unwanted and still felt as if she had no real place in the world.

She wondered if anyone would want to read a kids' book about an unwanted child who then grew up to be, somehow, an unwanted adult. She felt the tears well up in her eyes again, the now familiar occurrence of late, and quickly wiped them away with a ragged tissue she had dug out of her pocket. She looked at it and cringed at how long it must have been in her pocket. When was the last time she'd worn these jeans? And then she remembered, putting her hand instinctively on her belly.

No. She shook her head. She must not let herself worry. The past was the past. Just because the babies would not stay in her body before did not mean they would not now. No, this time, it'd be different.

She shook loose the thought of tragedy and put the laptop she'd been staring at on the coffee table beside her. She got up from the couch, tossed the tissue in the kitchen trash, and had a sudden flashback from several years before of John tossing a pregnancy test strip in the very same trash can. How they'd stood at the counter watching the clock, watching the time tick down until they were told whether they were pregnant or not, and for what seemed like the millionth time, having the pang of disappointment descend upon them like a thundercloud, making them shiver as if they'd been caught out in the worst of rainstorms without shelter. They'd clung to one another, trying to protect the other from the rainfall of disappointment, but every time they realized a third soul would not join them the entire house seemed to dim for days or weeks or months after.

At every negative test result, she felt unwanted again. Not from John, just the opposite. He seemed to think her more beautiful as each day came, and for the life of her, she couldn't figure out what he was looking at. The unwanted feeling of her childhood met at the secret place in her heart where she had stored her hope, and it taunted her again. Instead of her parents not wanting her, this time the world somehow did not wish her to be a mother.

She'd noticed a change in John after the last miscarriage. He refused to let her think she was anything other than special, and he encouraged her, but he didn't talk about a future with children any longer. As they both drifted quietly into their forties, he seemed content in their life together. Children would have been a bonus, he'd said, but there was nothing he would change about their life.

Why couldn't Grace accept it as easily? She wanted a child of her own. Growing up in foster care gave her a fear of hope. Each time she would get close to being adopted by her foster parents, her mother would come around, talking about her rights and about how Grace was her child and no one else's. The problem was, her mother went right back to drugs and men as soon as she'd get Grace back. Grace would go back into the system, and the whole process would start again.

Somehow, she couldn't handle the possibility of being a foster mother and loving a child and wanting to adopt that child and then not being able to. She couldn't dangle that kind of hope in front of a child, and she wasn't brave enough to forge ahead with confidence that it would be any different.

But she had been cautiously optimistic this time about her pregnancy. She had entered the fifth month, which was farther than she had made it before. She had allowed herself to think of the child this baby might become. Each time, she imagined a boy. She saw John's unruly hair and her eyes. They even talked about names casually, and Grace caught herself saying "Glenn's room," already picturing a little boy with that shrug and smirk that John always gave her in the face of a boy who was a combination of the two of them. She felt hope for the first time in a long time.

She could tell John was trying to be positive on her behalf. He even agreed to paint the extra room a robin's-egg blue, as Grace requested. What each pregnancy had done to her body and emotions had seemed to hit him harder than it did her. Or perhaps he was the mirror to everything she was feeling. Marriage was like that, she supposed. Each one reflected the other, either positively or negatively. Each showed the other what they looked like, sounded like, and how they came off to the world.

John seemed to adore her, which made her wonder if she was as great as he made her feel or if this was just the benefit of a good and happy marriage. She was not used to people in her life treating her as if she was special. Growing up, in the homes that weren't so bad, she would be treated as a nice enough girl who was easy to be around, and that's how she'd always thought of herself, before John.

Her mother had essentially disowned her. Grace had sent a note to her when she graduated high school but never heard back. When Grace graduated college, she tried again, sending one note and then another as they kept coming back undeliverable. Finally, she was able to find her mother's current address, and she sent one more note asking her to call.

Instead, she got a text that said, "I'm fine, Grace. I wish you the best."

Looking back, the text was meant to tell Grace that her mother had written her off, but she couldn't accept it at the time. She couldn't believe that her mother would refuse to raise her, refuse to allow someone else to adopt her, and yet also refuse to have a relationship with her. She clung to the idea that her mother would one day just embrace her and be interested in her life.

She had responded to her mother's text by saying, "I would really like to see you. I won't take up much of your time," hating that it sounded like she was making a sales pitch.

Reluctantly, her mother agreed, and they met at a greasy spoon in a suburb of Milwaukee. Grace had only been out of college for a few years. She'd been working long hours at a marketing firm, had no serious relationships to speak of, no close friends, and, since her grandmother had passed away, no family. She felt as if her life was in limbo. The morning she got ready to meet her mother, she changed her outfit twice and, for the first time in a while, thought about her appearance. She wanted to look nice for her mother, she realized. She wanted to make her mother see that she was worthy of love. Even if she hadn't felt it, she wanted her mother to see that in her.

What she remembered of her mother was that she was thin and often wore tight jeans and a T-shirt of some sort. Her mother had the same reddish-brown hair and green eyes that she did, and as Grace scanned the restaurant, she tried picturing an older version of that, still with the same features and body but, basically, similar to what she could call up from her childhood memories.

She glanced at a woman who was scowling at her. The woman was heavyset, with a flowing, red and yellow muumuu. Her gray hair was cropped short, emphasizing her puffy face. Grace saw her and continued scanning the place for her mother, and it wasn't until the woman turned on her heel and marched off to a table that she realized it was, in fact, her mother. She had the same stomping walk she'd had when Grace was a child. She'd remembered that stomp very well. It usually preceded a slap across the face.

Without a word, she followed her to the table, watching the fat rolls jiggle on the woman's behind. Her change in appearance shocked Grace, but it had been fifteen years since she'd seen her, and she knew those were not easy years for either of them.

Her mother had slid into the booth already, and Grace debated leaning over to hug her, but her body language told her she just wasn't open to that. Instead, she slid into the other side of the booth. Her mother looked at her appraisingly.

"Well," she said with a sneer, "you cleaned up nice." Grace caught a slur in her words and noted with disappointment that her mother was tipsy.

"Thanks," she said. "I didn't recognize you at first. It's been a while, I guess." She smiled, wanting to reach her hand across the table and just break this woman's hard exterior. She'd forgotten how icy her mother could be when she wanted.

"Oh," she laughed nastily, "you think you're better than me because you're younger? I used to be pretty, too. You'll age. You'll see."

"I didn't mean that at all." *Mom*, she wanted to say. I didn't mean that, *Mom*. Can you just be kind, *Mom*? Can you smile at me, and tell me you love me, *Mom*? "I'm glad you decided to meet me. I've missed you," she said automatically, and wondered if it were true. She had missed having a mother; she just didn't know if it was the mother she'd been born to.

As her mother scowled at her now, Grace silently wondered why her mother seemed to hate her.

"Well,"—her mother picked up her drink, which Grace

noted was some kind of alcoholic mixture she could smell from across the table—"you were persistent." She drank the same way she always did, a hunger that sucked at the ice in the glass and made Grace shiver. She remembered the noise of ice clinking against a drinking glass as one of her least favorite sounds from childhood.

Grace had seen alcoholism affect families in her years as a foster child. She had been in a couple of foster families where the drinking with one of the parents was lighthearted but concerning. The person drank too much and genuinely wanted to quit, but couldn't seem to. For other families, the person was held hostage by the booze, and in those cases, the family seemed to fall into negative patterns right along with them.

She'd also talked to therapists while growing up, about her mother and her drinking. She was thankful for one of her foster families, in particular, who recognized Grace's pattern of just wanting to be a "good girl" to make everything perfect and had sent her to someone who understood the challenges of being outside a real family and dealing with an alcoholic parent. The therapist talked about boundaries, how Grace didn't need to work so hard to be loved, and how her mother had a disease that might never allow her to be a real mom until she decided to work on her drinking. Grace remembered the therapist saying that she could never help her mother quit drinking by "being good" because if that were the case, she would have done it already. This, the therapist stressed, was a little girl's belief that Grace needed to overcome to be a successful adult.

And yet, here she sat in front of a mother, who she once again chased down, once again begged to get love from.

"Mom," Grace said, "do you love me?"

"What a stupid question." She rolled her eyes. "I'm your

mother. And you know what? Not everything is about you. I don't want to hear about your childhood. Is that why you brought me here?"

Grace shivered at the sound of her mother's voice, haughty and slurring.

"I didn't bring you here," she countered. "I asked you to come. I don't understand why you act as if you hate me."

Her mother downed the last of her drink and waved her arm in the air wildly for another. The fat on her arm shook like a flag being waved in surrender. The waitress came right away with a replacement.

"Ready to order?" She smiled at them.

"Not quite," Grace said. The waitress left quickly, and as she did, her mother downed the drink in three large gulps. One after another.

"You know"—her mother wiped her mouth—"they told me not to come and see you. You"—she pointed at Grace with her index finger, the glass still in her hand—"are a trigger for me." She had slurred the word trigger, and Grace found herself swallowing hard. She braced herself for anything when it came to her mother, including nasty words followed by a slap that would send her to the floor.

Grace wondered who her mother meant by "they." Maybe it was her friends. Maybe it was a support group. Maybe it was just the people at the bar she liked to hang out with. Or maybe, she thought with sadness, it was a new family, complete with replacement children.

Grace remembered the last thing her therapist had told her and found her voice. "I love you, Mom."

She waited, but her mother did not say it back.

"I love you, even though you don't love me," Grace said calmly and not accusatory. The therapist had told her that forgiveness would set her free, and she didn't realize how true that statement was until this moment.

"I didn't say that," her mother sneered, and Grace remembered how much her mother always enjoyed being cruel. She'd accuse Grace of something, and Grace would apologize to her over and over, begging her mom to forgive her, and all the while her mother would act hurt as if Grace were the problem, as if Grace were the adult. Now, Grace realized, she was the adult.

"I love you," she said again, sliding out of the booth and placing enough money on the table for what she thought would cover the cost of her mother's drinks, "and I forgive you. You have my number if you would like to contact me, Mom. But not with the booze."

As Grace left the restaurant, she heard her mother shout, "If I have to choose booze or my daughter, I'll happily choose booze!"

Grace had not heard from her mother since that day, twenty years before. While she had longed to follow up many times, she knew it would not help. If she hadn't convinced her mother that she was worthy of love by now, she never would.

She had hoped that when she got married, she could finally be a part of a family. But John's parents had already died years before when she had met him, and he wasn't close to his extended family. She knew from the experience with her mother that if people didn't love you enough to respect you, or want a genuine relationship, there was nothing you could do to convince them. The way someone treated you was often more an indication of their own character than anything else.

She shook loose the thought from her mind, trying to clear it out as she'd seen one of her foster mother's do with the laundry. Grace remembered the woman shaking out a wet shirt with a snap and quickly placing it on the line to dry outside, airing their laundry for anyone to see and not caring about who commented on what. She hung it out, nodded hello to whoever happened to be passing by, walked back in the house, and went about her business. Her approach to everything, from the wash to the way she could manage the schedules of the four foster children, had always impressed Grace.

She looked out their bedroom window at the vibrant green of the trees. She adored the changing seasons Wisconsin offered. How beautiful life could be when change brought something new. The trees could show us that letting go of the way you thought life would always be could bring an unexpected yet pleasant gift in its place.

Grace took two steps outside and stopped, closing her eyes to the bright summer sun on her face. She opened her eyes, reached into the mailbox, and noted a thick envelope and some junk mail. She felt the edges of the envelope as she walked back indoors, thinking there seemed to be a book inside. A book she had edited? A publisher giving her an advanced copy?

She tossed the junk mail directly in the trash and opened the envelope. There was a letter of some sort. Two handwritten pages, front and back. The book's title said something about learning to be a better person. She frowned, looking at the envelope again. She didn't recognize the sender or the return address. She read the note, scrawled in blue ink on notebook paper.

Hello Grace,

I'm sending you the obituary notice for your mother. She died several weeks ago and was buried next to your grandmother.

I have been wanting to write you for a long time, even before your mother passed away. When she died, that was my sign to finally contact you. For years now, everywhere I turned, I saw signs that I should write. Each time I turned around, Grace Grace Grace.

There are many reasons why I am writing. I have known your mother for a long time, longer than you ever did. She was so disappointed that you didn't seem to want her in your life, and if you don't mind my saying, it is incredibly selfish. She was your MOTHER. You only have one, and now it is too late for you. It is a special relationship, and you gave her nothing but grief growing up and then blamed her for your lousy life after you became an adult. How dare you? Do you even know what a wonderfully sweet, loving, attentive, imaginative, creative, and sensitive lady she was? Do you even know what a kind and loving mother you had? And now, you will never know. I hope that pain causes you to rethink your life and your choices.

And to withhold your children from seeing their grandmother, for shame!

Sincerely,
Susan Butterfield

P.S. If you ever want to chat with me about your mother, I am open to that.

Her mother was dead? She told people that Grace didn't want her in her life? That she was withholding grandchildren? Grace knew, with everything she had, that if this woman, this Susan Butterfield, believed that, then it was because her mother was drinking and telling lies. So, her mother had assumed Grace must have kids by now. She assumed Grace was fine and didn't want to see her, even after she had shouted in a restaurant that booze was her first choice.

Grace had not ended the relationship, as Susan Butterfield believed. She had not been a kid that gave her mother "grief." She was a kid who just wanted to be loved.

No, her mother had ended the relationship. She had ended it when she refused to stop drinking, when she hit Grace so frequently that someone at school had called social services. She ended it when she "wished Grace the best" in a text and when she made Grace beg to see her. She ended it in that restaurant, and she ended it by never, not once, trying to contact Grace in the twenty years since she'd last seen her.

And worse, Grace thought, she terminated the relationship every time she stepped forward to refuse to allow someone else to adopt Grace.

Grace read the letter again, so shocked that someone would be this ignorant and arrogant to send something like this. Even if Susan Butterfield felt she knew the situation, even if she had listened to her mother rage on and on for years, how did that qualify this woman to write such filth and deliver it to Grace?

And oh, by the way, Grace thought as she paced, here's an obituary. Your mother is dead.

Your mother is dead.

Grace knew that everything Susan Butterfield believed were lies, spewed from her mother's mouth. The lies were the start of why she lost Grace all those years before. She hit Grace and knocked her down, and when Grace got a black eye, she told the school her daughter was just clumsy. When an event at school needed a parent, she told Grace she would be there for her, and never was. When Grace's school started calling the social workers about Grace's injuries, she promised she would go to a rehab center to quit drinking so she could get her daughter back, and didn't.

When she drank, she lied. And obviously, she was lying about Grace.

She stopped pacing and read the obituary.

Katherine Langley passed lovingly from this world to the next on April 1st. She was born and raised in Milwaukee and loved the summer festivals, especially the ones where she could dance on a picnic table and enjoy free music. She enjoyed any event where she could meet new people, and all who knew her were inspired by her laugh, her sense of humor, and the kind way she sat and listened to each soul in need.

She was truly a remarkable woman who deserved better than she got in life, and she will be missed.

Grace read it once, then again. What an odd obituary, she thought. No cause of death and not much about her life. No mention of relationships. No mention of Grace. It was as if Grace mattered so little, no one even thought to acknowledge her.

She wondered if Susan Butterfield, whoever she was, wrote the obituary. It seemed like a possibility. She wondered why, if the woman knew who Grace was all this time, why she didn't get a call when her mother was sick or dying, or had just died, instead of sending this letter and notice weeks after. Did her mother know where to reach her? Or did Susan Butterfield do some digging to find Grace and send this letter?

And who would send a missive like this, filled with incorrect assumptions, and then end it with a desire to "talk" if Grace wished? Why didn't the woman just call Grace and talk? Why didn't she try to have a real conversation, instead of sending a nasty letter by way of introduction, then thinking she and Grace would have lots to discuss after that?

The more Grace thought about the letter, the angrier she became. For this woman to try and shame her, to make such terrible assumptions… it made her wonder if the woman had influenced her mother in not contacting Grace sooner. She imagined her mother spouting these lies about Grace, and Susan Butterfield piling on the negativity.

There could have been a way for this Susan to support her mother and be a friend, to listen but try and encourage her mother to look at it from Grace's perspective: as a child who was rejected by her mother. She could have said, "Imagine the pain Grace has had to live with," but no, this woman must have enjoyed being the negative friend who would add fuel to the fire, with anger and hate, thinking she was some kind of hero to Grace's mother, meanwhile making it worse.

But obviously, her mother had created this. All of it. This woman knew of Grace but had gotten the specifics of the relationship entirely wrong. Why was she chiding Grace when her mother had been the one to hit her and fail to pick her up at school? She had abused Grace and lost her, and no matter what, didn't seem to want to do what was necessary to get her back. And worse, every time she had the chance to be adopted by a foster parent, her mother would decide to step in, and Grace would go back to the endless wandering, the space where dreams can grow but never become reality.

Her mother had been absent. She and John had been alone all these years. Their lives had been about trying for a baby, trying to figure out this great mystery of married life, and trying to keep their sanity each time their hopes for a family vanished from her body. And they'd done it all without the support of family. They'd been alone, and she felt that loneliness very strongly now. Her legs felt weak and started to shake.

She sat on the chair by the door, still gripping the letter. Who was this woman? Why was she writing these hateful things, and perhaps most puzzling, why did she think it was okay to do this?

Grace pored over the words, the things her mother had said the last time they'd spoken: the slaps, the drunken rages, and then losing her. Being told about her this way with a nasty letter and a book, was too much. The stress of it all, this lifetime of not feeling wanted for doing nothing more than being born, it all weighed heavily upon Grace. She felt like she couldn't breathe.

This letter was the final seal on the envelope of hope she had foolishly kept open all this time, tucking in best wishes and good thoughts as if one day she could take them all out and show the world that she was worthy of love. That her mother had been wrong. What a fool she'd been. She felt sick then. She felt the hopes that had buoyed her descend on her like a thick fog. Tears formed quietly in her eyes, and her heart seemed to physically ache. The letter fell to the floor, along with the blood that gushed from her body, taunting her, letting her know that once more she wasn't going to be a mother.

CHAPTER 2 - JANE

Jane McDonald lingered after the staff meeting and walked alongside her boss as he went back to his office.

"So"—she tried to be nonchalant—"tomorrow is my tenth anniversary with the gallery."

She expected to be ignored, but he turned to her.

"Really? That's quite an achievement."

Her boss, Vince Washington, had asked the staff to call him "Bug". He explained during a staff meeting that he'd been given the nickname "VW" by his high school friends, and then it got shortened to Bug by his college pals. The name stuck, and he asked each of his employees to address him that way. After a few awkward starts—"Uh… Mr. … Bug?"—Jane finally embraced his request.

Bug paused for a moment in thought. "I think ten years might be the record with my staff."

Jane thought of the other long-term employees and knew instantly that wasn't correct. Henry had been there at least twice as long. Donna had passed her decade a few years back.

"You know what?" he continued. "Come on into my office. I think we need to talk about your future."

He gestured for her to sit in his office and dug through a file in his cabinet. His leftover salad from lunch was sitting on the table, and Jane turned her nose up at the aroma of wilted lettuce and warm ranch dressing, combined with garlic croutons. There was a plastic fork left in the container, and as Bug searched through the file, he pulled it out and picked his teeth with it. A small piece of what looked to be green pepper flew from his mouth to the file below. Bug flicked it off as if it were nothing. It landed on the floor near Jane's foot.

"Yes, here it is." He tapped the employment application and cover letter. "Ten years." He glanced at a few things in the file, then turned to her. "You know"—he pointed the fork at her—"I've been thinking about honoring the staff in a new way. Maybe even hire a few people. The morale around here…" Bug let the sentence hang as he shook his head. "Well, needless to say, people aren't happy."

Bug tapped the fork on the table while he thought, the tines that had just pulled the rogue pepper from his mouth now touched Jane's file.

"Jane, I want to transform this gallery space into one of peace, harmony, and happiness." He stared at her, and she stared back, frozen in her chair, unable to figure out how to reply. "Mostly happiness." He shrugged, putting away her file. "And I'm going to start with you." He twirled the plastic fork in his hand, then ran it through his salt-and-pepper hair like a comb. "In honor of your tenth anniversary, I'm going to do something very special for you."

What could she say? That she didn't believe him? That whatever he was doing with his fork was making her want to laugh and puke at the same time?

No, what she wanted to say was that he promised that kind of stuff all the time. She wanted to flick off these words like the piece of green pepper Bug had relegated to the floor. But the truth was, she did believe him. At least, she desperately wanted to.

Jane waited for Bug to elaborate on just how he would "start with her" to transform the gallery into a place of happiness. He seemed lost in thought for a moment, and then his phone rang. He looked through the bottom of his bifocals and spotted the caller ID.

"My wife. Better take this."

He ushered her out of his office with a wave of his hand, letting the plastic fork fall to the floor. She turned and headed back to her office, and as she did, Jane felt something she hadn't felt in a long time: joy. She wrapped herself in that feeling as if it were a favorite blanket that had just come out of the dryer, and held on to it all night.

The next morning, she rose early so she'd have time to say hello to her landlady, Mrs. Ferch, before she left for work. But her neighbor Eric Kincaid's voice, which she could hear even from her apartment upstairs, was distracting her. Jane could hear Eric telling a story that made their eighty-year-old landlady giggle. Their laughter floated right up through the vents. One more reason for her to take extra time getting ready today.

Jane put on her new gray skirt, sensible gray heels with a light-pink stripe on the side, and the light-pink blouse that always made her feel professional but pretty. She didn't have near enough days where she felt that way.

She gazed at her reflection in the mirror and frowned. Her father's note asking her for money was tucked in the space between the mirror and frame, taunting her. She didn't want to disappoint him, but she didn't make enough to keep giving him money, either. Her father created inventions he thought would make the family rich, but none of them ever made them a dime, and in the meantime, he didn't bring any income in. This had been the third time her father had asked her for money, and each time, the request got larger and larger. She knew she should say no. That's what Jane's sister, Charlotte, told her to do.

Jane looked again at her reflection, tilting her head at the honey-blonde hair that hung to her shoulders. Her blue eyes looked pale to her, even as she tried to put mascara on them to help them stand out. She didn't wear makeup very often; maybe that was the problem.

After a final glance in the mirror, Jane twisted her hair up in a clip and grabbed her purse, work bag, and keys. As she turned into the hallway to knock on Mrs. Ferch's door, she saw Eric chatting with the older woman in the hallway. Jane held back, not wanting to make conversation with Eric. He was certainly cute, but she was dating Brad. One day she and Brad would be married. At least, that's what she thought would probably happen.

Jane noticed Eric had on his trademark flannel shirt and jeans. At least Brad had a good job. She couldn't help thinking that Eric was probably just a slacker, like her dad. She didn't need another a guy like that in her life. Jane had made her mind up from the start that she wasn't going to be interested in someone who didn't believe in the power of work. She'd had enough of that with her dad, and if Eric, who seemed to just hang around all day and night, was that type of guy, she'd do her best to steer clear of him. Even if he did fill out his jeans rather nicely.

She watched from around the corner at the way Mrs. Ferch laughed at the things Eric said. She watched Eric's dark, curly hair bounce when he laughed along with Mrs. Ferch, and she supposed it was sweet that he took the time to chat with their elderly landlady. Still, Jane thought, he needed a haircut. And that red-and-gray flannel shirt he always wore was rather unflattering as well.

When Eric finally left, she walked down the hall and knocked on Mrs. Ferch's door.

"Come in," the older woman called from the kitchen.

"Morning," Jane said, trying to keep her voice down, in case Eric was outside lurking somewhere and could hear her. She spotted him out the window as he went to his car.

Mrs. Ferch followed her gaze. "That's Eric. Do you two ever talk? He's such a nice young man."

"I don't think we've met, no." And I don't want to, Jane thought to herself.

"Oh, pish, I think I've introduced you two, haven't I?" The older woman frowned and scratched at her white hair, looking at Jane for a long moment, and then shrugged. "Well, I'll have to do it next time I see you both together."

"That's okay." Jane sat in the kitchen chair that Mrs. Ferch offered. "I don't think we'd have much in common." Jane cringed at the snobbishness in her voice.

"Oh, but you're wrong, dear. I'm sure of it. You two would become great friends. Or"—the woman looked at Jane coyly—"maybe more."

"It's okay," Jane said to change the subject but then laughed as Mrs. Ferch continued the silly face she was making. It was hard to be irritated with Mrs. Ferch. The woman was just too good-hearted.

"Well, I hope you don't mind, I did tell him a little bit about you. Oh, and I mentioned you were single, so…"

Mrs. Ferch smiled with pride, but all Jane could feel was panic.

"You told him I was single?"

"Well, yes." Mrs. Ferch frowned. "Is that not correct?"

"No, I am dating Brad. Remember?"

"Yes," Mrs. Ferch said in a tone that was akin to having just tasted something rancid. "Brad." She paused a moment. "If you don't mind me saying so, dear, if you don't make a change, you will have 'She dated Brad' on your headstone."

Jane should have been taken aback, but Mrs. Ferch was never one to mince words. "And if I do mind you saying so?" She rolled her eyes, but Mrs. Ferch did have a point. It had been eight years now. She was almost thirty and was still assuming they'd get married one day.

The woman laughed. "Well, you and Eric could be friends, at least. You can never have too many of those. And who knows, maybe one day you and Brad will decide to go your separate ways." She held up a hand in protest at Jane's shock. "I'm just saying. Maybe. And if that ever happens, why not have a nice man ready for you to have some fun with? Hmmm?"

Jane loved Mrs. Ferch as if she were family, but there were times when her prodding became more harsh than gentle. She tried to think of a different subject, but before she could open her mouth, Mrs. Ferch continued.

"Oh, come on, now. He's cute; you're cute; he's single…"

"And I'm *not* single," Jane said again. "Besides, he wears those dumb flannel shirts all the time," she said irritably. "And he needs a haircut." She debated whether to mention his lack-of-employment status to Mrs. Ferch but stopped herself. She'd made her point clear enough: *not interested.*

"So, you *have* noticed him." Mrs. Ferch slapped her

hand on the table as if that proved everything.

Jane sighed. Maybe she hadn't made her point as well as she thought. "Let's change the subject."

"None of my business." The older woman nodded. "Got it."

She'd expected Mrs. Ferch to go on about it and felt a surge of disappointment that she was giving up so quickly. There was a part of Jane that wanted to be convinced, but maybe that was loneliness talking. Lately, she'd begun to feel as if her life had passed her by. It had been a long time since she and Brad had even been on a real date. They just stayed in most weekend nights at his place, each on their laptops browsing the internet.

Mrs. Ferch continued with a shift in topic. "So, what's on the agenda for today, dear?"

Jane put aside the thoughts of her romantic life and smiled to herself as she thought about her job. She'd gone over that conversation she'd had with Bug several times, and she hoped he would give her the assistant manager job she'd been after.

"I can see by that smile that it's good news." Mrs. Ferch smiled into her coffee and then asked the question Jane always dreaded hearing. "Maybe I was wrong in telling Eric you were single?"

"No, actually—"

"Oh, and before I forget. Have you seen my new coffeemaker? It's slick. Will you have a cup?"

Jane was used to these sudden changes in conversation with Mrs. Ferch. The older woman popped up and grabbed two mugs and a couple of coffee containers, and showed Jane how the machine worked.

"Sure." Jane had planned to go to the coffee shop, but she supposed she could have a cup with Mrs. Ferch and then just pick up a bagel on her way to work.

"See how it works? You pop it in, and look…" Mrs. Ferch pointed to the coffee that was quickly coming out the spout and landing in a coffee mug. "So fast. You can't even change your mind in the time it takes this thing to brew."

The coffee had finished, and Mrs. Ferch took the cup and set it down on the kitchen table with a satisfied smile. Jane sipped a delicious French vanilla cappuccino. "Coffee's good," she said.

"Yes," the older woman said, "and isn't it marvelous that you can make so many flavors? And so quickly!" Mrs. Ferch chuckled to herself, took another sip, and then set her cup down on the kitchen table. Her white hair was pulled back with barrettes, and her blue eyes stood out against her creamy-light skin. She still looked great, Jane thought, remembering at some point that Mrs. Ferch had told her she was in her eighties. She had a few wrinkles around her eyes and mouth, but even those seemed to make her more attractive. She supposed that living a full life had kept Mrs. Ferch young.

"Well, I do have something exciting to share," Jane continued, "although you might think it's dumb."

"Oh pish." The older woman swiped her hand through the air as if clearing the room of a bad smell. "I wouldn't think anything you do is dumb, my dear. You're a smart girl." She paused and then tapped the table gently with her index finger. "But it's okay if you don't want to tell me."

Jane hated to disappoint Mrs. Ferch. The older woman had become like a second mother to her, especially given the adversarial relationship she had with her mom. Mrs. Ferch cooked her meals and listened to her complain about work and the problems she'd had with her family, growing up. There was something about the woman that made Jane feel comfortable and loved. She wasn't used to that feeling, but she reveled in it.

She thought again about Eric standing in Mrs. Ferch's doorway earlier. Maybe he felt the same way about the older woman. She thought of his curly hair and flannel shirt again and reminded herself that she was dating someone.

"Do you think it's silly to still be dating Brad?" she asked Mrs. Ferch, surprising herself.

Mrs. Ferch didn't answer right away but instead looked at Jane with those kind eyes that always made her feel so accepted.

"I think you have stayed in that relationship for what you wish it was instead of what it actually is. Now"—the older woman glanced at the clock—"before you need leave for work, would you like to tell me your secret? You were smiling a minute ago at the thought of it."

Jane let go of the odd way Mrs. Ferch had answered her question about Brad, and decided to get back to the subject of her promotion. "Okay. About why I'm so happy. I think it's time I told someone about this. I've been holding it in." She paused, giving the announcement the weight she hoped would be worthy of her secret. "I think I'm about to be promoted."

Jane sat back and smiled. There.

If she expected Mrs. Ferch to be excited for her, she was disappointed.

"I see." She patted Jane's hand and sipped from her coffee mug.

Jane filled in the silence. "See, yesterday I made sure that Bug would know about my anniversary. It's been ten years. I mean, really, *ten years...* can you believe it?"

Mrs. Ferch nodded pleasantly but said nothing.

"What?" she finally asked. "You're not happy for me?" Her voice caught for a moment, reminding Jane of how much the woman's approval had begun to mean to her.

"Of course I am," Mrs. Ferch quickly assured her. "It's just that, I think you're too concerned with work. I don't see you having any fun, and someone your age needs to do that."

"I'm almost thirty, Mrs. Ferch. It's not like I go out partying anymore." Not like she ever did, but Jane didn't want to say that out loud. She was always concerned about work first. She supposed it was one reason she had not had a good, long think about Brad and their future, but now wasn't the time to underscore Mrs. Ferch's point.

"You've got a couple more months until you're thirty, but that's beside the point. You know, there is a very handsome young man in this building, and I don't even see you flirting with him. I don't even see you two talking. Now, maybe I forgot to introduce you two. But even so, you need to take it upon yourself, make an effort."

Jane was both disappointed that Mrs. Ferch was bringing up Eric again, and oddly excited. It had been too long since she could even daydream about a guy she liked. Still, her perception of Eric wasn't a good one.

"We don't talk," Jane admitted. She'd seen Eric around the building when he picked up his mail or sat in the backyard with a book, but she never saw him go to work. He was always dressed casually and never seemed to be in a hurry like she always was. "What does he do for a living?"

Mrs. Ferch tapped her chin with her index finger while she thought about it. "He's always on time with his rent. I'll tell you that much." Mrs. Ferch pointed at Jane to emphasize the statement. "He used to work a lot. All I know"—she lowered her voice as if sharing a juicy secret with Jane—"is that he's wonderful to have in the building. He does all my snow shoveling for me. I never even ask him; he just gets the shovel out and does it." She clapped her hands together as if she'd revealed the biggest detail of all.

With almost fifty inches of snow a year in Milwaukee, Jane could see why Mrs. Ferch thought Eric was so priceless. They all lived in a one-hundred-year-old house on Milwaukee's East Side, and snow shoveling was part of the territory. Now that she'd thought about it, her car had been scraped off the morning after the last blizzard they had. Jane wondered now if Eric had done that kindness for her. It never even occurred to her that he might. Jane's dad had not been good about shoveling, and she and her sister always had to do it before school so their mom would be able to get out of the driveway for work.

As if reading her thoughts, Mrs. Ferch continued. "Not every man is going to be like your father, dear."

Jane felt her eyes sting at the truth in those words.

Mrs. Ferch placed her hand on Jane's once again. "I'm sorry, dear. I didn't mean to upset you. I need to learn to keep my big mouth shut." She made the lock-and-key gesture across her mouth, tossing the imaginary key over her shoulder.

Jane chuckled at that. "You're right. Not every man will be like my dad, but I need someone that understands the importance of work. Brad does. That means a lot to me." And not continually ask me for money, she thought to herself. She wanted to help her father, but when would it end? She held her stomach, which had become more upset the longer she thought about her dad's request.

Mrs. Ferch studied her a long moment as if wanting to say more. Jane held her breath, wondering if she was going to go there, to the subject of her dad and her sister, Charlotte, and all the rest. She didn't need to get upset, and just wanted to get to work and see if she was getting the promotion she craved. No bad thoughts, please, she silently begged.

"Okay, let's change the subject. It's your ten-year anniversary at work. Is this... *Bug*... going to promote you? For sure?"

Jane realized then how big she'd made this possible promotion, in her mind. While she had been promised a promotion, it didn't mean Bug would follow through. Sitting before Mrs. Ferch as the voice of reality, the cold winds of truth were starting to come Jane's way. She shivered at the thought.

"I don't know if he's going to promote me for sure. He did seem"—she struggled for the right word—"*sincere* about it, for once. Actually, I just don't want to be disappointed." Jane looked at the clock, realizing she needed to go. She got up and hugged Mrs. Ferch. "I've got to go. I still want to stop at the coffee shop before I go in."

Mrs. Ferch stepped back from their hug. "For more coffee?"

"No," Jane said, picking up her purse, "for a bagel. My stomach is queasy. Plus, I like their cinnamon cream cheese."

Mrs. Ferch smiled knowingly. "It is good there. I wonder if I should pick some up so you'll have it here in the morning." She snapped her fingers before Jane could reply. "I'm going to do that. Now"—she put her hands on Jane's shoulders—"I want to tell you something. You're feeling good today, and that's the best time to introduce yourself to a man."

Jane blinked. "What?"

"I'm just thinking that Eric goes to that same coffee shop..."

Mrs. Ferch let the sentence drop and then wagged her eyebrows up and down so Jane could catch her meaning.

Jane rolled her eyes. "So, you want me to talk to him? Say hello?"

"Well, don't look too excited about it, dear." Mrs. Ferch giggled. "My, if youth isn't wasted on the young. Okay, now here's what you do. You walk up to him and just say good morning. Just introduce yourself."

"I don't know, Mrs. Ferch. He seems—"

"Just say hello. Flirt a little. Let him know you're a young, attractive girl and you're confident. That's all."

"What's the point of doing that if I'm not interested in dating him?"

"My goodness, what can it hurt? Do it for me, if for no other reason. Promise me? Besides that, you never quite know what can happen with someone until you meet them. That much an old lady knows. Don't be afraid to hope for things, Jane."

CHAPTER 3 - GRACE

Grace swung her feet over the edge of the bed, finally sitting up after days of trying to hide her grief under the covers. She wanted to disappear, to smother the feelings of sadness and confusion beneath her pillow. She could hear the floorboards creaking in the studio down the hall and knew her husband was painting.

They'd developed their own responses to grief. He, to his painting, which he took up after the second miscarriage, and she, to her room, where she would bury her head in a pillow and cry until she couldn't anymore: her body expelling her dreams of motherhood with every tear.

Grace could hear her husband's footsteps in his studio down the hall, one step forward, then back, then forward again, as he put the final touches on this latest painting. She could picture him adding dabs of color, light as air on the painting's surface, and doing it as lovingly as the kisses he painted on her neck every night as she stood before the mirror and contemplated each new wrinkle that had appeared on her face.

She listened as his steps increased, forward and back quickly, these last few paces his way of saying goodbye to the work. She found comfort in their rhythm, closing her eyes to the sounds that had become like music to her these last few days. As John's steps slowed to a stop, she left their bedroom and walked out into the kitchen, knowing he would meet her there and encourage them both to eat.

She paused before sitting down at their kitchen island, taking in the sunlight that came through the window. It was one of the things she loved about this house, but today, when her soul felt empty, the ray that shined on her face like a spotlight made her inexplicably angry.

"Hi," he said, pushing a cup of coffee with milk and a plate of scrambled eggs her way. She wondered how her husband always managed to make the food at just the right moment so it was hot and ready for her when her body was all cried out, and she needed to return to the routine of the world.

"Smells good." She sipped from the cup, wishing that small talk would not serve as the bridge between them after each disappointment. She wanted big, important conversations, not talk of eggs and food. If he commented on the brightness of the day, she decided that she would take her coffee back to her room.

Instead, he placed another plate with eggs on the counter and slowly ate, chewing so softly, it almost appeared that he was pretending. Even his fork moved soundlessly as he scooped up bits of scrambled egg. Grace watched him closely, his brown hair blending with bits of gray, his handsome face accentuated with five-day stubble. Even the lines around his eyes and mouth seemed to make him more attractive. After each disappointment, her anguish landed everywhere, like a bird flying desperately around a cage, looking for the tiny little door that would help it find freedom. John was always one of her targets, with silent anger at the way he dried his tears, got out of bed, and headed to the studio to assuage his grief. It seemed to her that to be productive after their losses diminished them. And yet, even this she knew was her anger talking.

She watched him eat, her heart softening to him as she saw the effort he took in this. Why did she always forget that his heart was broken, too?

They finished at the same time. Wordlessly, he took her plate and washed the dishes in the sink by hand. They had a dishwasher, but the movement of the water over the plates and cups seemed to soothe him. She waited until he was finished before she asked.

"Can I see it?"

"Of course."

He took her hand and led her down the hall to his studio space. When she was able to lock her anger away long enough to breathe again, she allowed herself to feel the anticipation of what he had created next. In the moments before she turned her gaze to his work, she felt a thrill enter her body. Even now, with sadness pushing her feet forward, she held excitement in her heart for what he had painted.

He moved to the easel first, and she waited by the doorway, knowing he would need one last look before showing her. After a moment, she moved forward, walking toward him.

He held his left arm out, an unspoken invitation to come to his side so he could pull her close. She wondered how many times her body had slid next to his, so perfectly close that it seemed as if she were made just for him. She placed her head on his shoulder and he kissed it, smiling at her as she raised her face to look at his painting.

She took in the image with a feeling of fear and exhilaration. There was something about this girl, the way she reached out into the night, the look on her face desperate and angry and yet innocent. She wanted to comfort the image, to tell her, whatever it was that made her so afraid, it would be all right. This painting seemed to speak to her in a language she didn't understand yet but desperately wanted to learn.

"It's…" She groped for words but found herself crying instead. Was it the pain of their latest disappointment? Or her reaction to the painting? She couldn't form the words she wanted to say, that the girl in the painting seemed familiar to her. She had John's smile and her eyes. Her face was a combination of the two of them; she was sure of it. She wondered when the image of this girl had shown up in her husband's thoughts.

He kissed the top of her head again, not saying a word. She appreciated that he let her gather her thoughts with as much time as she needed. He never asked her what she thought, like she'd seen some artists do. He knew she needed to experience the work before she could decide how she felt about it. But still, this pain in her chest, which seemed to ache the longer she took in the image, was new to her.

She turned to him and hugged him despite the anger she was also feeling. Tears streamed down her face, and she felt caught up in a sea of emotions, as if the heartbreak she carried along with her was suddenly out in the open. Had the painting found a hole in her heart that she hadn't yet cordoned off from the world?

He took her hand and led her to the couch at the edge of his studio, each of them knowing to duck before sitting down. The angled ceilings had roughly reminded them to do so enough times over the years. His studio had once been a large pantry from a long-ago era, where people kept enough staples and baking supplies to last them through a hard winter and beyond.

As they sat, he pulled her close again, her tears dissolving into his sweatshirt. She wanted to say something encouraging about his work, or about their loss, but she stayed quiet, unable to call up her voice to meet the day.

"It will be all right," he said softly, kissing her wet cheeks.

"That's what you always say."

He turned, facing her. "And I mean it. We will be all right. We will get through this."

She could picture this moment played out over and over during the years they had been married. Each time she remembered them, it was with the large tears that overtook her, washing her face with grief and aging her beyond her forty-five years. She looked at him then, seeing him as he was when they had first met, still with the dark hair and young face that had people guessing his age. Twenty years later, he still looked a decade younger than the fifty years he'd been alive. How had they managed to age so differently?

"How will we be okay?" She pulled away from him then, standing up and hugging her arms to herself. She walked toward the painting and stood before it.

He got up quickly and came to her, standing behind her and placing his arms around her waist. For a bitter moment she wondered if he did so to protect his painting more than to comfort her. She hated herself for thinking that.

"Look. Grace…" He sighed.

They'd learned to grieve differently in order to move forward, she to her tears and him to his painting. The first few years were all about hugs and gripping their hands so tightly, it was as if holding on to each other created a shield that kept the world from breaking their hearts any further. But somewhere in the years since, he had taken up painting, which gave him a sense of lightness that she envied and hated. Why wasn't he drowning as she was?

His painting time was a hobby at first, and then a way to heal. He'd get in time after his day job as an insurance adjuster, and it would help him relax. But eventually, she'd wake up from a night filled with tears and dreams of holding children to find that the bed was cold, and her arms held only his pillow. He had gotten up hours before, gone to the studio to paint, and left her alone. He had said it was to let her sleep, and she believed that for a while.

He said something about moving forward, but she was distracted by the painting. There was something about this one, this woman who reached out into the night as the light came through her window, which reminded her of someone she couldn't bear to look at anymore.

"This…" She turned to him, questioning. "It's me. Isn't it?"

"I was saying…" He stopped to look at her, then at the painting. "What?"

"I said"—her voice getting louder—"this is me. Isn't it?"

The thought made her angry. Was he putting her sadness on display? The desperate way the woman reached out… It was her… reaching for children, for motherhood… and finding her arms empty.

He looked at the painting with a frown. "Well, no. Of course not. This is just something… it's from my imagination. Why would you think that?"

"Why?" Her words were short and clipped. "Because. Certainly… obviously, this is me. You painted me."

She remained still, and yet felt herself get short of breath, as if she had been running up and down the hall shouting rather than standing next to him. What was he doing? Trying to show her how she looked when she clung to this desire so desperately? Was he trying to get her to look at her life and see it as he did? Is this what he thought of her?

He took a deep breath. "Why are we doing this? This fighting that happens? Please, Grace. Let's not anymore. We have each other." He placed his arms on her shoulders. "We love each other."

She turned her head, knowing he was right but not ready to admit it. Her pain needed to land somewhere, and it had found its home in him. She turned and went down the hall, feeling her knee buckle as she stepped. Was this another sign of old age? Creaking joints and knees that refused to bend as they should? She put her hand on the wall for support, gathering herself, as she walked down the hall to their room, one foot in front of the other, feeling the rough edges of the walls as she did. How could she move on again? Smile while shopping at the grocery store or having meetings with her clients? It was too much to emerge from this house as someone who had lost yet another child and no longer had the hope that it would change one day.

She reached their room, wanting to plop down on the bed and pull the covers over her head, but this room that she had spent the last few days in seemed suffocating now. She walked over to the window and opened it, pounding the spot with her palm where it always stuck.

He was in the doorway, looking at her with a mixture of sadness and pity. She turned back to the window, feeling the cool air on her face. She imagined her mother there, holding her, brushing the hair from her face and telling her to cry but don't shut out her husband. She imagined her mother saying she was sorry, over and over again.

She turned toward John, but he had already reached her, and they lay down on the bed and held each other until they were both strong enough to get up and face the world together.

CHAPTER 4 - JANE

There was something about the coffee shop that Jane really enjoyed. Everyone seemed busy, rushing to order, hurrying to drink their hot beverages, and taking quick bites of food. The fast pace gave her a rush that helped jump-start her day.

She waited in line for her raisin bagel with cinnamon cream cheese, daydreaming about Mrs. Ferch's final words to her before she left. She *had* been afraid to hope. Maybe she *should* just introduce herself to Eric and say hello. Just so they could at least be friendly when they saw each other in the apartment building.

Jane scanned the coffee shop and spotted Eric standing patiently, looking like he had all the time in the world. He smiled at the other patrons as he waited for his drink and when his name was called, she noted that the barista flirted with him shamelessly. She touched his arm and handed him a small bag that looked like it had a phone number on it. Jane partially envied the girl in her boldness and also cringed at it. When Brad had asked her out eight years before, she was a shy girl, fresh out of college, her nose in a book at the local bookstore and someone who barely noticed the world around her.

She pushed away thoughts of Brad. Jane just wanted to make Mrs. Ferch happy, so she tried to study Eric like her sister would. Charlotte would flirt first and ask questions later. She tried to see beyond the hair that needed a cut and the flannel shirt that reminded her of her father. Even Eric's laid-back attitude reminded Jane of her dad. Her mom always worked two jobs while her dad talked about the inventions he thought would make their family rich.

Eric had chosen a seat by the window. She picked up her bagel and approached his table. It would make Mrs. Ferch happy if she at least tried this once. She stood before him for an awkward moment before he noticed her. She could hear a bag rustling and realized it was the one she held in her hand.

"Hi, there. I'm Jane." She paused at the way he smiled at her. "McDonald." She cleared her throat and frowned. "I, um, live in your building."

Had it been so long since she'd been on a date that she didn't even know how to make small talk anymore?

"Yes," he said, shaking the hand she offered briefly as if they were entering a business meeting. "I remember Mrs. Ferch introducing you when you moved in."

Jane couldn't remember Mrs. Ferch doing this. Then again, she'd been focused on work the last few months and wasn't exactly paying attention. But standing before Eric, she hated to admit that Mrs. Ferch was right. He was handsome. Even through the five-o'clock shadow he sported; she could see a pleasant-looking face. As he and Jane shook hands, she noticed his green eyes.

Eric remained silent, a curious look on his face. He didn't appear concerned about filling the silence, which was too bad, Jane thought, because that meant she would have to.

"So… Eric," she said, moving the bag to her other hand, "what do you do?"

He'd had a smirk on his face as he had watched her up until then, but her question seemed to wipe it from his lips. He rubbed his face, his whiskers making an unpleasant scratching sound. "Ah, the big question," he mused. "What do I do?"

Eric was looking at her as if she had spoken a different language. She tried to clarify. "You know, what—"

"Do I do. Yes, I heard you." He scratched his head, causing his dark-brown curls to shake this way and that. He tapped the tip of his coffee cup and frowned. "I, ah, do a lot of different things right now."

That could mean anything, she thought. It could mean that he ran five Fortune 500 companies at once. Or he had invented a device that helped you get younger every time you sneezed. Or even that he did a lot of things that added up to nothing in particular, like her dad.

She knew Mrs. Ferch wouldn't be satisfied unless she had given this discussion some effort, so she went on with what she hoped was her light-and-flirty voice. "No, where do you work?" *There, was that so hard?*

Eric's smiled returned, and Jane felt a sense of relief that perhaps she hadn't managed to derail their entire conversation.

"Well, up until recently I had worked at Chapman Industries."

Jane waited. She was tired of playing conversational detective, but those green eyes of his convinced her to try again. "Oh, I'm sorry. Did you get laid off? That's been happening so much lately."

He tilted his head at her like she'd sprouted a third eye.

Jane instinctively scratched at her forehead while she waited for a response.

He continued, "I'm really glad you finally decided to talk to me. You know I'd been trying to get your attention since you moved in. You always look so…"

He searched for the right word while Jane's mind filled in the blank with all kinds of paranoid words in return: stressed out, weird, goofy…

Thankfully, he finished his thought. "*Busy*. In fact." He took a sip of coffee, and a little bit of foam ended up on his lip. Jane was just about to point to it when he absentmindedly licked it off before continuing. "I didn't think you were interested in getting to know me."

How could she tell him that she was only talking to him because Mrs. Ferch asked her to? Or that she suspected he might be like her dad, who liked to "tinker" around, as he called it, but never actually had a job. She must have showed the panic she'd suddenly felt because Eric came to her rescue.

"Hey, there," he laughed, touching his hand to hers in the briefest of moments. "Where'd you go?"

She blushed, but struggled to say something that resembled real conversation.

"I'm at my company ten years today," she blurted.

"Okay…" Eric tilted his head as if he were studying a rare breed of animal at the zoo, with a sign around her neck that said, *The female workaholic out of her natural habitat. Notice her blush and stutter as the male approaches.*

She tried to explain. "There might be a raise. I talked to my boss yesterday." She spoke even more rapidly now. "He wants there to be more happiness in the office, so he's going to start with me. I think it might be the assistant-manager job."

Eric maintained a curious look on his face as she

babbled. "Congratulations, then."

"Yeah, well…" Jane managed to burst her own happiness bubble with a bit of reality. "Nothing's for certain. But it could be…" She let the thought trail off while she suddenly pictured the opposite of this fantasyland she'd been dreaming about all night. There could be no party. No Happy Anniversary sign even. No raise. No…

"Hey, there, again." Jane felt Eric's hand on hers for a few moments more. It was warm and slightly calloused. Did that mean he did something for a living, after all? "I hope it is for certain, then. In fact, why don't we celebrate when you find out?"

"Oh, I don't want get too hopeful."

Jane got up to toss her cup in the trash and finally realized what he had said. "Celebrate?" Did that mean he was asking her out?

Eric stood also, crunching his cup with his fist and then tossed it in the trash. She knew the moment had ended and panicked for what to say next. Should she ask him if he really did just suggest they meet after work?

He looked at his watch, then back at her. "Jane," he said, extending his hand. She shook it, feeling the warmth of his touch as closed his other hand gently around hers. "It was nice to finally meet you properly. I hope your day is all you're hoping for."

He walked out the door, leaving her frozen in place as she watched him go. Suddenly, rushing into work was about the last thing she wanted to do.

As Jane walked into the gallery, she noticed, for the first time ever, she was late. Just fifteen minutes, but still, what a way to start her tenth year at the company.

Donna, the receptionist, was a no-nonsense lady who had three kids, two dogs, a turtle, and a husband who cherished her. She favored sweaters with cardinals on them and big, chunky jewelry that clanked against the phone each time it rang. She teased everyone in the gallery and expected them all to do the same back, but when they needed a hug or a kind word, she was there for them. Like when your boss forgets your ten-year anniversary, for example.

"Congratulations, honey!" She reached across the reception desk to give Jane a big hug, and as she did, her bracelet smacked Jane in the wrist. "I know how important it is to you, sweetie, but don't be too disappointed. Bug forgot."

Jane exhaled, closing her eyes and picturing the hope she'd kept bottled the last few weeks drift away along with her.

"Right. Well… no big deal." She wanted to cry, and feared she actually might. No raise. No promotion. Ten years. For what? She felt an additional pang of disappointment at the thought that she wouldn't even be able to celebrate with Eric. Not that she was interested in him. She couldn't let herself be interested, especially after he had acted so odd when she asked him what he did for a living.

Then again, she wasn't exactly the picture of grace this morning, either. She blushed again at the thought of how tongue-tied she became around him. Those green eyes were nice, regardless of what he did for a living.

Jane gave Donna a smile that said, *I didn't care about this anyway.* But who was she kidding? This was a very big deal.

Jane had looked forward to it to the point where it took on a life of its own, the notion of a promotion germinated into something big in her mind. She had allowed herself to hope, and was angry that she had even gone there.

Despite what Mrs. Ferch had said that morning, Jane feared that hope was for other people, like her sister, Charlotte, who just seemed to fall into good things as they skipped through life.

Donna broke into her thoughts with a sideways hug. "Now, sugar, you are an important part of this place! Don't you forget it. Honey, I don't know what I'd do if you weren't here. I made you these."

She handed Jane a plate with cupcakes on it. Donna believed in the power of sugar, both as nicknames and food. The sweeter the names she called you, the sadder you probably were.

"Thanks, Donna. You really are a wonderful person." Jane turned to go back toward her office, but Donna stopped her.

"Now, look, sugar," she said, her hands on her hips. "You should be promoted. But also? You spend way too much time here. You can't let your whole life be work. Okay? You can't put all your hopes in it. There has to be more. Remember, your life is a collection of things. Not one person, and certainly not one place. Don't put your life on hold until you like your job better. *Your life can start right now.*" She pointed at the floor to emphasize her point.

Jane gave Donna a hug and told her she was right.

"Of course I am," Donna said in return, then waved at Jane as she answered the phone.

Jane was disappointed, but between the cupcakes and Donna's words, she knew she was right. If she let herself daydream, she admitted to herself that she couldn't stop thinking of Eric's green eyes or the way his warm hand would land on hers. She felt guilty about it and but also wondered if Mrs. Ferch was right that she needed to be more open to the possibilities in life.

She held that thought for exactly one minute, the time it took to sit down at her desk and check her emails. The number of artists' emergencies she received first thing often dictated how the rest of her day would go.

She had not even finished reading the first email when Bug walked into her office.

"Jane! There you are. I need you to do me a favor," he said by way of greeting. No *Thanks for your years of service* or *Happy to have worked with you for the past ten years*, Jane thought. Instead, he grunted, "I need you to go to the Cream City Arts Fest next weekend and scope out some of the artists. We need new blood in this space. It's all about happiness from now on!" he exclaimed, extending his hands into the air like a football referee, indicating that the extra point was good.

She wanted to say that scoping out artists at fairs was a job for the assistant manager. That she would be happy to do that if he was promoting her. Instead, she nodded, and could hear him greeting guests in the gallery space, his loud but joyful bellow talking proudly about the art.

She thought about her father and the one bonus of not getting promoted was that she had a good excuse to say no to his request for money. Without the raise, she couldn't afford a loan. She'd put off making the phone call to him, but at noon, she finally got up enough courage. She dialed and waited as it rang. Six times… seven. She was just about to hang up when she heard her father's familiar voice.

"Hullo?"

His voice was scratchy, and he seemed disoriented.

"Dad? It's Jane. Are you okay?"

"Huh? What time is it?"

"It's about ten o'clock. Are you all right?"

"Ten! Well… I'll be. I was up late working on my latest invention. I have a prototype made, and now I just need some cash for inventory. Were you able to get my money?"

She bristled at the way he said "my money." "No. Dad, look, I was hoping I was going to get a promotion, which would mean I could afford a loan for that… but I didn't get it." Disappointment descended on her again, and she felt her eyes sting with the threat of tears. Saying it aloud made her feel the reality of it.

"But you still could get a raise, right? Then you'd be able to do it. Or, maybe you could sell something. I know your mother and I gave you that antique locket a few years ago, and that might be worth something."

She remembered the antique locket. A few years before she had sold it after her dad asked her for money.

"I sold that a few years ago. It only brought me a hundred dollars. Remember?" It wasn't the lack of monetary value that had disappointed her after she'd sold it. It was one of the few gifts she got from her parents that wasn't something she actually needed, like school clothes or notebooks.

After she sold it, Jane came home and cried about it. She never told Charlotte that story out of fear that her sister would tell her how dumb she'd been to do it. In the end, her dad used the money for "marketing purposes" for an invention that never came to be.

"That's all you got for it? You're gonna have to get smarter about who you sell things to, Janey. That should have gone for much, much more."

"I'm sorry, Dad. I just can't swing the money right now."

"Think it over some more and see what you've got. Your old man is onto something here, I can feel it. This could make us rich, kiddo."

She'd heard it a million times from her dad. The promises of hitting it big from one of his inventions.

"Yeah, Dad. That'd be great." She played with her ballpoint pen, clicking it in and out while her father told her about this invention he was working on. She interrupted him. "Dad, I'm sorry, I have to go."

She needed cheering up, and she decided she was going to take a long lunch. If she wasn't going to get a raise or promotion, maybe she could start a new career as a lousy employee instead. She'd already come in late, why not continue?

CHAPTER 5 - GRACE

Morning, you." John kissed Grace's neck as she lay in bed and snuggled in behind her. She could feel the warmth of his knees on the backs of hers, his chest hair tickling her back. Grace could have lingered that way all day. He felt so warm, and mornings like this were one of the things she loved most about them, about how comfortable they were with each other.

"Morning," she replied, eyes closed and too sleepy to say much more.

His kisses continued, down her neck, her back, his hands roaming. She turned over and smiled at him.

"I thought we had to get up early today for the art fair."

Between kisses, he replied, "We do. But I think we have time for this."

She ran her hands through his thick hair and smiled to herself as his hands and lips went to the places that made her forget about anything except how happy she was with him. During the roughest times, when infertility ripped a hole in her heart, she'd wonder how they could get through it all and move past it. But when she quieted her worries, her body and soul chose him again. Always.

After they'd made love, he slapped her behind playfully. "You want to jump in the shower first?"

She wished they could sleep in but couldn't complain about the way the day had gone so far. She got up, grabbed the clothes she had laid out the night before, and went to take a shower. She'd long ago learned to make it easy for herself on art fair mornings, laying out everything she needed to quickly get going. The night before she had washed her hair and twisted chunks of it into spirals, then she secured each little piece with a bobby pin. It was an old-fashioned way of creating waves in her hair without spending time curling or blow-drying it. She'd leave the bobby pins in until they were done setting up their booth. It didn't pay to take them out before then, all that moving around and sweating would leave her hair without any curl or style if she took them out too early.

Grace jumped in the shower and got clean, toweled off quickly and put some moisturizer on her face. Every once in a while, she looked at her reflection and wondered where the years had gone. She didn't look bad for someone about to turn forty-six, but the lines on her face reminded her that time was ticking. The thought made her sad, but she shook it off. She had no time to cry today, and besides, she done enough of that over the years.

She placed tinted moisturizer over the regular moisturizer and laughed to herself that she had now reached the age where she needed two different kinds. What next? Superstrength moisturizer? She hoped they made such a thing.

Grace got dressed, sliding on a maxi dress and short jean jacket. She went back to the bedroom and called out, "I'm out!" to her husband, who, by the sounds of it, was in the kitchen making coffee.

She put on a small dab of perfume, then regretted it. If there were bees at the fair, they'd be all over her. Too late now, she thought. She put on her favorite earrings, the silvery dangle ones he bought her for their tenth anniversary. She slipped on her comfy shoes and headed toward the kitchen. He had two travel mugs set out, her favorite one with the Packers logo on it and his with a Bible verse. It said something about trusting the Lord on it, and while he cherished it, she had struggled when it came to trusting God, especially as the years went on and she saw that the worst types of parents could have children so easily, while she and her husband struggled to get pregnant.

Both the mugs were full of coffee, and she could see that he had added the three tablespoons of milk she liked in hers. His was black.

She secured the lids of each, grabbed the bag that held their portable credit card reader, markers, scissors, and wholesale sheets. She picked up the directions for the fair and the map with their booth number on it, and waited for him.

"Ready?" He was already showered and changed. His damp hair hid the usual gray that highlighted his temples, darkening his thick brown strands and returning him to the boyish good looks that had first caught her eye. She marveled that in a matter of minutes he was dressed and set to go.

"Men have it so lucky. You got ready in no time."

He walked up, gave her butt another playful slap, and pulled her into an embrace. She almost dropped the coffee mugs.

"I have it so lucky because I get to wake up next to you."

"Oh"—she blushed—"you." She wondered if she

would ever stop thinking how cool it was that he loved her so. She guessed not.

He took the mug of coffee she held out, sipped it and grabbed the paper with the directions on it. They got in the car they had already loaded with his prints the night before.

As they pulled out of the driveway, she commented on the day. "It's sunny. That's good. I heard a slight chance of rain, but I'm hoping the weatherman was wrong."

He nodded, watching the road.

"I'm glad we loaded this stuff last night," she said, but realized when she said "we" that what she really meant was him.

"Saves so much time. Less hassle in the mornings."

They had been to this art fair a couple of times before and always did well at it, but it was Grace's favorite for other reasons. Set on a beautiful Wisconsin historical site, it held special memories for her. It's where she first fell in love with him, on a date set up by two of their friends.

"You think we'll see Linda and Ed today?"

"Gah." He grimaced. "Probably. Remember last year? How snarky they were?"

She remembered. It was odd to think that at one point they were such good friends. "I mean, she was my maid of honor." She mentally shook her head at how her friend seemed to change the minute Grace got engaged.

"When I think that she was the one who introduced us..." Grace shuddered. "How do friendships change so much? She wasn't even happy when we got engaged. Everything was a nasty comment. A jab about the dress I chose. Rolling her eyes when I'd talk about plans for the reception..."

He put his hand on her leg and patted.

"And then the wedding! She made that comment about how long she thought the wedding would last. Remember?

Not to mention how unsupportive she was when we couldn't have kids. She turned into some kind of frenemy."

"Frenemy?" He glanced over at her.

"Come on, you know that word. It's the friend who turns against you and becomes almost like an enemy."

He moved his hand back to the steering wheel. "Well, it's not just her. It was Ed, too. They both got a bug up their butt for some reason."

"I don't get it. I mean, when Linda got pregnant, I was so happy for her, and then she said…" Grace teared up at the way her friend seemed to turn on her. When Grace didn't get pregnant right away, Linda suggested that maybe she didn't really want kids. As the years went on, Linda laughed that obviously God didn't want John and Grace to have them, so why were they continuing to try? She made stupid, mean comments, and Grace could not figure out why she had turned so nasty.

"I know, babe." He reached for her hand and squeezed it. "But they're unhappy people. They don't have a good relationship."

She turned to him, surprised. She'd never thought about it like that.

"Really? I thought they were perfect for each other."

He laughed. "You've got a point there. Ed was nicer in the beginning, or at least I thought he was. I always thought his little insults were just him joking. But then I realized he was just being a jerk."

"And her. She was my best friend at one point in my life. But I guess that was almost twenty years ago now. Things change."

He gave her hand another squeeze. "I hope they skip the fair this year."

Grace had been the one to keep things going with their friendship, even from the start, before Linda had kids.

Looking back, their friendship was one-sided from the beginning. It took one too many nasty comments from Linda for Grace to finally pull away, deciding not to contact her again. She waited to see if Linda would call or email, and a year went by and then two without a word.

She wondered if she should have told Linda that she was ending the friendship and why. Did you really need to do that when someone behaved so badly? Grace's body had lingering physical effects after each fertility treatment, and she was constantly fatigued. Up until that point, she had a full-time job editing for a publisher, where she worked long hours, but during the treatments she went down to part-time, and even that became a challenge. She would practically crawl home from work, exhausted and feeling depressed at the changes in her body. That went on for months, and when the hormone treatments were over, many of the physical changes stayed behind. She realized she needed to make a job change to something she could do full time because her old career was too demanding for her, and they needed her income. Every penny was put toward medical bills and trying to start a family.

Instead of being supportive, Linda seemed to get meaner. She'd smile kindly but say something nasty, making fun of Grace for moving to part-time work. It was then that Grace pulled away, and it wasn't a hard decision to make. Despite Grace's efforts not to continue the friendship, Linda and Ed seemed to show up at the same fairs they did, where they couldn't very well tell them to leave since it was a public event.

Grace shook away the thoughts of hurt and anger that came when she thought of her old friends as she realized John had pulled up to the fairgrounds. They quickly unloaded the tables, racks, and stacks of prints. They started doing art fairs a couple of years ago after John became serious about painting. It had taken them doing a few fairs to get their booth set up the way they wanted, but now they had it down to a science.

They used old magazine racks, spray-painted in various colors, to hold the prints. Before each art fair they had a few more prints made up, and she flipped through them, making sure she had a nice variety in each holder. Then she placed colorful doilies under each rack and arranged a couple of them on top of decorative boxes so they had a variety of heights in the booth.

She took the old coffee-mug tree she had found at an estate sale and placed the necklaces she made from his artwork and draped them on the stems of the tree. She stepped back and took a look at the arrangement. Grace decided there was enough room for people to walk through the booth without getting jammed up in one specific spot. She liked the variety of items and colors, and was satisfied with the layout.

"Looks great." She felt a kiss on her cheek and smelled the citrusy shampoo he had used that morning.

"Thanks."

"Here." He handed her a breakfast sandwich with a piping-hot egg topped with bacon on a croissant.

She took a bite. "Mmm. That hits the spot. I didn't realize how hungry I was." As she said it, a big piece of cheese dripped out, dropping onto her dress.

He handed her a napkin from the stack he had brought. "I figured you'd need these."

"You know me so well." She wiped her mouth and then the spot on her dress, quickly ate the rest of the sandwich, and drank the last of the coffee. Then Grace took the pin curls out of her shoulder-length hair and fluffed up the strands. She pulled a mirror out from her purse to survey the results. She saw a few gray hairs poke through her natural reddish-brown color. "Ugh. These early mornings make me look so tired."

"You look great," he whispered in her ear. "I'm glad we got some time to enjoy the morning, actually."

She laughed and playfully swatted his arm. "Oh, you!" She finished fluffing her hair, took the napkins and wrapper from the breakfast sandwich and walked over to a nearby garbage can, tossing them in. She closed her eyes, feeling the autumn sun on her face. It was going to be a nice day. Warm, but not too hot.

When she walked back to their booth, John was chatting with the couple who had set up a booth next to them.

"This is my wife, Grace," he introduced her, and she shook hands with the couple. "This is Marta and Jack. They were just telling me that they have a record number of artist vendors here today."

They all agreed that they hoped it meant more people and more sales, too. This was something Grace enjoyed about doing the art fair circuit, talking to the other vendors and finding out their story. Marta and Jack made various kinds of lawn accents; each was one-of-a-kind.

"You do beautiful work," she told Marta. "They're all so individual and unique."

"Thank you. We make things from old parts, chains, kitchen gadgets…" She shrugged. "They're all different."

"You can tell how much work goes into it. We were by a vendor once who clearly had purchased their garden accents from some wholesaler, and then were trying to push it off as homemade. They got away with it, too."

"I think I know who you're talking about. Makes us all look bad when people do that." The woman picked up one of the prints from their booth. "Your artwork is beautiful, by the way. I love the colors. And the style."

"It's my husband's, actually. He's the artist. I'm just the assistant." She smiled over at him, proud that people noticed his artwork.

Marta studied the print, then put it back in the rack. "So much detail. Does he do it full time?"

"No. We wish. During the day he works as an insurance adjustor."

"And he still finds time to paint! How wonderful."

"Yes. It really…" Grace wanted to say that it helps him work through life's disappointments or that it keeps him sane. She cleared her throat. "It's really a passion for him."

"Well, good. Everyone needs a hobby like that. Me and Jack just lose all track of time when we're working on garden sculptures, too. What about you, hon? You have a hobby like that?"

Grace thought about it. "Not really. I work a lot. I'm a freelance editor. I used to work in an office, and then it just got too much for me, so I started doing it on the side with my own business, so I could have a more healthy schedule."

Marta nodded. "Better life balance. I'm all for that. Me and Jackie here travel to all the craft shows and whatnot, and it's our full-time thing now that we're retired. But we love it. The money isn't the same as when we were in the big working world, ya know, but we live simply. I actually feel better about our life now than when we had a big house. Well, I should scoot. Looks like it's time to open."

Grace fussed with the placement of the prints one more time, and after scanning the booth a final time decided they were ready for the crowds. Each art fair seemed to have its own personality. Some were busy early, and then the crowds died off. Others didn't pick up until later in the day. This one usually kept steady traffic throughout the day. She gave her husband a quick pat on the butt.

"I really am proud of you; you know that."

He smiled at her. "That means everything to me. Thank you."

She could have stayed there all day, smiling like a fool at her husband, content to be out at a fair, the breeze blowing, people browsing through the art, and the world calm and peaceful. Art fairs could be a gamble sometimes. You paid money to exhibit. Sometimes you didn't get in, sometimes the weather didn't cooperate, and sometimes the crowds just didn't like what you were selling.

But there were also times where she felt extremely happy and content in the booth. She'd watch the people, talk to them about art—something she was surprisingly good at—and feel a sense that this is what they were meant to do all along. It was as if the world became different at an art fair. People moved at a slower pace. They took time to look at things and see the small details. They felt positive about the world, just for a few moments, and the problems in their lives could be pushed away and replaced by beauty instead.

John gave her a quick kiss, but she could see him looking past her, frowning.

"Your face just fell like a lead balloon."

He gestured with his chin. "Don't look now, but…"

Grace turned to see Ed and Linda.

"Again?" Grace shook her head. "Do you think they actually want to buy art, or are they just trying to irritate us?

"Probably the latter."

"Great," she said. "I feel like I want to do something crazy just to make them go away. Like take off my shirt or something."

"I'd vote for that." He winked.

They walked into the booth, Linda with a frown and her arms crossed and Ed with a sneer. They had their son with them, who Grace guessed might have been about ten or eleven years old by now.

"Hi," she said, pretending that it was good to see them. Grace focused on the little boy instead. "Hey, I like that tattoo you've got there." She gestured to the fake rub-on tattoo he must have gotten from one of the booths down the aisle. "Did you get that here?"

"Yes! It's an alligator. Did you know alligators have been on earth for millions of years?"

Grace laughed. What a cute kid. "I didn't know that."

"And they swim really fast. Like, a gazillion miles an hour."

"That is very fast," she agreed. "Are alligators your favorite animal, then?"

He rolled his eyes at her in that adorable way kids do when they want to let an adult know how ridiculous they're being. "No. Way. Can you guess which animal is my favorite?"

Grace put her finger on her chin, considering it. "Dogs?"

"I do like dogs. But no."

"Chickens?"

"Not even!" He shouted now, and she was laughing with him.

"I don't think I can guess it!"

"Koala bears! Duh! They are so cuddly. Like, you could just hold them, and their bellies would make you warm, even if it was cold outside."

"I didn't know that. What about this one?" She pointed to another fake tattoo that looked like a monkey.

"Oh, that's Sir Walter. He's *royal*. He's the head of the monkey zoo."

Grace felt a laugh escape her throat that she thought had been gone forever. The child had lifted Grace's spirits, and she was grateful. She turned to Linda with a smile.

"Your son is adorable," she said, then asked a question she knew she would regret. "So how you are guys?"

"Good, good." Ed's sneer got even wider. "I'm working on a new business idea right now. Electronics." He filled her in on the intricacies of his work, which bored Grace to no end.

Linda turned to Grace. "And I suppose you are… still working part-time?"

Here we go again, she thought. Grace didn't wish the fertility merry-go-round on anyone else. Still, part of the issue with Ed and Linda not understanding was that everything she and her husband had gone through were things that came easy to them. Linda conceived within months of deciding to have children. Her pregnancy was easy, they never experienced health problems, and when money problems came their way, Linda's dad wrote them checks.

"No, Ed. I am a freelance editor, and it's full time." She changed the subject to something more pleasant. "Your son has grown from the last time we saw him. He's a sweet kid," she said to Linda.

Linda's scowl lifted slightly.

"Linda…" Ed spoke louder. "Grace here says she is working *full time* now."

Grace sighed.

"I went freelance a few years ago." She tried to change the subject again. "You knew that already."

"And Grace, what is it you do full time now?" Ed wasn't even looking at Grace as he said it, choosing instead to sneer at Linda, who responded to him.

"She's in *editing*, Ed. Remember? Apparently, it's busy. Full time."

"Right, right," Ed said back to his wife, and Grace

wondered how long these two would continue this fun little game of trying to make her feel bad. If they were so happy, why did they do things like this?

Grace looked at John, who was busy talking to two other people who had come into the booth, but he spotted her and rolled his eyes as if Ed and Linda were so ridiculous, he could not believe they were allowed to get up every day and interact with people. Later, Grace knew she and John would snuggle up on the couch and talk about how funny it was how some people come in and out of your life. When Grace had met Linda, she complained constantly about Ed, that he couldn't hold a job, that he was lazy. Linda joked that she never wanted kids because she already had her hands full with Ed.

Back then Grace was dating different people and would make Linda laugh with her horror stories about guys who were boring or showed up late for the date. Linda seemed sympathetic and would tell Grace that she wanted her to find someone special, but when Grace did, Linda seemed to change. She became sarcastic, and that ever-present scowl became more pronounced.

John always encouraged her to move on and forget about them, but it was hard to reconcile the things that had happened. She would replay every action and conversation, wondering what she had done to deserve such horrible treatment. Maybe her husband was right: Linda and Ed really were just miserable people. Linda changed for the negative when Grace got engaged. She asked Linda to be the maid of honor at her wedding, and the entire time she made fun of Grace's choices for hairstyle and shoes and made jabs about the house they bought. Every step of their new life together included snarky comments.

"It was so great seeing you both," Grace lied. "I've gotta get back to things here. Take care." She walked over to two women who were looking at some prints and chatted with them. When she looked back at Ed and Linda, she noticed they had moved on to another booth.

Things slowed down in the booth enough so she could catch her breath, but seeing Ed and Linda had sapped her energy. She felt a hand on her back and smiled, knowing it was her husband, someone so different from Ed that it prompted her to be thankful daily.

"You look like you need a break." His voice was low and tickled against her ear.

"Yeah"—she rubbed her neck, still feeling the sting of friends who seemed to delight in her misery—"I guess I do."

"Hey..." He placed his hands on her arms and turned her to him. "Don't let them get to you."

"It was the same old thing with them."

"I know. I heard. I couldn't get to you because a customer had me pinned."

"I saw that. They bought two prints."

"You don't miss anything." He grinned.

She nodded, distracted, still thinking about her old friends.

"Somehow being rude makes them feel better," John continued. "Not everyone is cut out to be a friend for life. I'm very thankful to them. They introduced me to you, and maybe that is the only reason we were meant to know them." He kissed the top of her head. "Why don't you take a break for a bit? You've been on your feet all morning. Get some air, and check out the other booths. I heard the coffee is good over at the main tent. I'm sure they have a tablespoon or three of milk for you, too."

She grinned at him. "You've been on your feet all morning, too."

"My feet are bigger. They can take it."

"Why don't you take a break first and I'll go after you," she said. "I'll take one of those coffees if you don't mind."

He left to get the coffee and Grace took a quiet moment to look out on the people attending the festival. She felt the cool autumn air on her face and it seemed to calm her. Her spirit could be taken down so easily these days, it seemed. She used to be so strong and could shake off anything from a snarky friend to a crappy mother. But that just wasn't so anymore.

She turned her attention instead to the fair. She would not let her old friends ruin the joy she felt at being able to show the world her husband's art. Grace took in the assortment of people walking past. There were friends chatting away (barely looking at the artful goods displayed in each booth), young couples holding hands (who seemed to only have eyes for each other), mothers with young kids, and an older couple that caught Grace's eye. They were holding hands and had stopped for moment, the gentlemen picking up a vase with his free hand and holding it up to his wife, who wrinkled her nose in return. He put it down with a smile, and they continued walking without a word said between them, their silent language mastered after years of marriage. They reminded her of herself and John.

She wished she could be more like her husband. He was so black and white about things. Once their friends had hurt them, he referred to them as jerks. He was done. Why hang out with them, he reasoned. She would linger in the gray spaces, wondering why their friends had said certain things, trying to show Linda that she was a good friend in order to get her to treat her better, and through it all she got more and more disappointed. Even now, years later, she wondered how a friend could turn out to be someone who didn't even seem to like you. Maybe she needed some new friends.

CHAPTER 6 - JANE

Jane woke up with excitement about the art fair combined with a lingering feeling of dread. She had been trying to connect with Brad all week, and had hoped he would come to the art fair with her. But no luck. She had finally received a text from him saying he "was busy" and that was it. When she mentioned the whole thing to Mrs. Ferch, the woman clapped her hands as if she were five years old and the ice cream truck had just pulled into town.

"Oh goodie! I haven't been to an art fair in ages! Would it be all right if I came with?"

Jane felt a wave of joy wash over her. She didn't mind doing events by herself, but it was always nice to share them with others, especially those who enjoyed art. She felt that part of the joy of her job was seeing how people reacted to art, how it moved them and allowed them to open up and experience life in a way that was different.

"Yeah, absolutely," she said. "I can pick you up at—"

"Oh no, hon, I will be out that morning. I have some errands. But I will meet you there. Is that all right?"

That was strange, Jane thought, but Mrs. Ferch did have an active life. Probably, if she were being honest, more active than hers. The thought inspired and depressed her.

"Of course," she said, and gave Mrs. Ferch the information so they could meet.

The morning of the art fair, she dressed in her comfy boots, a blue poet blouse, and her ratty, old jeans. She skipped the makeup and put her hair up, which hadn't been washed in a couple of days, into a series of ponytails, which when combined, looked like one long braid. She tied the scarf at the end to dress it up and further hide the fact that she hadn't bothered washing her hair. She'd seen a hairstyling video online of a girl with long hair who put it up into all kinds of interesting styles. It was what she did at night now. While some people spent time with their boyfriends, she was learning new ways to style her hair. She inwardly rolled her eyes, noting how content she'd become with the relationship she and Brad had.

She'd tried to talk to him about it the night before on the phone, and as usual he *had to go* and didn't explain what his plans were. She didn't ask, even though it was a Friday night, and most couples spent them together. Didn't they?

Jane shook the thought loose, grabbed her keys, and headed for the art fair. While this was a work assignment, she really did enjoy going to fairs and would do it even if it wasn't her job. Besides that, tooling around Milwaukee's Third Ward was always fun. The Third Ward was an older, artsy part of town that had gone through a renaissance over the last twenty years. What were once dilapidated, abandoned buildings had been turned into galleries and coffee shops and quaint, unique restaurants.

Art fairs were a good way to scout out new talent to include in the gallery. She waited at the entrance and checked her watch. Mrs. Ferch had said, "Promptly at ten a.m." and she was glad to be early. She hated disappointing the woman. As Jane waited, she smelled the aroma coming from one particular food booth and went to check it out. She ordered an egg sandwich on a croissant, which was so delicious it seemed to melt in her mouth, and, she quickly realized, on her blouse as well. She wiped at the buttery stain with a napkin, which only seemed to make it worse. Instead, she took off the scarf she had tied around her hair and placed it around her neck, hiding the stain over her blouse.

The fair was already crowded, and Jane watched as the couples arrived, holding hands and scanning the aisles for goods. Probably buying art for their homes, she thought, and then chided herself. Was she just looking for people coupled up like that now because it was what she wanted from Brad? Not for the first time she asked herself, what *did* she want from him?

"Good morning," she heard, and turned to find Eric standing there. What was he doing there? He had gotten a haircut, she noticed. And he did look nice in his khakis and golf shirt. For a moment, she wished she had gotten a bit spruced up that morning.

"Um, morning?" she said, looking past him. Maybe he had given Mrs. Ferch a ride.

He turned to follow her gaze. "Looking for someone?"

She stared at him a moment. No. It couldn't be. "Did Mrs. Ferch tell you to meet me here?"

"Yeah. She said you had a work event and needed

someone to accompany you. You were in a bind and—"

"A bind!" She hated how that made her sound.

He cringed. "Sorry, it's how she put it. She just asked me to come as a favor to her."

Jane let out a breath and looked at the sky. Then she stared at him, waiting for him to get it.

"Oh," he finally said, laughing. "We've been duped."

"It appears so. I love that lady, but—"

"Right. She's trying to play matchmaker."

"Yeah. Look," she said, "you don't have to come with me. I asked her because…" Jane let the sentence hang. *Because my boyfriend wouldn't go with me* was not something she wanted to say aloud. She shook her head. "Doesn't matter."

"Well, I do actually enjoy this sort of thing. Mrs. Ferch said you work at a gallery? I find that really interesting, too. So, if you wouldn't mind, I'd like to tag along with you and check out the art. To be honest," he continued, "this is something I probably would have done anyway. I've attended the Hampton Arts Fest for about twenty years in a row. Since I was a kid."

So had she, also since she was a kid. A thought popped in her head wondering if they had met as kids there. Wouldn't that be interesting? She quickly brushed it away.

"That'd be nice," she said instead, feeling herself smile.

They strolled at what Jane felt was the perfect pace. Attending an art fair with someone can tell you a lot about them. Someone who barrels through at the speed of light generally had no interest in seeing the nuances of the pieces. This was the type of person she didn't care to spend time with, but someone who poked around so slowly, asking endless questions of each and every artist, was equally annoying. These people could be know-it-alls who actually knew nothing about art but wanted to sound important.

They walked together, making small talk about the weather and the plethora of Milwaukee festivals, but they would each stop and look at whatever interested them. When more than one person visited an art fair together, they needed to be in sync, or one—or both—of them would miss things they wanted to see. There was a definite rhythm to walking a fair. Suddenly she felt at Brad once again that he couldn't just do things like this with her once in a while. It wasn't simply that he was always inexplicably busy, it was the fact he didn't seem to care at all about what she did.

Even though Eric wasn't attached at her hip, when she did look through a booth and come back into the center, he would be there waiting patiently. They would continue on, and despite herself, she realized she was enjoying this more than if she had gone with Brad, who would probably be on his phone and missing the whole thing.

Jane looked at the art in each booth and listened to comments people made as they shopped. Finding the right art for the gallery wasn't just about what she liked, but about what other people were drawn to as well. She happened upon a booth with a nice little crowd gathered around it and waited her turn to get a close-up look. She spotted a woman who answered questions and talked with people about what kind of art they were looking for.

The booth was laid out nicely, and Jane noted that they had found old wooden magazine racks, painted them a variety of colors, and used them as a way to display the art. It was clever and an idea she wanted to remember for the gallery. There were also decorative boxes that lifted the artwork up, so everything was at different levels, encouraging the eye to travel around the booth.

She flipped through the prints and liked the colors and

compositions. There were still-life images, pictures of men and women doing everyday things, like making dinner or planting flowers, and whimsical works filled with bright colors like aqua and red. The art was vibrant and fanciful, yet if you looked close enough at the subject matter, there was a seriousness to it as well. The style was unique, or at least, something she hadn't seen before. Art today could be so repetitive, with artists watching others do their thing online and then not finding their own voice. This particular artist had his own style, which was whimsical but also filled with longing. She was intrigued.

She picked up a print to get a closer look. The color scheme was dark browns and grays, yet the image was hopeful. A man sat at the table alone, hands clasped, with his eyes closed in prayer. There was nothing on the brown table but a white bowl. The man wore a gray shirt, torn slightly by wear in several places. Despite the muted tones, the man's eyes were closed lightly, not with concentration or anger, but almost with joy. As if he were happy to pray and be thankful.

"That's a popular one," the woman in the booth commented on the print Jane held. The woman had wavy, reddish-brown hair, which seemed to draw out her green eyes. She wore minimal makeup, and faint laugh lines were visible around her eyes and mouth. Jane guessed that she was older than her, but the jean jacket and maxi dress she had on made it hard to guess her age.

"I like the image," Jane told her. "Are you the artist?"

"Oh, no," the woman chuckled. "I can't draw a thing. My husband is the artist. He's only been painting for a couple years. He took it up…" She trailed off, her face pulling down, and Jane wondered if he'd started painting as a way to heal. It wasn't uncommon. Jane had seen some beautiful art created from emotional pain. She waited patiently, and the woman seemed to regain her composure. "He just picked up a paintbrush and found that he joyfully lost hours creating," she continued, and Jane thought it was a lovely way to phrase it. "You just missed him," she said, pointing to where he had headed.

"My name is Jane McDonald, and I work at the Cream City Gallery." She handed the woman her business card.

"Nice to meet you," she said in return, taking Jane's card. "And you," she said, turning to Eric.

"Oh, sorry," Jane hadn't exactly forgotten that Eric was there, but he had left her to do her business and talk, for which she was grateful. "This is Eric, my..." She blushed and stammered, feeling like a fool.

"We're neighbors," he said smoothly, extending his hand to Grace. "Your husband's work reminds me of Chagall combined with Henri Rousseau. It has a charm to it, along with"—he searched for a word—"hope." He shrugged. "I don't know much about art, actually. Other than I like it."

Grace laughed. "It seems like you know pretty much," she assured him. "And your assessment is spot-on. John, my husband, loves both those artists. Which reminds me, have you guys seen the Chagall tapestry at the Jewish Museum? It is truly magnificent."

Jane gestured to the print she held. "Your husband must be a praying man, then, huh?"

The woman nodded. "For sure. He likes to call it his personal hotline with the Lord." She put out her hand, and Jane shook it. "I'm Grace, by the way."

"And are you a praying woman, too?" Jane asked.

A darkness passed over Grace's face. "No. I used to be. But not so much anymore." She put on a fake smile, and Jane instantly felt bad. She wasn't sure why she asked the woman that. Talking about faith and prayer wasn't something she normally did with people, especially when she had just met them. Faith was something that needed context at the very least and a relationship between the listener and talker at the most. She had overstepped and caused the woman pain in mentioning it.

"I'm sorry. I shouldn't have blurted that out. Forgive me?"

Grace studied her a moment and smiled. This time the smile was genuine. "Forgiven. Don't think anything of it. I don't want to yap at you while you're browsing, but if you have any questions, let me know."

She started to go, but Jane didn't want the woman to leave. There was something she really liked about her.

Jane and Eric continued perusing, and then Jane asked her if it would be all right to take a picture of their booth.

"Yes," Grace said, "and thank you for asking first. We always appreciate that."

"I get it." Jane smiled. She knew how rude it was for someone to just snap pictures of an artist's work. She'd seen people do it in the gallery and constantly had to tell them to be respectful.

Both Jane and Eric chatted with her a few minutes more, and Jane took John Cambridge's card and held it up to the woman.

"I would love to talk with your husband further. Please let him know I'll be calling." She smiled, and Grace assured her she would.

"I liked her," Eric said as they left the booth, and Jane agreed. There was something about Grace that she found pleasant and comforting. How could a person get a sense about someone so quickly? But Jane had found her judgement of people was accurate much of the time. People were just like art; they gave off a sense of who they were if you just stood there long enough to take it all in.

They walked up several more aisles and came upon a food tent. Jane felt her stomach growl at the sight. She cringed, remembering that she'd already eaten an egg sandwich earlier. These early mornings seemed to jump-start her appetite.

"Hungry?" Eric grinned.

"You heard, hey?"

"I could go for a bite. And, I didn't tell you this, but Mrs. Ferch gave me twenty dollars to spend at the fair today."

Jane frowned at him.

"Hey," he shrugged, "I tried to give it back to her and she insisted. You know how she is."

"No," Jane said, "I mean, *why* would she do that?"

"For food and something she called, 'whatnots.'" He pointed to an open table under a tent. "Would you like to grab us a spot, and I can get our food?"

Jane told him what she wanted, a good-old fashioned Milwaukee brat with mustard on a Sheboygan roll. She sat down at the table and looked at her phone, surprised to see it was almost noon. She checked for a message of any kind from Brad, but there was nothing.

She took a selfie of herself and texted it to him, saying, "Having a great time at the art fair." She sent it and, within a second, received a thumbs-up. She sighed. That was so like him. "How is your Saturday going?" she texted and got silence in return. Not even the three dots that show up when someone is typing.

"Here you go." Eric put the brat down in front of her. "And chips. And"—he placed a giant brownie before her that appeared to be covered in caramel and nuts—"a big ole brownie. Just because."

Jane was pleasantly surprised that they had been having such a good time together. It had been easy to spend time with Eric. She watched him eat for a moment, trying to stop herself from wondering more about him.

He stopped eating and looked at her. "Do I have mustard on my face?" He raised an eyebrow.

She smiled. "No." She hesitated. "I was just thinking that I don't know much about you. Like, you know, where you work now, or…" She let the sentence trail off, hoping he would pick up on it.

"Right." His face seemed to fall. He wiped his mouth and sat back.

Jane regretted bringing it up. The subject of work dropped a heavy vibe on to the nice day they were having. She kept talking in an effort to wipe away the negativity she seemed to bring to their lunch.

"You know where I work," she acknowledged, "but really, sometimes I don't even know what I'm doing at that place. I work such long hours. I never"—she was going to say *have fun* or *see my boyfriend* but caught herself— "go out with my friends anymore. And I haven't had a raise in so long."

Eric nodded sympathetically. "You didn't get the promotion you were hoping for?" He guessed.

She'd forgotten how awkward she was at the coffee shop that morning. "Right," she laughed. "I forgot I told you about that. I love my job mostly," she continued. "I mean, things like this? Seeing art and talking to artists? But my boss is flighty most of the time, and lately I just feel… stuck."

He nodded. "That sounds familiar. I worked for a place like that. The corporate world can be tough sometimes. They make business decisions, and it's just—"

"Eric! Buddy!" A tall guy headed their way, and Jane noted that he was one of those people who seemed to know everyone wherever they go. He was high-fiving people and saying hello as he made his way to Eric. "Fancy meeting you here, bud. I was just going to call you tonight. We're almost good to go on the move."

Eric looked at Jane a bit nervously. "Uh… that's good, Wayne." Eric bit his lip. "Let me introduce Jane. Jane, this is my friend Wayne."

They shook hands. "Nice to meet you, Jane!" Wayne was gregarious, to say the least. He turned to Eric. "Maggie's working late tonight. I'm on dad patrol." Wayne waved at Jane. "Nice meeting you. Tell Eric to bring you to the barbeque" and headed back out into the art fair. Within a moment, he was already lost in the crowds.

Jane felt like they had been blown over by Hurricane Wayne and his big personality. "He's quite a character."

Eric nodded. "Yeah. He is. He's a good guy. And he's right. I should bring you to the barbeque. If you're interested, that is."

Now would be a good time to tell him I have a boyfriend, she thought. Instead, she said, "A barbeque?"

"Yep. Wayne and Maggie are having this huge cookout. Brats, chicken, barbecued pork… you name it. It's next Saturday, if you'd like to come."

Eric had such kindness in his eyes. Thoughts of Brad vanished, like dandelion wishes into the air, floating away from her.

"Can't actually," she heard herself saying, the now familiar refrain when people asked her to do something. She was constantly holding out hope that she would be spending time with Brad. "What's the occasion, anyway?" she added.

"What?"

She wondered if she had said something wrong.

"Are they having the barbeque for any particular reason?"

He blew out a breath. Something had changed in Eric just then. "Yeah. They're uh… moving. To another state."

"Oh." She felt Eric's disappointment then, and didn't want to press things further. Obviously, he was upset that his friend was moving away.

"Anyway… where were we?"

He seemed ready to move on from the subject, so she followed his lead.

"We were talking about jobs." She sat up. "How overworked we are, and how you were at your last job—"

"Oh right." Eric was playing with his straw. "Right. Well, tell me more about you. Do you have any brothers and sisters?"

Avoiding the jobs subject again. Why did she keep bringing it up?

"One sister," she answered him. "Charlotte."

"You two close?"

"Yes and no. We're very close in age. She's less than a year older than me. But she's more of a free spirit. Kind of like my dad."

"And you're not?" Eric pretended to be shocked.

Jane rolled her eyes, but it was fun to see him tease. "No. Not quite."

Eric got serious for a moment. "So, you don't like the fact that your sister is a free spirit?"

"Well,"—she thought about it—"like my dad? To be honest, I love him. I really do, but it was hard to grow up with him. He was fun dad"—she made air quotes, and Eric nodded—"and he was always thinking of schemes on how to make money, invent things, sell different things, but his ideas never quite panned out. He never really worked much."

Jane stopped and let the sentence hang there. She didn't want to tell Eric about his constant badgering her for money. She doubted he'd understand, and besides that, the subject embarrassed her.

"And Charlotte's like that?"

"No, actually. But, get this." She sat up straighter. "She took off when she was eighteen, to Seattle, and just hoped that it would all work out. Didn't have a job. Nothing."

Eric looked at her for a moment so deeply that Jane thought he might just lean over and kiss her. He finally shook his head and looked away. "Seattle, you say? She just decided to move out there?"

Jane nodded. "Crazy."

"And did it work out?"

"Of course, it did! She's Ms. Lucky Pants. She met a guy—on the plane, mind you—that just turned out to be her perfect man. She married him. They have a beautiful daughter. Sally. Fairy tale."

Eric considered this. "And you're jealous of that?"

"What? *Jealous?*" Was she? She'd never thought about it like that. "No. Not jealous. I mean, she's just so lucky."

"But you could have that kind of 'luck.'" Now it was Eric's turn to use air quotes.

"What do you mean by that?"

"She trusted her gut and made a decision based on what she felt in her heart."

"Yeah, well it could have worked out really badly for her," she grumbled.

"It could have, but it didn't."

"*Lucky.*"

"Maybe," he conceded. The subject had suddenly made him very quiet, and Jane wondered what the change was all about. "Jane, can I ask you a personal question?"

She nodded, looking into his green eyes. It was hard not to agree.

"Just… about your sister. I know something about

stepping out on faith. I'm trying to do that now. I know that it's hard to understand what to do next in your life sometimes. It's like… you're unhappy, but you don't know what to do to change it. Your sister… maybe she just had a feeling. Maybe she was just young, and as you said, she got lucky. But I think it's more than that.

"I do think life tries to steer us in certain directions. Sometimes it's difficult to know what to do next, and other times, it seems very clear. Even when it's a completely new situation, and we might be a little scared deep down, we still believe it's right."

She thought about what he said. "You sound like you're talking from experience."

"When my company downsized, I took it as a message for me to do something new. I worked too much. I had no life. I was engaged to a girl who was so ashamed of the fact that I lost my job, she dumped me. Then I had no job and no girlfriend. It was a really rough time. But I figured it out," he said, getting up to throw away the garbage from their table. "And you will, too."

He held out his hand to help Jane up. "Don't settle for a life you're not happy with."

CHAPTER 7 - GRACE

Grace liked Jane. Her long, blonde hair had been done in a cute ponytail that she wished she could pull off herself, and there was a sweetness about her. Grace felt that she was much younger than herself but was obviously very mature. It showed in the way she noticed Grace had been uncomfortable talking about certain things. Most people were so clueless when it came to that.

John came back into the booth and handed her a coffee. Grace thanked him, then relayed the conversation she'd had with Jane.

"She really seemed to like your work. So did her boyfriend. Or, I guess, he said he was her neighbor," Grace said, thinking about how cute they looked together. "And Cream City Gallery would be a good spot for your work. I mean, it's the perfect size, really. And location! Right in the Third Ward."

She reached for his hand and held it in hers.

"I can't wait for you to meet Jane. She seemed to understand your work, you know?"

John smiled at her. "I'm sure your sales skills were part of that."

When did he become so considerate? She remembered glimpses of it when they were dating, but he had grown more in tune with her as the years had gone on. It made her feel good that he noticed her contributions to the life they had built, even the ones that seemed like they were all about him, like his painting.

He leaned in close to her. "I love you, and I do feel you could benefit from a break." His voice was low and tickled against her ear.

"Yeah." She rubbed her neck, realizing how tense she had been since their ex-friends had shown up earlier. They said their jabs and left, probably never thinking about Grace or John until the next time they were prompted to cause trouble. But their constant negative influence left cracks here and there, as only the sting of friends who delight in your misery can do. "I guess I could use a break."

He went off to talk to a few more people who had come into the booth, and she took the opportunity do as he suggested.

Grace left to get some coffee at the food tent. As she strolled past the other booths, she thought about how much she'd changed over the years. She used to think that if she could just make it out of childhood, she'd be okay. If she could just survive her mother she would grow up and have her own life. But as she grew, she realized the damage that a life filled with rejection really did. It left her on unsteady ground so it would take her longer to learn how to live, to learn how to accept love like the kind she got from John. It took Grace time to actually learn how not to bow to people who treated you badly, and it was a lesson she was still learning.

She reached the food tent and ordered a refill, then

poured a generous helping of creamer in. Then she sat down at a small table inside the tent. She sipped slowly, blowing on the cup.

"Grace?"

"Oh!" She was completely lost in her own thoughts. "Jane. Hello."

Grace was happy to see her again. She'd left such a positive impression that it was a welcome surprise to see her again so soon.

"My husband is back in the booth now," she explained. "I mean, if you still want to talk to him."

"Yes, I do. It might seem totally weird, actually, but we're just about to leave," Jane gestured to Eric, who was standing off to the side. He waved as he realized they were both looking at him. "And I just had this weird sensation to ask you to coffee. I mean, I'd like to get to know you. I mean, Eric just reminded me that changing my life starts with steps. Like, asking someone for coffee. Getting to know them. Changing direction."

Jane shook her head, embarrassed. "I'm babbling like an idiot." She laughed.

"No, not at all." Grace laughed now, too. "I was actually just thinking that I needed to meet some new friends, too. It's hard to do when you get older," she confided. "And coffee?" She held up her cup. "I'm a fan."

They made plans to meet after Grace dropped off The Space Between Dreaming and a few other originals at the gallery the following Wednesday. She felt lighter, happier now that she had shaken off the bad feelings that their former friends had left behind. There was a cool breeze coming into the tent that she appreciated, and she closed her eyes to enjoy it fully.

She got up from her table and ordered a black coffee to go for her husband and a large water in case he wanted that instead. It was the least she could do after he encouraged her to take a break. He was right, of course. She needed to clear her head. Grace held on too tightly to these people who brought negativity in her life and caused her to question herself. Too often she'd let it interfere with her happiness.

The woman behind the counter told her she'd bring the coffee and water in a carrier out to her, and that was fine with Grace. She sat down again and soaked up the additional opportunity to catch her breath before rejoining her husband in their booth.

Grace noticed a woman with a baby rush into the tent and sit down. The child clung to her mother, bouncing as the woman hurried toward a table in the center of the tent. The baby's sandy-blonde hair was damp, with little curls plastered against her head. Her blue eyes twinkled at Grace as the woman held the baby up and kissed her cheek over and over with loud smacking sounds. The baby seemed annoyed by the smothering, or perhaps was just too warm with the heavy sweater she had on. Her red face made her light-blue eyes stand out, and she looked at Grace with a frown as if she were asking her to please stop her mother from sucking up her entire face. Grace smiled at the child, wishing she could tell her that her mother was in love with her and would never stop being annoying.

At seeing this mother, she once again thought of her own. She wished she had siblings she could call up to help sort out the complicated grief she'd felt. If there had been someone else who was born to her mother but raised by other people, they would understand the range of emotions she felt.

On one hand, she seemed detached about her mother's death. It was hard to care about a woman who had left her thirty years before. She'd had an entire lifetime without her.

In fact, her mother never even knew her, never knew what kind of person she turned out to be. But that was where the grief would grab her, jolt her. Her mother chose to leave her, to write her off, as if it were just too much work to care about her. She told so many lies about Grace that a stranger felt the need to send her a nasty letter, attacking her. That plunged her into sadness when she thought of it.

Since learning of her mother's death, she went back and forth between these extremes. It had left her feeling like a tiny boat rocking in a stormy sea. She didn't know how she would find the shore again.

Grace looked once more at the woman in the tent, who continued kissing her baby, adding a "mwa mwa mwa" sound after every screechy smooch, and the child gave Grace one last frown before wailing at the top of her lungs. The woman tried to soothe her with baby talk, using words like "my widdle gurl" and "who's Mommy's widdo beebee" punctuated by more kisses, which sounded more like slurping of soup than affection.

Little beads of sweat accumulated on the baby's red face as she wailed. The child grabbed her mother's hair and pulled, her chubby fingers working their way through the woman's perfectly straightened hair. She squirmed in her mother's arms, and rather than remove the too-hot sweater or refrain from wetting the child's face with her lipstick-coated lips, the mother continued the smooching until a worker came out from behind the counter to see what the noise was. The clerk walked to Grace's table and handed her the coffee and water, and with a nod in the woman's direction, whispered, "Sounds like she's trying to swallow that baby whole."

Grace giggled, nodding. The baby continued squirming, and she gave the child a little wave. The woman turned and smiled at Grace.

"I don't know what's got her so riled up this morning."

Grace didn't want to state the obvious, that the child looked to be sweating underneath too many layers of clothes. "She's beautiful," she said instead.

"Oh, thank you."

The woman added another smooch to the child, who gave her mother a yank with another tug of her hair. She kept smiling and gently tried to extract the child's sweaty fist from her hair.

"Now, Ella, let's be gentle."

Ella let out another screech in response.

"Do you have kids?"

The woman smiled as she said it, and Grace wondered how this question became acceptable small talk. Why didn't people ask every single person if they were married, or what their sex life was like upon first meeting them? Or maybe, what kind of credit card bills they'd racked up? But those items were deemed too personal for small talk. Talking about kids right off the bat should be considered too personal as well.

"No."

Grace said it lightly, learning after all these years not to elaborate. The woman waited, eventually frowning when Grace offered nothing else by way of explanation. But she'd finally learned that she didn't owe the woman that. She didn't owe anyone an explanation of her life.

Grace smiled at the woman and picked up her coffee and water, and left.

The next day, John got up early. Grace pulled the covers tighter as he headed to the bathroom to shower and change. The entire bed got cold when he left it. His warmth was why they were able to keep the heat off at night until December. She missed snuggling up to his back, wrapping her arm around his side and pulling herself close. She kept her eyes closed, but sleep stubbornly left her. Still, her head was filled with thoughts of the art fair.

It was interesting to Grace what a day brought with it. You got up, never knowing whom you'd see or talk with. Art fair days in particular were hard to judge. They'd had times when they hadn't made a sale. She'd feel so defeated afterward, all that work, with prep and setup, and yet John would shrug it off easily, already focusing on their next event.

But other times, like yesterday, they sold a lot and made some good connections. It helped that now they knew which fairs were right for the kinds of art they sold. Not every fair had a good audience for John's work. It was all a matter of taste, she supposed.

"Still sleeping? Or faking it?" He kissed her nose and she opened her eyes. He sat on the edge of the bed, smiling at her.

"Not faking it. I was just thinking."

"Uh-oh. What now? Do we need to rearrange the living room again?" He got up, taking the towel from his waist and changing into jeans and a green button-down shirt. His eyes were blue, but the shirt brought out flecks of emerald in them.

She laughed. "No, I'm not thinking about furniture layout. I was going over the art fair yesterday. We did really well."

She got out of bed just as he was buttoning the last button and slid her arms around him. They stayed that way for a long moment, with him rubbing her back and holding her close.

"I can thank you for that."

She pulled away and looked up at him.

"You can thank me? What?"

He pulled her tight again, kissing her on the mouth. Then he smiled down at her.

"You do all the PR for me. What would I know about getting people to our booth?"

He ran his hands through her hair.

"Oh stop. It's not me. It's your art. People are really starting to find it." She giggled as his kisses tickled her neck. He kissed her again on the mouth.

"I thought you were going to church this morning."

"I am."

"I'll go make you some coffee."

Grace grabbed her robe and headed down the hall to the kitchen. She put the coffee maker on and wondered what life would be like right now if they'd had kids. Would she be making a proper breakfast for everyone, rather than just coffee? Would she want to go to church with him, feeling more charitable toward God?

The years of infertility were hard enough emotionally, but the debt they incurred with treatments was almost totally debilitating. They were just starting to come out of it, finally getting a handle on it, but it would still be years before they were free. What then? Saving for retirement, she supposed. Saving for retirement in the years when others their age might already be retired.

She could picture a baby boy who grew to be a man, with her green eyes and John's dark, wavy hair. The combination of the two of them. She used to hear that from the foster families she stayed with, how his chin was his father's, how her music talent came from this person.

She wondered if the kids who wound up looking nothing like their parents still heard such things about the qualities each parent felt they had passed on.

The thought of their own children that had never come brought the sting of tears, but she pushed it away, pouring her husband a cup of coffee and wanting to get on with the business of their Sunday morning. She was tired of tears and the sadness that seemed to steal away the happy moments.

She put the coffee in a travel mug and wrote out a check for him to take to church.

He came into the kitchen, grabbed the mug and the check, and gave her a hug.

"Have a good… time. Or whatever."

"Or whatever." He winked at her, pausing to study her. Grace figured he could see the start of tears on her, knowing after all this time when dark thoughts grabbed hold of her. She didn't want him to ask her because the tears would surely come then.

"Pick up milk on the way home, please."

She could see his brow lift, mentally making note. They hadn't really needed milk, but she needed him to go, not comfort her. Not now. He needed to do his thing with God, and she needed time alone. She'd tried to be friends with God, but a lousy childhood hadn't made it easy, and years of heartbreak had made it almost impossible.

Grace used to question her husband, how he could possibly go to church when God hadn't done them any favors, but his response was always about how blessed they were. Just to be alive, to have each other, they were so blessed. Her husband used church as a way to learn more about God, and Grace avoided it, wanting to do just the opposite.

She grabbed a bowl from the cupboard, feeling like

some cereal for breakfast. She scanned the pantry for something appealing, noting with disappointment that all she seemed to buy these days were things with fiber. She chose a box and shook out some of the contents, then splashed some almond milk over it and hoped for the best. Sitting at the kitchen island, she thought about how nice it was to have the place to herself just to think and relax. They'd been so busy lately, with work and his painting business and just doing the everyday things in life, like running errands. Their life was definitely full. People had always told her that not having children would make their marriage boring, but it hadn't been the case. She was happy to spend the rest of her life with this man who continued to interest her and make her proud.

She finished half the bowl of cereal, deciding that it might be good for her, but it certainly didn't taste good. She spilled half the bowl on the table, cursing her clumsiness, then put the bowl in the sink and rinsed down the uneaten cereal. As she wiped up the table and counter, she heard something down the hall in his studio. She suspected that he had left the window open again in there and felt a slight irritation that after twenty years of marriage, there were some things that she repeatedly had to ask him to do. *Can you close the window, please? Will you please not drink from the juice container? Can you just pick up your socks and place them in the hamper?*

Grace walked down the hall, and as she opened the studio door, she could feel the September breeze hit her face before she even entered the room.

There were sketches on the table moving with each gust of wind, like a classroom full of children begging to be called on. She closed the window and looked at John's latest work, another woman, this time on a sunny path in what looked like a park. The painting was brighter than

The Space Between Dreaming, but the woman was just as sad, just as confused. There was longing there. This painting seemed to say that she had given up something very important to her and refused to leave her seat on the park bench now that she had it.

She'd always loved her husband's work, but lately she saw nothing but their life story played out in each painting. She wondered if it had always been this way or if it was something she purposely saw as she thought through things herself. For a moment, she wondered if he could read her so well that even her thoughts would find their way into his paintings.

CHAPTER 8 - JANE

Jane texted Brad the next morning.

"Meet for coffee?"

She added three hearts and a coffee cup and got a thumbs-up in return. She thought about suggesting the coffee shop near her apartment, the one she went to every morning, and then realized she didn't want Brad there. That space was sacred to her. It was where she went each morning to center herself for the day ahead. It was where she awkwardly tried talking to Eric the first time. At first, she told herself that Brad probably wouldn't like that place anyway with its artsy touches and mishmash furniture. There were paintings hung salon style, floor to ceiling, all over the shop, with old, weathered doors as dividers that allowed for the impression of a more intimate setting in certain areas.

Brad didn't care for much of what Jane liked, now that she'd really thought about it. But it was more than that. She didn't want him in her favorite space, with his manic energy, staring at his phone and not even stopping a moment to appreciate the inspired vibe that she felt there.

She suggested a different place, a national chain coffee shop located halfway between her apartment and his. Even in their living spaces, she noted suddenly, they differed. She lived on Milwaukee's East Side, in an old Victorian home that had been converted to an apartment building, with Mrs. Ferch on the ground floor, Eric on the second, and Jane in what was formerly the attic space.

Brad lived in a modern condo in Mequon, a suburb north of Milwaukee proper that'd had its own resurgence of late, with living spaces built above upscale restaurants. Jane couldn't imagine living above a restaurant. She suspected it was where Brad ate dinner most nights.

But did he? She wondered now, if the life she imagined him living during the week, when they didn't see each other, matched with her assumptions. Long ago, she had accepted that he worked long hours. But somehow it meant that they didn't spend time together, either. He cited the distance between them as the reason, but it was only twenty minutes on I43, and that wasn't too long to drive to see your girlfriend. Was it?

She glanced at her phone and saw that he was ten minutes late. She was going to wait for him but decided to order instead. She got an iced latte, and scanned through the pictures she had on her phone from the day before at the art fair. There were several she'd show Bug, suggestions she had for artists to add to the gallery. But she realized she also needed to get serious about asking him about a promotion. What was she afraid of?

Eric had also taken a photo of her looking through John Cambridge's art booth. Jane hadn't even realized he'd done it until later that night when he texted it to her, saying, "Enjoyed today. Thanks." He'd added a palette emoji.

The photo was of her looking at the painting called The Space Between Dreaming. It was of a woman in bed, moonlight shining on her face and dressers on each side of her. There was a blue blanket on the bed that seemed to stand out from the darker colors of the picture, and her arms reached out before her, as if she were grasping for something that the viewer could not see. The picture spoke to her so deeply, that longing of something you can't articulate with your voice but that which your soul will not relinquish. It made Jane feel like this woman in the picture desperately needed her friendship and, at the same time, was her. She shook off the feeling but needed to find out more. It had been a long time since an art piece gave her a shiver she could feel down to her bones.

Jane remembered how much she had enjoyed talking with John's wife, Grace. Grace had remained quiet and kept a respectful distance while she allowed Jane to process her thoughts. She liked the fact that Grace knew how to help customers buy art without being too intrusive. There was a thought process involved. You had to be ready to offer answers or encouragement for those who hesitated, but also allow them to imagine the picture in their home or figure out what the work was saying to them.

Jane smiled as she looked at how Eric had captured her, so engrossed in the art that she'd lost herself for a moment.

Her thoughts were interrupted as Brad roughly placed a kiss on her cheek and sat down opposite her. He drummed his fingers on the table and looked around the restaurant.

"Hi," she said, prompting him to look at her.

"Hey," he said, scanning through his phone, then putting it down on the table again. She thought he would get up and order a coffee of his own, but instead he kept looking around the coffee shop.

She followed his gaze. He was acting like he was

meeting someone else there. It was odd, she thought, then noticed for the first time that he was wearing a dress shirt and nice pants. Not his usual Sunday attire.

"You look nice. Are you planning on going somewhere?" She thought they might spend the day together.

"Uh… yeah. Going to the office."

"On a Sunday?" That was unusual.

He looked at her for the first time. "Yes, Jane. Are you questioning me?"

She sat up straighter. "Why are you so crabby this morning?"

He stood. "I'm not. You're reading into it."

"Okay," she said, noting that he still didn't have any coffee. "Want something?" She gestured with her cup.

He was texting, not seeing her gesture. "No," he said, not looking up.

"Brad?" she said, not wanting to ask the question but feeling she must. "Is everything all right? I mean, you're behaving rather strangely lately…" She let that hang, but actually, she realized with a heavy heart, he wasn't acting all that strangely. There were times when he was nicer, to be sure, but also plenty of times when he was exactly as he was now.

He waited a beat, finished his text, and looked at her. "Strange, how?" He frowned.

"Do you love me, Brad?" she blurted, surprising herself. "You don't even seem to like me. It's just that, we usually never even see each other during the week—"

"Which you have never minded," he cut in.

"Which I have *tolerated*," she corrected, feeling a new sense of strength. "And now you don't even want to see me on a weekend. Plus—"

"Why?" he spat. "Because I didn't want to go to some

craft fair with the other geriatrics? You have the dumbest hobbies, Jane. Probably from hanging out with that old lady in your building. You're more like her every minute."

That stung, mostly because Jane loved Mrs. Ferch. He stared at her for a minute, and then his eyes flicked to his phone. She could tell he really wanted to grab it, and after a beat, she saw him smirk in the nasty way he did whenever he was about to say something hurtful. Instead of talking, though, he just texted again.

"Why are you such an angry person?" she finally asked.

He put his phone away again and shook his head in disbelief. "Excuse me, now? I don't want to go to a craft fair, and now that means I'm angry?"

"You seem very angry. Yes."

"Well, Jane, if you had a real job instead of one where you go to craft fairs as part of your actual job, maybe you would understand the pressure I'm under."

She thought about saying *what pressure* but that would underscore his point. But she was still left with the haunting feeling that she had no idea what to make of his emotions.

"Why are you with me?" she asked instead. "Seriously, Brad. We've dated for eight years, and at this particular moment in time, I'm wondering what it is you even see in me, because you don't appear to even like me, let alone love me." She realized with a pang of hurt that he had never answered her question earlier about whether he loved her.

He sighed. It was a long, obnoxious, drawn-out sigh meant to tell her how much she bored him.

"Jane, you want some truth? Huh? I've been through all this before." He gestured his hand back and forth between them. "All the bickering. All the fighting. You know what I got out of it? A lifelong commitment for money, like I'm a cash machine. My ex has taken me to court multiple times to cough up money for our kid. Like you, she doesn't have a real job and can't support herself. Like you, she always wanted to know where our relationship was going. And then, guess what? One day she tells me she's pregnant. And that's it. Without ever wanting to, I became a dad." He laughed bitterly, grabbing his phone again. He flipped through the pictures he'd had on it and held out his phone so she could the one he'd stopped on.

"Here's my daughter. Magnolia. I hate her name. I didn't have a voice in naming her. I didn't have a choice on being a dad. And here I am, ten years later, forking over cash right and left. You want to know why I work so much? That's why."

Jane stared at him, feeling gut-punched. "You were married before?"

"No, Jane. I was engaged. Okay? It was no big deal. Obviously, the wedding didn't happen."

"When were you engaged?"

He rolled his eyes at her. "Years ago, Jane. I was young. She was young. It didn't happen."

"You never told me this before."

"What are you, jealous?"

"And you have a child? Why did you never tell me this?" She felt as if she were looking at a stranger. Did she even know this man?

"Because I knew this is how you'd react." He laughed in this nasty way, as if she were throwing a fit simply because she had asked him about his life.

"And how am I reacting, Brad? I'm asking you a question. We've dated for eight years. Don't you think I deserve some answers about who you are?"

He grabbed his phone and looked at the time. "Jane,

look, you know who I am. I am late for my daughter's birthday party, and my ex is a real witch when I don't show up to things on time. I need to go. We'll talk about this later."

"Brad?" she called to him as he was leaving.

He turned halfway, his strong nose and lips making what she thought was a perfect profile. She wished he were staying so they could talk more about this. The moment seemed to call for more than a casual mention of a previous engagement and a child.

"What else aren't you telling me?"

He sighed, a loud, long sigh to let her know how irritated he was. "Nothing, Jane. You know it all now. Okay? I've got to run."

Jane went back home and stared out her living room window. She felt as if she were in a fog, as if every movement was belabored and heavy. She thought about going down to Mrs. Ferch's apartment for comfort but couldn't bring herself to do it, not after Brad had made the comment about Jane living like an old person. What was the term he used? A geriatric?

To be honest, Jane always felt as if Mrs. Ferch was far younger than her in many ways. She acted younger. She seemed to have a more robust outlook on life. Jane wondered if that was her personality or did that happen to a person when they'd lived a certain number of years? Did the uncertainty that came with finding love and getting settled in your career leave you constantly wondering about the future? Was that why Brad was so angry all the time?

She got up, feeling resentment all over again. He was at his daughter's birthday party. A party she was not invited to for a girl she had never even known about until today. The anger rose in her. Maybe instead of worrying what Brad thought about her friendship with Mrs. Ferch, he should worry about being honest with Jane instead. She was doing nothing wrong and wouldn't be made to feel as if she were.

She knocked on Mrs. Ferch's door, all ready to launch into what happened, when she heard a dog barking. Mrs. Ferch opened the door and motioned her inside.

"Don't mind this cutie pie," Mrs. Ferch was saying about the dog, but she saw that Eric was also there. "He barks whenever he hears someone at the door. That makes him a good watchdog. Doesn't it, boy?" She stroked the dog on the head and it lay down at the woman's feet, watching Jane closely. She'd always wanted a dog, growing up.

"Hi," Eric had said to her. "Have a seat, Jane. I need to pop out for a bit." Then, to Mrs. Ferch, he said, "You okay with Pepper for half an hour or so?"

"Of course!" the woman exclaimed. "Before you go, dear, reach up in the high cabinet there." She pointed at a spot above the stove. "That's right. I've got some bowls in there from Mickey. I never got rid of them. Can you fill up one with water? That's right."

Eric did as she asked and placed the bowl before the dog, who took a long drink. "He was thirsty." He smiled at her. "I haven't thought about Mickey in a long time. He was the best dog." He waved at Mrs. Ferch and then at Jane and left. The dog finished drinking and looked at the door, then to Mrs. Ferch.

"Oh, he'll be back. Don't you worry," she assured him,

scratching his head.

Jane placed her hand down so the dog could smell her. She pet the top of his head, and he jumped up on her leg, wanting more.

"He likes you," Mrs. Ferch noted with approval. "I think dogs know things about people," she said.

Jane felt as if she was out of the loop. She gestured to the dog. "So, who is this little guy?"

"This is Pepper." At the mention of his name, the dog looked up at Mrs. Ferch. "Eric is watching him for a friend. Just last night and today, I think."

Jane nodded, silently noting how kind that was. How often did she do favors for friends like that anymore? Her whole life seemed to be about work and trying to figure out Brad.

"And also, Mickey? I don't think I've ever heard you talk about him."

"I wish you could have met Mickey." Mrs. Ferch smiled at the memory. "I loved that dog, but he was quite a yapper. Such a good companion, though. You know," she said, sitting back down at the kitchen table, "I think that dog is one of the reasons I was able to get through that time after Mr. Ferch's passing. It was rough. I couldn't sleep at night. Couldn't get used to coming home and feeling that quiet that just takes over your whole being, body and soul."

Jane understood that sense of quiet. She'd felt it every night when she came home, but she tried to drown out the noise with thoughts of work. If she worked until she couldn't anymore, she'd come home exhausted and sleep through the night. The quiet was still there, but by the time she'd fully realize it, another morning had broken, and it was time to do it all over again.

"I know what you mean," she surprised herself by

saying aloud. "I feel it, too, but I'm sure it's nothing like losing a husband."

Mrs. Ferch shrugged. "Losing a husband, searching for one… it's all about the desire to be loved. When Mr. Ferch passed, I was bitter and angry for a while." She looked at Jane and laughed sadly. "I was angry at the world."

Jane's heart went out to Mrs. Ferch, and she squeezed the older woman's hand. With the care she gave Jane, it had been too easy to forget that she was just another woman who could feel loneliness and hurt also. She thought about what to say next, but Mrs. Ferch sat up straighter and with that simple gesture seemed to take the moment back, shaking the sadness from her shoulders like an old shawl.

"Anyway," Mrs. Ferch continued, "I've had a wonderful life. No right to complain about a thing."

"I feel like that's all I do," Jane said.

"No, actually, you don't. You should, though. Get it out!" Mrs. Ferch made a gesture with her hands as if to say, *welcome to the party.* "Everyone needs an outlet for grief and hurt. That's what Mickey was for me. And you're looking very glum right now, my girl." She slapped the table, and Jane jumped. "Out with it!"

Jane laughed and then shook her head. It all sounded so stupid, that she had been so stupid. She launched into the events of the morning, all the details that were making her feel very foolish and naïve. When she finished speaking, she placed her hands in her lap, not sure what to say next. The dog jumped up and licked her on her hand. She picked him up and sat him on her lap, which seemed to delight the dog. He licked her again and then settled in on her lap, with Jane absentmindedly petting his back.

Mrs. Ferch had been leaning forward as she spoke, and when Jane had finished talking, the woman leaned back in her chair.

"My goodness," she said.

"You think I'm stupid for being with him," Jane said. It was a not a question.

"No," she said, "but I do think this is the perfect time to take a step back and evaluate. This can be a good thing in your relationship or a bad thing. It's either an opening, where you two will be more honest with each other, or something that will lead you to realize that you're not right for each other."

Jane felt very, very tired of her relationship with Brad. "Right now? I feel like I don't know where to go next. I am in a haze. Like a sleepwalker."

"Oh, I know how that is." Mrs. Ferch cleared her throat. "When Mr. Ferch died? I was in a world of hurt. But I'd been through some things, and despite my anger, God gave me a strong spirit." She hooted and slapped the table, amused at her words. "I went to bed one night angry as a hornet, and when I woke up the next morning, I had the strongest urge to buy a dog. I had never had a dog before. Can you imagine? I didn't know a thing about them. I headed over to the Milwaukee Humane Society and picked out a pup. There was this cute little Schnauzer that seemed to smile at me as soon as I came in. Now, I know dogs technically can't smile"—she glanced over at the dog on Jane's lap, who looked at the older woman as if hanging on her every word—"or maybe they can." They both laughed.

Mrs. Ferch went on. "I talked to a nice young man when I was at the humane society. He was a kid, just about to graduate high school, and a part-time volunteer there, and he was going through his own kind of grief. His father had just passed away. I told him about my dilemma, that I was an old lady and lonely, and I wasn't about to get married again. But I told this kid *something* had brought me there that morning. I thought he might just laugh in my face. I really wasn't making much sense in those days. With the lack of sleep, and the hurt in my heart, I found it hard just to get the words out.

"But here's the amazing thing. That boy and I became friends. We talked about grief, and in the process, he mentioned that he needed a place to live. I had never rented out this place before, but I had the upstairs space that you're in now," she told Jane, "and I told him I had this creepy attic space, and he could have it for free if he helped me clean it out." She laughed. "I told him after we did that, I'd let him live there for free if he helped me with the other space, and he did.

"And I took the dog home, and almost immediately, I felt a little bit better about life. I still missed Mr. Ferch. I do to this day. But I was able to stifle that quiet that I thought would overtake me. With Mickey, I had a purpose. I couldn't wallow because I had to get up, feed him, teach him to do his business.

"So then"—the older woman got up from the table as if to shake off the bad memories—"that dog just made it seem like it would all be okay. He reminded me that there's more to life than our painful memories. That's how I met Eric, and I became a landlady for the first time."

That explained why Eric and Mrs. Ferch seemed to have a bond. Then again, Jane had one with the woman, also. Her spirit was open and loving, and suddenly, it reminded her of someone she knew and hadn't spoken with in a very long time.

CHAPTER 9 - GRACE

Grace knew that when John returned from church, he would ask her how her morning went, and she would say *fine*, even though it was entirely unremarkable, the same as she did every Sunday. She always felt a little guilty not doing anything of any importance while he'd been away. Their routine was that they would make lunch, and when they cleaned up the dishes, he would tell her he was going to work on his latest painting. She was happy that he had found painting. But what about her? What was her passion?

One of her foster mothers was a gardener, and Grace remembered being outside with her occasionally as she toiled away on pruning buds and pulling weeds. It was one of the few times she'd felt at peace in her foster home, one of the few times she didn't think about her future and what happened if her mother wanted her back, or didn't.

Grace had started a garden when they'd moved to their house. She did many things, like paint the extra bedroom in preparation for a child that would come into their family, place her grandmother's teacups along the kitchen shelving, and sew curtains and pillows. She remembered being energic and excited at the prospects their married life would hold.

Somewhere along the line, the room she painted still remained empty, the curtains and pillows seemed to mock her, and her garden looked as if it hadn't been tended to in quite some time. She stood in the backyard, hands on hips, and took in the shabbiness of it, almost as if she were seeing it for the first time. The row of hydrangeas behind the garage that she had loved so much were nearly gone. The trellis that held the morning glory flowers was rusted, the vines withered and brown. The row of purple coneflowers that lined the walkway was full of dandelions, and the ragged robin was overgrown. What was it her foster mother had said about that one? That it attracted butterflies if you took care of it right. No wonder there wasn't a butterfly in sight.

It looked like the yard of someone who had been sick for a long time and couldn't take care of things properly. It looked like she felt on the inside. She tried to think of how long it had been since she'd been out there, really working it like she should, and she couldn't even remember. She decided to at least rake out the leaves that had accumulated there, which choked out all the flowers she'd once planted. She searched throughout the garage and even the house for the rake, feeling frustrated that she was unorganized and couldn't find it.

She thought of a former foster mother as she worked and wondered now if she could see Grace from where she was, in heaven, most likely, looking down—if she got to see their future, and if it were a pleasant one. She wished she could just ask her if it would be all be all right in the end.

Grace looked out at the neighbors' lawns. When she

was out in the garden with her foster mother as a little girl, it became about the two of them, with the sun on their faces and a private world that made her feel loved and protected. She never noticed the other people outside, the folks who lived near her, or who might have been working on their lawns or playing with their kids. It was just her and her foster mother, and it was enough.

Being out in this poor excuse for a garden, after all the work she had once put into it, shamed Grace. She should have been keeping it up. Grace looked up and saw her neighbor wave. She waved back but felt weird about it. Seeing them cutting their lawns, raking leaves… going on as if nothing in the world was wrong. She wondered how many of them also had broken hearts and were each trying to do normal things so they could feel like a regular person instead of someone who felt as if the world were against them.

She walked back inside and stood in front of Glenn's bedroom door. She hadn't been in there since the last miscarriage. She and John had closed Glenn's bedroom door and went their own separate ways toward banishing grief. They hadn't spoke of the child again or what they should do with the room now. Grace supposed that when they were ready, they'd decide, but for now, it brought her comfort to know there was a place in the house where the spirit of the child they lost could exist.

Grace put her hand on the doorknob, but stopped. She couldn't do it. Not today. Not yet. She needed to remember that there was a little boy who almost joined their family, whom they loved, even for a short while, that had a blue room and stuffed animals and too many toys. Maybe if she left the room the way it was, his spirit would stay around a little while longer. She knew it didn't make any sense, but she imagined the spirit of her mother caring for Glenn in that room, rocking him and singing to him, and giving him the kind of love that she couldn't give Grace.

She took her hand off the doorknob, and instead, decided to get dressed and get on with the day. She walked back to her bedroom, peeled off her clothes, and tossed them on the floor. She took a long shower, letting the hot water pour over her face and shoulders. She made the water as hot as she could stand it and stood, closing her eyes until she had the sense that time had moved on outside of her, outside of the shower and bathroom. When her skin started feeling pruned, she finally turned off the water, and dried her body with a towel.

She wrapped the towel around her and lingered in front of the mirror, staring at herself and seeing someone she didn't recognize anymore. There was a woman who had aged, badly, she thought. Deep lines in her forehead and around her eyes. Grace made a crying expression with her face, and sure enough, that's where the lines deepened. Grief had slapped her around, and the effects were all over her face. She noticed more lines as she frowned.

She shook her head. Making faces at herself was not going to help anything. She went back to their bedroom and flipped through her clothes hanging in the closet. She noticed John's smock hanging on the back of their bedroom door, and took it off the hook, running her hand along the multicolored paint stains, the finger marks where he'd use the smock as a cloth. She thought of all the moments he'd spent in his studio, all the time there away from her, where he exorcised his demons and chased away his pain.

He was handling this better than her. She knew that: deep down, in the part of her heart that held on to joy, the part she had locked away when she was first married, when she had first fallen in love, and the world seemed open and full of possibilities. When this world of children, of family, had been pulled from her each time, she had cried and walked aimlessly around the house, her anger bubbling up like a caustic fountain. At the same time, John became quiet, and painted. He was content to do that, to live a life that allowed him to put his grief and emotions out on display for others to learn from, and even, enjoy.

She'd noticed the fight had gone from him. She'd felt so much closer to him in the beginning, when he also struggled to find peace at night, when they both longed to sleep, fitfully, with silly, throwaway dreams that meant nothing. Her dreams got darker, with babies and children taunting her while his seemed to get lighter. Was it the paintings he'd created that showed him a different kind of life? One that would be a more brilliant masterpiece for them?

She flung the towel off and put on his smock. It was big on her, wrapping almost around her entire body. She tied it in the back and headed down the hall to the studio. Walking the steps one by one, she felt a need to see his latest work, to feel some of the lightness that had allowed him to get out of bed each day and see the possibilities in the world.

The Space Between Dreaming was leaning against the wall, and she picked it up by the edges and placed it on the table. She stood over it, transfixed. It was beautiful, to be sure. There was something about it, something that tugged at her. Was she imagining it? She couldn't be sure. But that woman who reached out into the night seemed familiar to her. Grace seemed to feel the longing this woman felt, and yet, there was a release she could feel as well. She wanted to reach out and hug the woman, yet at the same time felt the woman hugging her, as if her arms reaching out were especially for her, to comfort her and no one else.

Grace moved closer and closer, until she could see the brush marks, see the times John touched the surface of the painting with his fingertips. She could picture him, touching gently here and lightly dabbing there. Was he releasing his pain in those moments? Or sending out his love?

She reached forward, her hand shaking slightly, afraid to make contact. She'd been told many times that touching the work wasn't good form, yet she couldn't turn away.

She held her breath and continued reaching, farther and farther, until lightly, softly, she touched the woman's hand. At that moment, she could see a different life for them. One that started today, a new path to take them away from heartbreak. She could picture them laughing, sitting at a table, and clinking glasses of champagne, and in the background, music and soft lights that warmed their faces and made them look younger. The image made her smile. She looked down at her hand. The painting was dry, had been dry for days, yet she imagined the smallest amount of paint left behind on her finger like a secret code that could transport her to another world.

"This one is different. Isn't it?"

His voice made her jump, and she quickly closed her hand into a fist, hiding the secret of what it represented to her.

"I didn't hear you."

"I know. That's okay. It was…" He came closer, his shoes making tapping sounds on the floor. "It was sexy. Watching you. Seeing you lost in your thoughts."

She thought about moving away. She didn't want to let him know what she'd been thinking, about the alternate life that popped up before her eyes like a mirage. "Oh," she tried to sound light, "I was just admiring your work."

He stopped, as if her words had the power to put up a barrier that he couldn't cross. But his voice, his slight grin, told her he wanted her. She licked her lips, nervous, despite herself. He knew her so well after all this time, and yet she didn't want him to ask her about what she was thinking, about the vision that had popped up in her mind about moving forward, just the two of them.

"I just... I needed to see the painting."

She turned away from him, trying to center herself, to breathe normally, but he was behind her in an instant. His voice sent shivers down her spine as she felt his breath on her ear.

"And you decided to wear my smock. It looks good on you. Especially given what's under it."

His hands moved around her, under the smock, and caressed her stomach, her breasts. Her breathing became heavy, and she leaned into it, the kisses along her neck and the feeling of being wanted. His fingers got her ready, so expertly, as only someone who had made love to her thousands of times could do. When she couldn't stand it anymore, when she was just about to turn around and beg him to enter her, he did, without her saying a single word. He knew, just by the way she arched her back and the pace of her breath, he knew.

CHAPTER 10 - JANE

Jane went back upstairs, feeling lighter after talking with Mrs. Ferch. There was something about people who could be comfortable sharing their pain as much as their laughter that deepened relationships. It was what she had been so disappointed at with Brad, that he didn't trust her enough to tell her the truth about his life. It made their relationship feel one dimensional, and only left her more confused.

As she spoke with Mrs. Ferch earlier, she kept thinking about her sister. Mrs. Ferch was focusing on the good in her life, and Jane needed to do the same. She had been mad at Charlotte for leaving; she could finally admit that to herself. Maybe she was jealous, as Eric had gently suggested.

Charlotte and Jane were exactly nine months apart. While Jane was younger, she felt like the older of the two. Charlotte just seemed so immature to Jane, but maybe it was the fact that she just didn't agree with her decisions. The minute Charlotte turned eighteen, she up and moved from their Milwaukee apartment and across the country to

Seattle, Washington. Charlotte visited there once when she was in high school for a class trip and apparently never forgot it. She didn't even have a job or a place to live, just bought a plane ticket and said she'd figure it out when she got there.

But, of course, Charlotte being Charlotte, met a guy on the plane ride out there and emailed Jane as soon as she had landed, saying she had just met Mr. Right. Just like that. Jane didn't believe her. She kept waiting for the email telling her it had blown up and that the guy had dumped Charlotte. Not that she had hoped for that, but she really thought it would end that way. How could it not? She had just met him. But she said it just felt right. Within a year they were married, and another year after that, she had Sally, a beautiful baby girl with their mother's blue eyes and Charlotte's fiery spirit.

Jane reached for the phone and dialed her sister's number. One thing she loved about Charlotte was that they could go for long periods of time without talking and then suddenly pick up as if had spoken the week before.

"Why did we never have a dog?" Jane said by way of hello.

"Because that would mean we would have had to feed it?"

Jane smiled. True to form, Charlotte never even asked her why. She did want to know how Jane was, however.

"Man, it's good to hear your voice, Janey. How have you been?"

"I dunno." It was a little kid's answer, and yet, it was all she could come up with. Funny how talking to your big sister will turn you into an eight-year-old all over again.

"Janey? You okay?" She could hear the concern in Charlotte's voice. "Talk to me. I'm here."

Jane instantly felt the love in her sister's voice, and it

felt like a balm over the pain that was pushing up from this life she had created for herself. She wasn't sure how, but she had developed a routine where she just ran from day to day and in the process never made any progress. Just running in place and trying to figure out where to go. She was lonely. She could admit that to herself now, and worse, she wondered where her life was going. At the kindness in Charlotte's voice, she felt tears well up in her eyes.

"It's hard to admit, Charlotte. But… I'm tired."

"Of course, you're tired. You work all the time. Is Mrs. Ferch taking good care of you?"

"Yeah."

"Good. Oh, Janey, I miss you. I could just tell something was wrong the minute I picked up the phone."

"Could not."

Charlotte snorted. "Could so! What are big sisters for, if not to worry?"

Jane asked her the question she had always wanted to ask but didn't have the courage to voice before. "Charlotte? Are you happy? I mean, since you left here and got married and everything."

Charlotte knew what Jane meant: Was she happier than when they were kids? Since they had a rough upbringing, their childhood became the barometer for how they each measured things in their adult life. If they were happier than they were as kids, then they were headed in the right direction.

The problem now was that Jane wasn't happy. It wasn't the same as when they were kids, of course, but there was a hole missing in her life. She could chalk it up to loneliness, but it was more than that. She felt unfulfilled somehow. For years she thought if she made a certain amount of money, she'd be happy. Or if she achieved a certain position. She had received some of that, but she also gave up large parts of her personal life, toiling away at the gallery, and the rewards didn't seem to match. She used to think that if she was headed toward marriage, she'd be happy. She didn't need to be married, per se, but just headed there.

Charlotte pulled Jane from her thoughts, and she was glad. At this rate, she'd be crying all night.

"Yes, I'm happy, Janey. I met a man I love and had a wonderful kid that has changed my life. But I think I know what you're asking. Am I fulfilled? That's it, right?"

Jane nodded, then realized Charlotte couldn't see her on the phone. "I think that's what I'm asking. I don't know. I feel kind of…"

"Lost?"

"Yes," she said, and hated that a tear had slid down her face. Jane usually wasn't one to wallow. Neither of them was. Then she thought about Mrs. Ferch's story about Mickey.

"Do you think I should get a dog?" she blurted out.

Charlotte laughed. "Oh, sis, I think you'd be great with a dog, but I doubt it would heal whatever is hurting in you now."

Jane could hear the caring in Charlotte's voice. It was awful being so far away from each other. She wanted to tell Charlotte about Brad, but hesitated. She knew what Charlotte would say. Her sister operated on instinct. Jane wished she could be the same, but her instincts never seemed right. Maybe she should do the opposite of what she felt instead.

"Oh, Janey. I wish I was there with you, right now. I hate that you're there all alone. Listen, Janey, I need to get back to Sally now so she can finish up homework. You wouldn't believe what they hand kids to take home these days. It's nothing like the homework we had. Anyway, I miss you, and I really want to see you. It's been too long. I'm worried about you, Jane."

"Don't worry about me," she said, despite that it felt good to hear that Charlotte cared.

"Listen, I'm going to talk to Bill tonight about flying out. He can handle Sally for a few days, and I think some quality sister time is long past due."

Jane felt a smile coming up. "That would be great, Charlotte."

"I'll let you know when I'm coming. But I really want to do it soon. You need a hug, and a long-distance phone call isn't going to cut it."

The next day at work, Jane had showed Bug the pictures she'd taken and the artists she was interested in interviewing for the gallery. He studied the photos on her phone with interest.

"These are good." He nodded. "You have a good eye for this."

His compliment felt like rain after a long drought. But a quenching only lasted for so long. Jane knew she had to find out if she had a future here.

"I appreciate that, Bug."

He sat back in the chair, and said, "Jane, I'm hoping to add more hope and happiness to the office." He continued talking, and she tuned him out. Hadn't she already heard this?

"Sir," she interrupted.

"Please, please, call me Bug."

She took a deep breath. Even after all these years, it was hard to do that.

"Bug. When I told you about my ten-year anniversary, you mentioned a reward of some kind."

Bug looked confused. "Yes. That's why I sent you to the art fair."

"But Bug, that is what you would have the assistant manager do. I feel—"

"Yes. I made you assistant manager last week. Didn't I tell you that?" He scrambled through the pile of papers on his desk and found a stack in the center. A cookie sat atop of them, like a melty, sugary paperweight.

"Yes, yes." He slid them to her. "Here. You have the position and the salary, of course, and my goodness, you've earned it. Long overdue. And judging by the photos you showed me, I made the right choice." He nodded to himself in congratulations. His phone rang, and he held it up to Jane. "It's the boy. I'm guessing his mother forgot to pack his lunch or some such. I better get this."

He swiveled in his chair, turning his back to Jane, so he missed the smile that had made its way onto her face.

She went back to her office, excited about the promotion that she wondered now why she didn't ask for before. It had been easy. Well, as easy as things ever were with Bug. She wanted to share the news and knew exactly who she'd call first.

"Hello?" Mrs. Ferch said.

As she answered, Jane thought about what Brad would say with her phoning her landlady first instead of him. But instinctively, she knew Brad just wouldn't even be happy for her, and she didn't want his negativity to ruin this moment. He hadn't called or texted since she'd seen him for coffee, and she was trying to avoid thinking about him. She'd have to make a decision to either talk it through with him, or… she silently shook her head. He'd been a part of her life for eight years now. How could she just let all of that go?

"Mrs. Ferch, I have the best news," she started, and told her about the promotion.

"Oh, that's wonderful, dear! You deserve it! You work so hard. Oh, and you remind me so much of young Eric."

Mrs. Ferch put the phone on speaker, and Jane could hear her rummaging around in the background. Suddenly, a loud noise drowned out her voice, and Jane found herself shouting to be heard.

"Mrs. Ferch! What are you doing? I can't hear you!"

"Oh, I'm making myself a smoothie. Have you tried them? A little fruit, a little milk, they're just delicious."

Mrs. Ferch's conversation skills were like the sails on a boat. They changed direction based on which way the winds blew, and Jane knew she'd have to get her back on track if she wanted to find out more about Eric.

"You were saying that Eric reminded you of me?" she prompted.

"Oh yes, that's right. He worked so much. Just like you do now. You young kids, you give up your life to work. Not that that's a bad thing. But I feel bad for you. Time goes so fast."

"He told me a bit about his old job," Jane said, thinking of how he'd mentioned it at the art fair. "Sounds like he was grateful to make the change."

Jane smiled to herself at the memory of it. Just a couple of days before, she had spent an entire day looking through an art fair and was happy, and then the following day she met Brad for coffee, and within moments she was unhappy.

"This promotion makes me happy," she mused.

"If you love your job, that is a blessing," the woman

said, surprising Jane. She was thinking Mrs. Ferch had probably not heard her with all the noise in the background.

Jane heard more noises on the other end. "Did I tell you about the new flavor I'm trying for the coffee maker? It's a caramel something or other. You put a small container in that looks like a creamer, but it's really coffee, and within an instant you have a hot cup of coffee, and it's so delicious. Or tea. I suppose you could use it for that, too."

"Yes, I've seen them," Jane was thinking about how much they cost. She still used a tea kettle that she picked up at a rummage sale for a quarter. The coffee shop was her only splurge, but she was proud of Mrs. Ferch for treating herself.

"So, what does he do now?" Jane asked, remembering that while they'd talked about some things, Eric still hadn't really told her if he currently had a job.

"Oh, he's considering his options. Is that the right phrase? Anyhoo, I make myself a morning smoothie and cup of coffee," Mrs. Ferch was saying now, "then I get my fruit and the caffeine. I do like that." Jane smiled to herself at Mrs. Ferch's chatter. Somehow, she found it comforting. "I never used to eat enough fruit. Do you eat enough, Jane?"

"Fruit? Probably not. Or vegetables." Funny how Jane could get pulled along the winds of conversation with Mrs. Ferch. She marveled at how things could start off with talk about working and life and end up with smoothies and fruit. "I was thinking about getting a juicer," Jane confided, "but they're so expensive." Then again, she thought, maybe now she would treat herself.

"Oh, they are. But one of the ladies from my knitting club has one and she loves it. Oh, hi, Eric. Come on in.

Would you like a cup of coffee? I can put a new one on in a jiffy. Have you seen these new machines? Say hi to Jane. I'm on the phone with her right now."

Eric was there? Jane took comfort in the fact that at least she wasn't the only one who gravitated toward their landlady for friendship.

Jane could faintly make out Eric's voice in the background, and then it got clearer as he must have leaned closer. "Hi, Jane."

"Hi, Eric." They sounded like two kids in school who were too shy to dance with each other at the recital.

"Our Jane has just gotten that promotion she wanted," Mrs. Ferch was saying now.

"Jane, that's great!" Eric seemed to be genuinely happy for her. "We'll have to go out and celebrate."

It was the second time he'd mentioned going out to celebrate her promotion. He'd said it at the coffee shop that day. Was he interested in her? She needed to tell him she had a boyfriend, she thought. Then again, did she really have one? Or were her and Brad all but over? She'd have to decide and then talk to him about it.

She tried not to overthink the situation, but she didn't want to assume things with Eric. She also didn't want to lead him on. She stumbled on how to respond to him.

"That's a great idea!" Mrs. Ferch was saying now. "You know what I was just thinking? You both love art so much. And Eric, have you ever been to the Milwaukee Art Museum? It is one of Jane's favorite places. And don't they have a festival starting Friday? Jane was just looking for a chance to scoot out early from work one day and enjoy this gorgeous weather. Why don't you pick her up here after she gets out of work, and you can head down there together. You'll really enjoy it there, Eric. Does that sound good, Jane?"

Jane was caught off guard. Mrs. Ferch could be a forceful matchmaker if she wanted to. "Um…"

"Great! Eric is nodding on this end. He's in, too. Oh, how nice for you kids. Bring me a magnet from the gift shop. Will you, dear?"

"Um, I guess. It's just that—"

"The postman is here, dear. Gotta run. Congrats again! I am so proud of you."

And with that, the line was dead. Jane was both irritated with Mrs. Ferch and grateful. She would have never asked him to do anything with her, and she had so enjoyed their time together at the art fair. But she would need to clarify things with Brad before she went.

She took a deep breath and texted him.

"Brad. Let's talk more about the things you told me yesterday. Okay? Please call me."

She saw the three dots pop up, indicating that he was typing. And then, they were gone. There was no response.

CHAPTER 11 - GRACE

As protective as John was about his painting time, he seemed to take no interest in shipping his work to galleries or buyers. Grace took care of all that, from accepting the payments in person or via their website, to packaging and shipping.

The Space Between Dreaming was done on a thirty-by-forty canvas. She gently eased it into the van along with ten other paintings. Jane had asked her to bring a selection, and she wasn't sure about how large the space would be for his work, but she felt good about the sizes and variety of subject matter. She had written up a note about each painting, the medium used, year completed, and a short note about the composition. She didn't like to explain the art that much, as if she even could, but she did like to put her writing and editing background to work and give it some sales copy.

She had completed the notes for all the paintings but had saved The Space Between Dreaming for last. She wasn't sure what to write for that one. She'd been thinking about that painting nonstop ever since her husband had finished it. Was it about a random woman? Someone who needed help? Was it her? Another thought occurred to her that perhaps the woman in the painting was the imaginary mother she always wished she had. Grace could fantasize about a mother who held out her hands to her and invited her into a hug that would make it all better. But there was something in the way the woman's eyes seemed to look right at you that also unnerved Grace, as if she had the ability to step out of the canvas and walk right up to you. The thought made Grace shiver.

Maybe the fact that the woman seemed to be everyone and no one. Maybe that was the real key to the painting. Grace sat at the kitchen island and finally wrote out the description.

> *"The Space Before Dreaming illustrates the common themes in every woman's life, from wanting to be held to needing to comfort, from a desire for independence to a need to be cared for, and from recognizing her blessings to striving for more.*
>
> *She is every woman, and no woman, all at once. Because she, like each of us, is completely unique."*

Grace reread what she wrote. She liked writing marketing copy, especially as it applied to the paintings. She liked to sum up the picture in a way that would reach out to buyers. When she started writing descriptions for the work, she'd ask John endless questions about the subject matter, his process, and what he basically wanted to convey about his work. But he never had any input; he didn't want to think about what the painting might really be about because he said it took away from the viewer's experience. A viewer should make up their own mind about a painting, and decide for themselves what it was about the painting that moved them.

Grace agreed with that, however, when it came to sales, sometimes you needed to offer a definition for a work so people could decide what they felt. A good bit of sales copy could be just as illuminating as the work itself, although in a completely different way. She'd never compare what she did with John's work, and yet, she did feel they complemented each other. She was glad to use her wordsmith skills to help him sell paintings. It was good for both of them.

She gathered the notes she had written for each painting and placed them in her purse. Then she checked her reflection one final time in the mirror. Jane had looked so cute when Grace saw her at the art fair, and it inspired her to get a little more artsy in her own appearance. She wore an old minidress that she'd long ago banished to the back of her closet, thinking she was too old for it, but paired it with skinny jeans and red Mary Janes. She twisted her hair up in a clip with just a little bit down for some bangs across her forehead, and put on dangly earrings, with red and blue flowers on them. Then she grabbed her keys and took off for the gallery.

She'd been past the Cream City Gallery many times but had never been inside. It was located in an old building that contained Milwaukee's famous cream-colored brick that gave the building its name. The light bricks served as the perfect backdrop for the art inside.

Grace loved the space instantly. Bright, with large windows on the south side of the building and the perfect LED lighting to best show off the paintings. She noticed that museums and galleries seemed to be replacing their old halogen lights with LEDs. She'd read that LED lights were much easier to control with regard to color temperature, plus she didn't like the yellowing affect that halogen offered.

There was a retail area in front, with a funky display of smaller items like painted stones and necklaces. Farther in, the walls were tastefully covered with art that varied from modern to more classic Wisconsin types of pictures, like round barns and lighthouses. On white pedestals throughout the space were sculptures placed strategically that complemented the paintings.

She liked the variety the space offered, and noted that the main wall was blank. This would be the new home for The Space Between Dreaming. It touched her that Jane made space right in the center of the gallery for the painting. The additional works that she brought would fit well on the walls opposite.

John had his work displayed in different coffee shops and boutiques from time to time, but this space reinforced how awed Grace was at her husband's talent. There were times when it was difficult to see him lost in his own world when he was in his studio, but this was the reminder of why he needed to do it. His paintings were more than just a way for him to heal, they were a way to move others as well.

Jane greeted her, surveyed the paintings, and made notes. Two other people were hanging paintings on the opposite side of the gallery, at the direction of a man standing behind them, with his arms folded, offering comments here and there.

"Let me introduce you to Bug," Jane said, "and then let's grab a coffee next door. It's a bit hectic in here today."

Grace wondered what kind of name Bug was, but she wasn't going to ask. After a brief introduction, the man turned back to the process of hanging the other paintings.

"You're in good hands with Jane!" he added over his shoulder. "It's a pleasure meeting you."

Jane led Grace to the shop next door, another cream brick structure with loads of sunlight and bright, funky chairs spaced throughout. The board on the back wall listed all the different types of drinks available, mainly many different kinds of coffee, juices, and tea.

Jane offered to buy, and they took their drinks to a table. It was much quieter at the coffee shop than it had been in the gallery.

"They're hanging a new show today," Jane explained, "and everyone gets very loud and excited."

"Sounds like an interesting place to work," Grace said, thinking of how different her own job was. As a freelance editor, she worked mainly by herself with the bulk of her time spent quietly reading and writing notes on manuscripts. She felt happy in that moment, taking in the sunlight and being in the coffee shop filled with people, yet it was not so busy that she and Jane could still talk at a normal conversational level. She wondered if she could do this type of thing full time, where she promoted her husband's work and met with galleries and art buyers. The thought gave her a thrill.

Jane brought out the gallery contract and explained the specifics to Grace. They talked about an upcoming exhibit Jane wanted to have that would highlight John's work.

"This sounds wonderful," she said. "I'll take these papers home to John to sign. Sorry he couldn't be here. He works as an insurance adjustor. That's his day job. I work freelance, so my schedule is a bit more flexible."

"No problem at all. I would say most of the artists I work with have a day job. Unfortunately, art doesn't usually offer a full-time living. Although, there are more opportunities now. With print-on-demand and licensing and… well, the field is so open. Nearly every art career is completely different. I'm interested in learning more about you and your husband. Tell me about yourselves. Do you live near here? Have kids?"

Grace paused, feeling like someone had taken a needle and stuck it into her happy balloon. She wondered if this was the standard question she'd be forced to face for the rest of her life.

"Um. No kids. No pets. We did have a dog once. Harold. He was sweet. Got us through a very tough time." Grace inwardly cringed. How could she fault anyone on their small-talk skills when hers weren't the best? "We got Harold from a shelter. Before it was the cool thing to do." She laughed nervously.

Jane studied Grace a moment, sipping her drink.

"Does that question bother you?"

It was asked kindly, and for that reason, Grace was honest with her.

"About kids? It does, mainly because it never ends with a single answer. Although, I've started just to say no and leave it at that. Let them ask follow-up questions and be rude, if that's what they choose to do, but I'm not going to explain things to strangers anymore."

"You're right, you shouldn't have to talk about anything that personal. I'm so sorry to have asked that."

Grace felt bad, the guilt of shutting someone down when they were just trying to get to know you.

"Not that you're a stranger. I mean, you are... it's just that..."

That what? She felt so comfortable with Jane? It was too weird to say out loud. Grace gulped her coffee quickly, waiting for Jane to jump in. But Jane seemed happy to listen.

"What used to happen," she continued, "is I would say no and quickly add that we were trying." Grace shrugged. "I guess I wanted people to know that I loved kids and wasn't childless by choice. I felt like I was being judged. As years went on, and it was obvious that I wasn't going to get pregnant, they'd ask, and I'd tell them that we were trying to adopt. We went through all kinds of stuff with that, and everyone and their brother told me about how they did it. I think people just want to be helpful. Women, especially. But sometimes—most times, actually—they just go too far. One time, this woman rattled off so many questions, I felt like I was being interrogated. Like, *do you have kids? No? But you want them? But you'll keep trying? Do you have pets? A dog? Oh, you have a dog! Well, good, your dog is your baby, then.*

"And you know what? My dog *wasn't* my baby. My dog was my dog. I loved my dog. But it was a dog, not our baby. But this woman? It was like she couldn't be satisfied until she'd found something… I don't know, something that made her feel comfortable with me. As if, *oh, well you do know how to love something, so I guess I can talk to you.*"

Grace shook her head at the memory and sipped her coffee. Jane remained quiet, letting her talk. It felt good to be honest about this.

"And once you tell someone something, even a thought or intent like, yeah, we can't have kids, but we're considering adoption. Or, we're looking into things. Then that's all they can talk to you about from then on. I made the mistake of doing that with a client, and for three years after, she asked me every week 'Where are you'—Grace made air quotes with her fingers—'with things,' like suddenly I was reporting my progress to her. We had been in the midst of an overseas adoption, and it fell through. I was devastated. We both were. And then this woman just grilled me afterward. Who did I meet with? What agency? What were we going to do next? I realized that half the time I was just sharing my thoughts with these people. Not decisions. Not things my husband and I had decided, but things we were considering, all as a way to keep a conversation going.

"Finally, I learned to just say no when someone asked. It makes them wonder about me. Most of the time they think I don't like kids, which breaks my heart. It's their dumb assumption about why I don't have them. But even if they imagine something negative and avoid me, I'd rather have that than a barrage of questions with them offering solutions. As if we haven't tried a million things."

Grace paused. It felt good to vent, but did Jane really want to hear all of this?

"They don't know what you've been through," she said, pointing to Grace's cup. "You want another one? I've downed mine already, and I'm getting another."

"Sure."

She handed Jane the cup to throw out and waited as she got them two new ones. Jane returned in a moment with both their cups, handing Grace hers before she sat down again.

"Coffee and loads of milk, right?"

"Yes. Thank you. How did you know?"

"I paid attention." Jane winked and sipped her drink, instantly setting it down. "That's too hot right now. And you know what? Now I'm wondering how many times I have blurted out that question while making small talk. I shouldn't do that."

"And now I feel guilty that I unloaded like that. But wow, it felt good." Grace laughed.

"No," Jane put her hand on Grace's arm. "Definitely do not feel guilty. I'm really glad you did. You've taught me to see things from another perspective, which is always very helpful. And you know what? I'm totally projecting on you. I've been going over my own relationship in my mind so much lately, wondering if I'll get married and have kids. But I should know better, because people do get nosy with these life subjects. You know?"

Grace did. "I always thought I was just bad at small talk. But seriously, sometimes I feel like answering something ridiculous back. Like, *well, how much credit card debt do you have? Do you and your spouse have a good sex life? Do you ever sit and eat an entire bag of peanut butter cookies?*"

Grace cringed again, realizing she had actually sat and ate an entire bag once during an especially sad time. It was like she didn't know what to do so she shoveled cookies in her mouth to try and stop her grief. Still, Jane didn't want to hear all that. And here Grace was just dreaming about a day when she would meet with gallery owners to sell John's art! She'd have to step up her conversation skills if that was ever going to happen.

She tried to apologize again, but Jane but a hand up.

"Please. It feels good to be real for once. And I'm very casual. So is Bug. Oh, you're probably wondering about his name."

Jane filled Grace in, and they both laughed.

"He sounds like a wonderful boss."

Jane considered that. "He is. You know, I was so frustrated with him for a long time because I hadn't been promoted yet, and I realized I was just frustrated with myself. I'd been passed over for promotions, but I'd also not asked about the direction of my job, either. And now that I'm saying that, I can think of a few other areas in my life I need to get clearer about."

Grace knew what she was saying. "Sometimes just asking for directions about relationships or work or"—Grace paused, thinking about the future she was now considering of a life with just her and John—"or family. Well, that can be the hardest part. When you're totally open with things, you just move ahead, thinking anything is possible. And then life starts putting up roadblocks, and sometimes you have to make a tough decision just so you can stop wasting time when it's obvious the life you wanted is not the one you're being given. Not that it's a bad thing. It's just… it takes a while to get settled into a life or relationship you didn't plan for yourself. It's hard to see at first how a life you couldn't imagine could still be a blessing to you. Maybe a bigger blessing in some ways you hadn't planned on. But until you fully embrace it, you'll never accept the good things that are meant for you."

Jane stared at Grace for a long while.

"Oh man, I am so embarrassed," Grace said. "I am really babbling on today."

"No." Jane touched her arm again. "I am so in awe of everything you just said. Wow." She sat back, spinning her coffee cup in a circle. "You have no idea how that hits home for me right now." Jane smiled at her. "You are one wise woman, Grace. John is very lucky to have you."

"And I'm lucky to have him."

"It's so obvious you both were meant to be together. Tell me," Jane said to her. "How did you *know*? With John? How did you know he was the right one for you?"

Grace had been asked that many times by people over the years. She shook her head. "It's weird, isn't it? Such a big decision, and yet when we look back, it isn't the big moments that help you figure it out. I think with John I just felt comfortable. I mean, we could hang out and do just about anything, and often did." Grace laughed. "Trying to have kids for years meant we were broke most of our marriage, if you want more truths"—she smiled at Jane, who was listening intently—"and while it was a bummer, it also didn't make us less happy together. We had loads of challenges."

Grace talking to Jane about the things they'd endured, the miscarriages, her background as a foster kid, the problems with their friends, and even her mother's death. "Looking back, I guess I was just always looking for acceptance. To receive love." She thought about it. "A mother's love. You know? And I thought becoming a mother myself might help me feel that."

Jane slowly nodded. "I know what that's like. Not like you, not the same. It's my own mother I've wanted that from, actually. I think both my sister and I have."

Jane continued talking about her sister, Charlotte. It seemed to Grace that there was a lot of love between them as sisters, and she told Jane that.

"I think you are right. I didn't always see it that way. You know, Eric, the guy I was with at the art fair? He said maybe I was jealous of Charlotte, and the thought really upset me." She laughed. "But I think he might be right."

Grace studied her a moment. "You and Eric are just friends?"

Jane nodded. "He lives in my building. It's just him and me and our landlady, Mrs. Ferch. I think you'd like her, actually. I mean, she's eighty years old, but she's been like a best friend and mother to me."

It very much seemed to Grace that Jane and Eric had chemistry, but she wasn't going to say any more. Jane would figure it out in her own time.

Jane's openness encouraged Grace to share another truth. "I've finally started thinking about what my life might be like if I finally look elsewhere, instead of clinging to a dream that will never happen. As dumb as that sounds, this is a new thing for me. I'd never even allowed myself to think of anything other than family and children. It's such a new thing, I haven't even admitted to John that I've been thinking about it," Grace confessed.

Jane considered that. "What do you think will happen if you tell him?"

Grace thought about it. "That he'll agree, and this dream will really be dead, then." *Like her babies, like her mother.*

Jane was quiet a long while. "But," she said carefully, "a dream can't be truly alive until it steps out of the realm of possibility and into reality. Until then, it's just words and images that float somewhere in a place you don't live in yourself."

CHAPTER 12 - JANE

By Friday, Jane had still not heard back from Brad. She had to finally admit, her relationship was a disaster. What kind of boyfriend drops a bomb on you about having a child you knew nothing about and then doesn't call to follow up?

Still, what was she supposed to do? Text him that they were breaking up? It was one way to do it, of course. But after eight years, she wanted to just talk it through. What if this was a breakthrough for them?

She thought about Grace's words and how it wasn't the big moments that made you realize you should be with someone; it was the small ones. Everyday life. When she looked at it from that perspective, her daily life with Brad was anything but pleasant. It highlighted how much she had ignored the problems in their relationship, always wanting to believe it was better than it actually was.

She'd done the same thing with her father. She loved him. But that wasn't the same thing as him being a good dad. He wasn't. He didn't provide. He pumped her for money and favors. Many times, she didn't hear from him for long stretches, and when he wanted something from her, he'd show up. There were a lot of similarities between him and Brad, now that she was really looking at them as they were, instead of how she desperately wanted them to be.

She walked into the gallery space and stood before The Space Between Dreaming. It left her with the same feeling as when she had first seen it at the art fair, of wanting to comfort this woman, to tell her it would be okay.

It never ceased to amaze her what bringing art into a space could do. How it changed the energy of the entire room. The right piece could make you feel comfortable, turn you on, or remind you of the possibilities in life.

For a moment, she thought of the misconceptions about Milwaukee, the TV shows that depicted characters who talked funny or lacked sophistication. She hadn't found that at all. She loved growing up in the city, with its museums and theater and many festivals. It was one reason she wanted to work at a gallery. Visiting the art museum as a kid inspired her to work at a place where people could find the right art to fill their homes and lives. Art meant something to her, and she felt blessed to have a job where she could celebrate something she deemed so important to life.

Jane headed to the front of the gallery and told Donna she was leaving early. Donna immediately reached over the counter and felt her forehead.

"You sick?"

Jane laughed as she pulled away. "No. I'm taking an early day. Going to the art museum."

Donna studied her. "You know what?" Donna put a finger on her chin as she contemplated. "I can't remember the last time you took off early. I'm usually very good at remembering things like this."

"Actually? I've never left early. In ten years. Isn't that something?"

"Oh, that's something, all right," Donna said, then paused and looked her up and down. She put a finger up to Jane as she answered the phone.

"Oh..." Donna held the phone out to her. "It's for you." She mouthed, "a *guy*."

Jane frowned, thinking it might be her dad. He was the last person she needed to hear from today. Or worse, Brad, calling now, when she'd been trying to reach him all week. "This is Jane, may I help you?"

"Hey, it's Eric. Mrs. Ferch said you needed a ride to the art museum?"

Oh, she did, did she? Jane smiled at the thought of her landlady trying to orchestrate all this.

"Um, no, actually. I was going to meet you at home." Meet you at home. That sounded weird to her now that she'd just said that out loud. She glanced over at Donna, who raised an eyebrow, clearly listening in.

"Yeah. She said you didn't like driving in the downtown traffic."

Never mind that they lived on the East Side of Milwaukee, which was five minutes from downtown, and Jane was in that traffic all the time. But why argue at this point?

"Well, I don't mind the traffic, actually, so I'm not sure what she was referring to," Jane lied, thinking that Mrs. Ferch was trying very hard to get Eric to pick her up. "So why don't I come back and change, and then I'll knock on your apartment door. Say, half an hour?"

Jane handed the phone back to Donna, who was looking like she wanted every detail of the conversation.

"Well," Donna said, "out with it. Who's the guy?"

Jane looked at the clock above Donna's head. "You know what? I don't have time to tell you the whole thing because I need to get home and change. But I'll fill you in tomorrow." She headed toward the door. "Promise."

"Oh, just you hold on there, missy." Donna came around to the front of the reception desk and stood there, with her hands on her hips. "A cute guy calls who isn't your boyfriend, and you expect me to wait until tomorrow to get the scoop? I don't think so."

Jane cringed. "I know. Brad and I are having some issues."

"You and Brad never had anything but an issue. It's been long past due to break up with him."

Jane blinked. "How do you know that?"

Donna looked disgusted. "I can tell by his voice when he's called here. He's impatient. Rude. Condescending. Do I look clueless?" She pointed to her face.

"You are the least clueless person I know. But what makes you think Eric is cute?" Jane laughed. "You can't tell that by his voice."

"No, but I can tell by the way you blushed when you found out it was him."

Jane cleared her throat. "I'll fill you in tomorrow." She stopped to think, why was she blushing? She liked being around Eric, but she didn't like him like that. Not yet. She couldn't assume he liked her that way, either.

"Hah! And you're doing that thing you do, where you go off to never-never land with your thoughts. That means this is a juicy story."

"Donna…" Jane cringed.

"So… somebody special, after all. Okay, shoo, missy! Get on out of here, and don't you worry about work."

For the first time since she could remember, work was the last thing on Jane's mind.

Jane changed three times and finally settled on a maxidress, shrug, and sensible flats. She fiddled with her long hair, braiding it, putting it up in a ponytail, and then curling it in neat waves around her face. She needed a change. Nothing seemed right. Finally, she put her hair up in a clip and went down to knock on Eric's door.

He was wearing a teal golf shirt and khaki pants. She'd seen him so many times in that flannel shirt and with his straggly hair that this new Eric—she hated to admit—was looking cuter and cuter the more time she spent with him.

"Wow," he said as he opened the door. "Jane. You look amazing."

"Oh." She looked down awkwardly, as if she had just thrown the look together on a whim. "It's nothing."

Eric smiled at her a moment, and she couldn't help but smile back, too. Finally, he broke the silence. "Should we go?"

The car ride down to the museum was pleasant. Jane felt the sun shine on her face through the car window, and the warmth made her feel comfortable and relaxed for the first time in a long while.

"Thanks again for driving," she said, watching the scenery from Lake Shore Drive. The big houses were unique and varied. Some looked like they'd been built in the last century, and some were brand new. She favored the Cream City brick homes, the color of vanilla. She imagined herself living in one, making dinner. She suddenly wondered if Eric knew how to grill.

"Not a problem. Mrs. Ferch mentioned that you really needed a ride, and besides, I've never been there."

"The art museum? Well, this is so cool! I love being there with people when it's their first time. I can't wait to show you."

Jane was always surprised when someone from the city hadn't yet been to the museum. The building alone was a work of art, let alone the possessions inside. She was fascinated with the place.

"I enjoy art. As you know, from Saturday," he said, "I like going to fairs and all that. Although I couldn't tell you anything about painters or anything. I just know what I like when I see it."

"You knew about a couple painters at the fair, remember? I think you know more than you're saying," she teased.

He laughed. "No, actually, I don't. I'm not trying to be sly. But now that you bring it up, remember when that woman... was her name Grace?"

"Yes, the painter's wife."

"Right. She brought up the Chagall tapestry at the Jewish Museum. We should check it out sometime."

That sounded like he was asking her out. Wasn't he? It had been so long since she'd been on an actual date that she was doubting herself. She changed the subject to Grace and then to John and his painting.

"So then, you've been to the art museum, obviously," he stated, an invitation for her to share her experiences there.

"Oh yeah, lots of times. Charlotte and I used to go for field trips when we were in grade school, which was always really fun. The first time we were there was on a school trip. I saw an expressionist painting by Kandinsky, and I was hooked. I loved the color, the lines. And then I saw a Picasso, and that about did it. I was in love with art."

Eric kept his eyes on the road, but Jane could see a smile come across his face. "I envy that. That you had that passion from a young age. It sounds like you know a lot about the subject."

"I don't really, that's the thing," she admitted. "It's my job, sure. I watch for artists, and I know what will fit into the gallery. But really, it's all just bits and pieces. I found out a few things about paintings I liked, but really, I always feel like I should know more than I do."

"You sound so confident, though," he argued.

Did she? She'd never thought of herself that way, of being an expert or knowledgeable about anything actually.

"Well, thanks. I guess I just get excited when I really like something."

"I think you're being modest. But I'll let it go." He gave her a quick smile as they pulled into the parking garage.

"One thing is for sure... I'm very excited to see this place with you, Jane."

He took her hand, and they walked across the bridge from the parking garage to the museum. Jane just went with it, his hand warm and comforting. She closed her eyes a moment as they stood on the bridge that went to the museum's entrance, feeling the sun shine down on her face.

The view from the bridge was breathtaking. The blues of the water from Lake Michigan surrounded the white of the museum structure, and reflected the sun's rays above. Not for the first time, Jane noted how much the surroundings of the building were as beautiful as the art inside.

"Okay, now, this is the Reiman Bridge we're walking over," Jane said. "It's cool, right?" She pointed below them. "I love how we can look over the gardens and still see the lake view from here."

Eric took it all in. "Wow. I've seen the museum from far away, and it looked awesome, but it's really something up close. I've never seen anything like this." He glanced up at the exterior of the building. "It looks like a giant bird. But more majestic, somehow."

Jane nodded. "The 'wings' of the building"—she made air quotes—"actually move. They open at ten in the morning when the building opens. Then they close and open again at noon, and close when the building closes. Usually, five o'clock on most nights. If you sit and watch long enough, you'll see it."

Eric looked up again and back at her. "The building moves?"

"The wings of the structure, do, yes."

He looked shocked and amazed, and Jane laughed. She took out her phone and snapped a picture of the view, showing the blues of the lake and the white of the museum.

"Here," he said, taking her phone from her hand, "let's get a selfie."

Before she could protest, Eric was leaning close to her and holding the phone out. He snapped the picture before she was ready. She'd been lost in her own thoughts for a moment, thinking about how nice it was that his arm was around her.

"Aw," Eric jokingly chided her, "you look bewildered in this one." He held the phone out again and leaned in close to her. "Show us that gorgeous smile of yours."

Jane smiled into the camera of the phone, and when Eric checked the picture, he nodded appreciatively.

"This is a keeper. Check it out." He handed the phone back to her, and she looked at the picture, thinking that they made a cute couple. She took a deep breath and looked out over the gardens below the bridge. She reminded herself to enjoy this moment without any expectations.

She noticed Eric had been quiet, too, in the way that people who are taking in nature seem to be, standing side by side but lost in their own thoughts. She broke the silence.

"Don't you love the gardens below?" she asked Eric. He looked like he was enjoying himself, but Jane felt there was also a sadness to him. She remembered a quote she had heard somewhere once, that everyone was dealing with their own hard struggle. She supposed that was true of the two of them, as well.

"Honestly," he said, gesturing to the museum, to Lake Michigan in the distance, and finally the gardens below, "I feel like I'm speechless. This has been here all along, and I've never experienced it." He shook his head and said quietly, "I feel like I've wasted my time in this city. I could have been enjoying it so much more."

When he glanced back at Jane, he seemed to catch himself as if he'd shared too much. Jane held back the urge to question him more, just letting the conversations of the day take them where they may.

She gestured to the gardens below, one of her favorite spots in the whole city. "Do you want to know more about them?"

He seemed overwhelmed, taking in the beauty of the place. She'd seen it with other people she brought to the museum sometimes. They started out with an air of busyness, as if it were just another tourist attraction that they needed to check off their list. But when they saw the big, blue lake out the window and the gardens and buildings that made up the museum, it made them stop and feel their purpose in a whole new way.

The art museum was a safe place for her, somewhere she went to figure out her problems. She didn't want to dump all her knowledge on him at once, though. She wasn't sure if he'd appreciate it or find it annoying.

As if reading her thoughts, he turned to her. "Jane, I want to hear whatever you'd like to tell me about this place. I think seeing this with you is going to be an incredible experience." His green eyes encouraged her to go on. There was a crackle between them, an unmistakable attraction that she felt when she looked in his eyes and saw acceptance. It was a feeling she hadn't quite experienced before, and she turned away from him, toward the lake for a moment, closing her eyes to get her bearings before she continued.

Finally, she looked back at him. He didn't seem hurried or annoyed that she had taken a moment to think. She gestured to the building they had been standing in front of. "Now, behold the Burke Brise Soleil!" She threw out her arms wide, and Eric stood there in amazement. The building was known internationally for its unique design, and Jane couldn't wait to tell Eric all about it.

"The brise-soleil—" she continued, and Eric interrupted her.

"Okay, say that again. The what?"

Jane sounded it out phonetically. "Breeze. So. Lay."

He cocked his head. "Smarty-pants."

She giggled, emboldened by his teasing. "A little while ago, I mentioned that the wings on this building, which make up the brise-soleil, actually move. It folds and unfolds twice daily. The wingspan is over two hundred feet wide."

Eric looked up to take it all in. "You know what? Now that you say that, I do remember seeing it look different, depending on when I was driving by. When I drove by the first time, I could have sworn it was open. When I came by later, it was closed. I thought I was seeing things, but now I know."

"The extension was designed by Santiago Calatrava and built in 2001."

A look of recognition came across Eric's face. "So that's why people call this the Calatrava sometimes. I had no idea."

Jane couldn't suppress her joy, waiting to show Eric her favorite part of the whole museum. "But wait until you go inside."

Eric took her hand and kissed it. "Let's go!"

They walked in the door, and Jane could hardly keep the excitement from her voice. The kiss on her hand was unexpected, and she could feel the warmth of Eric's lips still on her skin. She couldn't wait to share this experience with him. Somehow, she knew Eric would love the entrance, which was her favorite part of the museum.

At over ninety feet, the glass ceiling allowed plenty of light to come in, while at the same time giving you the impression that you were on a huge boat in the middle of the water. Jane had seen many people come in and just stop and look up, frozen in place at the beauty of the architecture.

Eric reacted just as she'd thought he might. He dropped her hand absently and she didn't mind at all. Somehow, it made it more romantic that he could see the artistry of their surroundings just as she did.

He was quiet, taking it all in, but there was a grin on his face. She felt a thrill at showing him things he wouldn't have noticed if he'd come here alone, and it was more than just a physical attraction between them that she felt. Talking about the art and showing him the building fulfilled something in her.

"Before we go in the exhibit, let's stop and look at the Chihuly."

Eric turned. "The what?"

"Chihuly. Dale Chihuly." Jane gestured to a large blown-glass sculpture near the entrance. Blue and orange pieces were weaved together and hung from the ceiling.

The curves and twists of the sculpture drew your eyes outward. At over 180 feet tall by eighty-six feet wide and ninety-six feet deep, the Isola di San Giacomo in Palude Chandelier II, as the sculpture was called, was hard to miss. Jane thought it looked like a glass medusa, with curly tentacles that reached out like hair blowing in the wind.

The light was shining brightly through the glass sculpture, highlighting every variance of color and curve. "I wasn't sure if you had heard of him. Chihuly is known for his work in glass."

Light seemed to dawn on Eric's face. "You know what? I have heard of him. He, um…" Eric cleared his throat, and looked out at the view. "He has a museum in Seattle, I think." Something had changed in him, and Jane couldn't put her finger on it. She suddenly feared that she was boring him with her facts and figures.

"I'm sorry," she said. "I'm probably prattling on too much."

"No!" he said, a bit too loudly, as his voice echoed through the entryway. They both laughed as people turned to see where the noise was coming from. He lowered his voice. "Wow. Sound really does carry in here," he said quietly. "But, Jane, you are not prattling on or whatever you just said. I'm enjoying myself so much, and I just… I just happened to think about that museum I saw in Seattle. That's all."

"You've been to Seattle? You didn't say anything the other day when I mentioned my sister lived there."

"Yeah. I've… um… visited." He frowned for a moment, which confused Jane. She put aside her fears about what he might be thinking and focused on the fact she had just learned.

"And here my sister has lived there for over a decade, and I've never even been there. Charlotte could have told me about that museum." She made a mental note to bring up the point with her sister the next time they talked. "If I had known there was a Chihuly museum there, maybe I would have gone to visit her."

Eric looked surprised. "You've never been out to Seattle?"

"No." She supposed she just hadn't made time.

"Maybe your sister was worried that the museum was the only reason you'd make time."

She looked at Eric as if he'd suddenly entered Charlotte's brain. "What you just said? That sounds an awful lot like my sister, actually." She laughed. "And it's probably true. I should make more time to see her. Well, like it or not, I'm making time now." Jane vowed to put in a vacation request when she got back to work. "I'm going to do it. I haven't seen my niece in years, and I've barely used my vacation time. I think I might have even lost some of the days by now."

Regret filled her suddenly as she realized what she sounded like. She looked up at Eric, who seemed lost in his own thoughts. "You probably think I'm a terrible sister."

"No." He smiled at her. "I think you've been focused on work. I get where you're coming from." He gestured to the Chihuly glass sculpture again. "Does he have any other pieces in here?"

"No, and I've always thought it was such a bummer. After seeing that beautiful glass sculpture, you just want to see more. You know? Walk through a garden of them."

"I'm going to look him up when I get home. What amazing work."

It thrilled Jane that she was able to show Eric something that moved him so much.

He took her hand again. "Come on. What's next on the agenda, Miss Tour Guide?"

"How about some Impressionists?" She gestured to the Impressionist art exhibit across the hall and in through the glass doors, where people stood in line to enter.

They waited just a few moments, and Jane was almost sorry they had to drop their hands so they could go inside. It had been nice just standing there with him, the light from the windows making Eric's eyes seem even greener.

They entered the exhibit, stopping at each picture a long time and taking a seat on the benches to chat about the color and style. Jane thought that despite going to the museum dozens of times, this visit had to be her favorite. She smiled to herself. Maybe this guy wasn't so bad, after all. She had been able to see him for who he really was without judging him by his job or appearance. She chided herself for doing that in the past.

"Hey, there," he said, touching his hand to hers. "You went off somewhere there."

"I know." She looked down. "Just thinking about what a great time I'm having."

Eric hooked her chin gently with his index finger, bringing her face to his. "Me, too." Just as he leaned closer, a curator walked through the exhibit and startled them.

"Closing time!"

They both looked down, shaking off the spark that had developed between them.

CHAPTER 13 - GRACE

Grace was forty-six. She hated that thought. It wasn't the actual number; it was what it represented. She and John would probably never be able to retire, and here she was still clinging to the thought of having kids. Happy birthday to me, she thought, feeling incredibly depressed.

When Jane found out it was Grace's birthday, she insisted on taking her out to lunch. Grace agreed, as long as no one at the restaurant sung to her. She hated that.

"No singing," Jane agreed. "Unless you want me to. I can't carry a tune to save my life, but it could cheer you up to hear me warble a birthday song for you."

Grace laughed. Jane really was a sweet woman. "No. But thank you anyway. You never know when a skill like that can come in handy."

She picked Grace up at home and drove to Seventy-Sixth Street, into an older part of Wauwatosa, a suburb of Milwaukee. The restaurant was situated on a hilly drive that overlooked the city. Grace noted a bookstore nearby and a store that sold nothing but olive oil.

"Who would have thought olive oil would be a thing?"

Jane put the car in park, and they got out.

"I know, right? I don't think I've ever thought about olive oil to the point where I'd go somewhere special for it, but to each his own, I guess. That's what my grandma used to say."

They walked up the block, and just as they were about to step inside, Grace tripped. She would have gone down to the ground if Jane hadn't been there to catch her.

Jane released Grace's arm. "You okay?"

"Yes." Grace looked down at the ground. "I tripped over nothing more than my own feet, apparently."

"It happens."

Grace felt her face heat up from embarrassment. Falls like that were happening more and more lately. Jane didn't seem fazed by it, and pulled open the door to the restaurant. As they entered, Grace took in the smells of fresh bread and herbs. She looked around, noticing the vibe of a French bistro, with several small tables lined up in a row on the left and a bakery and bar on the right. A large chalkboard that contained the specials of the day was contained within a gilded gold frame and propped up on a stand just before the tables. They sat down and looked at their menus. Jane folded hers quickly and put it down on the small table between them.

"Know what you want already?"

"Oh sure. I come here a lot. They have good salads, especially. I'm hungry for one of those today, I think. But everything's good here."

The waiter came by to take their orders, and Grace decided to take Jane's suggestion and order the salade Niçoise, with potatoes, eggs, haricots verts, and salmon over a bed of mixed greens. Jane ordered a vegetable crêpe with leeks, mushrooms, and Gruyere cheese. They both ordered a fruity soft drink as well.

Grace laughed. "I thought you were going to order a salad."

Jane lifted her drink, and Grace did the same. "To friendship." They clinked glasses, and Grace was glad she hadn't said, *To birthdays.*

Jane continued, "I had totally planned to get a salad and then spotted that vegetable crêpe on the specials board. I changed my mind."

"A woman's prerogative, as they say. So, my dish has haricots verts? Is that…?"

"Green beans."

"Got it. Well, I have to say, this is really fun, Jane. Thanks for inviting me."

"You're welcome. I thought we could talk about the upcoming exhibit. And also"—she seemed to cringe—"I'm going out of my mind with men problems."

Grace nearly spit her drink out, and coughed. She laughed. "I wish I had men problems."

Jane laughed, too. "It sounds ridiculous, I know. But I've left many messages for my boyfriend, Brad, who never gets back to me. This is after he tells me he has a kid, for the first time, even though we've been together for eight years. Then, I have an amazing time at the art museum with Eric, and I don't know what to think about it."

Grace stated the obvious: "It sounds like you and Brad are done."

Jane nodded and then looked at her phone. "Look who just texted me." She held it out to Grace, who could not see the small lettering of the text, but she made an educated guess.

"Brad?"

Jane seemed exasperated. "After all the calls, he sends me a text."

"Saying…?"

Jane read it. "Get this! He is inviting me, and any friends I want to bring, to a Thanksgiving appetizer party."

Grace frowned. "Just appetizers?"

Jane rolled her eyes. "Apparently. Through text? What am I? One of his college buddies?"

"Are you going to go?" The drama of this was intriguing to Grace.

Jane thought for a moment. "Yes. You know why? Because then I can corner him and talk to him. Done. That's it." She wiped her hands against each other as if clearing them of dirt.

"So, you're going to a Thanksgiving party to break up with him?" That didn't seem like a good idea to Grace.

"When you put it that way, it seems ridiculous."

Then again, who was Grace to judge another person? "You know what? Don't mind me. You want to talk about ridiculous? I keep thinking of my mother, who is dead, and imagining her in my house, a place she never set foot in while she was alive. I even picture her rocking a child I lost to miscarriage. Like, I imagine her in the kid's room, taking care of him, and so I don't want to go in that room to disturb them. I feel like, if I step into the room and change anything, even move a piece of furniture, it will cause them to leave." Grace laughed and put her head in her hands. "It sounds like I've lost it. Completely, utterly, lost it."

"No," Jane said. "You're processing your grief. Besides, you want your mother to finally love you, and this is the only way you can picture it now."

She looked at Jane. "You are so wise."

"Oh sure." She snorted. "Just not with my own life." Jane frowned, looking exasperated. "You know what? I'm going to text him back." She typed and read what she was typing, aloud. "Brad, I would like to speak with you privately. When are you available?" She was about to hit send when Grace put up her hand.

"Stop. Before you send it…"

Jane waited. "Yes?"

"It seems like you have already given him enough chances to respond," she said, thinking of all the authors she tried to contact, who dragged their feet sometimes in contacting her back. Or the publishers who wanted her to hurry up and edit a book but then weren't as quick with payment when she dropped everything to meet a tight deadline for them. "Instead of asking when he is available, tell him you'll be stopping over before the party sometime, at a time of your choosing, to discuss your relationship. Tell him"—Grace thought quickly—"'I'll see you at that time, and we can discuss Thanksgiving after that.'"

Jane nodded, hit delete on part of the text and typed what Grace had just dictated, reading it aloud. She thought for a moment, and then sent it.

"I like that better," she told Grace. "Maybe I've been too lenient with him."

"Maybe," Grace said, sipping some of her drink. It was delicious. Fruity and light.

"Do you think that's it?" Jane asked. "That I've just not been good about boundaries? I ask, because, I was talking with my sister, Charlotte, the other night on the phone, and it got me thinking about my dad. I should say no to him sometimes and find myself unable to."

Grace thought for a moment. "I think you are at a point where you are thinking about your future and that you're probably being cautious, not wanting to throw away your relationship with Brad, if you're just about to come together but unable to make the decision to move on if you aren't."

Jane looked at her a long moment and then nodded. Grace hoped she hadn't been too forward in telling Jane her thoughts, but she did ask. She also recognized in Jane a girl who just wanted to be loved and didn't want to ruin it with Brad in case he could give her that. But eight years? To Grace, it was long past time to do it. How long could she possibility wait?

And then the irony of it hit Grace so hard, she almost felt like she couldn't breathe. She'd done the very same thing with children. She'd pushed and tried this and that, and waited and hoped, and despite the fact miracles sometimes happen, there were also times when it wasn't meant to be: when the good thing that everyone else seems to have, is not part of the plan for your life. Part of a plan you wanted, but not part of the plan God wanted.

John kept telling Grace that God only wanted good for them. Part of what kept her angry at God was her feeling that if it were true, God must really not like her very much to deny her children. But what if it were more than that? What if not having children, as hard as it was for her to understand, was part of the plan of goodness for her?

She used to think the reason she was being denied children was because the big, ole universe felt she wasn't going to be a good mother. But she knew now, with all her heart, that wasn't true. She would have been a wonderful mother. But she'd also worked long and hard to get over her childhood, to be able to love and have a relationship. What if having a child meant reopening wounds, she wondered. That every time she would be patient and loving with her child, she'd feel the pain of her mother who would drink and slap and taunt her? What if having a child, where Grace would sing to him or hug him and help him patiently when the dear boy was struggling, made Grace feel the pain of what she'd missed, from a new and unbearable perspective?

Jane showed Grace her phone again. "I got a reply." Jane read it. "I promise all will be explained at Thanksgiving. Hang in there with me." Jane frowned. "What on earth does that mean?"

Grace shook her head. Brad seemed like a confused guy himself. What an odd response, given all that had transpired between them.

"What do you think he is trying to tell you?"

Jane closed her eyes. "With Brad? Who knows? The last few months with him have been confusing. And if I'm being honest, he's never been easy to read. I just kept thinking it would get better, but now I look back and see that I've spent eight years with him, and if this doesn't end in marriage, I wonder if I've wasted my time."

Grace shook her head. "Don't do that to yourself. A moment ago, you were assuming things were over with him. Remember, marriage isn't the end-all, be-all solution, and I say that, having a very happy marriage. Marriage is rough. And if you have issues before you get married, they'll only increase after. I'm not trying to scare you," she added, noting the alarm on Jane's face. "I'm just trying to say, you need to decide what you want, regardless of what Brad does. And that's the hard part."

Their meals came, and Grace used her fork to mix up her salad, ensuring that the Dijon vinaigrette was evenly distributed. She took a bite, savoring the tangy dressing and crunchy green beans on her fork. When she looked over at Jane, she saw that she had just said a quick, silent prayer for her food. Now she dug in, continuing the conversation as if she hadn't just stopped to chat with God in the midst of it. Grace marveled at that. Her talks with God were usually when she was alone and practically shouting in desperation for help. A silent prayer of thanks hadn't occurred to her, and if anyone else but Jane had done it, she wouldn't have paid attention. But Jane had been through a lot in her life, and to still cling to her faith made Grace wonder why she couldn't seem to do the same thing.

After having a macaron for dessert at lunch, Grace couldn't resist getting a few to take home. They were just so colorful, with bright blues and pinks and yellows. And they were delicious.

When she got home, she took them out of the cute pastry box that the restaurant gave her and placed them on a plate in the center of the kitchen island. She arranged the brightly colored cookies and left them in the middle of the island so her husband would see them as soon as he came home.

Then she thought about some dinner. Looking through the fridge, she saw asparagus she'd picked up at the farmers' market over the weekend and had an idea for a pasta dish that one of her foster mothers used to make. Talking to Jane about her upbringing had left Grace thinking about the way different people had cared for her, growing up. One of her foster mothers loved to cook things Grace liked, and she wished she had paid more attention to how she created the dishes she served.

Grace put the asparagus on the counter and then rooted through the pantry for some angel-hair pasta and pine nuts. She found both and then went back to the fridge to see if they had any Parmesan cheese. She was in luck, and smiled to herself, that a nice meat-free meal awaited them.

John came home as she cooked. He spotted the macarons and picked one up and smelled it.

"What are these?"

"Macarons. I got those for you. Jane took me to this little French restaurant today for lunch in Wauwatosa. It was an amazing place. We'll have to go there sometime."

He bit into one and his eyes got wide. "Wow, delish. They just kinda melt on your tongue, don't they?" He gobbled another one down and then asked again, "What did you say these were?"

"French macarons. They are almond-meringue cookies with a buttercream filling."

Grace put on a pot of water to boil, adding a generous helping of salt. Then she took out a small sauté pan in order to toast the pine nuts. She grabbed the asparagus and rinsed it, blotting it dry on a paper towel. Then she brought the bundle to the kitchen island and cut off the ends. She'd add them to the pine nuts at the very end just to cook them through.

She glanced over at her husband, and he was still examining the plate of macarons. She smiled that the artist in him was studying the shape and color of the treats.

"They're pretty, aren't they?"

"They are. I've never seen them before. The colors…"

"I knew you'd like them. They are so vibrant and cheerful."

He popped another one in his mouth. She was going to tell him not to spoil his dinner, but thought against it. She was just happy she could give him something he enjoyed so much.

They'd just finished cleaning up dinner, when she turned and saw both a cake and a gift on the kitchen table.

She smiled. "You remembered."

He walked up behind her, kissing the back of her neck. "Did you honestly think, after all these years, that I would forget?"

Grace turned to him and shrugged. "No. But, since I didn't want a fuss—"

"And this isn't a fuss. It is me giving you a gift to tell you how much I love and appreciate you."

He kissed her, and she hugged him, feeling emotional. They were so good together. Why couldn't she just accept the things they didn't have so she could enjoy this fully?

"Hey, now," he said, kissing the top of her head. "No crying on your birthday. I believe that is a rule somewhere." He reached over her shoulder and lifted the lid for the box of cake. "Yellow cake, pink frosting, no frosting flowers, and the whipped frosting you like, not the other stuff."

She turned around, seeing the beautiful cake. It was perfect. Just like them together.

He grabbed the candles he'd bought, placing five around the edges of the cake.

"One for each decade of your life!" He said with a flourish, then shrugged. "Well, almost."

While Grace could have done without the reminder, she promised herself that her wish this year would not be for children, not for the family she'd begged God for through half of her thirties and forties, and instead, she wished to just remember this moment, and appreciate it.

CHAPTER 14 - JANE

Mrs. Ferch had texted Jane to stop over after she got off work and before heading up to her own apartment. As she reached the door, she smelled something wonderful cooking from within Mrs. Ferch's apartment.

She knocked, and Mrs. Ferch ushered her in.

"Oh good, you're here." She reached for a bag she had on the table. "Homemade bread." She handed it to Jane.

"Smells great." She sniffed the aroma coming from the bag. "For me? That was so nice."

Mrs. Ferch then reached for the other bag and Jane noted a small glass container, which was also warm. "And this. Beef stew. My own recipe."

"Wow! What a nice surprise. Thank you."

Mrs. Ferch looked at her expectantly.

Jane was confused. "Did you want to eat it with me?"

The woman laughed. "No, silly. Not me. I've already eaten. But that is a lot of food. And I mean, a lot. You might want to invite someone over for dinner."

Jane blinked. "You mean you—"

"No, silly!" Mrs. Ferch chuckled. "I want you to invite that young man over."

Jane rolled her eyes.

"Now, make it casual. Say, hey, why don't you pop over for dinner? Say it lightly. It's just dinner."

Jane began to protest, wanting to share the fact that she hadn't even heard from Eric in the last few days, but Mrs. Ferch shooed her out of the apartment with freshly baked bread and stew in hand.

When Jane approached Eric's place, she hesitated. Should she knock? Invite him over as Mrs. Ferch suggested? Would it be too forward? She thought of Mrs. Ferch's suggestion to keep it light. Could she do that without sounding stupid?

She didn't have to think about it because Eric opened the door.

"Hey, there! What a nice surprise!" He closed his eyes and took a whiff. "Mmm, I thought I smelled fresh bread. When did you find time to make it?"

"Oh, it's easy. I have a sweet, little old lady who felt like giving me an entire loaf of bread and"—she held up the other bag—"stew. Want to pop over for dinner?"

Eric smiled widely, and Jane caught her breath at how handsome he looked. When did he start looking so good? Or maybe it was just that Jane was beginning to look at the world as a single person again. In her head, she had broken up with Brad. The trouble was, in reality, she hadn't. That wasn't fair to Eric or Brad. Jane planned to speak with Brad properly at his mother's appetizer party the following week.

Eric smiled at her. "Homemade bread, stew, and a beautiful girl? Give me five minutes. I'll be right up."

"Great! See you in a few." Jane trotted upstairs with everything in hand, thinking about what she would wear.

She changed out of her work clothes, when she suddenly realized what he'd said. *Did he just say I was beautiful?*

Eric finished the last bite of stew and sat back. "That was delicious." He smiled at Jane appreciatively, and she felt a duty to remind him where that dinner had come from.

"It was delicious." She raised her glass of milk. "To Mrs. Ferch. Thank God we have such a kind lady looking out for us."

They clinked glasses and Eric agreed. "She takes good care of people, doesn't she? I've always felt really close to her. I can tell you do, too."

"With Charlotte in Seattle," she said, "Mrs. Ferch is really the only family I have around here. It's hard to believe Charlotte has been out there as long as she has."

Jane shook her head. Where did the time go? She could remember Charlotte and her going to Summerfest, Bastille Days, and all the ethnic festivals at the lakefront. Charlotte especially liked German Fest since their father came from German descent. It was a way for the girls to learn more about their heritage. Their father didn't tell them much, and their grandparents were already gone by the time they were born. Charlotte enjoyed the culture tent, where they learned about the German influence on architecture, art, and politics in Milwaukee.

Jane, on the other hand, liked the food. "Have you ever had a currywurst?" she blurted out suddenly to Eric.

He gave it some thought as if she hadn't just quickly

changed directions with the conversation. She liked that about him. He was just like Charlotte that way, she thought.

"German?" he guessed.

"Very good! Yeah, it's a bratwurst that is served on a stick—"

"All the best foods are served on a stick."

"Exactly. And it has a curry sauce that you dunk it in. I get one every year at German Fest. I was just thinking about how Charlotte and I used to go there when we were younger."

"No kidding? I've never been. I've been to some of the other ones, though. Like Festa Italiana."

"They have the best fireworks there."

"And food," Eric agreed. "I've been to Polish Fest a bunch of times. And I've been to Indian Summer with Wayne and the kids."

"It's been a few years since I've been to that one," Jane said, wondering what else she and Eric had in common. If he enjoyed the Milwaukee festivals, they certainly would have a lot of things in common they could do together.

"Man." Eric seemed lost in thought. He looked down at his plate and absentmindedly moved the remaining couple of bites of food around with his fork. "I do like how much there is to do in this town. I'm going to miss that."

Miss it?

Eric caught her look of confusion. He quickly got up with his plate and reached for hers as well. "Since you invited me to dinner, I think it's only fair that I clear the table."

Jane got up to help, but Eric gently put a hand on her back. "Why don't you go ahead and relax. You've worked all day and probably need to put your feet up."

She stood there stupidly at first, not believing that he

was actually clearing the table. That wasn't something she saw guys do that often, and while she was glad, she also felt like she didn't know what to do next. Her usual routine was to put her sweatpants on, thick socks, and an old, ratty T-shirt to relax in after she came home from work. She certainly wasn't going to do that now. Instead, she sat down on the couch, feeling awkward that someone was waiting on her like this. How long had it been since that last happened? She tried to think and could only imagine that it must have been her dad, making her and Charlotte breakfast on the weekends when her mom worked.

"Would you like me to make some tea?" Eric asked, dishes all rinsed and put away in the dishwasher. He pointed to the kitchen counter. "I see you have a teakettle."

"I'd love some. Thank you. Are you sure you don't need me to help?"

"No, I think I got it."

Jane wondered if their affinity for Milwaukee festivals counted as another thing they had in common. If she could count more things they shared, maybe she would see how perfect they were for each other, like Mrs. Ferch apparently could.

"Kettle's on," he said as he sat down next to her. "Hope you don't mind me staying for a bit."

"No, of course not."

"So, you're still using the older teakettles? Not like Mrs. Ferch's whiz of a coffee machine?"

Jane laughed. "She loves that thing. It allows her to multitask even more."

"Yeah, she's a pretty amazing lady. I'm happy I was able to meet her." He leaned in closer, and Jane found it hard not look into his eyes. They were just inches apart, and Jane held her breath for what might come next. "I'm especially thankful that she introduced me to you," he said.

Before Jane could reply, the whistle on the teakettle blew. Eric closed his eyes a moment and then shook his head. "What timing. I'll just go get our tea and be back in a second, okay?"

Jane nodded and unconsciously said, "Okay," like she was half in a dream. What was happening with her and Eric? Would they start dating? She could finally admit to herself that she found him attractive, and she did enjoy spending time with him, but she needed to find out more about his job plans. She needed to tell him about Brad and how she was planning on ending it with him. Well, maybe she was. She hated that she still wanted to talk with Brad one last time.

And his job. She sighed inwardly. She hated that she was even thinking about that, sizing Eric up over it. It wasn't that she cared what he did for a living, but if he was going to be a dreamer like her dad, now that he was laid off, it would mean stepping into the life her mother had of working constantly just to support their family. That was her mom's choice, but she remained resentful. Charlotte and Jane rarely even spoke to her mom now because once they were grown, she divorced their father and met someone new. It was like she wanted to forget all about their previous hardships, and forget about her kids as well. Jane didn't want to end up like that.

"Hey, there," Eric said, pulling her once again from her thoughts. "You drifted off somewhere else for a minute there." He smiled at her as he handed her a cup of tea. "Do you do that a lot?"

"Daydream, you mean? Or maybe it's not really daydreaming." Should she be honest with him? "I actually was thinking about my mom and dad just now. My mom used to work so hard, and she was always angry about things. I know she was mad at my dad a lot, but she also seemed mad and me and Charlotte, too. I just…" Jane looked down for a moment but continued. "I just don't want to end up like her. Dumb thing to have pop into my head, right?"

"Not at all," he said, not elaborating. He sipped his tea and looked at her over the teacup. "Plus, you're working a lot, and it's natural to contemplate your life and how you grew up. It makes sense that you'd be thinking about your parents."

Eric put his mug down on the coffee table and looked at her. "What you said just now? About your parents? I'm glad you did." He leaned toward her. "I've been thinking a lot about you. I mean"—he smiled—"you are a hard one to not think about. You know?"

Jane blinked. She was?

"Until now, I had the impression you were more concerned about money than you were about getting to know me. You just kept asking about my job. I get that, now. I understand where you are coming from. And, I want to be honest with you. I worked like a dog for a company that treated me like crap and I hated it. They gave me a big severance, and I've been taking some time to figure things out. I don't really know what I want to do. I'll be honest with you. But I do want to find a job I'm passionate about, Jane." He tapped his fingers on his leg, and Jane got the sense that he was nervous, that he had more to say but was struggling with how to say it. She didn't want to rush him.

"So…" He seemed to shake off whatever subject he'd been holding, for a moment. "What about your mom. Do you see her a lot?"

Jane felt as if she'd been holding her breath, waiting for him to tell her more. He'd told her some, but she knew there was more there. But she went with the conversation.

She really had no right to push him; they were still getting to know each other.

"My mom? No way. She really checked out when Charlotte left. She was so happy that Charlotte had moved on, and it seemed like she couldn't wait for me to do the same. The day after I graduated college, my mom said she was divorcing my dad and moving. She reconnected with her high school boyfriend and moved in with him. She travels a lot now, and once in a blue moon, Charlotte and I will get postcards from her, but that's about it. I haven't spoken to her, I mean, really had a conversation with her, in about ten years. But for the last month, she's refused to speak with me at all. I mean, she doesn't return my emails or phone calls… nothing."

Eric reached out and took her hand. "I am so sorry, Jane. That's really hard. You probably miss her."

"I do. She's mad at me right now because I agreed to give my dad money. I have in the past."

She could see Eric cringe, but he still looked at her with acceptance. "It's hard to say no, especially when it's with your parents. I actually have that problem with Wayne. I mean, the guy's been so good to me that I hate to disappoint him. I hope you don't blame yourself, Jane. Even if you have given your dad money… even if you do again, it doesn't mean she should cut you off completely. That's just not right."

"I feel like she blames me for the troubles she had in her life. Me and Charlotte both." Jane tried to blink back tears but once again felt them welling up in her eyes. Despite her best efforts, she felt one release, falling slowly down her cheek. Eric cupped her chin, wiping the tear with his thumb. He left his hand on her cheek for a moment, and she leaned into it, feeling the warmth he provided in his touch.

"I'm sorry to be crying like this. I've been doing that lately. I'm not sure what's come over me."

"You have nothing to apologize for." He stayed silent for a moment and wrung his hands. "Jane, I need to tell you something. I, ah…"

He blew out a breath and shook his head. His hand dropped to his lap.

"Up until a couple of days ago I was looking forward to the future. Toward different things. Things I was going to do now. A new life, if you will."

Jane nodded, unsure of where he was going with this.

"When I lost my job, it really shook me. I know you can understand that. I see the same things in you, the same tiredness and stress that I felt. I was in the wrong job to begin with, and then all I did was log hours."

She was fidgeting with her hands in her lap, and he took one of them in his. But Jane could feel his hand tense as he talked. She stayed silent, knowing he was finally going to tell her about his job plans. This was what she wanted to hear from him, but she hoped it wouldn't be something she'd regret knowing.

"I met my ex, Tiffany, at that job, too. We started dating. Got engaged." Eric took his hand off Jane's and rubbed his temples at the memory. "I thought it was what I was supposed to do. You know?" He turned to her, and she nodded, encouraging him to go on. "But I was unhappy there. Sales? It just wasn't me. I liked working with my hands, for one." He laughed bitterly; a memory lodged in his mind that went beyond Jane's understanding.

"And then," he went on, "I got laid off. Half the sales force did. Tiff worked in accounting, and they kept her on. But things were different between us after I lost my job. I told Tiff that I thought it might be a blessing in disguise. That I could finally figure out what I was supposed to do with my life. But she was angry with me. I'd already been feeling bad about the situation, and she was not very understanding. No, it's more than that. She was embarrassed by me or something. Then, she dumped me. Said she wasn't going to be with a guy who wasn't serious about work."

He turned to Jane now. Took both her hands in his. "I know what you're saying about your dad. I know you wanted to know what I did for a living. Mrs. Ferch told me that, and then just now, what you said… it all made sense. I was waiting for the right moment to tell you. At first, I thought maybe it was like with Tiffany… but it isn't. I get that you're working hard and want someone who is serious about life. I get that, Jane. It took me a long time to figure out what to do. But then I finally realized. It's what I've wanted to do since I was a kid. You know how you have these dreams of what you'll be?"

Jane nodded. "A doctor, a lawyer, fireman…"

"Exactly. I wanted to be a firefighter forever. I mean, I've even been volunteering for the Pine Ville Fire Department the last year and a half here. I thought that it was the perfect time to see if firefighting was really what I wanted to do. So that's what I've been doing. I'm gone at different times of the day and night, but I love it. And that's not all." Their hands parted, and he looked at her with those green eyes that seemed to see right through her. "I'm leaving. For Seattle. I got a job at a fire department out there."

Seattle? Another person leaving Jane to go to Seattle? She was stunned. "When?"

"In two weeks. Wayne and his family are moving out there, too. Wayne is a fireman now actually. He's been wanting to move to Seattle forever. Maggie, his wife, has some family out there, and I thought it all seemed to make sense. Wayne and I used to talk about firefighting all the time. It drove Tiffany crazy. She wasn't wild about the idea. When I got laid off, I figured it was my time to make a change. But then you and I have been spending time together, and Jane, I really like you."

Jane looked at him, with his sad eyes and handsome face. She felt like she could stay there forever, just looking at him and holding hands. She couldn't remember the last time she felt this content. "I like you, too" was all she could say. The admission sounded like it came from someone else. Did she really just say that out loud?

He gently pulled her toward him, and leaned in close. She could smell the lingering scent of tea on his lips, and as she closed her eyes, his lips met hers, and she tasted his kiss. Light, yet firm. Salty, yet sweet. She kissed back slowly, softly, and after a short moment, her kiss grew more urgent.

Jane couldn't process what he'd said, that he was leaving. Moving. Just like Charlotte. He really did have a job; he really wasn't a dreamer like her dad. None of that mattered at that moment, as her hands found their way to his neck, and his arms pulled her closer. She was aware of nothing but the two of them.

She was so absorbed in the kiss that she didn't hear the door or the sound of her sister letting herself in with the key Jane had given her.

CHAPTER 15 - GRACE

They ate the cake on the back porch, the autumn air cool on their faces. It was still warm during the day, which was unusual for that time of year. Milwaukee could be such a mixed bag of surprises when it came to the weather. When they'd finished, he took their plates and cleaned up. She stayed on the porch, listening to the birds sing and wanting to soak up everything the day had given her. Maybe that was the lesson now, to just appreciate every single moment of her life instead of wishing for what she didn't have.

John came back with a glass of champagne for her.

"My my my, what's this?" She smiled.

"Well, it's your birthday, and while you aren't happy about it, I am so happy to be here celebrating with you."

They clinked glasses.

"Thanks for cleaning up dinner," she told him.

"I can't very well let you wash dishes on your birthday. I would have taken you out—"

"I know." She patted his leg. "This is what I wanted. A quiet night with you."

She drank in silence, and replayed the day's events. She told John that Jane had invited them to Brad's mother's house for an appetizer type of Thanksgiving party.

"I hope you told her no," he said happily, looking out into the yard.

She laughed. He preferred to stay home and eat the Thanksgiving spread that Grace would make for the two of them.

"Honey, Jane is a sweet girl, and she's your new gallery rep; let's not forget that."

He looked at her. "You two have really hit it off. You have a knack for all that stuff, Grace."

She laughed. "For what? Talking to people?"

"Yes." He drank some more champagne and then refilled Grace's glass, too. "I'm going to get you good and drunk so you'll find me irresistible," he joked.

She accepted the champagne. "You don't need to get me drunk for that. You've been irresistible to me from the first minute we met."

It was true. She found him interesting and attractive from their first date and that had never changed.

"So, basically," he said, "I'm perfect."

"Don't push it," she joked. "And I'll make us our regular turkey dinner the day after. Okay? No biggie."

"I know." He drank, suddenly lost in his thoughts. He realized what she'd said and then turned to her briefly. "Thank you for doing that." He patted her leg. "Now, what is Jane's boyfriend's name again?"

This was always the series of questions she endured when they met someone knew. He barely paid attention when she talked about new people and then peppered her with questions at the last minute.

"Brad."

He nodded. She knew the next question would be

about Brad's mother.

"And the boyfriend's mother? What's her name again?"

"Constance."

Grace smiled to herself. She knew him so well. She looked at him, feeling so much love for this man, for everything they had been through. He was quiet suddenly. She could tell by the way he tapped his leg that he was going through his thoughts. Something was on his mind.

"Are you okay?"

"Huh?" He seemed surprised to be pulled from thought. "Yeah. 'Course. Just thinking about the party… trying to remember the names."

"It's okay to ask them to give you their name again, you know."

She laughed as she said it, and he smiled at her but turned back to look out over the yard again, lost in thought. She'd leave him to it. Maybe he was working through another painting idea.

There was a time, when they were first married, where Grace would get upset and spend days caught in depression. Between the childlessness and the betrayals of friends, she could not find her way back to the surface. Every day, she'd struggle just to get some air, just to get through a day as if she weren't drowning.

They sat quietly together until the sun went down. He seemed lost in his own thoughts, and she was in hers as well. She'd long ago found comfort in their silences, both appreciating the view of a sunset or simply enjoying spending the end of the day together, reflecting back individually, while they shared their lives.

CHAPTER 16 - JANE

Ahem! I see I'm interrupting! And here I thought you were lonely." Charlotte raised an eyebrow at Jane, and she was instantly embarrassed. She pulled back from Eric, but he just smiled and stood to greet Charlotte as if she popped by every single day.

"Hi," he said as he extended his hand and took the suitcase Charlotte was holding. "I'm Eric."

"Charlotte. Janey's sister." She shook his hand and smiled knowingly toward Jane. "I thought I'd surprise Janey here with a visit. She sounded like she needed some company, the other night."

Jane sat frozen on the couch, still feeling the touch of Eric's kiss. As he took Charlotte's suitcase to the other room, the two sisters exchanged a look. Jane rolled her eyes, and Charlotte let out a laugh. Finally, Charlotte held out her arms. "Come here, you silly girl." As they embraced, Charlotte whispered, "He's a hunk."

Jane couldn't help thinking how much her sister sounded like Mrs. Ferch. She had expected Eric to leave when Charlotte got there, but as soon as Charlotte spotted the tea they were drinking, she asked if she could have a cup. Jane got up to make a cup for Charlotte, and by the time she returned to the living room Eric and Charlotte were chatting away like long-lost friends.

"I was talking with my little sister here the other night, and she sounded kind of lonely. You should see how hard this kid works."

"Oh, Charlotte. Stop." Jane was uncomfortable with Charlotte spilling details about their phone conversation. After all, Eric didn't need to hear that she was crying, again, or that she was questioning her life choices.

"I know she does." Eric looked at Jane with admiration. "She's a remarkable person. So, Charlotte," he continued, "I understand you're from Seattle?"

"Yes. I love it there."

Eric gestured to the couch, indicating Charlotte should take his seat. Where he had just been next to me, Jane thought, still trying to recover from her sister's surprise entrance. She cleared her throat, mentioning the first thing that popped into her mind.

"Hey, you never told me there is a Chihuly museum there! I looked it up on the internet today while I was at work. That place is amazing! I so want to go there. I'm going to put in for a vacation request."

"Oh, sure." Charlotte crossed her arms in a huff. "You'll make time for that but not to see your only sister? Is that it?"

Charlotte had a playfulness in her voice, but Jane knew her well enough to see the hurt there also. She glanced at Eric, mindful of their conversation a couple of days before.

"I'm sorry, Charlotte. I know. I've been a terrible sister."

"No, you haven't." Charlotte smacked her on the arm.

"But you are a workaholic. Or whatever those people are called. You need to have a little fun once in a while."

Jane rolled her eyes. "You sound exactly like Mrs. Ferch."

"I knew I liked that woman," Charlotte said.

Charlotte continued talking about the sights in Seattle, and how much she had loved it when she first visited in school, years ago. Eric admitted that he was moving there in a couple of weeks.

"How interesting," Charlotte said, raising an eyebrow toward Jane.

Eric seemed to sense that the two sisters needed to talk. "Listen, why don't I head out? It'll give you girls time to catch up."

Jane was just about to say yes when Charlotte cut her off.

"Nonsense! I want to find out all about you. I'm going to ask you all kinds of nosy questions tonight, as a good sister should. Although I'm dying for some of that custard the shop on the corner sells. Charlotte jumped up off the couch and dug through her purse, pulling out some money. Flavor of the day. Do you mind?" she said, handing Eric the cash. "Then come back and hang out with me and Jane. Why don't we make some popcorn, too? I'm starving; can you tell? You know they don't feed you on planes like they used to."

Eric gave the cash back. "I'd be happy to. Custard sounds great. I'm happy to treat."

He left, and once again Jane felt like she was chatting with Mrs. Ferch, the conversation going to-and-fro, like winds on a sail. She exchanged a look with Eric, who seemed totally comfortable with Charlotte's forwardness. He smiled at Jane and said, "Be right back." Off he went.

Jane looked at Charlotte and laughed. "I love you,

Charlotte. But wow, do you make an entrance."

"Sorry." She hugged Jane again. "I didn't think you'd be all cozied up with a guy. And a cute guy, at that. What's the story? Give it to me quick before he comes back."

"Well," Jane felt herself whisper, "I didn't know he was moving to Seattle. I had no idea."

"How long have you two been dating?" Charlotte was whispering back now.

"Dating? We're not dating."

"Well, it certainly looked like—"

"I know what it looked like. But we just sort of… I mean, Mrs. Ferch…"

"He lives here in the building?" Charlotte was all about the facts.

"Yes."

"Mrs. Ferch introduced you?"

Jane nodded. "Yes. And I just found out about the Seattle thing now. Tonight. Right before—"

"Got it," Charlotte whispered as Eric came back in. "Eric, I'm all over the place tonight. Let's freeze the custard for later. Is that okay? Do you know how to make popcorn? With a kettle on the stove? That's the best way. Don't you think so, Janey? Remember how Dad used to make it like that?"

Charlotte took Eric by the arm and ushered him into the kitchen. Jane heard her telling him about the amount of oil to put in and how to know when the kernels were done. They talked more about Seattle, and Jane let out a deep breath. How can things change so quickly? she wondered.

The three of them talked for several hours. Eric made a giant bowl of popcorn with Charlotte's help, and they munched and chatted about everything from movies to their childhoods. Eric admitted that he was an only child, and after a grilling from Charlotte, he also opened up more about Tiffany.

"Do you still see her?" Charlotte blurted. Jane started to tell Eric he didn't have to answer that, but he told her it was okay. He seemed unfazed by Charlotte's constant questions.

"No, I don't."

"Does she want to see you now? Especially now that you're going to be a firefighter?"

Jane expected Eric to say no, but instead his answer surprised her. "I've heard that she wants to see me, but I have no interest in her. No."

"Has she contacted you?"

"Yes. She left a message."

Charlotte was unrelenting. "Did you return it?"

"No, I didn't. Then she called Maggie. Wayne's wife?" Eric looked at Jane as if to confirm his story. "To see if we could all have dinner."

"I see," Charlotte said, and Jane half expected her to get up and shine the lamp in Eric's face. "And did you agree to this dinner?"

"No, Charlotte, I did not." Eric looked at Jane now. His tone was matter-of-fact. "I'm not interested in having Tiff back in my life."

Jane sat stunned at the chain of events in the last day. The previous night she was wondering why he hadn't called, and then a great dinner and a kiss, and now this interrogation from Charlotte. This new revelation that Tiffany wanted him back was just too much.

"Well, what does it matter if Tiffany wants him back?" Jane said out loud, surprising herself. "He's moving. Away. To Seattle. Where apparently all the people I like, go." Jane shot a look at Charlotte, who then looked at Eric. "What is she going to do, date him while he's in Seattle and she's here?" She wasn't sure if she was saying it about Tiffany or herself.

Jane got up and brought the popcorn bowl to the sink. She was tired of this conversation.

"Well," Eric said, "that's true, except…"

"What?" Charlotte and Jane both said in unison.

"Tiffany claims she wants to move to Seattle. She and Maggie are close, and she doesn't have many other friends." Eric just looked from Charlotte to Jane and back again. "But that won't happen. She's just talking about it right now. Besides, I'm not interested in her. Remember?"

Charlotte gave her sister a sympathetic look, who took the cue and let out the loudest and most fake yawn Jane had ever heard. "You know what? That flight was really torture. I'm going to turn in. Eric"—she held out her hand—"I hope we can all spend more time together in the next couple days." Eric shook her hand and smiled at her. Charlotte turned and gave Jane a hug, "I'll see you in the morning."

Jane watched her walk away, closing the bedroom door behind her. She turned to Eric and couldn't hide her disappointment.

"You are moving to Seattle, and your ex-girlfriend… no, make that ex-fiancée, wants to move there, too. And you decided to tell me all this tonight. Tonight. Right before you__"

"Kissed you. I know. Bad timing. Worse. Lousy timing. Stupid timing."

Jane looked up at him, her hands on her hips. "Why did you kiss me? If you knew you were going to leave anyway?" The hurt was evident in her voice, and her eyes stung with the threat of tears.

"Look…" Eric motioned to the couch and held her hands in his as they each sat down. "I like you, Jane. I like you a lot. I wasn't expecting to fall for you. We've lived in this same building for a while now. You never looked at me before. I used to think you were just focused on work. I tried to talk to you when you first moved in, but you didn't seem interested."

He did? Jane couldn't remember. Regret had landed on their conversation, and the ups and downs of the past few days were taking their toll on her. Her emotions ran ragged as she tried to hold her tears inside.

"I don't know what to say. I almost wish I didn't like you, because moving would be a lot easier, then."

Jane asked the un-askable. "Can't you just work at a fire department here?"

Eric blew out a breath. "This move to Seattle? It's been a long time coming. I wanted a fresh start. Away from here. The bad memories. Away from Tiff—"

"Away from Tiffany—who you'll probably see all the time now anyway? Because she will move there?" Jane hated the way she sounded. She had no right to ask him to stay and no right to be jealous.

"I'm sorry, Jane. I'm so sorry. I even have my apartment out there already. I have my new job."

"Well, it sounds like the perfect place for you, then." Jane was trying to figure out the message in all this. She knew it wouldn't pay to get mad at Eric, and yet she couldn't help thinking that this whole situation only made her more confused.

"I used to think that," he said. "But now..." He shrugged helplessly.

She shook her head sadly. "I think you'd better go for now." She tried to say it without anger or hurt.

"Jane." Eric looked at her now with pleading eyes. "I have no right to ask you this. We've only been out a couple of times. But what if... what if you moved out there? Got a fresh start, too?"

"Move to Seattle? How could I possibly do that?"

"Well, it's not crazy, is it? Your sister lives there. Maybe you could move out there and we could date. Get to know each other better."

"Eric…" Jane thought for a moment. It sounded crazy. Quit her job? To do what? She needed to support herself. She couldn't just take off. She shook her head. "I can't. What if…" She didn't want to say what she was thinking, but she had no choice. "What if things don't work out? Or you and Tiff—"

"We're not getting back together. I swear that to you. I don't want her in my life."

Jane couldn't help but notice that he'd missed the opportunity to tell her that things would work out between them. To reassure her. But then, she knew that was asking too much. How could he tell her that when she had the same worries and doubts?

"I think you'd better go."

Eric stood, and Jane walked him to the door. He turned back to her before he left.

"We can figure out something, Jane. Let's think on this a little more. Okay?"

She nodded but felt lost and bewildered once again. When they were at the museum, she couldn't help but feel joy about their day, the way she was able to discuss art with him, about the prospect of the future... But now she felt even more alone. And then it hit her: the entire time with Eric she had all but forgotten about Brad.

The next day, Charlotte was up early, singing and making breakfast. It was Saturday, and normally Jane would have slept in longer. She was always so tired on weekends, the weekday stress catching up with her. But today, she dragged herself out of bed, feeling exhausted. She tossed and turned all night, thoughts of what her life was telling her had been taunting her from her dream life.

"I forgot that you were a morning person," Jane said to her sister. She tried to make it sound playful, but it still came out grumpy.

Charlotte, however, was used to the less-than-chipper Jane in the mornings. It didn't faze her in the least. "You didn't forget. You just hoped I'd have jet lag. Mwa hahahaha…" Charlotte tickled Jane just before setting down her breakfast.

"Hey… haha… stop it!" Jane hated being tickled by her sister. Still, it was nice of her to make breakfast. Jane looked at her plate, eggs over easy, just the way she liked them, toast with jam, and one pancake with maple syrup. "Thanks for cooking," she said sullenly.

Charlotte sat down with her plate and fanned out the napkin on her lap with a flourish. "You're at a turning point in your life, Jane, but I'm here for you. You know that."

Jane wondered about Charlotte's knowledge of life's biggest turning points. Somehow, her sister's attempts at comfort seemed to irritate her. "Turning point?"

Charlotte was nibbling on toast and watching Jane closely. "You didn't like that I'd just said that. Why?"

One of the things Jane both loved and disliked about her sister was that she knew her so well. She couldn't hide her emotions from Charlotte. "No. It irked me."

"I see that. But why?"

Charlotte seemed to really enjoy her breakfast, munching on toast and eggs and smiling at her. Jane, however, was in a bad mood. She couldn't put her finger on why. "Turning point? When have you ever been at a turning point in your life?"

Charlotte swallowed her toast, took a sip of tea. "Before I moved to Seattle."

"Exactly!" Jane slapped her leg for emphasis as she said it. "You had a random thought about moving, you did, you met a guy, and lived happily ever after."

Charlotte pointed a square of toast at Jane. "Be careful about assuming happily ever afters with people. Just because things work out doesn't mean there isn't struggle."

"Oh"—Jane snorted—"like you've struggled."

"Eat your toast before it gets cold. You have all morning to be mad at me, and this conversation needs a better setting than breakfast. You need to go to the grocery store, by the way. I had to borrow syrup and jam and eggs from Mrs. Ferch. All you had was a couple pieces of bread."

Charlotte got up, cleared her plate, and said, "I'm going to jump in the shower. Then you can take a shower, and we can figure out this divide between us. It's been a long time coming, and I've got some things to say about it, too."

With that, she went into the shower and left Jane at the table. She nibbled on the eggs and toast, but dumped the rest. She was too angry to eat. How could Charlotte be so nonchalant about her life? Just because things worked out for her didn't mean she could give advice. Then again, why was she so angry at her sister? Charlotte flew in to try and comfort her, and Jane didn't seem to appreciate it.

"I'm out of the shower!" Charlotte called. "You can go in now."

Jane shook her head in amazement. It took a lot for Charlotte to be angry with her, even times like now, when she was acting ungrateful and childish. She marveled at

Charlotte's ability to shake off unpleasantness and look for the bright side in any situation. Why didn't she get more of that ability?

Charlotte looked beautiful. Her honey-blonde hair was pulled high into a ponytail, and her face still glowed with the moisture from the shower. She looked fresh and young. Even though Jane was only nine months younger, she always thought she looked older than her sister. Her hair wasn't so honey-blonde as it was dirty blonde. She never knew what to do with it, and as a result, just kind of twisted it up in a clip.

"Why don't you take a shower and get dressed? You'll feel a lot better."

"Oh, will I?" Suddenly Jane was angry again. "I'm sorry, Charlotte. I'm irked at you today. I know I shouldn't be."

"Yes, I can see that. Take a shower. You'll feel better. Then, we'll talk. Okay?"

She knew Charlotte was right. She showered, got dressed, and felt better about life. There was something about laying around in your PJs that always made Jane feel as if life was too big for her. Getting dressed made it seem easier to take on the day.

"Okay," she said, when she was finished. "I'm here. I'm done."

Charlotte had been on the couch, reading from a magazine. She looked up at Jane. "You look beautiful."

Jane snorted. "Yeah, right!"

"Yes. Right. You know how beautiful you are, don't you?"

"Are we being honest here?" Jane asked.

Charlotte laughed. "I think we're about to have a major sister-to-sister discussion. I can feel it. So yes, let's be honest. It will make things so much easier."

"Fine." She sat down on the floor, too. "I've always felt that you were the prettier sister."

Charlotte snorted. "I've always thought you were!"

Jane shook her head. "Not even close."

"Wow." Charlotte looked her a long moment. "You really don't see it, do you? How beautiful and special you are."

"Oh yeah," Jane said bitterly, "I'm so special that you didn't even want to stay here with me." There it was. The real reason Jane had felt so much resentment about Charlotte over the years.

Charlotte's breath caught, and she looked up at the ceiling, trying not to cry. "Oh Janey." Charlotte scooted over to be closer to her sister. "I am so sorry. I suspected you felt that way, and I've had so much guilt about it. When we were growing up, it was so horrible. I just wanted out. I wanted to get away. Literally. I was eighteen, and thinking of myself. But, Janey, I didn't know where my life was going to take me. I know you think I got lucky; I was a directionless fool. I just trusted my gut. I had faith."

Jane looked earnestly at her sister. "Then why don't I trust that easily?" It was hard for her to admit. "I work hard. Isn't that what you're supposed to do? Why didn't my great guy just appear on my doorstep like yours did? I met a mediocre guy, and then I date him for eight years, and then I meet a good guy, and he's leaving the minute we try and start something up. Why didn't I get a raise? Or a promotion? Well," she amended, "I did eventually get one, but—"

"Janey, it doesn't work like that. And you know it doesn't. You didn't get a raise when you should have, and you most certainly deserved it. You didn't have a good childhood, and you deserved that, too. But I think that everything we get from life is also a gift of some kind."

Jane snorted. "Like our lousy upbringing was a gift?"

"You know what? I think it was. It taught us things. That lousy upbringing makes me that much more appreciative of my husband and family. I'm closer with my mother-in-law because I didn't have a mom to be close to. I cling to her, cherish her."

"Yeah? Well, what about my life? I don't have a huge support system like you. I don't have a family like you!" Jane sat back, realizing she was leaning forward and raising her voice. She hated the harsh way she was sounded with Charlotte.

Charlotte let out a sigh, put her hand on her arm. "Jane," she said softly, "you have so many people in your life that care about you. You can't even see it. You know how much Mrs. Ferch cares about you? She calls me every week, and we talk about you. We talk about what we hope for, that you're doing okay. She cares about you."

Jane was shocked. "She does that?"

"Yes. And Eric? Maybe you're just getting to know him, but it's obvious he cares about you. This morning when I was talking with Mrs. Ferch, he was genuinely sad. Here he's leaving for a new job and a new city. He's been planning this out and has been excited for months and months, and now, after a couple days with a girl he wished would have wanted to get to know him before now, he's torn. He wishes he could stay, and the two of you could just date for a while and see where this is going. But instead, he's upset, and sad."

Now Jane understood why he was quiet on the way home from the museum. Charlotte was right; Jane had every opportunity to get to know Eric before now, but she was too busy to pay attention. No, more than that, she didn't want to pay attention.

"I think all this time I just wrote him off because I

thought he was like Dad."

Charlotte nodded. "And me." Jane turned to her, surprised that she had guessed correctly.

"I guess I've been really hard on you, Charlotte."

"Jane, I'm still your family. I know you think I left you behind, and really, you're right. I was a young kid myself and could only think about myself. But I love you so much. You have no idea." Tears came to her eyes and it surprised Jane. Charlotte didn't cry very often. "I always thought after college you'd move out near me. Bill would always tell me not to assume that. That you needed your own life and to do things your own way. But I still held out hope. I'm so sorry you felt abandoned by me. I have such guilt about that. I know for the longest time it was just the two of us, and then I moved, and it hurt you. But I wasn't trying to do that. I just wanted a fresh start.

"I know you love it here, Jane, and I do, too. I always enjoy coming to visit, and Milwaukee will have a special place in my heart forever. But when I'm here, I think about the past too much. You can do things like go to the art museum, and it doesn't send you back to that little girl we each were, with a mom who seemed annoyed by us constantly, and a dad who was more like a friend than a parent. But when I spend too much time here, my mind does go back. For me, I needed a new place to live in order to really move on from all that past hurt."

All the guilt Charlotte held for all these years; Jane had never seen it. She instantly felt sorry for blaming Charlotte for her own feelings. She needed to make this right.

"Charlotte, I'm sorry about how I've made you feel. Please forgive me. I never meant to make you feel bad about moving. How selfish of me."

"Jane, can you forgive me?"

"Of course." They hugged, and Jane felt like a whole

new world had opened up to her, just in the span of that short conversation. "Charlotte," she said, "these bad feelings have been between us for so long. I'm glad we talked about it."

Charlotte looked at her with a smirk. "Didn't I tell you this was going to be a big conversation? Aren't you glad you showered now?"

Jane laughed and hit her sister playfully with a pillow from the couch. "You're a dork!"

"I know you are, but what am I?"

"Oh brother! We're back to that?" They both got up and hugged. It felt good to have Charlotte back in her life again without the feelings of negativity she'd had before.

Charlotte grinned at her. "So, I hate to ask, but what's going on with Brad? Have you dumped that guy yet?"

CHAPTER 17 - GRACE

Grace and John parked blocks away from Constance's house.

"This appetizer party must be popular," he said bitterly, marching through the street, hands in the pockets of his gray trousers. John reminded her of a sullen child, walking reluctantly, with his head down as if he were being forced into the most unpleasant situation he could think of. Grace supposed from his perspective, it was one of the worst things for him. He hated small talk, and she had already heard an earful when it came to the food. That morning, he had followed her from the bathroom to their bedroom, complaining about having to eat appetizers when he should be home eating turkey.

Finally, she turned to him and shouted, "We will have turkey tomorrow!" And then glared at him.

He laughed then, as if the whole thing were wildly funny. "What are you getting so upset about?"

She shook her head and finished getting ready. *That man.*

They walked up the long, winding driveway, and John turned to Grace.

"Now the boyfriend's name is Eric?"

Exasperated, she said, "*No.* Eric is the new guy who is moving away. The boyfriend's name is Brad. This is his mother's house. Jane is probably going to dump Brad today. Or, at least, I think she is."

Grace struggled to keep up John's quick pace, thankful that they had been blessed with a rare fifty-degree day in November in Wisconsin. She'd been so delighted not to have snow and ice that she almost had worn open-toed shoes. Instead, she opted for her blue boots again, and paired them this time with a black dress and a silk scarf with blues and a hint of orange. She wore her hair up in a French twist and wore her heavy black glasses.

"And the mother's name is Charlotte?"

"Have you even been listening to me?" she said, shaking her head. "How many times are you going to ask me this? The mother's name is *Constance.* Charlotte is Jane's sister."

He turned to her. "I have not been listening. I've been thinking about turkey. Also? Constance and Charlotte are basically the same name."

He kissed her on the cheek just as she was going to say something else. They reached the door, and before they could even knock, Jane opened it.

"I was watching for you guys. I didn't want you to get lost in the crowd."

"Jane, you remember my husband." Grace gestured to John.

She gave him a little wave. "Yes, of course."

John nodded in return, sticking his hands back in his pockets and looking irritable. Grace hoped he would at least try to fit in and mingle with the crowd.

She turned her attention back to Jane. She always managed to dress cute and artsy. Hanging around her had inspired Grace to step up her outfit choices. Today, Jane wore an orange maxi dress with a cream-colored sweater over her shoulders. She had curled her hair in beachy waves. The look seemed perfect for a fall day that was still mild.

"You look so pretty, Jane."

"Thank you, Grace. You, too." She smiled belatedly at Grace and continued to look around.

"How's it going?" Grace asked, following Jane's gaze. The place was packed. It was decorated with burgundy furniture and dark purple walls. The whole space looked like someone had accidentally spilled wine on itself.

Jane pulled her in close while they were still standing in the foyer.

"This party is a disaster. I'd understand if you wanted to leave early."

John, who had wandered back to the foyer, nodded sympathetically. "It's the appetizer concept."

"I wish it was just that." Jane looked near tears. "Brad and his mother have been fighting. We don't know why. No one is saying anything, but they were in the kitchen arguing really loudly. The rest of us, *me*, are out here trying to pretend that nothing is wrong. And everyone is drunk. It's been… well, not like Thanksgiving. That's for sure."

John whispered to them, "They're drunk because there is no food. Appetizers! Who does that?"

Grace swatted his arm, but he and Jane seemed to agree.

"I wish I could just leave with you guys."

"Come on." Grace took them both by the elbow. "We're here. Let's make the best of it. And Jane, I'm making a turkey dinner tomorrow if you want to come over. You and Charlotte or Brad, or..." She let the sentence hang. She still wasn't sure if Jane was going to keep dating Brad or not. Jane herself didn't seem too sure about it, either.

"You are? That sounds so good."

"My husband here cannot live without Thanksgiving leftovers, and the only way to get them is to make the whole dinner." Grace laughed. "It's okay, though. I like them, too, and cooking a turkey is surprisingly easy. So, it's not a bother."

John chimed in. "And I peel potatoes. Let's not forget that."

"As if I could." She playfully rolled her eyes. "So," she added to Jane, "are you in?"

"Oh, I wish I could. The gallery is open tomorrow for part of the day, and I need to be there. And unfortunately, Charlotte left for home already. She was only in town for a few days."

A waitress came up to them, passing a plate of appetizers. Jane giggled as Grace and John each took one, and each of them instantly made a face.

"I know. They *are* awful," Jane whispered to them.

John leaned in. "Who insists on hosting a party and then serves food that is gross?"

Grace smacked him on the arm. "Please ignore him." She leaned in close to Jane. "Did you talk to Brad?" She was trying not to pry, but Jane was biting her lip and looking around the room, and she seemed to desperately be searching for her boyfriend.

"No," Jane whispered back. "He disappeared after the ugliness with his mother. He never even greeted me when I came in. I waved at him and he sort of nodded." Jane rolled her eyes. "I feel like a fool even being here. And dragging you guys here besides!"

John shrugged. "So, you'll owe us."

Grace swatted him harder on the arm. He probably thought he was being cute right now, but he seemed oblivious to Jane's discomfort. Grace wanted to help Jane so much she was tempted to find Brad herself and talk with him, but she wouldn't do that to him. After all, despite everything she'd heard from Jane, she didn't know Brad at all. People need to stay out of other people's business. You usually never know what really goes on in someone else's family and relationships, no matter how close you think you are with them.

Jane turned to them. "I'm going to search for him again."

"Go ahead. We're fine," Grace assured her. She giggled as she watched John toss another appetizer into a nearby plant. He shook his head at her, mimicking a puking face.

Grace and John moved around the room, each one aware of what the other was doing. It was one of the things she liked about their marriage. They exchanged silly faces, saved each other from annoying people who had them cornered with poor conversation, and every so often touched: a quick kiss here, a quick joining of their hands there. It made it seem like they had a special language just for them.

Jane came back, shaking her head. "This is ridiculous."
Grace handed her an appetizer.

"It's pumpkin something with too much cinnamon."
She smiled. "Thanks."

"So, how many of these people do you know?"

"Nearly none of them."

"And no sign of Brad?" Grace really had to wonder about their relationship.

"I thought I saw him over there"—Jane pointed across the room—"talking to some girl, but when I got there, he was gone."

Constance appeared, clapping her hands to get everyone's attention. She had what Grace used to think of as helmet hair, the kind that was formed into a perfect, round ball, hardened with tons of hairspray. She had on a suit that went out of style in the nineties, high-heeled pumps, and pearls.

Grace sipped at a glass of awful-tasting white wine and thought, poor Jane having to endure this awful party and then still not able to have the conversation with Brad that she needed to have.

"Friends! Family! Thank you for coming. We've been picking up people from the highways and byways!" Constance laughed to herself, holding on to the pearls she wore as if they were a lifeline. "Wonderful, wonderful turnout! So many!" She clapped then, prompting the room to clap with her. Jane stood next to Grace and frowned.

"What is she doing?" Grace asked.

"I'll guess we'll find out."

Constance pulled a green box out and handed it to a young woman who was seated on a chair in the far corner of the room.

"My dear Brenda. You are like a daughter to me. Well, you are a daughter to me because you've given me my only grandchild! Happy birthday."

Grace's mind raced. Was the party supposed to be a birthday party or for Thanksgiving? The girl looked to be about Jane's age and seemed just as mixed-up about the gift as Jane was.

"Uh, thank you, Constance."

She opened the lid on the box, and lifted white tissue paper before pulling out a brilliant-blue sweater. It looked to be quite large, much larger than the girl obviously was.

"A sweater. It's nice. Thank you."

John had come up to Jane and Grace, whispering, "Nice? Only if that girl were ten sizes bigger than she is."

Grace gave him a look that said, must you. He walked off, grabbing a glass of cider from a tray on the bar.

"Do you know her?" Grace asked Jane, and kicked herself when she realized it was a stupid question. Obviously, the girl was the mother of Brad's daughter.

Jane stared at the girl. Her face was impassive. She obviously wasn't excited about the present but she said nothing. No one else seemed to make a sound, either.

Constance's grin, however, had turned dark. "Well, when I heard it was your birthday, I knew I had to give you something special. I do hope you like it, dear. I bought it for myself and then realized what a hideous color it would be on me."

She laughed drunkenly, and a few other people joined in. Grace wondered if they were laughing to cut the tension or because they genuinely thought it was funny to give someone what was clearly a used gift. The girl looked genuinely hurt, but not surprised.

"Thank you," she said simply, placing the box down and then heading upstairs.

Grace looked at Jane. "Well, that was weird."

"Brad's ex," Jane explained, but Grace had figured that out. She felt for Jane even more. What a strange situation this was.

"Well, now I can't seem to locate my husband," Grace said, looking around.

"Men," Jane joked, clearly wanting to cut the tension, but Grace saw through her brave front. They chatted for twenty more minutes, trying out different foods and failing to find a single hors d'oeuvre worth eating. Jane looked miserable.

John came up to them, grabbing Grace's hand and leaning in close to her and Jane.

"Jane, Brad is upstairs. First door on the right, at the top of the stairs."

"Thanks," Jane said, and quickly walked up the stairs to find him.

"How did you know it was Brad?" Grace asked him.

"Because I saw him sitting on the bed, and introduced myself."

"Husband, dear," Grace chided, "what were you doing upstairs in these people's house?"

He shrugged. "I wanted to see what kind of art they had. You can tell a lot about the kind of art someone collects."

"Or paints." Grace gave her husband a playful nudge.

"By the way"—he pulled an apple from his pocket and crunched—"that Brad seems like a jerk."

"You noticed that by just talking to him for a minute, did you?"

John looked at her like she was nuts. "No, he was up there with the girl. The one who got the big, fat blue sweater as a gift. Oh, and she introduced herself as Brad's fiancée." He crunched again, and Grace stared at him.

"You're kidding? And you just sent Jane up there without warning?"

He shrugged. "Can you say, awkward?"

"I can say, *no turkey dinner for you.*"

"Aw, come on." He tossed the apple in another plant. Grace was mortified. He pulled out a granola bar.

"How much food did you bring in those pockets anyway?"

"Not as much as I'll be eating when you make Thanksgiving dinner tomorrow, my sweet." He kissed her cheek and she rolled her eyes. They needed to get out of there before he managed to make things worse for Jane. But Grace wanted to wait and make sure she was okay.

She spotted Jane grabbing her coat.

"Hey," Grace said, "did you find Brad?"

"Yes," Jane said, looking embarrassed.

Grace cringed. "Are you okay?"

Jane shrugged. She looked both relieved and like she might cry.

"Did you guys talk?"

"Enough to know that I've been quite the fool," Jane said bitterly.

"I'll call you later," Grace assured her as she left. Jane gave Grace a quick hug and was out the door. "Well, husband"—she turned to John—"we can go, too, now. No point in staying."

"Sure," he said, "one minute."

Grace watched him walk over to Constance, interrupting her conversation and pointing over to the far bathroom. The woman put her hand on her chest dramatically, and raced over to the other end of the house.

John nodded his head toward the door. "Let's blow this pop stand."

They walked out, and Grace asked, "What did you say to her?"

"I told her the bathroom was plugged up to high heaven, and she better get in there and take a look."

Grace twisted up her face at him. "Why on earth would you say something like that!"

He laughed. "Because. *Appetizers*. And they weren't even good ones."

John stood at the kitchen island peeling potatoes.

"That was some party." He shook his head, chuckling. "What a family. That mother? With the drunken laugh?"

Grace stirred the onions, which were sautéing in brown butter. "Come on. That's not nice."

John continued making remarks about the party, laughing so hard it had started to make her giggle, too. It felt good to laugh again, to let their smiles run free.

"That really was awful. The appetizers!" He pounded his fist on the table with laughter.

"Who serves appetizers like that for Thanksgiving? Or was it supposed to be a birthday party?"

"And that tacky gift. For that girl?"

"Yeah." Grace stirred the food and thought about it. "I feel bad for Jane. She deserves better than that."

"Yeah. When I went to look at their paintings upstairs—"

"Which was very rude, you know. You can't just go traipsing around people's houses like that. Honestly." He could exasperate her sometimes.

He shrugged, the potato peeler still in his hand. "What was I supposed to do? That party was boring, the food was bad, and… it was just weird."

"Still, no excuse."

He sighed. "Okay, so anyway, when I went upstairs, that Brad was arguing quietly with that woman, and then she introduced herself to me as Brad's fiancée. Can you believe that?"

Grace turned to him. "And you're just telling me this now?"

He finished off the last potato. "I told you he was up there with a woman who said she was his fiancée."

She stared at her husband. "You didn't say they were arguing."

"The argument was about Brad not wanting to get married, and the woman wanting to announce the wedding date."

She put her hand on her hip. "Is that all?"

He placed the bowl of peeled potatoes next to the stove and she dumped them in the salted water she already had boiling.

"Why are you upset with me?"

"Because you snooped around and found something out, and now, I feel like I need to tell Jane."

"Why would you need to tell Jane? I don't even know what really happened."

"Well, I don't know. I suppose I'll see if Jane brings it up. Why do you have to wander around people's houses when we go somewhere? Can't you just make small talk like a normal person?"

"Apparently not."

The onions were cooked, and she added some flour to thicken the mixture.

"Well, I forgive you, but only if you take this turkey out for me so I can get at the drippings."

"That's a deal I can get behind."

He did as she asked, moving the small turkey she had cooked for them to the kitchen island and placing the drippings in the fat separator. She poured the drippings into her gravy mixture and added some cream for smoothness, and finished by whisking it all together. She poured the mixture into a gravy boat and placed it on the island.

"Want me to carve the turkey now?" He started picking at it, and she playfully slapped his hand away.

"Not yet. Let it rest first."

Grace set the table, adding the cranberries, stuffing, corn, muffins, and mashed potatoes. Finally, John cut the turkey, placing the pieces on a chop plate and bringing them to the table.

They sat down, and he bowed his head and said a prayer.

"Lord, thank you for this bounty and for blessing us with a happy marriage. It is a gift I am grateful for daily. Thank you for bringing Grace into my life. Amen."

Grace did not bow her head, did not say amen. She stared at her husband for a long time, but his eyes were fixed on turkey and gravy. She wondered if she would ever heal this rift she had with God. Her husband thanked God for blessing them with a good marriage, and she chided God for not blessing them with children. Who was right? She couldn't bring herself to think like her husband did, although in the deepest part of her soul, she desperately wanted to. There was a freedom in letting go of anger, and she could taste it as clearly as if she had sprinkled it on the mashed potatoes before her.

John ate heartily, gobbling up the turkey and cranberries as if he had not tasted them before.

"The dinner is wonderful, Grace. Thanks for making it. This gravy… wow."

Just when she wondered if her anger at life would ever subside, her husband did things like thank her for making gravy and openly thanked God for her.

"You're welcome, babe. I like cooking for you."

She found herself unable to say anything else, for fear that she would spill her doubts and worries about the future on to this holiday table and ruin their entire meal. Instead, she picked up her fork and celebrated a belated Thanksgiving with her husband.

CHAPTER 18 - JANE

Jane rushed out of the gallery, placing her long, blonde hair into a ponytail as she headed to the car. The day had been crazy with people, and she couldn't have been happier. They sold a lot, proving Black Friday worthy of its name, but it was the one sale in particular that she couldn't wait to tell Grace about. She had sold one of John's canvases. In the painting, a woman was standing at the stove cooking, her back to the viewer. It was smaller, an eight by ten that she had framed out in a large gilt frame, with a blue stripe that matched a shadow on the woman's skirt.

There were people who complained about their jobs, and in the past, Jane had been one of them. She worried about getting a raise, about being recognized by Bug, and about what her life meant. After seeing Brad the day before with that woman—his fiancée, no less—she felt like a fool for ever worrying about any of that. She'd been looking at her job with a magnifying glass and just occasionally glancing at her relationship with rose-colored glasses. She should have been paying more attention to what the last years with Brad had really been about.

Seeing Brad at Thanksgiving in the upstairs bedroom of his mother's house made her realize she was seeing his life, not hers. The moment looked so common, a man and his fiancée arguing. The two of them looked like they belonged together.

Jane thought about how many times he was unavailable or how they'd rarely spent time together on weekends. She'd been at the top of her class in college, and yet she could not have felt more stupid. What had she been thinking?

She left that party and went straight home to call Charlotte. Her sister sat on the phone with her for two hours, and while the talk had done both of them good, it didn't help her get back the eight years she felt were lost. She could have been dating other people; maybe she would be married by now. She couldn't even imagine where her life would be if she'd only had the courage to let go of whatever she thought she wanted with Brad. She was so afraid of losing him that it never dawned on her what she was giving up by continuing to have him in that remote, detached way that defined their relationship.

Of course, after weeks of him not answering his phone or calling her back, he tried reaching her several times after she'd left the party. The entire time she was on the phone with Charlotte she would see the call coming through and listen to her sister shout, "If that is Brad, do not answer!"

Charlotte was right. She listened to her sister. This time, at least.

Charlotte also had plenty to say about Eric. She enjoyed meeting him, and had even given him her and Bill's info for him to get in touch once he moved to Seattle. Charlotte's constant refrain from then on was, "Have you thought more about Seattle?"

She did want to visit Seattle now. She wanted to pay more attention to her relationship with Charlotte. Jane supposed she'd been ignoring her, too.

She had this overwhelming exhaustion come upon her. She yawned, shaking loose the ponytail she had in her hair. And then, stood before The Space Between Dreaming, taking it in. It had become a source of comfort for her these past few months. She looked forward to seeing the woman who held out her arms as if to say it was all going to be okay, like a mother would do with a child. The painting reminded her of Grace, the way the woman's eyes were warm but vulnerable, the lines on her face which showed her age yet at the same time framed her mouth and eyes in such a way that showed the viewer what she would have looked like as a young woman.

Grace had told her that she felt the woman was reaching for something, longing for a piece of her that was lost. In Grace's version, the woman was sad. Jane knew it was a testament to John's talent that people could look at the painting and each see something different.

"You look exhausted," Donna said to her.

Jane laughed. "Thank you."

"Oh." Donna cheerfully giggled. "You know I blurt things out. I mean, you should get home and get some rest. You've already worked later than you were scheduled."

It was true. Jane had chosen to stay late to avoid going home. She usually loved the quiet of her apartment, but she was feeling unsettled and lonely. She had people around her, like Mrs. Ferch, and she could always call Charlotte, but she wanted a connection, like what she had witnessed with Grace and John. They seemed made for each other. She hated that they had struggled so much in their marriage with family and children. If any couple deserved peace, it seemed like they did.

And they'd both been so wonderful to Jane. Grace had called her last night to check on her, and even when she said she didn't want to talk, she'd been kind and understood.

"Yeah," Jane admitted, "I guess I will head out. I was just taking in this beauty"—Jane gestured to the painting—"one more time."

Donna agreed. "It has added so much to this place. It's changed the vibe, in a way. I'll admit, I know we are in the business of selling art, but I will be very sad when it's time to let this one go."

Jane agreed, "This painter really has talent."

"And Bug is very impressed with you," Donna added.

She turned to her. "He is? He's barely said a word to me since he promoted me."

"Ugh." Donna looked disgusted. "That's so him. He's a bad communicator at times. And don't even get me started on how gross he is with that daily salad of his! I end up cleaning bits of dressing and vegetables off the notes he has me type up."

Donna shuddered at the thought of that, and Jane laughed. She told Donna about how Bug had used a fork to both pick his teeth and comb his hair as he talked to her about wanting to add happiness to the office.

"Oh yes." Donna cringed. "I've seen that as well. And look, aren't we just the happiest of happy?" She made a face that made Jane laugh.

They said goodbye, with Jane thinking about a quiet evening, snuggled in a few blankets and reading design magazines. Her hopes were dashed, however, the moment she pulled opened the door of her building and saw Brad standing there, looking at his phone.

"Texting your fiancée?" she said by way of hello.

He had the audacity to look hurt.

"Jane, I know this looks bad, but I can explain."

"That you have a fiancée? That you just told me you had a daughter a few weeks ago and then refused to talk to me more about it? That you ignore me half the time because you're too busy with the mother of your child?"

She pushed past him and walked up the landing toward her apartment. He followed, grabbing her by the arm.

"Let go of me!" she screamed.

"Jane"—he looked annoyed—"calm down. I can explain. My mother wanted to announce that Brenda and I were getting married, but I put a stop to it. I told her I couldn't go through with it. My mother is pressuring—"

"Oh, your mother is pressuring you, is she? Because she wants your daughter to have a father? Because she wants to enjoy her grandchild? You poor thing."

"Will you let me talk? I'm trying to tell you—"

"That's all you've done is talk, drop some little emotional bomb, and then make yourself unavailable. Whatever the excuse, whatever the explanation, I am *done*, Brad. Just leave me alone."

"Jane, you are not acting like yourself. You don't understand—"

"I'm not acting like the mouse I've been with you; you mean? Yes, that's right!" she yelled. "Get out of here and leave me alone."

She turned to head into her apartment, and he grabbed her arm again.

"Do not touch me!" she screamed, so angry that he would dare think he could treat her as his.

Eric had opened the door of his apartment and came out onto the landing where they were. He eyed Brad.

"Everything okay here?"

"Yes, Eric," Jane said. "I'm fine. He was just leaving."

"No, Jane." Brad folded his arms and shook his head

like a toddler being force-fed vegetables. "I will not leave until you hear me out. I want—"

"Whatever it is you want, Brad," she enunciated as if he were a child, "I am not interested. Now. Leave. Me. Alone."

She turned again, and once more, he grabbed her arm.

"Hey, pal," Eric intervened, "she says she wants to be left alone."

"Look." Brad had dropped her arm and turned to Eric. "This is none of your business. I will speak to my girlfriend any way I please, got it?"

Eric looked to Jane with confusion and hurt.

"This is your boyfriend?" he said to her.

"No, he is not. He is—"

"Yes, I am!" Brad shouted at Jane, and reached in his jacket pocket, pulling out a small box. "Jane," he said, getting down on one knee, "I want us to get married. I have finally decided."

Jane stood three, openmouthed.

"I'll leave you two alone, then," Eric said bitterly. He went back into his apartment and quietly shut the door.

"Get up," she said angrily to Brad. "How could you do that just now? After everything? Do you think this makes up for all of it—keeping your daughter a secret from me for eight years, you ignoring me all the time, all the rude ways you treat me. Do you really think this makes up for it?"

He got up, rubbed his knees, and held out the ring to her. She refused to even look at it.

"This is what you wanted," he spat. "Isn't it? It's what you've been hanging around for? Just waiting for the day you finally had your ring! I chose you over her! You win!"

She glared at him. "I win? Like this is some game to you?" She thought about what he'd said before. "And what do you mean, you finally decided? You don't get to decide. If this was a real relationship, we'd have decided together."

"Ugh, Jane, I thought you'd be over the moon about this. That's why I told my mother no, that I was not going to marry Brenda."

Jane stared at him. The pieces had finally come into place. "Oh, my…." She felt herself swallow hard. "You…" She went over the events of the last few weeks. "That's why you invited me to that appetizer fiasco. You wanted me to find out you were actually going to marry *her*. That's how you were going to tell me." She was stunned just thinking about it.

"Well, I changed my mind. You *won*, Jane." He smiled at her, and she felt the urge to slap that grin right off his face. She clenched her palms.

"I didn't win a thing, Brad. I lost…" She shook her head just thinking about it all. "I lost eight years. I lost my sense. I lost my dignity somewhere along the way."

"Oh Jane" He scrunched up his face, annoyed with her—"don't be so dramatic."

"And that ring"—she immediately had the horrible realization—"was for her. You were going to give that very same ring to *her*."

He snapped the box closed and put it back in his pocket. "If you want a different ring, I can give you that. Fine. Whatever. I'll take this one back."

The thought of spending a lifetime with him made her stomach feel sick.

"Please leave, Brad," she said quietly. "I do not want to marry you. I do not want to hear from you. We're done."

She turned to go upstairs, feeling very low.

"You'll change your mind!" he called up the landing to her.

She got in her apartment, closed the door, and didn't

come out for the rest of the weekend.

CHAPTER 19 - GRACE

Grace had begun the process of doing PR for her husband's upcoming exhibit. She had contacted every name on her media list and even added a few more. This reception for her husband's work was actually happening, and it felt like a beautiful dream.

While Grace had been busy trying to drum up interest for the exhibit, John had been busy painting. He came home from work and headed directly to his studio to paint. It was all Grace could do to get some food in him at suppertime. Even though he had been painting for years now, creating The Space Between Dreaming had ignited something in him, a passion she hadn't quite seen in him before.

She closed her laptop, giving her husband a few more minutes before she went to see if he wanted to have dinner. Grace and Jane had been talking a lot about the reception for the exhibit, and Jane had welcomed her input. While she enjoyed her editing job, this new aspect of John's business had put Grace into overdrive.

She worked from the kitchen island, which looked out over the backyard. She preferred working like this to some stuffy office, although with being in the kitchen, she also tried not to focus on the refrigerator. She'd never had a problem maintaining her weight before, but the infertility treatments seemed to change her body. In the last ten years, she'd managed to gain fifteen pounds.

On a whim, she walked out to the breezeway to see if they still had that old exercise bike. The last Grace remembered, something broke on it, and she couldn't remember now if they had ever gotten it fixed. She spotted the bike in the back of the crowded breezeway with a pile of old towels on it, which she guessed had become her husband's paint rags at some point. Leaned up against the old bike was the rake she'd been looking for that day she was working in the garden. She wondered how long ago she'd abandoned it to the breezeway, which used to be a cute little space between the garage and kitchen door, and now looked like a cluttered mess you couldn't even walk through.

She realized the breezeway was one area of her home that had been neglected, just as Glenn's old room had. She had closed the door on the room and that was it; it had stayed that way, in some perennial state of delayed hope for a reality that didn't exist. Grace had to admit, she was tired of the somedays and possibilities. She had to start dealing with now and the realities of life instead of clinging to something that might never, or would never, happen.

She went back to the kitchen, slouching on the barstool she sat on, making her gut stick out. To her dismay, she could pinch an inch, and more.

"Are you searching for the meaning of life or just trying to drive yourself crazy?" John kissed her neck and then went to the fridge, pulling out some juice. As he poured himself a glass, she stared at him. He hadn't aged like her. He was still fit, the wrinkles he did have only made him cuter, and his hair had spots of gray that seemed to make him look wise, not old.

"I think men have it much easier than women."

He laughed, nearly choking on his juice. He finished the glass, rinsed it out, and set it in the dishwasher.

"Without a doubt. But we also die sooner. So having it easy isn't all it's cracked up to be." He pulled out the barstool next to her and faced her. "Now, why are you looking at your adorable little tummy?"

He tried to tickle her but she swatted his hand away. "It's not so little. Do you know I've gained fifteen pounds?"

He grabbed her hand. "I don't care. I love you just as you are. Plus, didn't we have fun this morning?"

He'd woken her up in the wee hours of the morning, nuzzling her neck and moving his hands all over her body. They made love with a passion that seemed to grow stronger the longer they were together. Grace wondered if having children would have changed this between them. Afterward, she slept in later that morning, waking up tired but happy.

"I should blush, Mr. Cambridge. Those things you did are not something the average, middle-aged man would attempt."

He waggled his eyebrows. "I'm not your average, middle-aged man."

"You certainly aren't." She reached over and kissed him, then paused to look in those blue eyes she loved so much. "I'm a lucky woman."

"And I'm a lucky man. Now, enough with the pity-party talk." He nodded his chin toward her laptop. "What are you working on?"

"I'm working on the reception. I just finished contacting everyone I had on the media list. I also wrote up two pitches for magazines that I plan to send to after the reception. I have a good feeling about this. And I know Jane is working on contacts on her end, too. I think between the two of us, we'll have a nice mix of buyers, media, and art afficionados for the party."

"You amaze me. Allow me to take you out for dinner."

"You just want me to stop talking so you can eat, don't you?"

He shrugged. "I'm starving."

He grabbed his car keys and she stopped him. "Are you wearing that out?" He still had on his painting jeans and a white T-shirt stained with a variety of different colors.

He looked down. "What? Who is going to see me?"

"I'll see you."

"You could think of it as advertising for the reception. Picture this. Someone walks up to me." He pretended to be a stranger walking by. "Why, hello. Looks like you've got paint all over you. Are you a painter? I wonder if you're exhibiting anywhere."

"And then I could tell them about the reception? Maybe even hand them a flyer?" She pulled out one of the flyers she had printed the day before.

John took the flyer. "Hey, I haven't seen this yet."

She snatched it back. "That will give you something to look forward to at dinner." She gestured to the bedroom. "Now, go. Please? Change your pants, at least?"

He winked at her and went to change. She went back to thinking about the messy breezeway and how she could clean it up again. Maybe she should make it a gardening area of some kind. She could store all her tools in there, and that way she'd have a chance to reach them easily. She wondered suddenly if that's why the rake was there to begin with. She'd probably come in from the garden, walked straight into the breezeway to take off her muddy boots, and then left the rake.

And then what, Grace wondered. Did something happen that caused her to abandon gardening for years after that? Another phone call with bad news? Another nasty letter from a stranger? And she remembered what came after that letter, the last time she'd been pregnant, too. She doubted she would ever forget it. She could see herself abandoning a rake and her dreams and just leaving it all behind as she headed for bed to cry and forget about the world.

She shook her head at all she'd endured, and how difficult it had been for her to shake it all off. Was that what people were supposed to do when others wrongfully attacked them? Did they just laugh and say *oh well* and go on about their lives? If so, she envied them.

She was pulled from her thoughts as John was kissing the back of her neck. She turned to look at him—changed and smelling great. Did he just take a shower? She looked up and saw that he had. She ran a hand through his damp hair.

"You got ready quick," she said.

"I sped through my beautification process."

She laughed. "Your beautification process? What does that involve exactly?"

"Oh, you know, hours of looking at my shirts until my wife tells me *wear that.*"

"Your wife sounds like a smart woman," she joked.

"My wife," he said to her, slowly kissing her neck and then down the front of her shirt, "is the kindest, sweetest, sexiest woman I have ever known."

She giggled but squirmed out of his reach. "I thought

you were hungry."

"I am, and I'm also turned on by my wife. I think dinner can wait." He stripped off his pants right there in the kitchen.

"John!" she said, surprised and thrilled at the same time. "Someone will see."

"No one can see in the kitchen window. Besides, painting isn't the only thing I can use my imagination for," he said, kissing her more hungrily than before.

"You're an artist in so many ways," she teased, before being swept away in the moment herself.

"Where should we go, then?" he said, driving.

She laughed. "I thought you had an idea. You just got in the car and drove."

"I was distracted," he said, reaching over to move his hand up her leg.

"Watch the road," she giggled, moving his hand back toward the steering wheel. "I was thinking Lake Park Bistro for dinner. What do you say?"

John thought for a minute. "Is that the place overlooking the lake? The one with that French food?"

"The place we went on our first anniversary. Yes."

She thought he might say no. It was a bit expensive, after all. It was the type of place you went to celebrate events, but she was determined to celebrate things differently now. To not wait for special dates to appear while she longed for events that might never happen. She was done with all that and wanted to live differently.

"Great idea," he said. "I was craving escargot."

She looked at him. "You were not."

"Was. Getting it on with your wife will do that to a person."

She laughed.

"What made you think of it?" he asked.

"I was talking with Jane the other day about family stuff. And she told me how her dad used to take her and her sister there on Sundays. Apparently, he would ask his wife for grocery money and tell her he was taking the girls out with him to shop so she could relax and enjoy the day. The mom was the breadwinner," Grace reminded him, "and he worked on inventions. So, anyway, once they got in the car, he'd announce that they were going to brunch instead. I guess it was a favorite time for her until her mom found out and then got mad at all three of them."

"Ouch," John said. "Sounds like Jane's father put a lot of pressure on their mother."

"Yeah," Grace added, "and to have a really nice parental memory like that, but then to have it turned upside down because your dad was dishonest." She shook her head. "That kind of stinks."

"Oh, I can relate to that," he said. "My mother would start Sunday dinners by making a huge meal. A roast or turkey, something really big. She'd drink through the whole meal, overcook it, and then by the time we sat down she'd glare at me the whole time while also telling my dad how useless she thought he was."

Grace knew the sting of that. "One of my foster families was like that."

She went on with Jane's story. "Her dad was trying to be 'fun dad,' but their mom resented it. They never knew whether to enjoy things or be mad at him."

John shook head, disgusted. "That's an awful burden

to lay on young girls. And so, the restaurant probably has bad memories for her," he remarked.

"No," Grace said. "It's still one of her favorite places. I mean, the food more than makes up for anything else."

"It does," he agreed, pulling into the parking lot. He took her hand as they walked in. After a short wait at the bar, they were seated in a room with windows framing Lake Michigan. John pulled out the chair for Grace, and smiled at her as they sat. He reached over and kissed her lips briefly, then turned the conversation to the view. The sun was going down, and Lake Michigan glinted with the remaining bits of light. It was a beautiful time of day.

She leaned in close to John, smelling his cologne, and noting how handsome his profile was. He turned to her, and his blue eyes nearly made her heart melt.

"Thinking of how good this is. You here with me. We are so lucky, Grace."

She could not argue with that. "We are."

CHAPTER 20 - JANE

Jane met Grace for lunch at a new place, one that served famous Wisconsin cheese curds and the best burgers around.

"Thanks for meeting here," Jane told her. "I've been craving a burger all week."

Grace smiled at her. Jane could tell things with Grace had shifted slightly, but she couldn't put her finger on it. They'd been friends for months now, and it felt as natural as it was with her and Mrs. Ferch or her and Charlotte. Or even, Jane thought sadly, her and Eric. She'd really ruined that.

Jane had explained the whole mess to Grace, how Brad had shown up, how Eric had found out she had a boyfriend.

"The thing is," she was saying now, "I hate that Eric thinks I was being dishonest with him. I know that I was, wasn't I? I hung on to one reality and yet tried out this new reality with Eric before I had fully left the one I had with Brad. It wasn't fair to Eric. And I did tell you his other girlfriend cheated on him and then dumped him, didn't I?"

Grace gave a sympathetic nod. "Sometimes we hurt people without trying. Have you heard any more from Brad?"

"Oh yeah," she admitted. "He's called a bunch of times. Ironic, isn't it? When I wanted to talk to him, he was just too busy."

"I know the feeling. Had friends that were like that, actually. I wouldn't hear from them for a very long time, and then when they wanted a favor, they would call and tell me how busy they are, but they were taking the time to call in order to ask me for something. As if I should be flattered. And I hate to ask... but Eric? Have you talked to him?"

Jane let out a huge sigh.

"Sorry." Grace winced.

"No, it's a valid question. I haven't. I guess… I guess I realized I blew it with him. So, why try?"

"Well, because you liked him so much, that's why."

"I know, but… I feel like now that I goofed up, it's just… there's no point."

Grace laughed. "Oh, Jane, wait until you get married. Every day is a series of goofing up and then forgiving your spouse for goofing up. Things can be mended, especially with what you guys went through. You were in a weird overlap." She chewed some fries. "You knew you needed to end it with Brad but didn't feel strong enough to do it, and he knew he should have told you he was moving to Seattle, but he was obviously having second thoughts."

Jane hadn't thought of it like that. "You think there might be chance he would stay in Milwaukee?"

"Eat, eat," Grace urged her. "I'm almost finished with my burger. I'll talk while you eat." She smiled. "Think about it this way: Is staying here in Milwaukee the only option? Your sister lives in Seattle, and you could move.

You're young. Try it out."

Jane snorted. "I'm thirty! Not so young."

"Oh my goodness," Grace laughed. "You're still young."

"Okay," Jane conceded. "Let's say I do move to Seattle. Wouldn't it be weird to do it because I met a guy? Plus, I was hoping…" She sighed. "I guess I was hoping to get some kind of sign on what would happen with me and Eric either way. But now that I have one, it's not the answer I want."

Grace leaned in closer. "You think having Eric leave for Seattle is an answer to whether you should be together? Why?"

Jane looked at her incredulously. "Isn't it obvious? With Eric leaving, we'll have no more time to spend together. It's pretty clear that we're not meant to be together."

"Well, I have to be honest, when I first met you two at the art fair, I did think you were together. As a couple. And it wasn't because you just happened to go there together. I mean, you looked like a couple to me."

Jane thought about that day, how it had flown by, how natural it had been to spend the day with him, just looking through the fair and talking.

"And he's not leaving today, right?" Grace persisted.

Jane rolled her eyes, annoyed. "Let me guess; you think it's gonna be all happily ever after."

Grace shook her head. "Happily ever after depends solely on where you end your story. No, I'm talking about listening to your gut here. You think you're seeing signs, but you have to be careful with that. Those outward signs have to match what's going on in here." She pointed to her chest.

Jane looked at her skeptically.

"What do you feel in your heart, Jane?"

She shook her head. "I honestly don't know anymore."

"You're too close to it right now. You're thinking too much. You're a thinker. John is like that. Sometimes that's good. But other times, it makes you sit back and analyze your life instead of living it. Here's my advice. Which I know you didn't ask for, but what are friends for, right? My advice is to relax. Have fun with Eric for the next week or two or however long you guys have. Don't make a rash choice. I know how afraid you are to do that. But just… step back. Listen to what life is saying. You'll have an answer that will be satisfying to your heart when you do that."

"You mean you think somehow this thing with Eric will work out? Will he change his mind about going?"

"No, that's not what I mean." Grace sighed, and Jane could tell she was thinking about her own life in addition to giving Jane advice. "You will come to the decision you're meant to once you take a step back from trying to force an outcome. With Brad, you were hanging on to a bad relationship because you thought in time you guys would get married, or at least you'd have a better idea of your future. You didn't pay attention to the present state of your relationship, let alone what the past had already shown you. Sometimes, you need time to take a step back and think lightly, not overanalyze and not try and will an ending for yourself."

Grace got very quiet, and Jane knew that the things Grace had endured were far greater than this thing Jane was experiencing.

"Grace?" she said gently. "I really do appreciate you trying to help me. Is there anything I can do for you? Even if it's just to listen?"

Grace smiled at her. "You are an incredibly

compassionate person."

"No," Jane said between bites of her burger. "I notice things in other people that I ignore in myself. You look sad and speculative today. Want to tell me?"

"Well, I feel rather stupid offering advice to you, because I've been stuck in one long season of waiting and insisting on a situation myself."

She shook her head, the tears started to form, and Grace angrily wiped them away.

"I know you've had everyone give you advice from here to Timbuktu on this, so I will just say I wish you had not experienced all this negative stuff."

Jane was quiet, thinking about Grace's situation. She watched Grace enjoying the cheese curds, not wanting to say what was on her mind. Unfortunately, her frown gave her away.

"What..." Grace stopped. "Do I have a curd in my teeth?"

Grace made an exaggerated smile so Jane could see her teeth. It made Jane laugh.

"No! But you do have nice teeth."

"Aw shucks." She rolled her eyes playfully at Jane. "What's hard about these random friends that cause trouble for us, is that John and I are so often alone at holidays and during big life events. We really feel as if we don't have a family. It makes this kid thing even more difficult."

Jane nodded. "I get what you're saying." She knew the feeling all too well. When Charlotte moved away, Jane felt abandoned. She felt it more when her sister moved than even when her mother did. And yet she'd found Mrs. Ferch, and despite everything, she did feel a sense of family with her. And even though Charlotte lived in another state, she knew she could always call, and Charlotte would be there for her. That was the difference between having a family that wasn't perfect and not having a family at all.

Jane felt for Grace. She'd been drawn to her since the moment they met. "You know," she said, "I really do feel you would click with my landlady, Mrs. Ferch. She has made me feel like family. There are times when we have had holidays dinners, just the two of us. Or, she'll invite a group over, with friends and people she has met…" Jane trailed off, realizing Eric had even been at a few of those dinners. She never bothered to really get to know him.

"Thank you," Grace said. "It's okay."

"No," Jane said, "really. I'm not just saying that to make you feel better. I really do think you guys would click."

Jane made a mental note to introduce Grace and Mrs. Ferch. "And you know what else? I think you're right. I am going to spend some time with Eric, if he's still interested, until he leaves."

After lunch, Jane headed back to work, where she stood before The Space Between Dreaming again. There was a part of her that saw the mother she wished her own mom could be in her life. A mother who didn't look at her as if she was disgusted with her all the time, she thought bitterly. But Jane also saw herself in the painting. At least, the feel of her spirit, someone searching and reaching for whatever was supposed to come next in her life. As she pondered the work, she decided to call Eric before she thought about it too long and talked herself out of it.

"Hello?" he answered. He sounded rushed, and Jane could hear a flurry of voices in the background.

"Eric, hi, this is Jane."

She expected a greeting of some sort. Like, *Oh hi, how have you been?* Or, Hey, *I've been meaning to follow up with you after that whole scene with your ex.* Instead, all she could hear were the sounds of the voices in the background. Where was he right now?

"Well, yeah, so…" She cleared her throat, realizing again how terrible she was at talking to men and at small talk in general. "I wanted to catch up with you to explain the whole thing that happened on the landing a few weeks ago. I mean, that was—"

"Your boyfriend," he said icily. "Yeah, I got that."

Ouch. "Right. I'm sorry, Eric. I just…" The background noises were distracting to her. "Where are you right now?"

"I'm at the airport. I'm on my way to Seattle."

"Oh," was all she could say.

"Jane?" he added, the contempt obvious in his voice. "I'm hanging up now."

"Right."

And they didn't say goodbye.

She felt a pang of disappointment. Grace was right, she'd had weeks to apologize to Eric or get to know him, but she shied away because she just assumed his leaving was a sign. She tried to shrug off this feeling that she had lost out on something special. But really, she didn't know him. She couldn't put her hope in something that hadn't even begun.

Still, she felt her emotions sinking low. She dialed her sister.

"How come you didn't tell me Dad had asked you for money again?" Charlotte said by way of hello, although her tone was gentle and not accusing.

"I dunno. I guess I thought you'd yell at me."

"Yell? When do I ever yell?"

Jane smiled to herself. "Never, actually. I don't know why I'm always so afraid you will."

"Probably because I'll tell you something you don't

want to hear, and no matter how quietly I say it, you'll hear it loudly."

What a way to put it, but Jane agreed.

"Also," she added, "whenever I talk about Dad, you bring up moving to Seattle."

Charlotte laughed. "That doesn't have to do with Dad so much as it has to do with me wanting you to be close. That's all."

"Oh," Jane said, "well, I also thought you were going to bring it up with this whole Eric thing. And Charlotte, he sounded like he hated me just now. Like he just could not stand me."

"Oh, sis," Charlotte sounded distraught. "I'm so sorry."

Her sister was quiet, and Jane was, too. They could do this, she realized, talk on the phone without saying a word. Finally, Jane broke the silence.

"What should I do?"

For the first time in a long time, she had genuinely wanted her sister's advice.

"First, figure out how to tell Dad no. I know it isn't easy. I've wanted to give him money many times myself. I love him. But it's always the same thing with him. Inventions that never seem to happen. Money that seems to fly through his hands. This isn't new. It's twenty years' worth of avoiding real work. And it's easier for me. I know that. It's easy for me to tell him no because I have a daughter and we're saving for college and besides that, I'm far away. I can't just pop over and hand him money.

"I know how hard it is, Janey. And you're a good daughter. Don't buy into this thing Mom has dropped at our feet. This guilt. We weren't to blame. We were kids. And just because we love our dad and want to him help doesn't make us bad daughters, either. We'd help her, too, if she ever asked. If she ever let us. Never forget that, Jane. It isn't just him, it's her, too. She helped created that environment in our family."

"She's not even talking to me right now," Jane said with sadness. "It shouldn't bother me. I hardly see or talk to her anyway. But it does."

"Of course, it does. She's your mom. And just so you know, she's not talking to me, either. She called me to complain about you, and I told her I didn't want to hear it. I figured it was about Dad again. It usually is. I told her we're her daughters and we love both of them. I told her you didn't deserve the silent treatment from her. She hung up on me, and I haven't heard from her in a month."

"You stuck up for me?"

"Are you surprised?"

"I guess. I dunno." Jane hated that she always sounded like a little girl when she was around her sister.

"You have to stop thinking I'm against you, Janey. I love you so much. Okay?"

"Okay." Jane's voice sounded small.

"Now tell me what else Eric said."

She told Charlotte about her afternoon, the call with Eric, and before that, the lunch with Grace.

"He's coming out here earlier than he'd planned," Charlotte said.

"Right. I didn't think it was happening yet."

"Maybe that scene with Brad made him want to get away from that place. Can't be fun for him to witness that, after all."

Jane knew her sister was right. "I feel terrible about it."

"I mean," Charlotte was laughing, "Brad proposes right there in front of Eric! Can you imagine?"

"Yes, Charlotte, I was there."

"Right. Of course. I'm not laughing at you but at Brad.

I'm glad you finally saw the light, with him."

"Charlotte?" Jane's voice seemed far away.

"I'm here, Janey. Are you okay?"

Jane could feel a teardrop fall. "I don't think I am."

"Oh, man, I just knew you were feeling down. I could sense it."

Jane rolled her eyes. Her sister always thought she had some kind of physic power when it came to Jane. "Could not."

"Could so! Look, you need to come here and see me. Give your niece a hug, tell your brother-in-law hello, enjoy some sea air—"

"I do have *lake* air here, you know."

"Not the same thing. And, you need to come here and let me spoil you."

She couldn't argue with that.

CHAPTER 21 - GRACE

Grace came home and paused at the stillness of the house. John was at a seminar for the day and would be back in the morning. When her husband was gone, the silence had the power to grab hold of her, making her feel out of place and time, as if she were a stranger to this life she lived. An empty room could call up a memory from her imagination of some child that she thought she would have had by now. It jeered at her infertility like a schoolyard bully, and all she could do was catch her breath and try to be on her way, as if she didn't hear the blaring taunt of silence mocking her echoing footsteps.

When she was getting ready earlier to meet Jane, John had still been home. He'd been acting strangely, she thought. He worked from home that morning, saying he was going to finish up a few things and then head to his seminar. They kissed goodbye, and yet Grace felt like something was off. She supposed he was working through his own thoughts, his own grief, and they couldn't always do it together. If they were going to get through it, they needed to team up to defeat the negative feelings and then also work through them individually.

The lunch with Jane was soul filling. Their friendship had been like that, and Grace realized that the last few years she had pulled back from most of her women friends. It wasn't that she was jealous of the families they had, it was how they treated her. They seemed to shut her out, or worse, they wanted her to celebrate their own life events and worries but didn't want to hear about hers.

One lunch involved friends from her old job. They were acting strangely toward her, making small talk loudly, until one of them commented on having been sick and then covered her mouth as if she had revealed this huge secret that wasn't meant to be shared with Grace. Another friend loudly chided the girl for talking about being sick, and Grace finally asked, "Are you pregnant?" It hurt so much when she admitted she was and that she didn't want Grace to know. What did they think she would do, fly into a rage? Dissolve into hysterics? Why couldn't people just be real with each other?

But people were imperfect. If she wondered why someone else had hurt her, then she had to admit that she probably did some of the same thoughtless things that hurt others, too.

John had admitted to her that when Jesus says to forgive everyone, including your enemies, it means even people like Ed and Linda, who continued to be mean-spirited and didn't think they'd done a thing wrong. Your enemies were sometimes right in your own family, people who not only would never apologize but who blamed you for their bad behavior.

Forgiveness, she realized, was easier than continuing to live in a bad situation. That's where things got tricky.

She paused, noting that the air had a distinct smell that

was giving her a headache. Paint? The odor was strong, much stronger than she occasionally smelled when her husband had work drying. She reached for some aspirin and a glass of water, took a good, long drink, and set the glass down on the kitchen island. She sniffed the air, then followed the smell into John's studio, noting that there were several new paintings lined up on the floor and on his easel. Once inside the room, she realized the paint smell seemed to be coming from somewhere else. She was about to leave when she noticed a small bird. It flitted over the papers on his table, which contained his notes and even landed on an edge of one of the canvases, knocking it over.

It flew past her, its wings brushing her face roughly, and headed to the kitchen. Grace followed it, cupping her hands uselessly in an effort to catch it. It landed on the counters and then flew to the living room. She tried to shoo it out gently without scaring it. She followed it, running from the living room to the studio, and back to the kitchen. It continued flying frantically from one room to the next, knocking over Grace's favorite antique saltshaker that she had on the top shelf in the kitchen. It smashed to the floor, scaring the bird further. It darted to the living room again and flew from the couch to the TV cabinet to the bookshelves. Once on the bookshelves, it flopped around trying to find its way out of the knickknacks, and landing against the fine-bone China teacups that were her grandmother's.

Grace felt a tinge of fear that the bird would thrash through the entire shelf, breaking each cup until it found its way out. She felt her irritation rise, thinking about the window that must be open in the studio. Sometimes that man's habits were too much to take. She'd just had the argument with him again this week to stop leaving that window open. He liked the breeze when he was painting.

Well, she liked to keep things like her grandmother's teacups intact!

She used her lightest, sweetest voice to coax the bird down.

"Come on, little one. That's right."

She grabbed a sauté pan and lid from the kitchen and came back into the living room, moving slowly to somehow catch it in there gently, so she could safely release it outside. She took one step, slowly took another, and then the bird started thrashing, rustling behind the teacups. It managed to push one right to the edge.

"No!" The softness in her voice gone, she grabbed for the cup, and in doing so, the bird thrashed behind another, which fell with a crash to the floor. Grace felt her heart thump in her chest. That cup held the memories of her afternoons with her grandmother, and she felt them tumble out onto the floor along with the tiny glass shards that seemed to go everywhere. The teacup was ruined.

The bird edged its way behind another teacup, pushing that one forward, and as Grace reached for it, the teacup next to it came out quickly, tipping over the edge of the bookshelf and flying to the floor. Bits of pink and royal blue lay everywhere on their hardwood floors. The bird hopped twice and then miraculously flew out, landing, exhausted, on the couch. Its wings spread out like an angel bowing down, and Grace was able to grab it with the pan and lid and release it as she had originally planned. She walked with it to the kitchen and let it out the back door.

She tossed the pan and lid in the garbage, then grabbed the broom and dustpan and cleaned up the mess. She went back to the studio to shut the window John had left open, when her knee caught. She flew forward, knocking against a canvas and getting paint all over herself and the floor. When she tried to stand again, her knee would not allow her to walk properly. She hobbled to the kitchen, grabbed her phone off the island, and called Jane.

Jane glanced at Grace as she drove. "You're being awfully quiet. Are you sure you're okay?"

"You caught me daydreaming. I'm sure the medicine is helping with that." Grace felt a little woozy, with the warmth of the car on her face as she took in the scenery. She watched the people on the sidewalk, a mother helping a small child zip her jacket, a guy in his own world jamming out with headphones in his ears, and it made her feel as she had failed to notice some of the sweet, ordinary things that happen on an average day.

"Are you feeling better?" Jane turned onto the street where Grace and John lived.

"Oh yes. The drugs were especially good." She laughed. "Truthfully, I think I'm more embarrassed than anything. And Jane, thank you for picking me up. John was at a semmmin… semmmin…" Grace found it hard to pronounce. Oh yes, the pain pills they gave her were working well.

"A seminar. Yeah, you told me at the hospital. I called him actually. He's at home waiting for you."

"Huh." She *tutted*. "I'm mad at that man." She folded her arms, remembering the window and the bird and all those precious teacups, smashed on the floor.

The fall was another reminder to Grace that she wasn't young anymore. Grace suddenly had a vision of herself chasing after a little one and falling, her knee locking up, and unable to stand up by herself. The thought made her shiver. She wrapped her arms around herself.

"Are you cold? I can turn the heat on."

"No, no. It's fine."

Jane pulled into the driveway and helped Grace into the house, putting Grace's arm around her shoulders and easing her along, one careful step at a time.

"We're home!" Grace called out, figuring that John was in his studio. She wondered bitterly if he had opened the window back up.

He came right away, his T-shirt covered in paint, his fingers and hands filled with different colors.

"You remember my husband, the painter?" Grace gestured to his messy clothes.

"Of course. Hi." Jane waved.

He rushed to Grace's side. "What's this? Are you all right?" He pulled out the kitchen chair and eased her into it.

"I'm fine. Torn meni… min…" She looked to Jane for help, feeling the effects of the medicine.

"Meniscus," Jane supplied. "They gave her some pain pills and scheduled an MRI for next week." They had run through the pharmacy drive-through on their way out of the hospital, and Jane took the pills out of her purse and put them on the table. She lowered her voice: "But they are thinking surgery."

"Honey!" He kissed her forehead. "Why didn't you call me? I'd have picked you up. I had no idea." He looked a little angry at Grace.

"Are you seriously mad at *me*?" The pain pills were giving her courage.

"I wished you would have called me. But I'm happy you're okay."

"Okay? I need to have surgery!" She dragged out the

word surgery and slurred just a little. Grace was feeling the pain pills in full force now.

"I know, Grace."

He kissed her forehead and gave her a worried look. She was glad about that. He had a tendency to not react in these kinds of situations, and this time she wanted to see a reaction. She needed to feel that his emotions were tied with hers. He reached across and pulled a chair out for Jane. "I'm so happy you were there to take her to the hospital. Now, what happened?"

Grace and Jane told him everything. He listened, getting them both some water. He stood at the edge of the counter and took it all in.

"Oh!" Grace put a finger up in the air, punctuating the point she had been stewing about all afternoon. "Plus, I have a bone to pick with you!" Her words were louder than usual. She knew that, and yet she couldn't seem to turn down the volume on her own voice. "You broke my grandmother's teacups! The antique ones! From my grandmother! The ones that are…" Grace felt her lips moving in a funny way. "The ones that are antiques!"

He frowned at her. "I broke your grandmother's teacups?" He looked at the shelf where they were. "What happened?"

"Nice! Question!"

"Grace…" He winced, gesturing toward Jane. "Honey, you're being awfully loud. I doubt Jane wants to hear you yelling in her ear."

She knew she was being loud, but suddenly she seemed far away from herself. The volume didn't seem to matter. "You left the window open! After I asked you not to. I reminded you, and you just rolled your eyes at me."

He frowned at her, his face getting red. "Grace, let's talk about this later."

Jane stood up. "I should go."

"Sit!" Grace put a hand on her leg. "And you!" She turned to her husband. "You left the window open, and now those teacups are broken! I've been saving them. Our whole marriage! I was waiting…" Grace paused, feeling a pain of regret bubble up inside her so strongly that she feared she might choke. Why had she kept those cups? Her grandmother used them every Sunday, sitting with Grace and listening to her stories and concerns. They would talk for hours. She remembered her grandma sipping slowly and blowing on the tea as she listened to Grace go on and on about school and friends and dreams. It was a time before her mother's drinking, before her world spun upside down, and she was shuffled off from one home to another. When her grandmother died, the last real family she ever had died with her.

Her grandmother had lovingly used them, taking care to wash them by hand and place them gently on the table between them, but they didn't sit and get dusty up on a shelf. When her grandmother died, she left a note saying that all her teacups and China should go to Grace, and yet, what had Grace done with them? She put them up on a shelf and barely remembered that she had them.

"Honey?" He put his hand on her shoulder. "Are you all right? Let's get you to bed. I think you've had a long day."

"I should go," Jane said again, standing, but Grace pulled her back down again.

"No." She turned to her husband. "Jane drove me to the hospital!"

"Yes, I know."

"But those cups! It's my fault! I did this!" Despite herself, Grace started to cry. "I should have just used them. What was I waiting for? I put them away until the perfect time came, when we could relax and enjoy them." Her tears got more pronounced. "A special occasion. But that moment never came!"

She was wailing now, and her husband and Jane were trying to help her up.

"We've had lots of good moments," he said, that soothing voice that seemed to come from somewhere else.

"Yes. What I mean is, all those good moments? They were good enough. More than good enough! And yet, I didn't appreciate them. I didn't think they were worth pulling out my best china for. My best..." She groped for the words. "My best *stuff*."

"Honey, let's just let it go for now. You can tell me all about it later. I'm sorry I left the window open and let the bird in. It was my fault. Now, babe, you've got to get some rest."

"No!" She looked up at him, at the concern on his face and thought of how often they had perfectly wonderful days when they could have used those cups just as her grandma had done. How many moments they had in the course of their ordinary life that she wished she could have again, just to savor them, swirl them around and enjoy them again, just like her grandmother had done with the tea.

The tears came hot and angry down her face. She looked at him and choked out the words. "I'm sorry that those moments were all so good and perfect, and I didn't see it until now."

Grace blew out a breath. Meniscus surgery was fairly minor as far as surgeries went, but still, she was nervous.

"The hospital is right up here on the left. Apparently, all they do is ortho stuff."

"I know, honey," John said as he pulled up to the front door and helped Grace out. A valet parked the car and got them set up with a wheelchair. John pushed it to the registration desk.

"Wow." Grace tried to keep her voice happy and upbeat. "A valet and everything. They've got this thing down, here."

The nurse behind the desk certified Grace's name, then put a band around her wrist and walked out from behind the desk.

"Follow me. I'll show you to your room."

She walked briskly, and John was almost jogging to keep up with her and push Grace in the wheelchair. The woman stopped just as quickly, causing John to stop the wheelchair abruptly and Grace to lurch forward in the chair. John put his hand on her shoulder to make sure she was okay.

"Now..." The woman gestured for them to come in the tiny room. "This is where you'll be hanging out before surgery. You'll be weighed; the doctor will come in; the anesthesiologist will come in; the physical therapy nurse will come in. The PT nurse will show you how to do the stairs and get you set for crutches. You"—she nodded at John—"can stay here with her until surgery, and then you'll be in the waiting room. That room you passed on the way here?"

She held up a gown and some stockings. "These are your stockings; you'll be putting them on before surgery. They are tight. You'll struggle. They are meant to be tight. You'll keep them on after surgery and wear them for the next three days. Keep the extra one for when you wash the first one." She put them down on the table, picking up the gown. "This is your gown. You can keep your bra and panties on. Everything else off. Gown on. Ties in back. There is a robe here." She held up another garment. "Robe on after all this. Do you have any questions?"

It all went by pretty fast, but Grace just nodded.

"What's your question?"

"Oh, sorry. I mean, no. I got it. Thank you."

"Thank you, Mrs. Cambridge. Have a good surgery."

She left, and Grace and John just looked at each other. "Wow." John gestured to the pile of stockings and clothes. "She's got this whole thing down. Do you want me to leave so you can get into your stuff?"

"No, please. It's fine."

As John helped Grace tie the back of the robe, she sat down on the room's small bed and noticed it had railings on either side. "Do you think this is the thing they wheel me into surgery with?"

"Probably."

Grace blew out a big breath again. "I'm nervous."

"I know. I am, too." John cringed. "I mean, they do a lot of these, and the doctor said—"

"I know what you meant." She smiled at him.

The physical therapy nurse came in with a burst. "Morning! How are you doing today?" Grace opened her mouth, but the nurse continued without waiting for an answer. "How many steps in your house?"

Grace thought about it. "We have a ranch home, so just three steps up the front stoop to get into the house."

"And what about work? How many steps there?"

"I work at home. Freelancer."

"Oh? How interesting." She put the clipboard aside as if she were going to sit and chat a while. "And what do you do as a freelancer?"

"Editing." Grace thought about all the work she was doing for John's upcoming exhibit. "And promotion stuff."

The woman looked like she had all day. "And what are you working on now? Anything fabulous?"

Grace glanced at John, who raised his eyebrows. This woman was a hoot.

"I'm planning a reception for my husband, who is having an art exhibit." Grace nodded at him.

"Your husband is a painter? Very cool. So, you guys work together. Or, at least, you're a team. That's nice. And I suppose you pose nude for him all the time." She cracked herself up, and Grace laughed along but gave John a *do you believe her?* look.

"So, any kids?"

Grace's laughter stopped. "No."

The nurse waited a beat, then another. Grace let her sweat it out. Finally, the woman nodded and got back to business.

"So, let's show you how to get up those stairs."

While the nurse demonstrated the stair technique with crutches, Grace wondered if this was how it was going to be for her now. Always having to wonder where the next question about kids came from, like a roaming dart that followed her everywhere. This was how people made small talk, women, especially; it was the thing they thought connected everyone together. But they didn't seem to understand that for some people, this question, and all that came with it, wasn't like talking about the weather. This one had weight to it, one that carried years of hurt and longing with it. It was a question no one had the right to ask.

Grace's knee surgeon came in next. He was a small

man, five feet tall and slight in build, but loud. Grace was holding a magazine, and when he came in the room shouting "Good Morning!" she jumped and dropped the magazine to the floor. The doctor asked her how she was and told her the knee would be as good as new before she knew it. He left as suddenly as he had burst in.

"He's a man of few words," Grace told John. "I like him, though."

An anesthesiologist came in, followed by a nurse, followed by the physical therapist who had forgot to remind Grace about icing her knee and moving her feet every hour to limit the chance of a blood clot.

"I'm glad you're here to remind me of all this," she told John. "So much information at once." She narrowed her eyes at him. "You are getting all this, right?"

He gave her an *of course I am* look in response.

"After surgery, I hear they kick me out fairly quickly."

"I'll get you home and make sure you're okay."

She looked at the clock. "Any minute now." She could feel the apprehension building and just wanted to get on with it. Finally, a nurse came in to get her and take her to surgery.

Surgery had gone well, and within days, Grace was back on her feet. She was glad she could work from home and still be productive. She lay on the bed and did her knee exercises, thinking of John's exhibit. She placed one leg flat and bent the one that she'd just had surgery on. She pulled her knee up to her, feeling the tightness in the joint. It was hard to imagine the ache going away, but she supposed in time all pain either got worse or better, depending on what you did to soothe it.

After doing her knee exercises, Grace sat up straight on the bed, massaging her leg and thinking again about all the lost children, the ones her womb could not carry. They never mentioned Glenn's name after the miscarriage. It was as if her husband wanted to forget there had been a child growing in her and being a part of their family, even though he had not been born. They had closed the door of the robin's-egg-blue room, right along with their hopes.

Grace finally felt ready to clean up the room however. She needed to open the door and release her unborn child's spirit and the spirit of her mother, who she'd imagined in that room as if it had become a door to another dimension. She needed to release them from the prison of this dreamland that existed only in her mind, so she could finally start living the life she had been given.

She opened the door, expecting to see the crib they had bought and the blue paint on the walls, and instead, it was all gone. A single chair stood lonely in the corner, as if it had been punished and forced to be in this cold, white room alone. But there was nothing else, not the crib and not even the adorable butter-yellow dresser that they picked up at the thrift store. Even the paint, the robin's-egg blue, was gone, hidden beneath a thick coat of white. It must have taken at least two coats. When had this happened?

She thought of the times she was gone from the house for an extended period of time. Could John have pulled this off in so short a time? And yet, he must have. Who else would have come in here and removed everything, and painted it all away? She sat on the chair and took it all in. He did this without asking her? Without discussion? That seemed foreign to her. They were a team. It was what had buoyed her during the dark times. He was her friend, along with everything else. He was the only other person in the world who could understand exactly what she had been through.

She remembered how often she'd commented angrily that the windows had been left open. She thought it was because he wanted air in his studio, but what if it was for this? To get the smell of paint out of the room so she wouldn't notice. Would he do that behind her back, even going to this length?

A bolt of fear charged through her, like a knight racing at her with a javelin in his hand. What if this was his way of saying that he didn't want to do this dance anymore, this constant torture of putting your emotions out on a flag so someone could come and bombard them again? If he felt this way, then the reality of it would be certain for her as well.

But no, that couldn't be it. She stood up from the chair, seeing the room differently. What if he was just trying to make it clean and new for the next kid, for the one that would stay this time? Yes, that had to be it. She felt a sense of joy wash over her. He was being thoughtful. She smiled as she looked around the empty room. It wasn't cold at all to her now. It was fresh and clean, ready for a new start.

CHAPTER 22 - JANE

Jane made plans to fly out to Seattle. She marked off her vacation time on the gallery's master calendar and got a hug and "Good job" from Donna, who'd been telling her to stop wasting her days and use them. She called for flights and then texted Charlotte with the information. She felt good about finally getting out to see her sister.

She left the gallery and picked up some flowers for Mrs. Ferch on the way home, figuring that if she felt awful that Eric had left, Mrs. Ferch had to be missing him like crazy.

When she knocked on the woman's door, however, she was greeted with loud music and chatter.

"Oh Jane! What a wonderful surprise. Come on in, dear."

"Here." She handed her the flowers. "I thought you might need a little pick-me-up after Eric left for Seattle."

She ushered Jane into the living room and introduced her to the older gentleman who was already there. He had on a newsboy cap and jeans, a crisp, pressed white shirt, and the most genuine smile she'd ever seen. He stood as Jane approached.

"Neels, this is Jane. She's my upstairs tenant and just one of the most wonderful people you will ever meet."

"That's a hard introduction to live up to," Jane said, shaking the man's hand. "Neels, is it?"

"Yes, yes," he said, gesturing for Jane to sit. "Short for Cornelius. An old-fashioned name, even for my time."

Jane noted that he seemed very close in age to Mrs. Ferch. She put him at about eighty but didn't want to ask.

"It's a nice name," she continued. "I've always kind of hated mine. So boring."

"What?" Mrs. Ferch had placed the flowers in a vase and joined them in the living room. "Your name is wonderful, Jane."

Neels agreed. "I'd rather have a"—he made air quotes—"'boring' name. You wouldn't believe how people get your name wrong when it's one like mine. Anyhoo, Avery, I'm off. I'll see you tomorrow at game night?"

"Of course," she said, seeing him to the door. Jane tried not to watch but did notice him kiss her cheek as he said goodbye.

"Well, well, well," Jane said as Mrs. Ferch returned. "Is that your boyfriend?"

The woman laughed, slapping her knee. "Oh, I don't know. He has called upon me a time or two. But we visit now and again and enjoy each other's company. It works out for us."

Jane knew she shouldn't pry, but she couldn't help herself. "Do you ever want more from him?"

Mrs. Ferch frowned at her. "As in, marriage? Oh no, dear. I had my one true love. Would you like coffee?"

"No thanks," she'd said, but Mrs. Ferch was already up and out of her chair, making a cup. Jane wondered if she'd ever get to a point where she'd be satisfied to have had one true love, and wouldn't even think about needing more. "I actually stopped in to see how you were feeling about Eric being gone."

"Oh, well," she said, drinking the cup she'd brewed and then setting it down. "Too hot right now. Eric? He told me about the fuss with your Brad here, and he took it as… what did he say"—she snapped her fingers in the air as if that would pry the memory loose—"a sign or some such that he should leave."

Jane blinked.

"A sign?"

She drank her coffee again but nodded.

"I"—Jane put her hand on her chest—"took it as a sign that his moving to Seattle meant we weren't right for each other."

Jane sat back in her chair. She and Eric really did have the worst timing. And luck.

"Well, how marvelous!" Mrs. Ferch was saying now. "That means you are surely meant to get to know one another."

Jane frowned at her. "What's that, now?"

"Oh, my dear, do I have to spell it out?" She seemed exasperated.

"Apparently."

"You are both looking for signs to be together because you're both afraid. All you need, both of you, is some courage. I listened to Eric moan for a good long while after his Tiffany behaved so poorly, and finally he found the courage to go after his dreams and change his life. You can do the same. I know you can."

"I'm so tired of hearing about moving to Seattle."

"Well, who is saying to move. Call him first. Talk. You can court over the phone, you know. You young people, you've lost the ability to talk to one another." She tut-tutted out her displeasure as she sipped her brew.

"Okay," Jane said. "I'll call him," she promised. "But I would like a promise from you, too," she said, and told her about Grace. She really hoped Mrs. Ferch and Grace would hit it off.

"She sounds marvelous!" Mrs. Ferch seemed excited to do it. Jane hoped one day she would have a disposition like her, so joyful and full of life.

Mrs. Ferch got up again and gestured to the coffee maker, her silent question to Jane about whether she wanted a cup. She nodded. Why not?

Mrs. Ferch set the coffee down in front of her, and Jane took in the sight of her white hair, pulled up with tiny clips, just a hint of powder on her still pretty face. As Jane thought about how beautiful she looked, a thought occurred to her.

"Mrs. Ferch, how did you meet Mr. Ferch? I don't think you've ever said."

"Haven't I ever told you that story? It's a good one. We met on Valentine's Day, if you can believe it."

"Aw, how sweet!" Somehow Jane knew Mrs. Ferch would have a romantic story like that in her history.

"Cheesy," Mrs. Ferch supplied. "But very sweet. I went to a dance hall with some friends of mine. Pearl and Sal. Oh my, those two fought like cats and dogs. As opposite as two people could be. But they loved each other. They were dating then, but you just knew they were going to get married. They were cute to watch, so in love.

"Anyway, I never had a regular boyfriend. Every time there was a dance or someplace to go as a couple, I was the tagalong. But Pearl and Sal never minded. They'd drive me there, pay attention to me, and treat me like I was special. They never once treated me like a bother. I appreciated that.

"When the Valentine's Day dance came up, I was sweet on Harry Novak. Oh, that man was handsome!"

Jane giggled at her story. Her excitement was so sweet, just like it all happened yesterday.

"Pearl and Sal didn't like him, but I thought he was a dream. So smart. At least, that's what he always liked to tell people."

"He told you how smart he was?"

"Yes." Jane thought she saw Mrs. Ferch blush. "It sounds ridiculous, doesn't it? If he had to tell me that, then he probably wasn't." She laughed at the memory. "But I was smitten. So, the day of the dance was approaching, and I had my dress and these adorable Mary Jane flats, but I'm getting worried now. He hasn't asked me to the dance."

"Did he ask someone else?"

"Well, that was the thing about him. He didn't have another girl, but he never could just pick me up and take me out on a date. He always wanted to meet me there. It drove Pearl crazy. You know Sal always picked her up, even if they were going back to his mama's house to listen to the radio.

"I was used to getting a ride to some dance, usually with Pearl and Sal, and then spending the night dancing with Harry. But then I'd leave with Pearl and Sal."

Jane frowned, trying to keep it all straight. "Did he have a car?"

"Yes. But that wouldn't have mattered. Pearl and Sal and I all took the streetcar. I didn't care whether Harry had a car or not."

"What did you wear to the dance?"

"Oh, I had the most adorable red dress. It was really beautiful. It had lace all around the collar. Then I borrowed a silver shawl from my mama. I thought I was the bell of the ball. As it happened, Harry never did ask me to meet him at the dance, but since Pearl and Sal were going, I decided to go, too. When we got there, at first, I wasn't sure what to do. I didn't know if it would be proper to dance with anyone else."

"Was Harry even there? And besides, he didn't ask you."

"Oh, I know, honey. It sounds so old-fashioned now, but I wasn't sure what to do. For a long time, I just stood and watched the other couples dance. Finally, Seth—that's Mr. Ferch—he walked up to me and asked if he could have this dance. They were playing "Yellow Rose of Texas." I'll never forget it. He looked so handsome." She smiled at the memory of it.

"Did you dance then?"

"Absolutely not!"

Jane laughed. That wasn't the answer she was expecting.

"I had seen him come in with another girl. Well, you just don't come with one girl and ask another to dance. I told him so, too. And do you know what he said?"

Jane shook her head.

"He said, I've never brought one girl and danced with another before, but when you see your future wife, it doesn't matter who you came with." Mrs. Ferch put her hand to her chest, cherishing the memory. "Can you believe that?"

Jane was riveted.

"And did you dance with him, then?"

"Ha!" She slapped her leg. "I did. I couldn't help myself. I danced with him every dance after that. And do you know what? He took me home that night, too. Pearl and Sal wouldn't let me go alone. They walked right behind us to make sure he didn't pull anything funny. But he was such a sweetheart. Kissed my hand at my door and asked if he could take me out proper next time."

"Wow." Jane realized she'd been leaning forward, eager to hear more of the story. What a romantic way to meet. "And what about the other girl?"

"The other girl?"

"The one Mr. Ferch originally came with? Was she upset?" Jane tried to picture herself getting left at a dance while the guy who brought you went home with someone else.

"Well, that's another funny thing. You know what? Rose and I became very good friends after that."

"No way!" Jane couldn't imagine.

"Rose said it was obvious Mr. Ferch and I were meant to be together. She was a sweetheart. In fact, I set her up with my cousin Bud after that. Of course, it didn't work out. Bud never could hold a girl. But do you know what else? Rose was at our fiftieth wedding anniversary party. You remember that little place over on Water Street? With the heart decorations on the window and the blue shutters?"

Jane frowned. "No, I don't think so."

"Maybe it's gone. That was almost ten years ago now. Anyway, they made the best broasted chicken, and Mr. Ferch always loved that. I never cared for it too much. I'm a fried-chicken girl myself. Still, you compromise in marriage. Even with food. Well, anyway, Rose gave a toast at our party and told the whole story about how we met. She had the crowd in stitches."

"That's amazing. What a story." Jane felt even closer to Mrs. Ferch now that she knew. "Thank you for sharing that with me."

"Oh, I've got a million stories! But none like that one, for sure."

"Whatever happened with Harry?"

"Oh, how could I forget? I finally spotted him, all grumpy and mad"—she made a face to illustrate and folded her arms over her chest to show Jane what he was like—"just as we were leaving. Can you believe it? He never said one word to me, and I never said one to him. I just walked out with Mr. Ferch, and that was that."

"You never heard from Harry again? Never explained why you left him there and went home with Mr. Ferch instead?"

"No, of course not. Why should I? What's done is done. No use going back over a broken road when I had freshly paved one right in front of me."

There was something that was still bothering Jane about the story. "But how did you know? How come you were so sure going home with Mr. Ferch was the right choice?"

"Oh, that's easy. Because I didn't overthink it. I made the decision, it felt correct, and that was that." Mrs. Ferch acted out a motion of brushing the dirt from her hands to emphasis her point.

Jane sipped her coffee and eyed the woman, who had suddenly got a knowing look on her face.

"And with you, well, I already know it's going to work out. It's done. No turning back now."

Jane shook her head as if to clear the cobwebs.

"What do you mean it's done? What's done?"

"The wheels have been set in motion. I'd like to think I had something to do with that, but I know it's the good Lord's doing. Still, I was happy to help. You two were both so clueless. You can name your firstborn after me to thank me. I'm only partially kidding." She laughed to herself as Jane got up to rinse her coffee mug.

"You seem pretty sure of this. You're talking, what,

marriage with me and Eric?" Jane rolled her eyes. "He's not even speaking to me. We are living in separate states."

"Well, that's just it, honey. You're thinking about it too hard. Let the situation pull you along. Don't fight it."

Jane shook her head. "I love you, Mrs. Ferch. I really do. But I have no idea what you're talking about."

"It's a good thing you have to be on your way, then, isn't it?"

Jane grabbed her purse and put her hand on the doorknob to leave.

"Oh, and one more thing, dear..." Mrs. Ferch called to Jane.

She turned. "Yes?"

"Avery. That's my first name. Now that works for a boy or a girl."

Jane stood there, openmouthed.

"See you later." Mrs. Ferch giggled, and closed the door.

A week went by, and Jane had been busy getting ready for John Cambridge's exhibit. Even with her busy workload, however, she made a point to leave on time for once. She no longer had a boyfriend to help fill up her free time, but that actually worked out for the best. She needed some time to herself.

She found herself going back to the art museum, her comfort zone, and looking out at Lake Michigan from the windows. There were window seats along the east side of the building and she sat on one, sometimes for hours, just daydreaming and thinking. Each time, she remembered her day with Eric, how much she enjoyed being in this space with him. She tried not to overanalyze the feeling but just let herself feel it.

On a particularly gray day, with clouds that seemed to make Lake Michigan's waters a very dark blue, it struck her that just weeks before, the biggest disappointment she had was that Bug hadn't remembered her ten-year anniversary at work. Looking back now, that fact was so small, she hardly cared. She had decided to make space for more in her life. Sure, she would still work hard in her job but there was still plenty of room for more.

The next day at work, Bug stopped her as she was heading to her office. He had a tie with what looked like a print of giraffes highlighted by a stain of chocolate, which seemed to make his belly protrude as he sat.

"Jane," he said, looking at her with his glasses pulled down. "I noticed you're taking vacation right after the Cambridge exhibit."

"Yes," she said, the plans had been made weeks ago.

"My wife told me last night that she'd like us to take vacation that same week." He shuffled through the paperwork on his desk, and Jane was expecting him to show her a piece of paper or something.

She waited, and he looked up after several moments, surprised to see her there.

"Did you have a question, Jane?"

She frowned. "What are you saying? That I cannot take vacation now? I followed procedure for vacation time, and you approved it, remember?"

He sighed. "Yes, well, that was before my wife pulled this stunt on me. I'll be out of town that entire week, and as the new assistant manager, you'll have to fill in with the business end here. Sorry to do this to ya, kid."

He waved her off with a flick of his hand, much the same as he had done the morning he told her he wanted to create happiness in the office. A collection of thoughts raced through her mind: the tickets she'd already bought and paid for, the ride to the airport she had already arranged, the fact that she'd been looking forward to this since the moment he had approved her time off, and the fact that in most of her ten years with the gallery, she had not taken any time off at all.

"No, Bug," she said, a new resolve in her that seemed to come from outside her body, "I'm afraid that will not do."

He looked at her, frowning. "It will have to do, Jane. Sorry, kiddo."

"And I am not a kiddo. Or a kid. I am a grown woman, and I would appreciate it if you would address me as such."

"Look, I just promoted you, didn't I? Those are the breaks sometimes."

"And I have more than done my job to earn and be worthy of that promotion. No, my vacation plans will not be moved." Then she added, before she lost her nerve, "I'm sorry that you'll have to make other arrangements."

She left in a hurry back to her office, walking quickly but wishing she could run, throw herself in the chair, and hide. Would Bug fire her? What had she done that was all that bad? Still, there was a part of her that felt as if he did fire her, she'd pack up and move to Seattle and leave this whole place without a second glance. She'd enjoyed it here, but there were parts of it where she'd also had enough.

She waited all morning for Bug to come into her office. He didn't. Instead, she went about her job and was even more determined to make the Cambridge exhibit successful. Jane was impressed with Grace's efforts in getting the word out about the event.

It was funny how life could change in the span of weeks or months. It seemed years ago that she first saw Grace and her husband's work at that art fair, and now they were friends.

And yet she hated the way time could make you look at your life. Years could pass by with barely a care, and then you suddenly find yourself past a certain point, too old to make the same choices you would have made before. Other times, moments dragged on, causing you to wish you could disappear. She'd spent so many years as a kid just wanting to be an adult. Now that she was, she felt uncertain again. Even this reception, which really was no big deal, was something that made her question herself, and she wasn't sure why.

CHAPTER 23 - GRACE

Grace smiled as she approached Jane. "See? Nothing to worry about. Just look at this crowd."

The gallery was packed with people, but not so many that it seemed overcrowded. Everyone was viewing the art, and they seemed intrigued, pointing at different paintings and taking flyers. There was a guitar player singing in the background, who Jane had hired, and his music was uplifting but also blended into the chatter of the crowd, which helped set the tone of the space to a relaxed vibe.

Grace noticed a redheaded woman in high heels and a slim skirt walk their way.

"Oh my." Grace tried not to point. "That's Margo Carmichael, art critic for the Milwaukee Journal. I'm so glad she came. I hope she asks lots of questions. I should get my hubs over here in case she wants to interview him. I hope he behaves and gives a decent interview. He can be very blasé about this kind of stuff."

"I'll find him," Jane told her. "You introduce yourself."

Jane left to find John, and Grace watched as Margo

came closer to The Space Between Dreaming. She stood before the painting and inhaled deeply. She crossed her thin arms and slowly paced, back and forth, looking from the painting to Grace and back again.

She'd been reading Margo's column for years, since she was a little girl. But she supposed telling her that would just make her sound foolish. Instead, she opted for a simple introduction.

She held out her hand. "Hi. I'm Grace—"

"Shh!" Margo put her hand up like a traffic cop.

She felt like a schoolgirl getting scolded. She was going to introduce herself but obviously the woman had her own process when viewing art. Grace thought it was a little dramatic, actually more than a little dramatic, but who was she to judge? When it came to art, everyone had their own way of taking it in.

Margo stopped pacing, clasped her hands together before her, and said quietly, "It's simply… *perfect*." She had breathed the word as if she were blowing a kiss.

Grace had leaned forward slightly to take in her statement, then backward as she realized what she had said. So, Margo had felt that way, too. It wasn't just Grace thinking that this one was different. Margo was someone who could be very critical if the moment, and the work, deserved it.

She turned to Grace. "Where is the painter of this work?"

By then John had been hovering, a frown on his face as if he hated the fact that he was going to have to talk about his work. He didn't seem nearly as thrilled as Grace was.

Grace pulled him gently forward and gave his hand a final squeeze as she introduced him to Margo. He looked uncomfortable, and Grace's heart went out to him, knowing he would rather just be in his studio creating and not out talking with people.

Margo gestured to the painting. "When did you finish this?"

"A few months ago."

It seemed to Grace that he was going to say something more but stopped himself.

"This piece…" Margo said, allowing the space to frame her words, "I can feel the pain here."

Grace noticed him wince ever so slightly.

"Talk to me. What happened that caused this piece of brilliance?"

He paused, and Grace wondered if he was thinking of telling her off or trying to come up with something to say. In general, John hated to describe his process. His paintings just were, he said. He didn't want to define it for fear that if he thought about his process too much, he'd forget how to paint.

When he spoke, it was with no hint of a smile. He was letting Margo know it pained him to answer. "What happened is whatever you think happened."

His tone wasn't hostile, but if someone didn't know their story, she would have thought his response rather rude. But Margo seemed all the more pleased about it. She paced again, taking in what he'd said. Despite the noise of conversations and glasses clinking, Grace could hear the sensible square heels Margo wore rattling the walls as she marched to and fro with clipped steps. Grace noticed for the first time her legs, like the ends of tiny wooden spoons moving beneath a skirt that looked like a dish towel. She wondered if Margo always wore such ridiculous outfits, this one a skirt that mimicked a tablecloth she'd seen on her grandmother's dining room table years ago.

"That's an interesting skirt."

Margo looked down, torn from her purposeful marching, and smiled. "A new artist sent it to me. Isn't it delicious? Made from those old kitschy towels you see? With the states on them? So much color and life!"

Grace smiled at John, in the way that tells someone they'll have a lot to talk about with this person later on. John bit his lip to keep from grinning like a Cheshire cat. Margo was quite a character. Grace suddenly recalled a set of drinking glasses her grandmother used to have, which matched a kitchen towel in her house and wished she had them tonight just so they could toast this moment. It was clear that Margo was pleased with the painting and its creator.

"I'm going to view the rest of the exhibit," Margo said, "and then, if you're willing, I'd like to chat with you a bit more."

Grace gave John the *Be kind, say yes, say you want to talk* look.

John simply nodded, and it seemed enough for Margo.

"I'm going to grab a drink," he told Grace. "Want something?"

"No thanks." She was too nervous. Grace spotted Jane across the gallery, looking out at things, giving direction to the staff, adjusting flyers and business cards, which had been left on small stands at the edges of the room.

Grace could see that Jane had done quite a bit to prepare the gallery for this night. There was food, two bar areas, and a few standing tables where people could congregate. She noticed the flyers she had made were placed in various spots in the gallery, so no matter where someone went, they'd have the information about her husband's work right in front of them.

She walked up to Jane and hugged her.

"This looks great. You can tell you're a pro at these."

"I don't feel like it." She seemed nervous and frenzied. "I've been running around trying to get everything just so. I know this is important for you, too. I don't want to disappoint you, or screw something up—"

"Oh my goodness, you really are in your own head right now, aren't you? Jane, you are so accomplished, I don't even think you realize how much you have going for you. And you can't avoid bad things from happening. You just can't. If they do, we deal with it and learn from it. Right?"

Jane let out a breath. "You're right."

"You've done great. I just wanted to thank you."

John had joined them, walking up to Grace and giving her a quick kiss on the mouth. He was chewing something.

"What are you eating?"

"Little sausages." He pointed over to the bar. "Good eats, Jane. Not like that horrible appetizer party."

Grace rolled her eyes at Jane. "He'll never forget that, apparently."

Jane cringed. "And neither will I."

"Jane..." Grace realized how painful that party was to her. "I'm sorry—"

"No," she laughed, "it's fine. Just a really crazy memory. I'm good, Grace, really."

The look on Jane's face convinced Grace that she was good. She was feeling better, more confident.

"Thank you, Jane." John smiled at her. "I'm thrilled to have a showing here. Thanks so much for taking an interest in my work, like you have—and in your friendship with Grace."

"You're welcome. I've been enjoying your paintings for months now."

Jane noticed a few more people had arrived, and she excused herself to greet them. Grace turned to her husband. There were times when those blue eyes of his could really take her breath away.

"You look handsome in that suit."

He leaned in close to her. "I wish no one was here right now but us." He kissed her on her neck, which brought out a girlish giggle Grace believed had long been locked away.

"If no one else were here, this reception would be a dud." She interlocked her fingers in his and looked into his eyes. "I'm so proud of you."

He squeezed her hand and looked at the space where his paintings were hung. "It's pretty surreal, isn't it?" He sighed. "I kind of feel unnecessary, though. I mean, really, why would they need me here?"

Grace rolled her eyes. He never knew how special he was. "Because, silly, people want to see where all this creativity came from." Before things got too busy, she wanted to let him know that she had found out about Glenn's room. "By the way, I saw what you did in the extra bedroom. In… Glenn's room."

His eyes widened in surprise. "I didn't think you'd look in there yet. I wondered if it was too soon. I—"

"No." She squeezed his arm. "It's not too soon. I'm with you. Totally."

He seemed surprised. "You are? I was too afraid to bring it up. Grace, I don't want you to be hurt anymore. Or me."

"I know. We won't be hurt this time. I just know it."

He took a breath and stepped back. "Right. So, you're ready… to…?" He let the sentence hang, and she noticed the questioning tone. She cocked her head at him.

"To try again. I wasn't sure you were. I'm glad you gave the extra bedroom a fresh start. I wasn't sure why you got rid of the crib, though. I mean, we could have still used that."

She smiled at him and he swallowed hard. He looked nervous, and she figured it was because of the reception.

"Oh look," she told him. "Margo is back looking at The Space Between Dreaming."

"I'm going to the bathroom," he said suddenly, frowning at her. "I'll be back."

He left abruptly, and Grace felt for him. This whole thing was probably very surreal to him.

She wondered how many painters got a bad reputation just because they wanted to be left alone to paint. They never thought of the reality, that in order to be successful in any business you needed to market. She'd always assumed that her husband was just being sweet when he told her how valuable she was to his business. How she got the word out about his work, and the art shows they did, and how he could not have done it without her. She had brushed off the compliments, but now she saw the value in the work she did, too. She wondered why this dream she carried of getting people to notice his work didn't seem to include her until now, when she could finally stand before that painting everyone was so in awe of and see her effort in this, too. Like a kind of destiny they shared together.

Grace wondered if we didn't each live in our own dreamland, each of us viewing life as we want it instead of how it actually is. She had stood before the painting many times in the last few months, from that first time when it called up feelings of anger, to now, when she felt such satisfaction and pride. It was like a newly lit fire in her soul. She wondered if that meant the flame had been burning steady all these years, or if this was a new flame, one that would extinguish the other goals and wants she had for her life.

A waiter had come over with glasses of champagne.

Margo picked one up and handed a glass to Grace, who noticed she had been hovering stealthily.

"To… The Space Between Dreaming!" Margo said dramatically, glugging it down while simultaneously laughing at something only she seemed to know. She laughed with her whole body, causing the drink in her hand to spill on the towel skirt. Grace thought that rather appropriate, wanting to make a joke about it but stopping herself.

A couple of people applauded Margo's toast, but the chatter resumed quickly.

After Margo had downed her glass of champagne, she then grabbed another off a passing tray.

"My husband is a man of few words," Grace said as they both stood there before the painting.

A pencil and a small notebook had appeared in Margo's hand as Grace spoke. Grace wondered where the champagne had gone and how she had managed to hide the paper until this moment.

Margo scribbled something quickly. It had been easy to forget Margo was still a journalist as well as an art critic.

"Who writes the descriptions?" Margo pointed at the cards next to each painting.

"I do."

"Fascinating. So, what do *you* think this painting is about? I can feel the pain here," she said, for what seemed like the hundredth time. "I can tell this was something big in his life. I am wondering if this woman is a person, a lover, a—"

"Let me interrupt here." Grace couldn't believe she was doing it. "But I think John's words really do sum it up. After all, isn't the true meaning of art whatever someone sees in it? I have heard it said that art was just a receptacle of sorts." She tried to think of the quote. "It comes from all the elements, both manmade and the ones created by God. From the sky, the earth, or even throwaway pieces of paper we might use to jot our grocery lists on."

Margo put down her pencil and frowned at Grace. "You're paraphrasing Picasso. Badly, I might add. But there it is. Now, Grace. Tell me more about your husband."

"Of course." Grace cleared her throat. "He's a self-taught painter, who enjoys working in a variety of media. He generally starts with acrylic and adds oil at the end, in places."

"I see. And his personal life?"

"We've been married for twenty years."

Grace kept her face impassive, but she was bracing herself for the small-talk chatter about kids and family. Grace herself could feel a simmer of anger rising up in her, the thought that someone could easily invade a person's most hurtful life experiences just because it was something they tossed out carelessly as a matter of conversation. Weren't there etiquette police somewhere to tell someone it simply was none of their business? But she supposed even answering it that way gave people a happy little point of gossip they could chew on like an overdone cut of meat.

Within moments, the question came, as Grace knew it would.

"And kids?"

"No."

Grace waited a breath, hoping Margo would move on to another subject.

"No?" Margo made a sad face, much like a child would if they were being told that they couldn't have cookies for dinner. "Didn't want them? He was probably focused on his art, then?"

"We couldn't have them." Grace took a large sip of the

champagne.

"Oh, how sad!"

Margo reached out and grabbed Grace's arm in a bizarre gesture of female solidarity, almost spilling her drink once again in the process.

"But have you tried adoption? My friend adopted a baby from…" She frowned, looking around her, and snapping her fingers, as if someone at the party should run to her, supplying her with the name of the country she groped for. She let out an exasperated breath, finally turning back to Grace with a shrug. "Mambia. Or Zambia. Or Port… swalla… or something like that. She tried for years to get pregnant…"

Grace looked over at John, now at the back of the room snacking on olives by the reception desk. She knew her husband was not into this fuss, but she was getting angry that he had just left her to fend for herself. It was one thing to be artsy and not want to talk to the press. But couldn't he have predicted how this type of mingling would go for Grace? And then she realized, no, he probably couldn't.

She envied the male population, how the question of "Do you have children?" was answered with a simple yes or no before moving on to other subjects. Because women were nurturers; they needed to show you all your options to solve your problem.

"But you're still looking into options, then?"

Margo's pencil was poised above her pad as if hanging on every word of Grace's infertile testimony. She wondered if any of this was going to go into the article she would write about her husband's art, and hoped it wouldn't.

She floated the idea of telling Margo that they were fine, just as they were. It wasn't a lie. But she also had not abandoned the idea of a surrogate or other option. Maybe they would try again with adoption. She'd been thinking of it more and more since she noticed John had cleared the extra room of the ghosts Grace's mind had placed there. But before she could say anything, she felt her husband's hand on her back.

"Excuse me for running off, Margo. You had some questions for me?"

Grace let her back ease into his palm, feeling the comfort of his touch. Just knowing he was there, and she didn't have to stand there alone, made her feel good. She imagined them talking about this later. Maybe she would cry and he would comfort her. Or maybe this time, she would laugh it off, and he would laugh with her.

"Oh, Grace and I were just talking babies." Margo gave her a conspiratorial wink, which she did not return.

"Oh? I thought you had questions about my work, Margo. Perhaps we should stick with that."

Grace felt the pressure in his palm as he said it, as if he were using her to brace himself. She supposed it was what they both did, leaned on the other in order to get through it all.

Margo made a steeple with her fingers and looked at him thoughtfully. "I thought, perhaps... how shall I say this? That this subject has to do with the reason there is so much emotion in your work."

Grace saw a glimmer in her eye then, and realized that she was just doing her job. This was one reason she had longed to have Margo recognize her husband's work, because she could get to the heart of the painter and convey meaning in the work that the average viewer would miss. She never imagined that while Margo was mining for the heart of the painters she profiled, she was also digging up their pain as well. How many times had Grace been attracted to a certain work knowing that a tragedy had inspired it? She had not acknowledged how that painter must have felt having his or her personal anguish put on display, not just in their work but in Margo's profiles as well. She had longed for this moment, for Margo to meet her husband and see his life story, their story, through his paintings. She bitterly wondered how it was that God could grant this wish about her husband's art career rather than the one thing she had wanted with all her being.

"We are good with whatever direction God is leading us."

Grace looked up at him as he said it, without a hint of anger or regret. She wasn't sure she could have pulled that off without her face getting red and sweaty.

Margo considered that for a moment. "And how will your paintings change if you give up, do you think? Is there an element you will leave behind when you change the direction of your desires?"

It was one of those questions Grace always loved about her interviews with painters, but hearing it now felt intrusive.

Grace knew these types of questions would never end. Even when she was long past childbearing years, she'd be jackhammered with questions about *Did you ever have children? No grandchildren? No family at all?*

Every woman Grace met seemed to pound the subject into the ground, with *You'll get pregnant once you adopt* or *You can't give up* or *You'll see, next time will work*: advice that friends and acquaintances tossed before her like landmines disguised as rose petals. Pretty words that blew up the minute they touched anything real. And yet why did Grace herself keep holding this dream in her heart? Why hadn't she just given up and accepted what they had? As long as John was still on board, she was, too.

Margo was still talking, but Grace had tuned her out. She looked down at her drink, watching the bubbles dance before her and wished she could dive into her glass and swallow them all at once.

CHAPTER 24 - JANE

Jane wanted to talk with her dad and clear the air before leaving for Seattle. They had agreed to meet for dinner. He would meet her at her apartment and they'd head over to the restaurant. She got ready and noted that she had some time before he arrived, so she dialed Charlotte's number.

"Hey, Charlotte," she said, as her sister answered. "Only a couple more days now."

"Helloooo," Charlotte called out, acting odder than usual. "How can I help you?"

"How can you help me? Are you all right? It's me, Jane. Can you talk?"

"Yes, well I do want to talk with you. We've got a household full of people here right now." Jane heard laughter and the clinking of glasses in the background. Charlotte lowered her voice. "Hold on a sec. You're never gonna believe this."

She heard Charlotte call out to the group. "Hey, everyone. My sister is calling long distance from

Milwaukee. I'll just be a minute."

She heard muffled conversation and the phone being passed from one person to another, and when Charlotte came back, she was breathless.

"Janey?"

"Yes. What's going on over there?"

"Eric is here. We invited him and his friends over."

"Eric? How did that happen?" A million things rang through Jane's mind. She thought of how fun and engaging Charlotte was, how if Eric liked her sister, he would like Seattle better and never come back to Milwaukee. She shook her head in an effort to focus on what her sister was saying.

"Remember that night I walked in on you two making out?"

Jane snorted. "We just kissed briefly." But she could still feel that kiss on her lips, the way it sparked something in her.

"Right, sure. I just about believe that. When we were all talking, I gave him our number for when he moved, so he would have another couple of people he'd know here besides those friends of his."

"Wayne and Maggie," Jane supplied. "So, has he come by before? Are you friends with Eric now? I mean, not to sound jealous, but... I guess I am. Are Wayne and Maggie there right now, too?"

"You're jealous? I'm glad. Maybe that will motivate you to make some decisions for a change, instead of just waiting for everything to happen to you."

"You sound mad at me."

Charlotte let out a hiss. "Oh shoot, I can never stay mad at you, but yes, I'm a little irked. We invited Eric and those two, Wayne and Maggie, over, and guess who else came? Guess who else decided to fly out from

Milwaukee?"

Jane drew in a breath. "Tiffany?"

"Yes."

"I thought Eric didn't want her in his life anymore."

"Well, that doesn't mean she isn't trying to change that."

Jane put her hand to her forehead, trying to take it all in. "Is she staying there? As in… living there?"

"I don't think so. But she's been dropping hints all night about living with Wayne and Maggie, so maybe that's her plan."

"Oh boy."

"Oh boy, is right. I'm irked at you, Janey. You practically blew him off, and he probably thinks you don't care. Have you even tried to call him since he moved?"

Jane felt a jolt of regret for what she was putting Eric through. All because of her fears. "Only that time I caught him in the airport. Has he talked about me at all?"

"Of course he has! He likes you. When are you going to get that through your head? I have spent the last few days talking about nothing but you."

"Eric!" Charlotte called. "Do you have a minute to talk to Jane? She wants to say hello."

"What? I do not! What are you doing?" Jane hissed at her sister.

She hissed back, "You need to talk to him. *Be nice.* I love you, by the way. I'll call you tomorrow."

Before Jane could say goodbye, Eric picked up the phone.

"Hi, Jane. How are you?" His tone was at least warmer than when she'd caught him in the airport a few weeks before. How was she? She was scared that she had goofed up any chance of being with him; that's how she was.

"Hi, Eric. It's really good to hear your voice," she

found herself saying, surprised at her own boldness. Maybe Charlotte had rubbed off on her. It wouldn't be the worst thing. "Listen, Eric, I'm so sorry about all this. About what you saw with Brad and—"

"I know. Charlotte explained it all to me. She has really helped me see things clearly."

"Oh? What all has she said?"

"Charlotte says you're coming out here soon. Jane, would it be all right if I took you out? Anything you want to do. Seattle really is a beautiful city. I'd like us to spend a little time together. If you're up for it."

"Yes," she said, without overanalyzing for once. "I'd like that."

Jane heard a female voice near the phone. "Eric, who are you talking to? Come back to the party. We're talking about the firemen's' picnic next week. I've taken off work, so I can stay and go with you guys. Isn't that great?"

Tiffany?

"Look, Jane," Eric came back on the line. "I have to go."

With that, he hung up.

Jane stared at the phone for a full minute. She might have stayed that way all night if her father hadn't knocked on her door for their scheduled dinner.

"Hi, there, daughter of mine." He leaned over and gave her a kiss on the cheek. He had on a dingy, old sports coat, jeans, and a cream-colored T-shirt. Jane remembered the jacket from years ago. She and Charlotte had given it to him for Father's Day one year.

"I just talked to Charlotte," she told him. To her surprise, she filled him in on everything, her upcoming trip, her job, and even Eric. She hadn't realized how badly she'd wanted to talk to him about it all until that moment. So often, their conversations were about his inventions rather than her life.

"Is it serious?"

All the things she'd just told him and the only thing he picked out of the conversation was Eric.

She pulled on his arm. "Come on, Dad, let's grab some dinner. We can talk about my love life later," she laughed. "You're as bad as Charlotte."

"That bad, huh?" He chuckled.

They walked to the parking lot, where he usually left his car.

"Where'd you park?" She looked around the lot and onto the street.

"I had to park farther down. Why don't we go in your car instead?"

She agreed, pulling the keys from her purse. She wondered if he knew Charlotte was in town a few weeks before, and asked him.

"Yes, she called me. Said you needed some sister time, so she was devoting the entire stay to that. I understood."

"You did?" She'd have been upset if Charlotte had flown all the way out to see their dad and not her. "I think I would have been hurt if she hadn't made time for me."

"Well, it's different for you two. You've always been tight. That's good. I always wanted my girls to be friends, and I'm glad you are. Charlotte did call me, and we had a nice chat. She said she was worried about you, and I'm afraid I might be part of the reason why."

Jane wasn't sure what to say. She had planned to bring

up the issue of his multiple loan requests at dinner, but since he'd mentioned it, she followed his lead.

"I wish I could give you money, Dad. I wish I had more of it. But I don't."

"I didn't know you were taking out loans from the bank for that. I'm sorry."

They were quiet as they pulled up to the restaurant. "We're here. Remember this place?" Jane had taken them to a tiny hole-in-the-wall pub that served a Wednesday night fish fry.

"I sure do. Boy, this brings back some fine memories. We used to come here for a fish fry because your mom was working Friday nights for a while."

"I was thinking about it the other day. Let's grab a seat."

They sat and he held up his glass of water to clink with hers.

"To old times."

"Old times." She imagined her view of her childhood was probably very different than his. "Do you miss the past, Dad? I mean, from when we were kids?"

"I miss you girls being little. That was so much fun. I miss some of the Christmas dinners and just being part of a family. It's rough being on your own at my age."

Jane hadn't thought of her father as single until that moment. She guessed that it was probably very lonely for him sometimes. "Do you ever date at all, Dad? We're always talking about my love life. I haven't even thought to ask how you're doing."

The corners of his mouth tugged into a smile. "I do date sometimes. Yes. But I don't have much luck with any of the lovely ladies I know wanting to stay with me for very long. Seems I'm not very much of a catch."

She wasn't sure what to say. She thought maybe she

could help him figure it all out, but she didn't want to offend him, either. "Why do you think that is, Dad?" She looked down at her napkin and then adjusted the silverware in front of her.

"Oh, I suppose it's because I'm not made of money. Women can be so fickle nowadays."

Jane weighed her options. She wanted to tell him straight out that his "tinkering" without a job probably turned women off. She wondered if he was even asking the women he dated for money.

"You know, Dad," she ventured, "at first, I was not interested in Eric. I didn't want to get to know him, even though he lived right in my building. I assumed that he didn't have a job, and then it just turned me off because"— she paused, not wanting to tell her dad it was because of him—"because I wanted him to be solid. You know? Like, someone that took care of himself. But then, after a while, he explained to me that his company had downsized, and he was taking some time to figure out what he wanted to do. That's why he's in Seattle, actually. He has joined the fire department out there, along with a friend of his."

"Well, it's good that he has a job now. Being out of work is hard, but he's gotta suck it up."

She looked for signs that he might be joking, but her father was serious. Thankfully, the food came at that moment. They dug in and were quiet, savoring the first taste of their meal.

"Great fish fry," her dad commented between bites.

"Yeah, it is. Dad, Eric actually has a job. He's going to be a firefighter in Seattle," she repeated, thinking he hadn't heard her. "He's been training for it for several months."

Her father chewed his piece of rye bread, eyeing her carefully. "Seattle, you say? So, are you moving with him?"

"No, Dad. I mean, we aren't dating. I can't think about

it right now. I still have my job. I dunno…" She hated being asked that over and over. She was unsure, for many reasons, and she doubted her father would get the hint.

"Well, if you ask me, I wouldn't move to Seattle if I were you."

This actually surprised her. Everyone else had told her she should go. "Why do you say that?"

"Well, you've got a good job. What if this thing with his fire department doesn't work out? Then you're stuck. You need someone with a job. Someone reliable."

The irony was too much. "Dad, why are you saying this?"

"Well, I mean, it's not like with me, where he's trying to accomplish something big, and that's why he's not working a traditional job. He's got dreams of being a firefighter, but what if that doesn't work out? What's he going to try next?"

"Dad"—she put her fork down, hoping she would use the right words—"it's not like he's *trying* different things. This is what he's wanted to do for a long time. He's been volunteering at the fire department here for months. He worked in a job that wasn't right for him, and he gave it a lot of thought. This isn't some flash-in-the-pan thing."

"Okay, okay." Her father put his hands up. "I'm sorry. I shouldn't have said that. I just don't want to see my little girl hurt."

She resisted the urge to tell him his influence had almost ruined things completely between her and Eric. Her assumption of Eric's job status went beyond the normal, and it was partly because of her history with her father. But as he spoke, one thing bothered her.

"Dad, did you get rid of your car?"

"Yes."

He finished the last of his fish fry, took a forkful of

coleslaw, and pushed his plate away.

She had the weird sense that something was up when he had asked her to drive. "Why?"

"I needed the money, Jane. I told you, I'm very close on this one. The Boomeralk is going to be huge. You can doubt me if you want. Your mother certainly did. But she's going to be eating her words."

"But how will you get to work? I mean, are you working right now?" She realized how little she knew about her dad's finances. She knew he always needed money, but he couldn't live on what she gave him, alone.

He shrugged. "I get by. Your mother's maintenance gives me some. I get some from odd jobs—"

"What a minute, Mom pays you maintenance?"

"Yes. I thought you knew that. I was a stay-at-home parent. That's the way it is."

She saw how different their views really were then. He wasn't a stay-at-home parent at the choice of their mom. She always wanted him to get a job, and they had grandparents that could help out. But in his mind, he was at home waiting for his kids to get home from school. Funny how we all lived in our own reality, she thought.

CHAPTER 25 - GRACE

John was in his studio. They still hadn't talked about the reception from the night before. They had come home exhausted, went straight to bed, and in the morning went about their routine again. As she entered the studio, she was surprised to see a canvas filled with sunny colors of red and yellow, a grouping of flowers on a table.

"Still life?"

He stepped back and looked at the painting, as if for the first time. "I guess you could say that. How are you?" He put his brush down and embraced her, then kissed her. He asked her again. "How are you?"

She knew what he meant. Not just how was your day but how are you surviving? Will you be okay? Margo's questioning had shaken her a bit, but after all the disappointments they had endured, it was easy to move on. Grace had decided that no matter what Margo managed to write about her husband's work, it was something that she just couldn't worry about. She had finally learned that some things weren't worth the weight of carrying them along with you.

She wondered how often they'd had to ask each other this question over the years. How often she thought she couldn't go on as things were, but then again there they were, together still. Still in love. Still happy, despite the pain.

"I'm okay. What do you want for dinner?" She mentally went through the list of what they had. Leftover meatloaf. A warmed-up boxed meal. She could always whip up an omelet and pancakes if it came to that.

"We'll think of something."

He studied her, hesitating on what to say next. She knew him too well for that.

"What?"

He let out a breath. "Grace. I love you."

Oh dear, where was this going? A declaration of love could mean something good or something so awful, she wouldn't be able to recover. She feared it was the latter.

"Yes. I know you do. I love you, too."

He gestured to the small table he had in the corner, an old flea-market find they'd picked up for ten dollars. Two rickety wooden chairs they'd found along the way were on each side. He moved a jar where he kept water in for his brushes, to the side, and sat in one of the chairs. He smiled at her sadly as he pulled out the other chair.

She wanted to get angry suddenly. Demand that he spit it out, whatever it was. But she couldn't. She feared his next words so deeply that it prevented her from speaking.

"Honey…" He took her hand, and for the first time, she noticed the tears in his eyes. Were they there when she came in? "I love our life, Grace. I love it, exactly as it is."

She felt herself relax a bit. "Of course, honey. I love our life, too."

"I love us. You and me. This life we have built. The family that we are together."

Tension eased from Grace's shoulders. She felt herself sit up straighter, and smiled at him. He was so sweet. "Yeah. Me, too. I'm happy with our life together." Who could deny that they were happy? They had a strong marriage and were best friends. It was something she didn't see in all marriages, and she didn't think about it too closely, but yes, she was lucky for that.

The tears streamed harder down his face. Grace frowned.

"I can't do this anymore, Grace. I can't. Not one more time. How many times has it been? How many times have we placed our hope out there? I can't… I can't…"

He sobbed into his hands. She knew she should comfort him but her anger took over. "You can't what? What are you talking about?"

"I can't keep chasing this dream, Grace. It's all we've done. In twenty years, we haven't taken a vacation. We've accumulated so much debt. We're broke."

"But we're making it work. It's working—"

"We've made it work. We live frugally. Both of us. But Grace, aren't you tired? Are you feeling it now? This tiredness. This—"

"Stop saying 'tired.' What are you trying to declare here? That you don't want children? That—"

"That I like what we have, Grace. That I want us. I choose us, and whatever that means. I have always been grateful for you and me. For what we have."

She got up then, paced around the room. She knew it irritated him, but she couldn't help it. He reached for her arm and she pulled away.

"And what?" She felt her voice rising. "That you're just done? What does that even mean?"

"Grace. Let's be realistic here. We're in our forties now. We need to think about what's next. As it is, we'll never be able to retire. But we can still have a good life."

She stared at him, the finality of his words putting a stop to her dreaming of possibilities.

"Okay, so we won't try international again. That was a mistake. It was just bad luck. But we can do—"

"I'm spent emotionally, too, Grace. Money is part of it. How are we supposed to pay to raise a child? College? How about regular expenses? Grace, we're tapped out. We're more than tapped out. This is it for us, Grace. We have to accept this."

"You said cost." She was repeating herself now, trying to add up figures in her head.

"It costs *here*." He pounded his chest. "*Here*, Grace! I can't do it again. I can't get my hopes up again."

Her voice had turned to pleading. "We have had bad luck. More than once. I'll give you that. But it's not going to be like that again. It can't. Everyone says if you want to have kids, you will. It's just—"

"Well, *everyone*... These fools who give us advice, are *wrong!*" He was shouting now. "I don't know why people comment on this. I don't know why we are constantly defending ourselves to anyone. People just don't know.

They repeat things they hear. They know one couple that does this, one couple that does that. But they don't know us. They don't know what we've been through!"

He was following her pacing, like slow-motion chasing. She didn't know who was chasing whom at this point.

"But look..." She needed to calm him down. Get him to see reason. "You're just disappointed. I get that. I am, too. It's all I've been able to think about—"

"That's just it, Grace. It's all we've been able to think about. It's like our lives have been on hold for twenty years. We have to face facts. And, Grace, come on, it's not so hard to settle into this life we have, is it? We're good together. We're happy, happier than most every couple we know, and we're a family, you and me, even if we don't have children."

She wanted to slap him. To place her hand across his face so hard, it would leave a mark. But she couldn't. She knew how much he hurt because she hurt the same way.

"And so, what? Every idiot on the face of the earth can be a parent, can be a shitty parent, but we can't get a try at it?"

He reached for her again, but she pulled away. "Don't, Grace." His voice was soft. Full of love. "Don't go down this road."

But she was already on the way. "And so God can give all the horrible people who treat kids badly and abuse them, they can all have children, but not me, huh? I'm not good enough for that?"

"You know that's not how it goes. You can't be mad at God."

"Oh, I can! I can be as mad at Him as I want to be!"

"It's not God's fault, Grace. It's not ours. It's not even those shitty parents who don't understand the gift they have. It's not the people who are arrogant about parenting, who think they're better than other people." He put his hands on her arms. She remained stock still. "It's not anyone's fault, Grace."

She couldn't look at him. It was her fault. Of course, it was. She couldn't have children. God hadn't made her that way. Apparently, God didn't love her enough for that. But she knew better than to say it out loud. She didn't want John to pity her.

She stood before his painting and pointed at it. "I don't understand it. How you can so readily put your pain out there for the whole world this way. You can paint your feelings, and everyone can see them and feel them, and how is that okay? That is just fine with you. But you can't put your hope out there. You can't do the same thing with your hope!"

He stood slowly and came toward her. His voice was measured and low. "My pain, and my hope… they are one in the same, Grace."

Grace spent the rest of the week in a haze. She couldn't have imagined everything she and John had been through when they first met and fell in love. Back then, before their problems trying to have kids, before the debt, before the way her body was put through so much… *before, before,*

before. Back then, everything was open; everything was a possibility. When they saw friends who had kids, they'd smile at each other, both of them thinking *that's our future.* How could they have known what their future would be. How can anyone?

She knew John was probably in his studio, painting madly, while she headed for the bedroom. She opened her laptop and tried to work. Then closed it. This was a new kind of grief for her, one where she missed John even though he was in the next room.

They'd spent the last week like this, for the first time ever in their marriage. She couldn't remember a time when they hadn't found each other across the plane of their grief and held on tight, giving one another all the strength and love they had. They hadn't sought each other out, and that angered and scared her. And yet, she couldn't bring herself to approach him. She didn't want to have the conversation, didn't want to hear him say it again… she just couldn't.

The only sounds came from the daily habits of their lives, brushing teeth, taking showers, mentioning the small details they needed to know, but no conversation, nothing real. Before she left to do her errands, she had just told him she was running out and he had said fine. He didn't ask where she was going and she didn't volunteer.

She was in their bedroom and picked out an outfit for tonight. Did he even remember? The PR she'd done to help promote his exhibit paid off, and Bug had called her, asking if John would come to the gallery and meet with a second group of buyers. They were still waiting for Margo's article, but in the meantime the other PR efforts she had done increased the visibility of John's art. She had done her job in getting him noticed, and he had done his in painting something wonderful.

They made a great team. In work, in life, they just did. It pained her to be like this with him. She liked the life they had created. The realization descended on her like a thick fog. She needed and wanted him. He was her best friend.

She stood from the bed, realizing she'd still had her shoes on. She kicked them off, sending them with a clunk into the wall. She always took them off so daintily, as if the noise of removing them was too much for their sweet little house. Well, she wanted to make noise now. That's what she wanted most of all.

She marched into the studio, expecting to see him lost in his work, caring more about his paintings than he did about trying again, about her, about their family. All that time in the studio, all that time creating little worlds on canvas with people who were unlike them, people who could have children because their world was make-believe. She could pretend those people in the paintings John created were anything. They could be parents; they could fly; they could turn into anything and live anywhere. It was a world outside of this one, and she envied that.

She purposely made her steps loud on the hallway floor, *stomp stomp stomp* into the room, where she opened the door and saw... nothing. He wasn't there. Disappointment and relief flooded her. She closed the door, wondering if this was how easily a marriage could unravel. Just tug on one cord, a small one that is wrapped up in the beginnings of your life together, so one good jerk could make it all fall to pieces.

Grace heard the front door open and walked into the kitchen. He had bags of groceries in his arms and placed them on the counter.

She waited for him to say something. So, this is how it was going to be? He started putting things away as if it were the most normal thing in the world. They'd shared so much, and for her to have this rage inside her alone seemed very disconsolate. He opened the cupboard and placed two boxes of cereal in, then closed it quietly. He opened the fridge to add some fruit into the crisper and gently pushed it closed. It was enough to drive her mad.

"Where were you?"

Her voice sounded hollow, as if she were by herself, talking to a ghost.

He stopped putting items away, but she could see him thinking. He had the butter in his hand, and she could picture him placing it in the door of the fridge without a word of response. Instead, he placed it on the kitchen island and leaned forward, his knuckles taking the brunt of his weight.

"I was at the grocery store."

He said it without a hint of irony, without the usual humor they shared. She knew it was a dumb question, but that wasn't the point.

"You couldn't leave a note?"

She expected him to shrug, to move his stance, but he remained in position, like a boxer training his entire life for that one fight that will make or break him.

"I thought I would be home before you got back." His tone was even, and even more annoying, *fair*. She hadn't said when she was going to be back and had probably given the impression that she'd be gone a lot longer than she was.

"I would have appreciated a note, all the same."

He took his hands off the island and placed them at his sides. "Okay. I'm sorry."

She waited and so did he. It was like a gunfight, who would flinch first, who would draw their weapon and fire a bullet of truth, something about their age and money and how long they had been trying and heartbreak. The same old discussions, the things they both thought about constantly but tried to pretend weren't at the forefront of their minds.

He picked up the butter off the island and placed it in the fridge.

"Thank you for grocery shopping," she said kindly, and it came out of her mouth before she could stop it. They'd both always been so courteous to each other over the years, recognizing the small things each of them did in the minutia of their lives. He thanked her for making the bed; she said please and thank you when he asked if there was anything he could get her before they sat down to watch TV. Over and over, they made it a point to show gratitude for every small thing, and it had made her feel comforted and blessed, despite everything else that might be weighing them down.

He closed the fridge and stood before her, looking miserable. She wanted to reach out and step into those arms that had held her for twenty years. They had been strong enough to heal her spirit time and time again, but she paused, unable to take the step forward. He looked like he wanted to say something, his mouth making the movements of a sentence that she knew, without a doubt, she did not want to hear.

"I don't want to talk about it," she warned him. His body seemed to pause, and finally he nodded.

"We don't have to. Not right now."

She wanted to scream, *not ever!* But she changed the subject again.

"Do you have your outfit ready?" She glanced at the clock on the microwave. "We need to leave in about an hour."

He frowned at her. Of course, he had forgotten. She'd not been speaking to him the last week, and therefore she wasn't continually reminding him day after day, *Did you get your outfit? Remember we have the party on Saturday? Did you gas up the car?* Oh, how that ticked her off. That man! His forgetfulness.

"The. Party," she said through gritted teeth. "For. *You.*"

The look of recognition on his face almost made her laugh. He remembered then, and it was clear a party, even for his own art, was the last place he wanted to be.

"Right," he said quietly. "Of course."

He walked past her, squeezing her arm, something she'd probably do for a coworker who just found out about some bad news. She felt exhausted suddenly, but there was no way she was canceling this. This was something they'd both worked for, and they would show up for it and manage to enjoy it, even though things in their life weren't perfect.

They drove to the gallery in silence. When they arrived, he spoke.

"What is the name of this guy again? The one who owns this place?"

Her exasperation rose to the surface. Did she have to tell him everything five times?

"*Bug*," she said simply. She opened the door to get out of the car, and he put his hand on her leg.

"Grace."

She closed the door. Folded her arms. Waited.

"If you want to try again, we can. I had no right to just paint over everything without talking to you. To make a decision like that without you. I'm so sorry."

Her tears fell, and she angrily wiped at them. She agreed with him. "I'm sorry, too." And she was, at everything that had brought them to this moment. "I have missed you this week."

"I'm here, Grace." He took her hand. "I'm here, and I always will be."

"Do you hate me for not being able to have children?" she burst out, angry with herself for crying.

"My God! No! Why are you carrying this, Grace? I don't even think about that. Do you not realize that? *You* are the only one that does—that voice you hear in your head? The one that tells you this is some kind of punishment? It is not from God!"

"Oh," she said bitterly, "we're going to bring Him into the conversation, are we?"

"Yes," he said. "You want to know why? Because *circumstances* and *people* have been against us. Friends have not been there, and they've made it even harder. We don't have extended family. And it is as simple as that. And do you know what? I have not regretted marrying you ever. Not once! I love you, and nothing in our lives, *nothing* has made me regret it."

Her tears flowed freely then. "I've never regretted marrying you, either. I can't imagine my live without you. I actually get up every single day and thank God for you." She surprised herself at the truth in it. She looked at him. "Really. I do."

He smirked. "So, you *do* talk to Him, then?"

She playfully slapped his arm. "Most of it is angry talk, but yes."

"He can take angry talk. You know—"

"I really do not care to have a big faith discussion right now, in this car. And thank you," she said, looking in the mirror, "for making me cry. I look like crap now."

He took her hand and kissed it. "You look like the beautiful girl I married two decades ago."

"Oh"—she shook her head—"shush. I do not."

He looked at her a long moment. "I wish you could see yourself as I do. Or better yet, as God does."

"Right. Well, let's not push it, okay? You ready to get in there"—she nodded toward the gallery—"and talk about art?" she said with exaggerated excitement.

"Any chance we can run home and have make-up sex?"

"Not right now." She grinned at him.

"Then, I'm ready."

CHAPTER 26 - JANE

Jane had a late flight out to Seattle, but she was packed and ready to go early that morning. This trip had meant more to Jane than she first realized. She'd been hanging on to anger because Charlotte had moved away from her, and it was only now that she saw how petty it was.

She wondered if she would ever feel like a mature, confident woman. She longed to be like Mrs. Ferch, who would wave her hand at unpleasantries as if wiping them away without a second thought.

Jane paced her apartment, feeling restless. Her bags were packed, but she still changed her outfit three times. Why was she nervous? She hated her hair, for one. That morning she had put her long, blonde hair in a clip. Then braided it. Then left it down. No matter how she fixed it, she didn't like the way it looked. She'd been bored with it, putting it up in clips and ponytails. She wanted to do something different.

She looked at the clock and saw that there was plenty of time to get a haircut. She pictured herself with a cute, new cut for this new phase of her life, where she did things like take vacation days she had coming to her. She laughed at herself. Even small changes seemed huge to her, especially after she'd spent years holding her breath, waiting for Brad to propose and waiting for Bug to promote her. A new haircut seemed like the right next step.

It had been years since she'd been to a stylist. She had shoulder-length hair and just trimmed it herself now and then. She wasn't even sure where to go at first, then she remembered seeing a shop just around the corner from the apartment. Jane looked them up and they could take her right away.

She printed off a picture of a celebrity she spotted recently and headed out to the salon. On the way, she knocked on Mrs. Ferch's door.

"Come in," she called out.

Mrs. Ferch was reading a book in her big chair by the window. She smiled at Jane.

"I'm heading out. Getting a haircut. Need anything while I'm out?"

"Oh, how nice, a haircut. No, dear, I'm good, but stop and show me before you go. I want to see your new 'do.'" She frowned. "Don't you leave today?"

"Later. I have an evening flight."

"Oh." The woman put her glasses up on her head and put her book down. "I meant to tell you; I spoke with Grace. She seems like a doll! We are meeting here tomorrow. I invited her over for coffee."

Coffee. Jane chuckled to herself. Mrs. Ferch did love her coffee maker.

They said their goodbyes, and Jane headed to the salon. The girl assigned to Jane was about her age, with a beautiful round face and cute spiky brown hair that had a pink streak in the bangs. Somehow, she'd managed to make it look hip but still tasteful. Jane handed the girl the picture she'd printed off and told her that's what she wanted.

"See how her bangs are angled like that? I like that. And the length is way shorter. I need a change."

"Uh-huh. Okay." The girl tossed the picture aside and spritzed her hair with water. "I'm Jasmine," she said without a smile. Jane noticed her blue eyes were rimmed in red.

"Jane. Nice to meet you. Are you, um… okay?" she said, not really knowing how to make small talk with her. Jane wondered if she sucked at small talk in general.

"What? Oh, fine. Sure, yeah." The girl's tone was bitter. "Fine." She put a hand to her belly, and for the first time Jane noticed she was pregnant.

"Well," Jane continued, wincing as the girl tugged at her hair, "you looked a little upset. If you don't mind my saying."

"Yeah. I am. Sorry." She put a tissue up to her eyes, and Jane awkwardly rubbed the girl's arm. "It's just… never mind." She seemed to gather herself, taking a deep breath and putting the tissue in her pocket. "Put your head down, please."

Jane did as the girl asked. She heard the snips of hair coming off, but the stylist was quiet. "Okay," she tried again. It was hard to talk when she was facing down. "I'm, uh… flying out to see my sister today. Haven't been out to visit her since she moved." It had been a while since Jane was in a salon, but from what she remembered, the stylists usually yakked the whole time while Jane remained quiet. This felt odd.

"Head to the side, please," she said, pushing Jane's head in the direction she wanted. She heard lots of snipping from the scissors. "Seeing your sister? That's cool. Head to the other side."

She pushed Jane's head the other way, which hurt. "Yeah, um… well, there's a guy out there, too. I have a date planned with him." She was trying not to think about it too much, but the fact that Eric had suggested they go out was encouraging to her. She missed him.

"Oh, a date," she girl said between snips. "Cool. Yeah, cool. But just wait… just wait until you fall in love with him, and you get married, and you try for a baby, and you get pregnant, and then when you're six months pregnant, just wait… Turn your head the other way again, please."

The girl pushed Jane's head to the other side. More snipping.

"Then, when you're six months pregnant, and your sister-in-law throws you a shower, you get pulled aside by some woman who says she's slept with your husband. While you were *pregnant*. And when you confront him, all he can do is ask how you found out. That's it! 'How'd ya find that out, honey?' That's it. No denial. *Nothing*."

She twirled the chair around quickly so Jane faced her.

"I'm going to trim your bangs. That's what you wanted, right?" Before Jane could answer, she heard scissors quickly fly around her face: *snip snip snip*…

Jane closed her eyes and pictured Edward Scissorhands.

"Then," Jasmine went on, "you ask why. *Why*! He says it's because, duh, you got fat. *Fat*! That's what he called it.

Not pregnant. Not, having a baby. *Pregnant.*" She pumped the chair so it went down and pulled out a hair dryer. Jane's hair whipped around her face, and again, she closed her eyes. Jasmine had a brush and scraped it against Jane's head as she used the blow-dryer. *Tug, tug, tug.* It hurt. Jane wondered if Jasmine was picturing her husband at that moment.

"I'm sorry that happened to you. That's awful." Jane winced as another tug pulled her head to the side.

"Yeah, well... just don't ever fall in love. That's all I can say." Jasmine turned the chair around so Jane could face the mirror. "It's a little shorter than you're probably used to, but change is good. Embrace it. You can pay at the front." Jasmine stomped off to the back room, leaving Jane staring at the worst haircut she'd ever received in her life.

She put up her hand to her head. Her hair was gone. Her bangs were ragged, inches above her eyebrows. The sides were at a weird angle, not even the same length. It was too short to put up, and there was no way she could cover it up. She wanted to cry, but she was too stunned.

She got up from the chair and noticed the piles of blonde hair on the floor. Her hair. The hair she was bored with. How she wished she could glue it all back on.

Jane went back home, letting out a huge sigh as she knocked on Mrs. Ferch's door.

"I'm back," she called out.

Mrs. Ferch came around the corner from the back bedroom. "Hello! Oh… my…"

The older woman stopped short at the sight of Jane's hair.

"I know. It's awful." Jane ran her hand to where her hair used to be, and was shocked that once again it wasn't there. She'd been doing that all the way home.

"Is that"—Mrs. Ferch motioned to her head—"the… um… *look* you were going for?"

"No. It's really as awful as I think, isn't it?"

"Oh, now." Mrs. Ferch gave her that familiar wave of her hand. "Hair is hair. It grows back. No biggie."

"No biggie?" Hysterical laughter filled the room. It didn't even sound like it was coming from Jane, but it was. "No biggie?" She sat down, laughing and crying at the same time. She turned to Mrs. Ferch. "You think Eric is going to hate it?"

"Eric likes you," she said too quickly. "Hair is hair. It grows back."

"Right. He's going to hate it."

"But he likes *you*."

"Charlotte told me Eric wanted to take me to a barbeque while we there. To meet his friends Wayne and Maggie."

"Oh." The older woman sat down at the kitchen table. "Well… hair is—"

"Hair. Yeah."

"Yeah." The woman patted her leg. "You'll be fine. You wanted a change. You just use your attitude to convey that. You are in control."

Jane reached at the back of her neck again, surprised that all her hair was gone. "What?"

"It's all in how you carry yourself. Sure, it's not the best cut, but who cares? You got a cute guy on your arm, and he likes you. You are a beautiful girl with a sister who loves you, and you are smart and—"

"Okay. I get it. I guess I just need to get my head around this."

"Get your head around it." Mrs. Ferch slapped her knee and laughed. "See? Like that. You make a joke of it. You're in control."

"I wasn't joking. But I see what you mean. It's just hair. Some people lose their hair. I still have hair. It's just..." She ran her hands through her short, ragged bangs. "It's just a little shorter than usual. And uglier."

Mrs. Ferch waved her hands in front of her like someone trying to stop traffic. "Don't say uglier. Say... *chic.*"

"Chic. There, I said it. But will Eric?"

"Sure he will."

"We'll see."

Jane went upstairs to call Charlotte.

"Janey! I was just thinking about you."

"Were you thinking of me with incredibly short, uneven, ragged hair?"

"Oh no. What happened?"

"Here…" Jane snapped a selfie with her phone and sent it to her sister. "I'll show you."

Charlotte was quiet. Finally, she said. "You're beautiful. Doesn't matter."

"Matters!" she yelled so loud; she didn't recognize her own voice.

"What happened?"

"I got a stylist who was angry that her husband was cheating on her."

"Ouch. That's rough."

"While she is pregnant."

"Awful!" Charlotte said, and Jane could picture the anguish on her sister's face. She was someone who could sit and cry with someone or enjoy their stories and laugh. She really had a knack with people. Jane wondered if it was their upbringing that made her so empathetic, and if it were, why was Jane so reserved all the time?

"Well," Charlotte added, "I hope you didn't tip her at least. I know she's going through something, but wow…"

"Come to think of it, I gave her twenty percent." Jane ran her hands over the back of her head again. Maybe if she willed it to come back, it would.

"Janey!" Charlotte was laughing now, in that really hard way that told Jane she wished she could make it better for her. Jane remembered that laugh. She'd heard it many times over the years. When their father announced that they'd be having turkey for Christmas dinner and came home with four microwave meals for them instead. Or when he invented a new way to wash clothes that ended up shredding the only two dresses Charlotte and Jane owned. When things were bleak and Jane wanted to cry, Charlotte would somehow get her to laugh instead. It's how they kept going.

"*Edward Scissorhands.*" Jane was laughing now, too. "That's what I kept thinking of. Remember that movie?"

"I do. That was when Johnny Depp was hot. Was she going as fast as Edward Scissorhands?"

"Yes. I'm lucky I still have both my eyeballs."

They were both laughing so hard now that Jane had tears in her eyes. She was thankful they were from extreme joy rather than sadness.

"Mrs. Ferch kept saying 'hair is hair.'"

"Hair is hair. It grows back. A quarter of an inch a month."

Jane stopped short. "That's *it*? Are you serious? At that rate…" she looked at her bangs and tried to calculate how many months it would take to even get them to her eyebrows.

"Or maybe I have that wrong," Charlotte quickly amended. "Maybe it's like *half* an inch. Or an inch. Yeah, that's probably it. An *inch*."

"Nice try, Charlotte. But the worst part? Eric is taking me out. I wanted to look nice for him. He wants me to meet those friends of his. His *friends*." She cringed, hoping Tiffany was not part of the friend group.

"Oh, Janey…"

"I know." Jane paced in front of the mirror in her room. "And to think, just a couple weeks ago, my promotion and Dad's loan were the only things I was thinking about."

"Puts things in a new perspective. Look, we'll have a blast here. Sally is so excited; she even cleaned her room. Do you know how often that happens? Never. Bill even bought a brand-new bed for the guest room. We just cannot wait for you to be here. And Eric has been talking nonstop about it."

"You guys bought a new bed for me? Thank you for that. I mean, you didn't have to—"

"Oh, stop it. We love you. It feels like we've just been holding our breath, waiting for you, for years."

Jane ran her hands through her hair again, then pulled them away. "You know what's funny? I just thought the same thing. That I was holding my breath for things here, like my promotion and Brad's proposal. And I got both. But, what you're saying, is different."

"Like a satisfying exhale instead of one where you catch your breath and try again."

Jane sat down on her bed, smiling. "You really have a poetic way of looking at things."

"Thank you, Jane! You know what? I have actually been writing poetry again."

Her sister never ceased to amaze her. "I'm glad. You were always really good at it."

"You're sweet. The point is, you will enjoy your time here so much, you'll just forget about everything else. I know you will."

"It's not just that. The other things is… you know how this kind of stuff is for me. With new people? His friends? I'm not very good at all that. I hate big crowds." She felt the whininess coming back into her voice. "I'm not good at this party stuff."

"It's not your thing, that's true. You never liked big crowds. Remember Bruce Kerry's party when we were kids? You went off in a corner by yourself while the rest of us played musical chairs. Then you hung out with the family dog."

"That was an awesome dog. I was jealous that they had one."

"You're wired differently. But that's okay, Janey; it's who you are."

"It's who I am, but how am I going to do this? I feel uncomfortable at parties even when I know everyone there. I kind of just wanted to get to know Eric, one on one. Besides, what if they don't like me?" She put her hands over her eyes, feeling overwhelmed at the prospect of meeting new people.

"If they don't like you, they're nuts, because Eric does."

"Why are you saying all the right things?"

"Because I am the big sister, and I'm always right."

They said their goodbyes, and Jane stood before the mirror once more. She seemed to be looking for things to worry about. Eric's friends. Eric. A party. Her hair. Her stupid hair. She fussed with it, but it was no use. It would take months for it to grow out, and there was nothing she could do about it now. She might as well just embrace it.

CHAPTER 27 - GRACE

John? Grace? Nice to see you both again," Bug greeted them warmly as they walked in the gallery. Grace noticed they had rearranged John's paintings. The Space Between Dreaming was now hung on the wall right when you walked in. As she saw it, she was surprised to find herself pausing again, pulled into the image. She could almost feel it speak to her.

"You changed things up."

"Yes." Bug ushered them in and followed her gaze. "We try to rearrange things at least once a month in the gallery. I've moved some of your work to the front, and the rest to this side area." They followed Bug as he showed them the rest of the work. Their new arrangement seemed to highlight different aspects of the paintings, the light hitting them in certain spots, which made Grace walk up to them to get a closer look.

"Looks great," John said. "Thanks for all this, uh... Bug."

Grace giggled to herself that he was having a hard time calling Jane's boss that. Jane assured both of them it's what he preferred.

John and Bug went off to discuss the sales he'd had, and Grace thought she overheard Bug ask for more paintings. She was happy that his work was getting recognized. She walked back to The Space Between Dreaming and just stared at it for a long while.

One of Jane's coworkers hovered a bit at first and then walked away. Grace knew it took a special person to sell people art. You couldn't be too intrusive. You had to allow people to see the work, to feel it, and then to picture it in their homes. It was unlike selling other merchandise, and often involved people coming back again and again before they bought a certain painting to take home.

The gallery worker seemed to sense that she just needed some alone time with the painting, even if she didn't understand the reason. How could Grace explain that this painting had invaded her mind somehow, leaving its own fingerprints all over her face and breath. She couldn't stop thinking about this work. From the moment her husband had finished it, the image had lingered.

Last night, she had dreamed of it. The woman who reached out in the night with those eyes, which she had once thought looked like a plea for help, now begged her to pay attention. The woman whispered, *wake up, wake up, wake up…*

And Grace woke up. She shook at the image she saw in her dreams, so very real, it was frightening. She sat up, trying to understand what it all meant, and found that she was shivering in her bed. Her husband awoke, thinking she was cold, and threw a blanket over her. She didn't shake from the cold, but from a desperation that had left her hollowed out and empty inside.

Grace was glad The Space Between Dreaming had not sold yet. After her argument with John, she felt a need to see it again, to stand before it and find out what it had to say to her.

She felt someone behind her and noticed that the gallery worker had placed a chair there. She looked for the girl, who had walked away. Grace smiled to herself at the kindness of it. She turned to see where the girl had gone and caught sight of herself in a mirror that sat on the floor of the gallery. What Grace saw surprised her. She was frowning and had fully thought she was smiling. Was it just on the inside? Was that even possible?

She shook her head, the confusion of the day continuing. How could someone look so unhappy on the outside yet feel a sense of comfort inside? Or vice versa? How could the way she felt and act be so very different from each other?

Grace turned back to the painting, staring at it for a long time, allowing her mind to go places it hadn't before. She thought of her marriage, of the two of them together, their life filled with everyday tasks, of holding hands at farmers' markets, of art shows displaying his art, of nightly dinners and morning breakfasts. She thought of the way he touched her back as he led her to a seat at a restaurant, or how he kissed her tears away when she opened up her heart and showed him the hurt places that were too stubborn to heal. She thought of the two of them, over and over, doing nothing more than being happy together.

She walked up close to the painting, looking at the brushstrokes and fingerprints. He had left his mark on this work, and even if this woman was her, she felt okay with it. She reached forward and touched it. You weren't supposed to do that, but somehow, she couldn't help it. And just like that day when she'd touched it in his studio, she could envision a different life for them. The same life, yet one without the emotional weight of wanting and trying and wishing for something different. She sat back down, and for the first time, felt she could let go of the dream she had wanted, to let it fall from her grasp so she could finally hold whatever it was that life, that God, wanted her to embrace next.

Grace sat at the kitchen island, sipping coffee, and looking out over the backyard. She loved this house, truly, but there were also times when she longed for a change. This house held expectations. It held pain. She put down her mug and walked to Glenn's room. And that's how she thought of it. That's how she would always think of it, despite that he had never lived to see it, to sleep a single night in the crib they had bought. She opened the door, seeing the room again with fresh eyes: the lack of furniture, the white walls. It was John's way of sending a message to her. She didn't get it then. Didn't want to get it.

She sat on the lone chair in that room and thought about everything. She was tired. It wasn't just the trying over and over, it was the emotional ups and downs, the disappointments. Losing that last baby had changed things. Before, it was cost, the letdowns of children who never came, the physical toll on her body, but they could rebound after each time because the image that remained behind was a child someday, someone they could imagine. But Grace finally admitted, he lived in a space that didn't exist for her. And it was time to allow her grief to travel off to that space as well.

Grace looked around the room, feeling as hollow as the

sounds that bounced off the walls with every movement of the chair she sat on.

She heard John come home, wondering why he was back in the middle of a workday. He called out, and she told him, "I'm in the extra room." Even saying that seemed to hurt.

"Talking to God?" He nodded to her hands, which were clasped before her as if in prayer. She hadn't realized they were like that, and put them down.

"I suppose I never really stop talking with Him. Every thought is directed His way."

He stood at the doorframe, waiting.

"I want to hear what it is you are thinking," she said.

He gestured for them to leave the room. She was grateful for that, and followed him to their bedroom. She sat on the bed, pulling a throw pillow to her lap. They'd had so many important conversations in this room. They'd talked of how to get through their debt and what to make for dinner and what color to paint their kitchen. They talked about their day and the small things that happened they found funny or frustrating. Their bedroom had provided much needed rest, a room to retreat to when her grief made it hard to stand, and even a place for them to find comfort and pleasure. There was no TV in their room, no radio. Just them, their bed, and the safety of being able to be trust each other with anything.

He joined her on the bed, one foot off the edge and the rest of his body facing her.

"I'm ready to hear you, now," she said. "I want to hear you."

He nodded, and she thought he might pause and stumble, but he talked fast, his words pouring out of him as quickly as the brushstrokes moved when he was painting. His emotions moved him quickly into action. She envied him for that. Hers always seemed to make her slow to a complete stop.

"Grace, our lives are pretty wonderful. Sure, we have problems. We've always been broke." He chuckled. "Every time we get a little money, it goes toward our debt. Medical bills and infertility, failed adoption costs…"

"I know."

"And I was in it, I wanted the same thing you do, Grace. But let's face facts now. We're both in our forties. And I think about how long we have done this, Grace. Since the beginning. This has been our whole marriage. I was ready to give up before the last baby. I wanted children, too, very badly, but Grace… I don't hate what we have. I don't think anything is missing. A child would have been a blessing beyond belief, one that I would have welcomed. But we are a family. You and me. We are complete."

His eyes teared up, and she reached for his hand. She felt his pain and wanted to comfort his aching heart.

"I'm sorry that this didn't happen for us, Grace. I don't want to try again. But if you do…" He paused and brushed his tears away roughly. "If you do, then—"

"I don't. I've thought about it. I have to let it go. I want to let it go." She was tired of crying and wanting and longing.

"Do you know I dream about him?" John added. "I picture me holding his hand and walking outside, hearing him laugh and running ahead to show me something. Do you know why I spend so much time in the studio? Because sleeping is so difficult. I don't want to close my eyes and see him because it hurts. I don't want to have another child taken from us like that. And I can't do fostering only. I can't welcome a child in my home and then have to say goodbye. My body can't take any more disappointment. I can't…"

His sobs were strong, louder than she had ever heard them. She reached forward and held him, and before she knew it, her tears mixed with his and washed away the guilt of trying to keep hope alive.

They lay on the bed, fully clothed, and just held each other. Every once in a while, he kissed the top of her head.

"When I saw that room painted white, all the furniture gone…" She stopped. Why bother bringing it up?

"I should have talked about it with you first. I'm sorry. I guess I wanted you to be on the same page with me."

She looked at him. "Babe, I'm on the same page. But I will still have a hard time getting through it. I need you to be patient as I let go. Okay?"

"It's different for you," he acknowledged. "You get hammered with this. All the time. I see it."

She was grateful he could acknowledge it, but even though she didn't know exactly how to let go of the ache that seemed to overpower her, there was also a feeling of freedom that snuck its way into her heart. She could get up tomorrow and be content with what she had rather than feeling like a piece was missing. It was as simple as that. She could quietly decide to be happy about the things she had in life rather than giving all her energy to the one thing she didn't.

She wasn't sure how to proceed. Didn't know what this new life looked like, but lying there with John, holding each other silently, reminded her that their marriage had become the most beautiful and safest relationship she had ever had.

He put his hand under her shirt and caressed her back. "I want to make you happy, Grace."

It pained her that he would think that being married to him wasn't enough.

"You have always made me happy. Always. I am very

thankful for what we have. I love you."

There were times when the words "I love you" seemed weak in comparison to how she really felt. She often wondered how she existed without him. They married when she was twenty-five, and at the time, she felt she had waited a lifetime for him. Her early history was a blur, dimmed by the light of their relationship.

CHAPTER 28 - JANE

Charlotte picked her up at the airport, and despite having already seen the picture of her hair, did a predictable double take.

"I know, I know," was all Jane could say.

"That poor stylist."

"Yes, at least she gets my sympathy. If not, I'd have to be really mad at her for doing this to me."

"Well, change is good."

"So, they say."

They drove to Charlotte's house, and even through the darkness, she could see the beauty that Seattle offered. She watched the trees and scenery as Charlotte drove, and when they pulled into her driveway, she was struck by the view they had from their house.

"I didn't know you got to look at this every night."

"Just wait." Charlotte said. "Tomorrow we will go to Kerry Park. Oh, Janey, you will love it so much. You can see everything from there, the whole city, including Mount Rainier."

Jane thought. "You know what? I don't think I've ever seen a mountain in real life. For real."

Charlotte laughed. "Of course not! Why would you? Milwaukee is a beautiful city, but it's not known for its mountain ranges."

Jane eyed her sister. "You are going to try and wow me while I'm here, aren't you? Get me all wanting to see mountains and stuff now?" she joked.

"I am going to *spoil* you," she said, hugging her. "You'll never want to leave after that."

Jane couldn't imagine leaving Milwaukee, but a hug from her sister was a good start.

They had spent the next day sightseeing. They took in parks, stopped at a delicious vegan restaurant for lunch, and a cute artsy area, with galleries and artisan gift shops. By the time they got back to Charlotte's house, Jane was exhausted.

"Why don't you take a nap?" her sister suggested.

Bill agreed. "Get your rest, because tonight I'm making a big bonfire, and we're roasting smores."

Between the air travel and the sights, Jane went to sleep, happily dreaming of open green space, art, and endless miles of blue water. She dreamed of the girl in the painting, reaching out to her, holding her, and singing her to sleep. She dreamed of flying, with clouds that sang "Yellow Rose of Texas" to her as she passed them by, and when she awoke, it was already dark outside.

She was glad they were staying in that night. She rubbed at her eyes and scratched her head, still surprised each time she realized her long hair was gone. Funny how you could get used to something like that, she thought. She put on a pair of yoga pants, a long-sleeved tee, and her big, fuzzy slippers, and ambled out of her room and into the living room.

"Jane!" Charlotte and Bill said together. She laughed at their enthusiasm until she saw Eric just behind them. She scowled at Charlotte as she realized she looked a mess. Why didn't Charlotte come and get her so she could spruce herself up?

Charlotte caught Jane giving her the stink eye. "Eric popped over to say hello. Why don't you two get caught up outside? Bill and I have a lot to do to get dinner ready."

Bill was nodding enthusiastically. He was as bad a liar as Charlotte was. *Those two.* They went outdoors, and Charlotte made a motion to her from inside that looked something like, *Talk to him.* She rolled her eyes and turned to Eric.

"They're as bad as Mrs. Ferch." She could see that Eric was taken aback by the change in her appearance. "I know. It's terrible."

"No, it's not. It's... it shows off your face."

He recovered nicely. She had to hand it to him.

"It shows half my scalp, but that's beside the point."

She reached to give him a hug, and felt his breath on her neck. It sent a thrill through her body, and she shivered.

"Cold?" he asked.

"No. I just woke up. Sorry. I look a mess." She scratched at her head. "And my already terrible hair must look even worse."

They sat down on the patio love seat outside. She sat next to him, and they were both faced away from the front window, so Jane was happy Charlotte couldn't read their lips while they were out there, although she wouldn't put it past her sister to at least try.

"How do you like your job?" she asked.

"I really like it," he said, which disappointed her. She knew she shouldn't be, but there was a part of her that wished he hated his new job and would want to move back to Milwaukee.

"You know"—he had a mischievous smile—"Charlotte has actually told me quite a bit about you over the last couple weeks."

"Oh brother." She put her hand over her face.

"No." He took her hand away gently, and the warmth of his skin sent a tingle through her. "It's good. She helped explain the misunderstanding with your ex—"

"Brad," she interrupted. "I'm so sorry about all that."

"Yeah. I wasn't thrilled about it." He leaned forward, looking down at his lap. "I understand; things aren't always perfect in the beginning. The thing is," he said, inching closer to her, "I want to hang out with you while you're here and get to know you, without pressure, but I also wish things hadn't been so messy to start off with."

She sighed. "I was too afraid just to end things with Brad properly. It really wasn't even until Mrs. Ferch created that forced setup between us at the art fair that I began to see it could be different with someone else. And then the day went on, and—"

"And we went out again, and I kissed you immediately after telling you I was moving away. Yeah, not great on my part, either."

She hadn't stopped thinking about that kiss ever since.

"It's just that, for months, I liked you and just never got up the courage to ask you out or just to ask if you wanted to hang out," he said, catching her off guard. "Mrs. Ferch kept telling me to keep trying. She told me Brad wasn't right for you, and I took that to mean that you were done dating him, and then when you weren't... I felt stupid, I guess."

She blinked. "You liked me?"

He laughed. "And you didn't notice me at all. Or if you did, it was nothing positive."

She wished she could contradict him, but it was true. She'd barely noticed him, and when she did, she thought he was like her dad.

"Did Charlotte tell you more about our dad?" she asked.

He nodded. "I get it all now, Janey."

She giggled. "*Janey?*"

"I've been talking with Charlotte so much, I guess I picked up her nickname for you."

"I like it. And I understand what you're saying, Eric. Believe me. I don't like things to be unclear, either. I do want to get to know you. I'm looking forward to tomorrow, and I also hate that you're here, and I'm in Milwaukee. But, let's just see if we can spend some time together and get along? We might hang out for a bit and drive each other nuts. Or, you might take me to your favorite place that is, like, my least favorite. Or, I might show up with such a terrible haircut that it makes you do a double take."

He laughed. "It's not so bad."

"You're a terrible liar."

She kept him entertained with the rest of the haircut story.

"That is really bad luck. That poor stylist. So did she say anything else besides *You'll get used to the short hair?*"

Jane thought about it. "Yes. She told me never to fall in love."

Eric tilted his head and looked at her a long while. "You really do have the most beautiful eyes." He quickly added, "And the stylist just gave you about the worst advice ever." He held her gaze a long while and then cleared his throat.

"Well,"—he stood up, and she did as well—"you've had a long day with Charlotte and I need to work in the morning, so I should go. I just wanted to stop in and say hello and also"—he leaned in close to her and lowered his voice—"I am so glad you are here." He held her gaze and turned to go. Just before he reached the door, he called back, "Remember, tomorrow I'm picking you up for a surprise."

She waved as she sat back down, staring at the door long after he had left. She felt as if she were reaching on her tiptoes, waiting for the wind to come up and help her fly. She was being silly, she knew, but there was a flutter in her stomach she wasn't sure she had ever felt with anyone else.

Jane had changed four times. Various shirts and skirts and jeans were tossed around on the bed. Charlotte knocked on the door.

"Come in!"

Jane frowned at herself in the mirror.

"What time is Eric coming?" Charlotte took in the pile of clothes.

Jane glanced at the clock. "Fifteen minutes. I suppose you have a comment about my outfit," she said, seeing the look on her sister's face that said *Let me help you.* Jane watched as Charlotte appraised her outfit: a skirt that came to her knees, sandals, and a summery top. She made a motion of locking her mouth and tossing the key over her shoulder, much as Mrs. Ferch had done weeks before.

Finally, Jane kicked off the sandals and looked at Charlotte pleadingly.

"I wasn't going to give you feedback until you asked. If it were me, I would go with the jeans, those cute boots you like so much, and"—she paused, looking over the bed at the discarded outfits—"this top." She picked it up out of the pile and handed it to Jane.

"Really?"

Charlotte nodded. "Periwinkle looks nice on you. Brings out the color in your eyes."

Jane blew out a breath. "I'm nervous."

"I can tell. But you don't have a thing to worry about. It's just a fun day with a guy you've already been out with, remember?"

Jane rushed to put away the clothes she'd tossed on the bed.

"Leave them. I'll put them away. Come here, look at me." She took Jane's hands in hers. "You've already spent some time with Eric."

"That was when I had the whole relationship with Brad to hide behind. You know? And now… I can actually date him. And I like him, like, way more than I ever did with Brad, which sounds ridiculous, considering how long I dated Brad." Jane cringed just thinking about it. "And what if I *really* like Eric? Then what? Am I supposed to change my whole life for him? Move here? You'd probably tell me to, but—"

"Whoa, whoa, whoa," Charlotte said, sitting on the bed. The doorbell rang. Jane looked to Charlotte like she was going to be sick, but her sister patted her hand. "Change your clothes. Bill can let Eric in and do some chitchat." She turned as she reached the door and pointed at Jane. "Stay right there."

Jane changed into the periwinkle shirt her sister picked out, and surveyed her reflection in the mirror. She still hated her hair, but overall, she felt confident. She was about to meet Eric when Charlotte came back into the bedroom and closed the door.

"Now," she spoke in a soft voice. "No, you will not turn your life upside down for a guy. You will not *move* for a guy. Just as you will not do it for your sister. I would never want you to move here for me. I would want you to do that for *you*. If you ever make a change like this, it has to be for you. Remember how I decided to move here and *then* met Bill? If it hadn't worked out with him, I would have still stayed, for me. So"—she took a breath—"go out there. Enjoy your day with a cute guy who likes you, and don't read more into it than that."

Jane nodded and followed her sister out of the bedroom. Eric was seated on the couch, his arm placed casually over the edge and clearly feeling at home. Jane wondered just how much time he had spent here in the last few weeks. It looked like he and Bill had become good friends. She watched them joke around before she made her presence known.

"Hi, Eric."

He turned, and the look on his face registered happiness, desire, and relief. He popped up from the couch and gave her a quick hug.

They pulled away from each other and she smiled up at him. He took her hand, and they each gave Bill and Charlotte a quick wave.

They got in his car and chatted about the last few weeks. She told him about finally getting the promotion, about John Cambridge's exhibit, and how she hoped Grace and Mrs. Ferch would become friends.

"You know," she added, "I almost wasn't able to take this trip. My boss, Bug, suddenly wanted me to cancel my plans. And I would have, if I hadn't bought plane tickets and if I were someone that took vacations all the time. I even worried at first that Bug was going to fire me for that."

"It sounds like you were just being confident and defending yourself in a way you've never done with him before."

"That's true," she confirmed, "but I doubt Bug liked it very much." She uttered the thought she had kept down since landing in Seattle. "What if he makes it worse for me there now because of it? Or even, puts me on notice?"

Eric grinned. "I know I should feel bad about this, but all I can think is that if Bug lets you go, there'd be nothing holding you back from moving to Seattle."

"Eric!"

"I know, it's awful."

"No." She grinned. "I've been hoping you'd hate your new job and come back to Milwaukee."

He was quiet the rest of the drive, and so was she. Talking about moving was too much for them. Jane wanted to just get to know Eric without thinking about the future. Just now. Today.

They arrived at a restaurant, got out of the car, and he took her hand as they stepped inside. The décor was filled with kitschy, bright colors and fabrics on the tables. Old dishes and pictures from the fifties were on the walls.

"Ha! I love it." Jane took in everything. It was the right vibe of casual and fun. Just what they needed to keep things from getting too dark and serious. "You chose the perfect place."

"Thanks." He led her to a booth in the back.

"Have you been here before?" The place looked

familiar to her somehow.

"With Charlotte and Bill, a couple weeks ago," he said. "Charlotte explained that she is a real kitsch fanatic. She buys old dishcloths at flea markets, collects old cookbooks, and even has some of the clothes from back then."

"True," Jane confirmed. "Sometimes I wonder if she is trying to recreate our grandmother's house."

"When women vacuumed wearing their pearls, like on *Leave It to Beaver*?" he joked. "I suppose that wasn't the case in your house, huh?"

"With my mom working and my dad off dreaming somewhere? No. Not quite." Jane realized she didn't know much about Eric's background. "What were things like in your house, growing up?"

"I'm an only child. My mom died young. Breast cancer. And then my dad remarried, and he died when I was in my late teens."

Jane put together the information from what Mrs. Ferch had told her. "And that's when you started working at the animal shelter?"

"Yes. Mrs. Ferch told you that, hey? Yeah, and I moved out of my stepmother's house and into the apartment in Mrs. Ferch's building. I was there all this time until now."

Jane was quiet a moment. "That must feel really weird. To be living somewhere new."

"It does. It's hard. I miss Mrs. Ferch. And you." He smiled. "But I had reached a point where I felt unsettled and needed a change."

"I'm so sorry, about both your parents." Jane instantly felt bad for talking so much about her family. Here she didn't even know Eric's mother had passed away.

"It's okay. She was a good mom, though. My dad was not a good parent, however. He drank a lot. Was mean. He took off when she got sick and then came back after she died and got married and…" He shook head, the memory of it adding a darkness to his face. "And, I realized I needed to think about family differently."

"Any other family?" she asked him.

"A couple aunts and uncles. Cousins here and there. But really, Wayne and Maggie have become like my family. That's one reason I was glad to have dated Tiffany. Even though we weren't right for each other, she introduced me to them, and without Tiff, I wouldn't have Wayne and Maggie and their kids in my life."

Jane thought about the first time they went out, just a few weeks ago. She wasn't nervous at all but had actually felt annoyed that Mrs. Ferch had meddled and gotten Eric to take her to the art fair. That seemed like a lifetime ago now.

"What you said about being glad you met Tiffany? That's a healthy way of looking at it. Honestly, I don't look at things enough like that." She wondered what she would be thankful for years down the road when it came to Brad. A renewed sense of purpose? A new way to look at her life? "So, I keep wanting to ask you. *Why Seattle?* You know I'm beginning to think this town is out to get me. It keeps stealing my favorite people."

"Maybe that's because it secretly wants you here, too." Eric smiled. "Sorry. I'm joking." He paused. "*Half* joking. I had come out here with Wayne when he and Maggie were thinking of moving. At the time, I had no intention of leaving Milwaukee. But I liked it here. Then, I started thinking about what I wanted to do, and it all just sort of fell into place, I guess."

She kept looking at the various plates and napkins on the tables. "I feel like I'm at home with Charlotte again as a little girl, and we're wondering what concoction our grandmother is going to throw together for dinner. We used to stay with her sometimes when my mom was working and our dad was in what he called his studio, working on inventions."

Jane looked through the menu and instantly got excited. "Creamed corn and sausages!" she exclaimed.

"What now?" He frowned.

"Okay, hear me out. When we were little, our grandma would make maple breakfast sausages with creamed corn. It sounds weird, I know, but it's actually delicious."

"Seriously?" Eric cocked his head at her. "I've never tried it. And yes, it sounds awful," he laughed. "But somehow, I knew you'd appreciate this place."

Jane closed her menu and he followed suit. The waitress asked for their orders, and Jane put in for her favorite nostalgic dish.

"That's a good one." The waitress pointed at her with her ballpoint pen. "Not enough people try that one, but they're missing out." She turned to Eric. "And for you, sir?"

"I'll have the cheeseburger and fries."

"Uh-huh," the waitress scribbled, barely looking at him. "Wisconsin cheddar or American cheese on top of that?"

"Wisconsin cheddar. *Of course.*" He grinned at Jane.

The waitress closed her order book and nodded. "Be right up."

They chatted about Milwaukee and Seattle, about their families, and shared about their exes. The waitress returned with their food and they continued the conversation.

Eric shook his head. "Sometimes I look at my past choices and wonder what it was I was thinking. I mean, with Tiffany? I knew it was a disaster even as I starting dating her. I knew my job was wrong for me. But I just kept thinking that if I tried harder, it would all fall into place. I chalked it up to growing up, and this is what people did. I made everything more difficult than it had to be."

"Oh, please," she added. "Don't beat yourself up. What about me? I stayed with a guy for eight years, not even knowing he had a daughter or that he was keeping the child's mother on the same string he kept me on. I met her at this horrible Thanksgiving appetizer party"—she laughed just thinking about it—"and I couldn't find him anywhere, and here he was in a bedroom arguing with a girl who introduced herself to me as his fiancée."

"Yeah." Eric wrinkled his nose. "Charlotte told me. You know what I think?"

"Huh?" She finished the last of her dish and asked him if he'd like to try it.

"Oh no." He put his hand up. "It still looks really horrible to me, but I'm glad you liked it," he laughed. "I think Brad might be, and it's just my personal opinion here, one of the biggest fools in the entire world." He took her hand in his.

"You know what I think?" she said, feeling bold. "The way you crinkle that nose of yours is very adorable."

"Why, thank you, miss," he said, doing it again. "It is a patented move, designed to make the ladies swoon."

Well, she thought, it was working pretty well on her.

CHAPTER 29 - GRACE

Grace met Mrs. Ferch at a bistro that was focused on healthy foods and vegetarian dishes. They sat at a small booth right next to a large window, and each had a glass of juice in front of them as they made small talk, mostly about Jane, their common bond.

The seating area had a beautiful view of Lake Michigan, and Grace imagined her husband taking in the colors, the blues and greens that blurred together like an Impressionist painting. He'd probably be sketching in his mind even while he sipped his drink. "This is really a gorgeous view. I think if I worked here, I would spend my entire day in this spot."

"As would I," Mrs. Ferch agreed. "Jane tells me you're married to a painter. That must be so wonderful."

It was interesting to her that people thought of John as a painter rather than someone who worked a day job and painted. Another part of the power of art, she thought, that people would label you a certain thing, just by the creative activity you loved most. It would be the same, she supposed, with someone who was a cook or photographer.

"It is," Grace agreed. "We get to do things like exhibits and shows. I enjoy helping him promote himself, so it has become something both of us enjoy. I do like seeing his process and what comes from his imagination."

"And it's good that you can do your own hobbies and then also come together for other things," she said. "My Seth and I were like that. He was an ace mechanic. He'd find car parts at various places and then here and there fix people's cars and make them like new. It was his sideline, something he just did because he enjoyed that. But, oh my"—she clapped her hands together at the thought—"there were times when our backyard looked like a junkyard!" She laughed at the thought. "My mom hated Seth, felt like he was a good-for-nothing. But he was a good husband to me, and well"—Grace studied her and found a wonderfully happy look on her face—"the love of my life."

Grace stayed silent for a moment, not wanting to add her own words to such a beautiful sentiment. She wanted Mrs. Ferch's memory of her husband to stay there, front and center.

After a few seconds, Mrs. Ferch looked at her. "I've heard you and your John have a relationship like that. An honest-to-goodness, true-blue love."

"Did Jane tell you that?" She smiled.

"Oh yes. All I know about you both really is that she thinks you and your hubby are adorable, and she likes you very much. And that was all I needed to want to meet you."

"I can tell why Jane values you, Mrs. Ferch."

"Call me Avery. I joked with Jane that she needed to name her firstborn after me. But then you know what? I hated that I said that. Why is that always the expectation when a couple gets together?"

"Jane told you we were childless, did she?" Grace frowned.

"What? No, dear." Mrs. Ferch put her hand on Grace's across the table. It was surprising, but Grace found comfort in it. "I'm talking of myself. Seth and I did not have kids. In my day people would ask sometimes, but today I hear such judgment on the topic." She made a tsk tsk noise. "Seth and I wanted them, and it just never happened. We were disappointed, of course, but the worst part was having people ask me about it. I would say we were not blessed with kids, and that was that. I didn't realize how hard it was talking it about until Seth died, and then all people could ask me about was kids. One woman, I hardly knew her, but she came to the funeral and right there told me it was such a shame we didn't have kids because now I was all alone. My goodness." She shivered at the memory.

Grace felt for her. "I'm so sorry. People are awful sometimes."

"And you know what? I found that my family, of all people, were the worst when it came to that. There was a time I was very sad after Seth died, and when I mentioned about that woman at the funeral to my cousin, who is married with five kids, no less, she just barked at me that she was sick of hearing me drone on. She actually used those words, 'drone on,' about children. As if my grief was just so boring to her. Then, she went on to tell me about her granddaughter and how the child was learning to walk.

Now, of course, that's a lovely thing, but why is that a better conversation topic than helping someone you love with their grief?" Mrs. Ferch shook her head at it.

"People don't understand grief. It's true," Grace remarked. "We've lost friends because they either excluded us from things, as if we somehow wouldn't want to hang around their children, or they've just made fun of us."

"I've learned," Mrs. Ferch continued, "that it doesn't matter a lick who you were born to. You really have to make your own family. Friends can be that. I have a better group surrounding me now than I did when I was your age, Grace. I'll tell you that."

Grace smiled at her. "I hope I can be like you when I grow up."

"Oh pish," she said, and swiped her hand through the air, a gesture Grace had seen Jane mimic once or twice when talking about Mrs. Ferch.

They chatted some more about hobbies and life and Milwaukee.

"I've been here all my life," Mrs. Ferch said. "You?"

Grace nodded. "I've never wanted to live anywhere else. I just hate the reputation that Milwaukee has. There is so much art and culture and you just never hear about it."

"Which reminds me: I'm wondering if you'd be able to take me to see your husband's work. Jane said they had some sort of display at her gallery. Well, I think of it as her gallery, but it's really owned by that boss of hers. *Bug.*" She added his name with distaste.

"Not a fan of his?"

"He works her like a dog. And you know what? She allows it. I'm hoping she will begin to see work for what it was meant to be."

Grace waited. "What's that?"

"Something that fulfills you but isn't your whole life," Mrs. Ferch said, as if Grace should know this already. She supposed she should have realized this by now.

Mrs. Ferch stood before The Space Between Dreaming for a long time, eventually leaning on Grace to help steady herself.

"It is simply marvelous," she breathed. They stood for several more minutes, with Grace feeling proud and happy that Mrs. Ferch was enjoying her husband's work. She wondered what Avery was seeing in the woman who reached out into the darkness. Was it herself? A woman ready to embrace a child, as Jane thought? Grace resolved herself that she wouldn't ask her and would wait until she decided to share her thoughts herself.

As Grace dropped Mrs. Ferch off at home, the woman turned. "I have had a simply wonderful time with you," she said. "I would very much like it you and John both would like to come to dinner. Let's talk," she said, and hopped out of the car with a wave.

Grace waved and found herself smiling. To have met two special new friends like Jane and Avery was something she could indeed call a blessing.

"Okay," she acknowledged to God. "I'm not sure what you're up to here, but I feel your hand in it." She thought about telling Him more, laying it all out so He knew her heart, but she'd done that so many times over the years, she didn't want to do it again. "You know how I feel about things," she added to herself. Both Jane and Mrs. Ferch were not the type of friends she would have necessarily chosen for herself, but she could feel how special they both were, the type of bond she felt with them right from the start. "Thank you for these two new friends," she added, then headed home.

Margo Carmichael's review had finally been published. She got an email from Margo herself, stating again that it was great to meet her and that her husband's work was lovely. Grace shook her head. Lovely? She wouldn't exactly describe it as that, and that little word gave her a shiver about what Margo was about to say in her review.

Grace printed out the attachment Margo had sent and smoothed it out on the kitchen island. She sat back. Was she ready for this? It was what she had wanted since the beginning for her husband's work. She put on her reading glasses and tried to absorb the words. She read it once, then twice. She paced before the counter and read it again:

Some people live their lives fully, paying attention to every moment. For others, they open their eyes for certain snippets of time when they can handle the realities of things like pain, love, or even joy, only to close them again when the feeling gets too intense. And that feeling, the one that is too much for anyone to handle, is exactly where The Space Between Dreaming lies. It holds you there, in the most uncomfortable expanse of time, the spot where you cannot enjoy it or look away from it, and all the while you are thinking of everything you wished you were… the wife you wanted to be, the mother you hoped you'd be, the woman you wished you'd be. But when you open your eyes and step back, looking at it again, it is just paint on canvas, a mirage of colors and design like any other. And yet, it is unlike anything you will ever see.

Grace read it aloud this time, the sound of her voice going up a notch with each sentence. It was a typical Margo Carmichael review, one that reminded people of the value of art, also, maddeningly mysterious. It was a review that encouraged you to see the painting, which was the point. Grace felt it was a win for John. A win for both of them.

She called up Jane. "Did you happen to see—?"

Jane yawned.

"Oh, I'm sorry!" Grace realized Jane was in Seattle, and the time difference meant she had probably just woken up. "I forgot. You're on vacation. No, I will call back—"

"What's going on?" Jane seemed alert now. "Is it published?"

Grace smiled at the fact that Jane knew exactly what she was talking about without saying.

"Just now," Grace confirmed, "but look, I forgot you were on vacation. We'll talk when you get back."

"No, it's good. I was up, just lying here thinking about what I'm going to wear. Remember that song that talked about that?"

"Remember it?" Grace laughed. "I think a boy from high school made me a mix tape with that on it once."

"I wish I had been around during the mix-tape days."

"Ha! No, you don't. Frosted jeans and spiral perms. But look," Grace said, worried that she was keeping Jane from her day, "I should let you go."

"It's good to talk to you. I'm having a blast here. I can't wait to tell you about it. But wait, I want to read the review while I have you on the line. Let me look it up. Hold on."

Grace waited and found herself dancing before her kitchen island, feeling silly and happy all at the same time.

"Wow. This is exactly what he needs," Jane said. "I wish I was there to give you a hug. I know you must be flying high right now."

"I am," she said. "I can't wait to tell John."

"When you tell him, be sure to mention that one of his paintings just sold yesterday."

Grace's ears pricked. "Someone bought one of his paintings? Was it…?"

There was a moment of disappointment when she imagined The Space Between Dreaming hanging on the wall of someone's home, a stuffy couple who hung it in a room with no light. Or worse, another gallery that wouldn't give it the display space Jane had. Or worse…

"Are you there?"

"Sorry. I was daydreaming. A part of me was actually disappointed that it sold."

"The Space is still there. Before I left for vacation, more people were coming in to look at it. I'm technically on vacation, but I've already heard from Bug about a couple other things. He mentioned yesterday about that other painting having sold, the one with the woman on the park bench. I've got to run; time to get dressed."

"Enjoy your time away."

Grace wondered which painting had sold, before she realized the good news. A painting had sold! She dialed her husband at work.

"Hello, this is—"

"Babe, you're never going to believe this. One of your paintings sold!"

"Hey, that's great. Thanks for letting me know."

His tone was even, and Grace knew he could have cared less. He could be so blasé about things sometimes. "Don't you want to know which one it was?"

"Sure. Which one was it?"

Grace sighed. "Well, I don't know."

He laughed then, a hearty hoot that Grace had missed. They'd been mired in clouds the last few months, and his laugh was like a ray of sunshine that fought its way through.

"I assume it isn't The Space Between Dreaming," he said.

"You're right. How did you know that?"

"Because I think, dear wife, you might have fallen in love with that painting so much that you don't want anyone else to have it. You'd have been disappointed, and you sounded excited instead."

Sometimes he knew her so well, it sent a shiver down her spine.

"Oh, you. You think you're so smart. Of course, you're right. But I was also calling about the review. Margo's review. Do you want to read it?"

"Not particularly."

"Really? Don't you want to know what she thought?"

"I don't really care. It doesn't change things for me, so what's the point? Listen, babe, I've gotta run. I'm just about to go into a meeting. I am so glad you called. It was nice to hear your voice."

"You, too."

"I love you."

She said she loved him, too, and this time it wasn't automatic, but something she knew more than anything else.

CHAPTER 30 - JANE

Jane had enjoyed the last couple of days. She'd had movie nights with Charlotte, Bill and Sally, lunches with Eric, and even time to spend on her own, just enjoying the view from her sister's back porch. Seattle was beautiful, she had to admit.

More than that, she felt a sense of belonging there she hadn't anticipated. She missed Mrs. Ferch and Grace, but she didn't miss her job as much as she thought she would. In fact, she'd been looking at some of the galleries they had passed and made a mental note of those that looked like the size and vibe she'd be interested in working for. Just in case, she kept telling herself—just in case.

She was someone who thought about things, but sometimes she needed to act. She had learned a lot about herself since the breakup with Brad. She also thought she would miss him, but she didn't. She could not miss what they had together because they didn't have a good relationship. Jane was relieved not to question the choice of breaking up with him. Her only regret was in waiting so long to do it.

Spending the last few days with Eric didn't hurt, either. They were casual lunches, where they talked and flirted but kept things low-key. Still, she felt a spark whenever they were together, and she couldn't help but think he did, too.

He picked her up and said, "Hey," as she got in. She smiled, knowing that was all part of the Milwaukee dialect, and he'd probably never lose it. People would say things like, "That was a good movie, hey?" Or "Hey, did you go to the store?"

"Hey, yourself." He kissed her cheek, and she felt herself blush. The simplest of actions from him could make her melt.

"There's one place we definitely need to see together. I'll keep it a surprise, but I think you can guess."

"Okay." She grinned. Within minutes, Jane knew where they were going. "The Chihuly Glass Museum?" She was so excited, her mouth was suddenly dry. "Oh, Eric…"

"Yes, and I had to beg Charlotte to let me be the one to bring you. I really wanted to experience this with you."

They parked and walked in. They paid for their tickets and started their tour with the Glass Forest, a series of long glass sculptures lit up with neon and argon. Instantly, she was transported.

"I've waited to come here until I could hold your hand and take you here with me," Eric said, squeezing her hand briefly. "I read up on Chihuly before we came here," he said.

She looked at him. "Seriously? For me?"

He pulled her aside and let other people pass. "Of course, for you. I wanted to have some knowledge of what

I was looking at, and the more I read up on Chihuly, the more I wanted to come here with you." He stepped in closer, talking low. "I don't know if you've caught onto this or not, Jane, but I think you're pretty amazing."

She felt her cheeks flush. The way the green sparkled in his eyes made her wish she could stay there, staring at him. His voice was low, and she leaned closer to him.

"I think you are amazing, too," she said quietly. She felt shy and wanted to look away, but those eyes kept pulling her in.

He cupped her face with his palm, and all she could think of was kissing him, pulling him close. Instead, she put her hand on his, gently taking it away from her face and holding it instead.

No, she told herself, I cannot fall in love. No. I cannot.

"Let's get to see these glass pieces," she said, barely able to get the words out.

He smiled at her and kissed her hand. They continued walking in, hands interlocked like longtime lovers. How could it be so easy with him?

"I… um…" Eric cleared his throat, undoubtedly feeling as turned on as she was about Chihuly's creativity. "I never knew glass could make such an art statement. I'm really blown away by some of the work he does."

Jane laughed. "Blown away is a good way to put it. It's part of his process, too."

Eric cringed. "Glass blowing… blown away… I'm such a poet."

She patted his arm to let him know it was okay. "It's hard to find the words for something so beautiful." She pointed to the pieces in the Glass Forest. "I've read that these are created by blowing hot glass and at the same time, pouring it down from a ladder. Then, as it cools, it creates these shapes and hardens."

"I think the sea life sculptures are my favorite," Eric commented. "I dig the blue color, and the sea urchins and starfish are cool." He pointed to his favorite, an octopus with glass extending out.

"Oh good," Jane commented as they walked to the boat sculptures. "I've been wanting to see these." She told Eric about how these sculptures began. The two of them wound up facing each other, inches away, as they continued to hold hands. "When Chihuly was doing the Venice project, he tossed glass pieces in the river to study the way light touched the glass as it hit the water. As the pieces floated away, students collected them and put them all in boats. That gave Chihuly the idea for a new way to display the glass."

He kissed her hand when she finished talking. She was uttering details about art like a madman, trying to keep her mind off how much she wanted to kiss him. She was talking too much, which seemed to amuse him. But how could she start something new with him and then leave?

They continued walking, her hand still in his. They entered the Mille Fiori, which was Italian for "a thousand flowers." The exhibit featured glass in the shapes of leaves and flowers of every size and shape. It was like walking through a vibrant forest.

In the glasshouse, they looked up at the red-and-orange glass sculpture all along the top of the building, with light shining through each piece, making it glow throughout the building.

"These are called Fire Orange Baskets," Jane said. She and Eric were transfixed, their eyes looking up at the large orange, red, and yellow sculptures. They looked like huge umbrellas from below, just about to float down to where you could reach them.

"I've heard these light up at night," Eric said. "Maybe we can stop by and see that sometime."

She'd wanted to say, *when?* She was leaving soon. But she wanted to keep it light.

"I'd like that."

After they'd seen the exhibits, they got a bite to eat at the Collections Café. Jane took in the décor, which seemed to fit with Chihuly's style of color and light. As they sat, she admired the chairs, which were a modern, bright-green color.

"If I ever redecorate my apartment, I think I'd like to incorporate some of this style," she said.

"Including the accordions on the ceiling?" He pointed up. Sure enough, dozens of accordions hung from the rafters.

She laughed. "I didn't even see that!"

"I think Chihuly collects accordions," Eric said, frowning to remember what he'd read. "I know he got started with glass just by collecting it as a boy," Eric told her, recalling the information he'd studied. "He used to look for beach glass by Puget Sound. Can't you just picture him picking up a piece of glass, holding it up to the sun, and studying it?"

Jane was impressed. "You did your research, didn't you?"

"Do I get a gold star?" He smiled an impish grin, leaning in closer. "Maybe… a kiss?" He pointed at his cheek.

She could smell his cologne, that citrus-and-wood fragrance that pulled her in. She leaned in, and they locked eyes. She could see his eyes crinkle with a smile that automatically made her do the same. She kissed him on the cheek, letting her lips linger, the she pulled away and smiled at him. He moved closer to her and brushed his lips with hers. He continued, his lips sending a spark through her. He pressed his mouth to hers hungrily, and she accepted, their tongues flirting. They continued that way until they heard someone complain.

"Get a room!"

Embarrassed, they pulled apart.

"Yeah," he said, clearly trying to regain his composure. "So… hungry?"

She giggled. "Starved."

All she was hungry for was more time together, more kisses, more of him.

He cleared his throat again. "I liked the way you described the Chihuly glass sculpture at the Milwaukee Art Museum when we were there. You were so passionate. Without you there, I might have looked at it and appreciated it, but not felt that fire to learn more." Eric paused and smiled at her, taking her hand as they sat at the table. Eric read from the menu. "The food here is inspired by the places Chihuly has traveled to."

After lunch, she sat back, sated. "I'm afraid I won't have room for the brats and burgers Bill is going to grill tonight for the cookout."

"Is he really making brats? Bringing some Wisconsin to the Northwest, hey?"

"I think that was a requirement when Charlotte agreed to marry him," Jane joked. "Brats at cookouts, or no deal."

"So," Eric looked at her thoughtfully. "Any of the exhibits you'd like to go back and see again before we leave?"

"You really do need to look at it all a couple times, don't you? I don't think I was able to take it all in. It was all so amazing, although the one thing I really need to see again before we go is the Glasshouse."

As they entered the Glasshouse once more, she was taken in by the size of the sculptures at the ceiling. Eric took her hand and looked up at the art pieces.

"It really is a special space, isn't it?"

She closed her eyes, feeling the sunlight on her face. She sighed. "It is. I think this should be a place we come back to often."

She opened her eyes with alarm, realizing what she'd just said: "Come back often." But before she could correct herself, he responded.

"I agree," he said, taking her face in his hands. She looked up just as a brief kiss landed on her lips. He looked into her eyes, and she felt that heat again, the spark that was there from the very beginning. He kissed her gently and said in a low voice, "Whatever this is, Jane, I don't want it to end." Then he kissed her until people throughout the Glasshouse applauded. Embarrassed once more, they left.

They got in his car, and he turned toward her.

"Well," he joked, "I doubt they'll want to see us back here anytime soon."

"Oh, I don't know. We did get applause the second time we made out like teenagers."

He shook his head. "I've never been like this… with anyone."

"Me neither," she admitted. "I dated a guy for eight years and didn't long to hold his hand or just hear his opinions or…"

She looked at him.

"Or want to kiss him every time you thought of him?" he said, bringing his lips to hers again.

When they pulled apart, the windows had fogged up.

"We have to get out of here," she giggled.

"On it." He pulled out of the parking lot, and they drove to a sunny, wooded park that overlooked the entire city. "I want to show you one more thing before I drop you off," he said. She got out of the car, and he took her hand, looking out over the view.

"Remember that day at the art fair?" he asked.

How could she forget. "It was the first day I realized I could have a different kind of relationship. Than what I'd had with Brad, I mean. Here, you and I were just friends, but it felt so…"

"Natural."

"Right. The day flew by. We talked about so many things. I really enjoyed myself and forgot about everything else."

He squeezed her hand. "Me, too. Wayne could even see it. He called me after seeing us there and asked me about you. He saw how I looked at you. I haven't been with anyone since Tiffany, and he could tell I really liked you. He wanted to know the story. About how we met and everything."

Jane thought of Mrs. Ferch. "You know how often Mrs. Ferch was throwing us together?"

"Probably every single time?" Eric guessed.

"Pretty much. I was annoyed at first, but now I realize I should probably apologize to her." Jane paused, unsure if she should share her thought. She figured it needed to be said. "She thought we were perfect for each other. And she was right."

Eric looked into her eyes and just nodded. When he looked down, Jane knew he was thinking the same thing she was. If they were so perfect for each other, what would they do now?

"But I mean… what am I supposed to do? We've only been dating a short time. And I mean, are we even dating?"

"I know what you're saying, Jane. I'm shocked at how this turned out, too. I know it's only been a few weeks since that very first coffee shop encounter."

She giggled. "I acted like a fool at the coffee shop! And then you had that girl behind the counter ask for your number," she teased.

He cringed. "You saw that, huh? I was trying to be discreet in turning her down."

She leaned up and kissed him. "You poor, adorable thing, getting hit on by all the girls."

He shook his head. "Yeah, it's a tough job, especially when you're only interested in one girl who won't give you the time of day." He nudged her. "It really does feel like we've known each other forever. I know moving would be a lot to ask of you. You've got more in Milwaukee than a job, and I know that. Your life is there."

"Right." She turned to look into his eyes. "So, let's not think about it. I've been driving myself crazy thinking about it. I don't have any answers, but let's just appreciate what we have right now. This minute. I don't know about you, but the last couple days have been better than years that I've spent with anyone else."

"I feel the same, Jane. That's what makes this whole thing so hard. I feel cheated, somehow. I've enjoyed every minute we've spent together. No matter what we're doing. Hanging out like this or doing nothing. Or going to the museum… or whatever. I just enjoy being with you."

"So, let's just enjoy it. You know, Charlotte and I had some really nice conversations while she was in Milwaukee. And one of the things she mentioned was that everything is a gift. Even something like our rotten childhoods. I argued with her then. I didn't see where she was coming from. But now I do. Eric, getting to know you, even this short time, it's been a gift. I treasure it."

He leaned over and whispered, "You are an amazing person, Janey." He held her gaze, and she felt the heat between them rise.

She turned to admire the sunset that had just begun, then she stepped up on a rock at the edge of the path and was taller than Eric. She pulled him to her and looked down at him.

"I'm beginning to miss you already."

"Don't miss me yet. I'm still here."

They kissed long after the skateboarders came by again, jeering and making whooping sounds. It didn't matter to her. She focused on Eric and held on to that moment for as long as she could.

That night she dreamed of beautiful red-and-yellow sculptures stretched out like giant flower petals; she saw light shining through glass sculptures, and purple glass sticks set among driftwood. She woke up, thinking of the museum, the juxtaposition of clean and modern with old, traditional, and suddenly, she knew what she had to do.

CHAPTER 31 - GRACE

Grace had started knitting again, a hobby she had tried a few years ago and abandoned. Spending time with Mrs. Ferch inspired her to get out her old knitting needles and try again. Mrs. Ferch introduced Grace to her knitting group, and while they were all Avery's age, she found she could talk with them easily. There didn't seem to be the generation gap she sometimes found with people older than her. They were busy knitting things for a woman at Avery's church, who was about to have a baby. She was young and single and could use every bit of help and care she could. Grace decided to knit an outfit for her.

She pulled out a pattern for pink booties and a hat to match, and got to work. She knitted the first bootie, but the one she worked now was at least twice the size of the first. Her husband watched her, and held the first bootie up.

"Do you think this baby is going to be born with different-sized feet?"

She grabbed it back. "Oh, stop. I'm still trying to remember how to do this. I haven't knitted in ages."

"I know." He kissed the top of her head and then grabbed a Diet Coke from the fridge. As he opened the can, he watched her. "I'm glad you're knitting again."

She had given it up after the second miscarriage. She had been making tiny baby clothes, booties, and little sweaters, and she boxed them up and sent them off to the donation bin. That was the first realization that they'd never have a baby in the house. Even if they had adopted a child, he or she would probably be a toddler, or older. She remembered adjusting her vision of what parenthood would be like, from a baby you raised from the start to a little person who had already experienced something before they met you. To now. A dream that would never take place.

They had changed their expectations again and again over the years. She knew now that was part of what made it hard. She wondered if she had only stopped envisioning things like she had, maybe they would have been easier to handle. But then again, hope was something that snuck its way in, and sometimes it moved you forward, and other times it held you prisoner in the same spot for years.

Grace was not ready to let go of hope, but she knew she needed to change the way she held it in her heart. Gripping on to her idea of hope, so tightly that it nearly choked out the joy she currently had, was no way to live, and she had done that enough.

John sat opposite her. "So… pink, huh?"

"I'm picturing a girl. I just can't imagine this young girl having a boy."

Her husband laughed. "I can. They do come in two varieties you know."

"Yes, smarty-pants, I know. But I picture a girl."

"What if she has a boy?"

"Then he'd better like pink."

He eyed her some more. "You've spent a lot of time with Mrs. Ferch, haven't you?"

"Avery," she said.

"What now?"

She put down her knitting and looked at him, exasperated. She'd told him the woman's name several times already.

"She asked that we call her Avery."

"Right." he nodded, taking a slurp of his soda. "And when do we have dinner with her again?"

She glared at him. "I've told you this already. Tomorrow. Night." She shook her head, picking up her needles again. Honestly, that man.

"Sounds good," he said, unbothered by her exasperation. "I'm going to paint. Let's meet in the bedroom in half an hour." He waggled his eyebrows at her.

"It's a little early to go to sleep," she teased.

"Sleep will have very little to do with it."

They met Mrs. Ferch at her apartment. Grace couldn't wait to show John the building. There was something about it that charmed her. She understood why Jane enjoyed living here so much.

"And it's so close to all the downtown activities," she said. They were driving downtown more and more lately for John's art. He'd given a talk, had another exhibit, and been invited to a presentation for Gallery Night. All because of Margo Carmichael. Grace marveled at the kind of influence the woman had.

They knocked on Avery's door and heard the "Come on in" welcome from within.

"So nice to have you!" she said, wiping a bead of sweat from her brow. She wore a charming blue dress and had her hair up in a chignon.

"I hope you haven't gone to too much trouble." Grace took everything in. There were salads and beef stew, and from the aroma, homemade bread.

"Oh, it was a delight," she said. "Sit, sit."

Grace introduced John, and they all sat for dinner. Avery asked John if he'd like to say the prayer.

"Lord, what a blessing to be able to share this meal with our new friend, Avery. Thank you for her, for this food, and for Jane, who introduced us. Help Jane in this stage in her life, where she is trying to figure out the next steps. Thank you for my wife, who shines your light even through the dark times. Thank you for the gift of creativity. Amen."

"What a lovely prayer, John," Avery said. "I agree with everything you've said!" She raised her water glass in a toast, and they all clinked glasses. "I got a phone call from Eric yesterday. He said he and Jane are having a lovely time. I do hope those two kids figure it all out. I feel like the wheels are in motion for them to get together; they just need to realize it themselves. Don't you agree, Grace?"

"Yes," she said. "When I first saw them at the art fair, they looked like a couple. Some people just seem to be perfect together. Although, John, I have to admit I'm surprised you've been paying attention to the things I've told you about Jane," she laughed. The fact that he understood the details surprised her. He mostly responded with "hmm" when she brought it up.

"I listen to you, my dear." He winked. "I just like to throw you off by making you think I don't hear you."

"Like when I ask you not to leave the window open in the studio?" She eyed him.

"Especially then."

Avery laughed at them. "My, you two are adorable. This banter reminds me of me and my Seth. We used to bicker constantly, and as we did, someone would hear us and tell us how cute we were! I think it goes back to what you were saying, Grace, that some people are just meant to be together, and you can tell from the way they hold hands or even argue."

Grace quietly ate. Being mentioned in prayer when she felt such confusion and anger felt wrong to her. She didn't feel she deserved it.

John and Avery chatted through most of dinner. Grace knew he would enjoy Mrs. Ferch's company. There was something about the woman that was welcoming and loving. Sitting there, having dinner, felt like the family she'd always wanted. What she wished she had with her own mother.

"This meal is delicious, Avery." John gobbled away, and Grace smiled at him. He did like a good meal. "Grace is an excellent cook, too." He smiled at her as if reading her thoughts. "My mother, though?" He shook his head and made a face.

Avery laughed. "Oh my, not a good cook, then?"

"It's wasn't just that," John added. "She never seemed to enjoy preparing a meal for us. After a while, she hired a woman to help us, to clean and prep meals and all that, and even then, when we sat down to eat, it was like she didn't enjoy it."

"Did she cook more when your dad was alive?" Avery asked, and Grace thought perhaps John would be hesitant to talk about his father with her but he wasn't.

"No, not at all. And he was more like me, where he did appreciate it when someone prepared a meal for him. His mother, my grandmother, would bake for him, and every time, no matter what she made him, he would gush."

"With some people," Avery went on, "they feel most loved when someone cooks or cleans for them. Not because they don't want to, but because they just feel cared for then."

"You're right about that," he said. "And you should have seen my dad! He was thin as a rail."

He and Mrs. Ferch laughed. Grace saw how easily John seemed to open up to her, and it touched her heart. He deserved the love of someone who really appreciated him, too. His mother had been long gone, but from what he had told her, she, too, drank too much. She knew that John sometimes longed for a mother who would simply cherish him.

"I do think cooking is just another way to be creative," Mrs. Ferch said, "and you put your personality in it like you do painting or writing."

Grace knew that to be true. A good meal made with love was felt as much as it was tasted. Her husband's egg sandwiches were simple, and yet one of her favorite dishes, mostly because of how thoughtful he was in making them. She loved watching him move the eggs around the pan slowly, or how he gently scraped the butter across the surface of the bread. He took such care.

They finished the meal, and Grace offered to clean up.

"Oh no, dear, I'll do it later," Mrs. Ferch said.

"Come on, now. I would be happy to," John said. "You and Grace can relax. I've got this."

John started grabbing plates and cups and taking them to the sink. She thought Mrs. Ferch would protest again, but she said, "How wonderful! Thank you." She walked into the living room and Grace followed. She gave John a grateful smile and he returned one of his own, a look so filled with happiness that she wondered the last time she saw a smile like that on him. This constant pressure about family, children, and all the rest had taken their toll on both of them. She was happy to see him enjoying himself.

"You know, I have been angling to get Jane and Eric together," Mrs. Ferch confessed to Grace. "Not pushing, exactly. But encouraging. They seem as if they'd be perfect together. And he's liked her since the moment she moved in. He was with that horrible Tiffany then," Mrs. Ferch made a face as if she'd sucked a lemon.

"What will you do now with Eric's apartment?" Grace asked. "Do you want me to ask around to see if I know of someone who needs a place to live?"

"You know what? I've been praying about that. I'm not sure what I should do yet, with that. When Eric moved in, I felt a sense of relief in having someone else here. It was right after my husband died"—she leaned in—"and I was feeling a bit lonely. And then Jane came along, which was lovely, but I'm not sure what the future holds for that. Going to wait on it," she said. "Although," she mused, "I will miss Eric's snow shoveling for me. He was such a doll about that."

"I can come and shovel for you," John was saying now as he joined them.

Grace looked past him to the kitchen area, which looked neat and clean. He had tidied up quickly.

Mrs. Ferch shook her head. "Nonsense. I don't expect you to do that. I only mentioned it because I was thinking about Eric."

"No, really. I'd be happy to. Why not?" He smiled. "I'll let you in on a secret. I actually love shoveling and plowing.

Mostly plowing. I have this extra little snowblower, which would be perfect for here. I like being out in the cold after a snowfall and just taking in the quiet as I shovel, too.""

Mrs. Ferch seemed relieved. "That would be wonderful, John! I'd be ever so grateful. And I'd be happy to do something for you in return. Baked goods? I have an excellent snickerdoodle recipe."

"Baked anything is always appreciated, but not necessary," he assured her.

Yes, Grace thought, John seemed very light and happy suddenly, and Grace, too, felt so at home with Mrs. Ferch. They chatted for hours, and it felt like just a few minutes. They'd even talked about the hard stuff, kids and family, without it bringing down the conversation. Mrs. Ferch was happy to talk through it all, which Grace admired.

"I keep thinking about Jane," Grace said now. "I'm trying to remember myself at her age. She is so much more mature in many ways than I was."

"She is mature." Mrs. Ferch agreed. "But also struggles in other ways. Just as we all do, I suppose."

"When I was her age, I wanted everyone to like me. Not for popularity," Grace clarified, "but to be loved. So, I put up with people treating me unkindly."

"Trying to act a certain way to be loved by the people who should already love you is never going to work out," Mrs. Ferch concurred. "When I was younger, I desperately wanted to be liked by my mother. Oh, she seemed to hate me something fierce," Mrs. Ferch chuckled. "I was always running myself ragged, trying to please her. It wasn't until I met Seth that I began to see my mother as a person. She wasn't happy with my dad, and she poured all her frustration on me. Luckily, he was able to help me get some distance with all that. And that's how it seems to go as you get older. You realize who is on your side, and you're not so ready to surround yourself with people who bring you down." She smiled at them both. "And you learn more quickly to see the true character of people. That is one reason I'm so delighted to have met you both."

Without even planning to, John and Grace answered in unison. "We feel the same."

<h1 style="text-align:center">CHAPTER 32 - JANE</h1>

J ane stood once again before the mirror in her sister's guest room, deciding what to wear. Charlotte came in.

"Dress comfortably but in something that gives you confidence. Remember, you've already met these people before."

"I've met Wayne before, but not Maggie," she corrected.

"Right. I've met Maggie, and she seems *fine*," Charlotte noted, holding up a white cotton T-shirt with long sleeves and a fluttery collar. Jane thought it would look stupid on her, but when she tried it on, she realized her sister was right.

Jane turned to her. "Fine? She seems *fine*?" There was more to that tone.

Charlotte ignored her and focused on Jane's outfit. "I'd wear this"—she held up a long jean skirt—"and these." She held up tan-colored boots. "But it's up to you."

Of course, these looked great together, and Jane would

not have chosen them otherwise. "Thank you, sis," she said. "I am nervous. More than I should be." Jane felt that familiar apprehension. She couldn't put her finger on it, but she felt like she wanted to disappear.

"You'll be fine," Charlotte said quickly. "Big shindigs like this are not your thing. But you'll be okay. You're an introvert, sure, but if you find one person you can talk to for a bit, you usually do better."

She hugged Charlotte, harder and longer than she had in a while. "I forgot how much I had missed you."

"Same," she said, and hugged Jane back until they were both ready to let go.

The entire ride there, Jane noticed how happy Eric seemed. He was even singing in the car, out of tune and badly, as he drummed his fingers on the steering wheel.

"This will be great," he said, thinking out loud on the way there.

Jane was quiet, trying to calm her nerves. Parties with new people weren't necessarily her thing, but knowing there was a chance for Eric's ex to be there made it even worse. She felt the back of her head, trying to embrace her short hair. She heard Mrs. Ferch's words in her head: *Be confident.*

Over the past few days, she and Eric had talked about many things. He already seemed to know her so well.

"I won't leave your side if you don't want me to," Eric whispered to her as they approached the crowd.

"No, I don't want you to do that. You don't have to

babysit me. I'll be okay."

"I know you will," he said. "I've met introverts before, you know," he teased her. "In fact, I knew you were an introvert before you told me. I noticed how you paused and thought about things, even on that first date at the art fair."

Looking back, she also thought of the art fair as their first date. On the surface, they enjoyed themselves and had a great time, but beneath all that, she had a boyfriend, and he was moving.

"I'll clue you in on a secret," Eric said, coming close to her before they entered. "I like watching you think. It's very cool." He kissed her neck and she giggled, feeling ticklish and turned on all at the same time.

"Maybe we can go somewhere and make out later?" She raised her eyebrows.

"I'm counting on it."

They entered the party, and Wayne spotted them, waving and then coming up to greet them. *Hurricane Wayne*, Jane had begun to think of him as. He had that same big, gregarious spirit as before.

"Hello, there! So nice to see you again." He reached over and gave her a big, burly hug.

A beautiful girl with long, blonde hair and blue eyes stood before them. She gave Eric a hug which he half-heartedly returned, patting her side as she pulled away.

"Hello, Eric," she cooed, "And is this a guy from work?"

Jane felt at the lack of hair on her head once again.

Eric ignored her jab. "Tiff, this is Jane."

"Jane? I'm so sorry!" She put a hand to her heart. "I thought you might be one of Eric's work colleagues."

Eric took a deep breath, and Jane could sense that he was going to defend her, but Mrs. Ferch's words whispered in her thoughts once more: Be confident.

"No," Jane laughed, "there was a sale at Super Cuts, and I thought I'd take advantage. Now I don't need a haircut again for another two years. Nice to meet you, Tiffany."

"I like this girl!" Wayne clapped Eric on the back. "And your sister is cool, too," he said to Jane.

"Thanks," she agreed. "Everyone seems to love Charlotte."

Eric leaned into Jane, whispering, "You really are amazing; you know that?"

Tiffany stomped off, apparently bored with the conversation.

"Nice girl," Jane quipped, wondering what Eric saw in her, besides the beauty.

"She can be. But sometimes it takes you a while to get to see the real person under that snooty exterior. Oh, there's Maggie. Let me introduce you to Wayne's wife."

He took Jane by the hand and led her to where Maggie was setting out buns for the hot dogs and hamburgers.

"Mags..." He gave her a hug when they'd reached her. "I want you to meet Jane."

"Hi, nice to meet you." Jane reached out her hand and Maggie reacted slowly, looking at it as if it were a dead fish. Finally, she shook her hand while staring at her hair. "Nice haircut." She rolled her eyes and then turned to Eric. "Tiffany is looking for you."

"Yes, I saw her."

"She wants to have a private conversation with you." Maggie looked at Jane as she enunciated the word "private."

Jane could see Eric's jaw tighten.

"Well, you know what, Maggie? I'm not doing that. So, thank you for inviting me to this party, but Jane and I will leave now. I will call Wayne later."

Eric took her hand and led her back to the car.

"We really don't have to go on my account." Jane had never seen Eric angry before.

"We're not going on your account. We're going because my friends are behaving rudely. I'm not going to deal with it."

"Wayne was nice," she offered.

Eric stopped, and Jane noticed they were both getting out of breath from walking so fast. "He was. That's true."

"Eric! Buddy!" Wayne came running over. "You leaving?"

"Wayne, I'm going to call you later." Eric gave him a pointed look, and Wayne got a pained expression on his face.

"Okay. Jane..." Wayne reached out and gave her a sideways hug. "It really was nice to see you again."

"You, too."

"I don't know what happened, but I'm sorry."

"We'll talk later." Eric waved over his shoulder as he led Jane out of there. They got in the car, and Eric let out a deep breath.

"Have you been holding that in?" she ventured.

"I must have." He turned to her. "I am so sorry."

"It really wasn't that bad."

"No. It was. Because if we had stayed, it would have been much worse. I won't put up with people being rude to you. Maggie, especially. I expect that out of Tiffany. Maggie and Tiffany are friends, and I guess Mags thought she was being a good friend or something, but I'm not going to deal with snarky whatever-ness, when it comes to you."

"Whatever-ness?" She smiled.

"Pretty much covers everything."

"That was kinda dramatic. You know, the whole, *we're leaving unless you're nice* thing."

She was teasing him, and he laughed. "Yeah? You like that? Did it make me look cute?"

"I don't think you could get any cuter."

Eric had spent the rest of the day with Jane at her sister's house instead. They told Charlotte about Tiffany, and instantly, she felt bad for the girl.

"You really have to feel sorry for her."

Jane rolled her eyes at Eric.

"Um, I know you're trying to be nice, Charlotte," he said, "but Tiffany really is an unkind, *fake*, type of person."

"Yes," Charlotte agreed. "That's why I feel sorry for her."

Jane just shook her head. She wished she could be as forgiving as her sister sometimes. As they all sat around talking, Jane wondered what would have happened if she had ever followed through with any of her attempts to visit her sister over the years. Would she have wanted to move there? Would she have still, somehow, met Eric? Life had so many twists and turns that it was a wonder we managed to follow the right path at all, she thought.

They all settled in to watch a movie, with Eric and Jane holding hands on the couch and Charlotte and Bill each in a chair. Sally sat on the floor, snuggled up in a blanket. It was the calmest and safest Jane had felt in years. More than that, it all felt like home.

The next day, she packed and dressed for the plane, and then sat down on the bed and called Bug. She explained to him that she had decided to move out to Seattle and would be giving her notice. He said he was sorry and was disappointed. But that was it. It was done. She walked out by her sister, who was cleaning up the kitchen.

"Charlotte, guess what?"

"You realized you adore Eric, you love Seattle, you love me more, ha!, and you're moving here." Charlotte said it in the most bored, passionless way. She was wiping the countertop after making a late breakfast for Sally. She was joking, but Jane would be the one to get the last laugh.

"Yes."

"I wish. So what time is your flight? When do we have to leave?"

"Charlotte. I'm serious. I just called Bug and gave him my notice."

Charlotte was quiet.

"Charlotte?"

"If you are joking about this, Janey, I will never forgive you." It almost sounded like Charlotte was near tears.

"Charlotte," she said softly, "I've been a fool. I miss you like crazy. The last few days have showed me that. I have loved exploring this city. I need a change. And, I want to get to know Eric. I don't care how long we dated. I'm done trying to reason it all logically. I'm taking the leap, Charlotte. And I'm so, so happy about it."

CHAPTER 33 - GRACE

Jane told both Mrs. Ferch and Grace that she had "big news" to share with them, so Grace invited them over to her house for lunch.

"Coffee?" Grace asked Mrs. Ferch, gesturing to her new coffee machine.

"Did you buy one of those, too?"

"I'm afraid it's all your fault," she admitted. "Your variety pack of coffee flavors sucked me in."

"You'll love it," the woman promised. She pointed to the one she wanted, and Grace made the drink and placed it before her.

"So," Mrs. Ferch started, "do you think Jane's news is anything other than that she is moving to Seattle and is in love with Eric?"

"Not a chance. That's definitely it," Grace replied.

They shared a laugh at that while they waited for Jane.

"I'm glad you asked me over, Grace. I've enjoyed seeing your place. The teacups on the shelf are simply charming."

"What's left of them." Grace shared the story of the day with the bird who broke cup by cup. Mrs. Ferch laughed and cringed and covered her face. "I can just see you trying to stop the little guy from kicking them off, one by one."

"We've had a lot of good memories here," Grace said, "but we're actually getting ready to put the place up for sale." She couldn't believe she had said it out loud.

"You are?" The woman drank the coffee and eyed Grace. "Change of scenery. New place, new memories."

She nodded. "You've got it. And, now that we've decided to, um… move on… with things, it'll help to clear out some of this debt. We accumulated a lot between adoption fees and medical bills. We want to get out from under it, and the only way we can see it is by selling."

Mrs. Ferch listened closely to her. "Are you sad about that, Grace?"

"Yes," she admitted, "and also, no. I am looking forward to the next step and whatever it brings. It's been a long haul, and while I'll always be sad that we didn't have the family we wanted, I will not complain about our good life. And it is good. I am looking forward to living, finally just living, and enjoying life with John.

"If we can sell this place and pay off our debts, that will help. While I love this house, there are also things that bring back haunted memories. The room our baby was supposed to be in, the living room where I had the first miscarriage, and even the mailbox where I got the letter that led to my final miscarriage."

Mrs. Ferch frowned. "You mentioned that. Tell me more about that, honey."

The woman was quiet and listened to the entire story: the happiness at that pregnancy, walking to the mailbox, the letter, the mean-spirited words from someone she didn't even know, and when Grace finished, she was quiet.

"I guess," Grace went on, "I just wasn't prepared for

something like that. Maybe I wasn't tough enough—"

"Stop." Mrs. Ferch put her hand on her arm. "You should never have to be prepared for a letter like that. My God." She shook her head. "You two have been through it. People should support you in these troubles, not add to them with negativity and attacks and putting so much pressure on you that the family you are trying to build cracks little by little.

"In my day, when Seth and I couldn't have kids, my mother-in-law was actually very kind. It was one of the things that helped me through. She sat with me, cried with me, prayed with me..." She paused as she remembered. "How different things could have been if you could have just had that."

"Thank you for being so understanding and for listening. And with this house? There are things I see that I've just neglected, like that garden and that crazy breezeway full of junk, and"—Grace shrugged—"I just want to start over."

Mrs. Ferch was contemplative. "Will John still have a studio space when you move?"

"We're hoping for that. He has a very tiny room right now, so if we can get a two-bedroom house or condo or apartment"—she shrugged again—"it will just have to be the right place. I don't know. We're open to possibilities."

"Hello, hello!" Jane called out from the back door.

"Come on in."

Grace offered her coffee, and she started laughing instantly. "You know, this whole thing started with coffee. Remember, Mrs. Ferch? You told me to talk to Eric at the coffee shop."

The woman winked at Grace and nodded at Jane, encouraging her to go on.

"Well..." Jane blew out a breath. "You're not going to

believe this…" She smiled so big, it made both the ladies laugh. "I'm moving to Seattle!" She held her arms out wide, as if to say, can you believe it?

Both Mrs. Ferch and Grace said in unison, "We're happy for you."

"Aw, come on," Jane whined. "Were you not surprised at all by that?"

They looked at each other a moment and turned back to Jane, shaking their heads.

She laughed. "I guess it was a pretty obvious thing to do. But you know what? I'm doing it for me," she added. "Being with Charlotte, hanging out with Eric, it just all seemed right. And there are a lot of artsy places out there, so I feel good about trying to find a gig. I have to be honest," she added, drinking her coffee, "I kind of had a feeling I would love Seattle."

"We had the same feeling," both Mrs. Ferch and Grace responded.

After several weeks, John and Grace began the long process of clearing out their home. They were still looking for places to move, and while they had twenty years of accumulation and memories in their home, both of them were anxious to get something smaller.

Jane had moved to Seattle and still talked to Grace often. She was happy for the girl. It was funny to think a year earlier she'd first met her at that art fair. How different their lives were back then. John was now at a gallery and regularly selling paintings. Jane was dating Eric and had no idea what her future held with him, but she felt more at home in this new life she had embraced. Grace wondered if God was at work in all this, clearing out the old in their lives and offering them each a new future.

She'd been talking with God more lately. She still could not bring herself to go to church with John, but now he regularly took Mrs. Ferch with him, and the two seemed to bond over that. She was happy for them. As a little girl, Grace had genuine faith, and then it seemed to change, with anger making every prayer more like an argument than anything else. She now spoke to God often, sometimes still with anger, sometimes with confusion, and sometimes, with gratitude. For the first time, she felt comfortable bringing it all to Him and each time, she asked Him to help her with whatever she was struggling with at the moment. She wished she could be like those people who praise God and always believe that He will fix everything, but for now, she was content to tell Him all her thoughts and listen to what He told her in return.

Grace had cleared out a couple of cabinets in the kitchen. The remains of bowls and glasses were scattered on the large kitchen island in the center of the room.

"Thatsa lotta bowls," John said, joining her.

"Is that supposed to be some kind of Italian accent?"

"The silly kind. The one they use to sell mozzarella cheese."

"I don't think they do," she teased him, "but nice try."

"I want to show you something," he said, leading her into his studio, which was now empty except for the old couch he kept in there.

"Where's your stuff? Your easel?"

"I'm glad you asked. Why don't you go out to the breezeway?"

She frowned at him. "What's going on?"

He pointed in the direction of the small space that was between their back kitchen door and the garage. It wasn't big enough for a room but was sizeable enough to store plenty of junk, like the skis they no longer used and the exercise bike that broke four years before.

"Out to the breezeway, woman!"

She did as he said, feeling his hand playfully swat at her bottom as she walked. She tried to grab his hand between swats, but she couldn't catch him.

The breezeway was completely transformed. All the exercise equipment was gone, and his easel and paints were set up instead.

"What the...?" She walked in, looking at how deftly he had positioned things. It was a tight fit, but she could see him working in there. She looked back at him, mouth open and feeling so much love for him that she thought she might just burst.

He nodded, pleased with himself. "I'm glad you like it, Mrs. Cambridge." He walked up behind her and kissed her neck.

"Are you sure you want to give up your painting room?"

He smiled down at her. "Well, the way I look at it is that I can paint in any small space. This is proof. So that will help when we're looking at new places. And, this will help when it comes to selling this house. We'll have a couple full bedrooms to show off our house, instead of one cluttered with painting stuff."

Grace looked around the space. "It is really tight in here. You won't even be able to store your finished pieces."

"It'll be fine, Grace. It's what we need to do for right now, right? If by some miracle we can purchase a new place that has enough room for a studio, then great. If not, I'm perfectly happy painting wherever I can."

She smiled up at him but was struck by a thought. All the items that used to be in the breezeway were suddenly gone. "Wait. Where did the rest of this junk go?"

He pointed to a spot behind the breezeway, to the backyard.

"Oh, come on!"

He laughed. "The guys are going to help me move it. It's only temporary."

She thought of how many changes they had made like this, moving furniture, anticipating one thing and then dealing with another. Sometimes "only temporary" could be very permanent.

He continued kissing her neck and moved his lips down her throat to the tops of her breasts. His hands roamed, working their way down her sides and up under her shirt. He had her bra undone before she realized that the breezeway wasn't exactly a private space.

"You do know we have windows in here, don't you?"

"We'll make sure no one sees."

He removed her shirt and moved her to the wall so their neighbors couldn't see in. She giggled as his hands roamed.

"Are you sure you want to dirty up your new painting space this way?"

"I can't think of a better way to christen it."

Grace finished the last swipe of paint in the old studio space. She opened the windows to let some air in and went out to the kitchen, where John was pouring himself a Diet

Coke.

"Can I get you one?"

"Sure."

He handed her a can, and she popped the top and took a sip. "I finished the walls in there. Thanks for cutting in for me. That's always the hardest part."

"Painting went fast in there. No furniture, I guess that helps."

He nodded, and they were both quiet, lost in their own thoughts. He always seemed to go with the flow, something she needed to do more of. It seemed to her that she had fought too much in the past, going against the tide of her life and feeling exhausted and confused when she washed up onshore.

"You're sweet, you know that?" she said suddenly.

He smiled at her. "So, I've been told a time or two. A fresh coat of paint always manages to make things better."

"You would say that. Ready to go?" They were having dinner with Mrs. Ferch later.

"Oh, this is fun." He rubbed his hands together. "For once I get to tell you to change so you look decent."

"Yes, Mr. Painter, you do."

"Need some help in there?" He gave her a playful look.

"We'll be late, but rain check." She swatted him on the butt and changed her clothes.

They knocked on her door and heard the familiar, "Come in, you two. Come in!" They'd been having dinner with her every week since they first met. It brought a comfort to Grace she thought was impossible before.

"We brought some flowers," she said, reaching for the vase Mrs. Ferch kept in the cabinet.

"How wonderful. Thank you both! Sit, sit," the woman urged. "I have chicken and dumplings tonight. My Seth used to love this meal."

It was another delicious feast. Week after week, Grace had been impressed that Mrs. Ferch seemed to want to do this for them. She would cook this big meal; they would clean up for her; they'd talk, and she'd send them home with leftovers. It had become an unspoken ritual for them over the last several weeks. They now blocked off their schedules for this dinner, and Mrs. Ferch no longer invited them but expected them. Somewhere along the line, it had become a new tradition for them all.

John and Grace had cleaned up and joined Mrs. Ferch in the living room.

"Can I get you two anything?" she asked.

"Are you kidding?" Grace said, "I'm so full, I might explode." She smiled. "You are a wonderful cook. Thank you for doing this for us."

"Oh pish," she said, swiping her hand through the air in the gesture Grace had now become so familiar with. "It's my delight. And this is what I want to talk to you both about tonight. I've been thinking."

She told them her plan. They were looking for a new place to live, and she had two apartments open and available. They were already there several times a week, helping her with chores or the yard, and she was grateful to spend time with them.

"I enjoy your company, both of you, so much," she finished. "And I'd love it if you moved in here. Now"— she held up her hand before they could speak—"I thought about what I'd like, and I hope it will benefit what you want in your life right now, too."

Mrs. Ferch told them if they would pay the taxes each year on her house, they could live there, with both apartments, rent free.

"You see," she went on, "I offered free heat and water as part of the rent package for Jane and Eric. I pay for the whole house anyway," she said, "and it was never a bother. It worked out well for all of us. And this way, John, you'll have an entire apartment for your studio. You can paint there, store your work, or even, Grace, you could set up a little desk for the work you do for the business."

It was true. Grace was now spending a great deal of time promoting his work, applying to shows on his behalf, and creating videos of him painting. She enjoyed it immensely, and while she still took on editing jobs, she hoped to work with John full time one day.

John, for his part, still enjoyed his day job, but he loved coming home and disappearing into the studio for a couple of hours here and there. While he did, Grace would read or knit or daydream. She was still trying to figure out her own passions, and having the time to herself allowed her to do that.

John and Grace looked at each other now. They had been searching for places on the East Side of Milwaukee, so moving in with Mrs. Ferch would be perfect for them. But they both had the same thought.

"Paying your taxes"—John calculated in his head—"does not equal rent, though. It's not enough. We would have to pay for more than that."

"Oh no, you see, that is where you are wrong," Mrs. Ferch added. "My Seth did very well in his job, and I have enough to pay for all that. But I do forget to put away for my taxes each year. So having you pay that part of it would help me, and I'm hoping the reduced cost in living will help both of you. You've been through so much, and it's about time someone helped you. And you know what? I would be pleased as punch if you would allow me to do that! You have both been such a blessing to me."

And she was to them, Grace realized. All because of a girl who went to an art fair, who lived in a building owned by an older woman with a generous spirit. How their lives were all blessed now because of it.

EPILOGUE

My journey started in a room filled with sadness, in a town called Milwaukee. I was painted by a man who had allowed his soul to open up and imagine me into existence. He poured his pain and hope into my canvas, and I showed the world that they could exist together peacefully.

I had lived for a time at a gallery, where every loving touch of my painter's brush allowed me to shine, to comfort each viewer and help them see their life clearer.

And then there was a day when the painter's wife stood before me in the gallery. She had seen me many times by then, each time with a mix of confusion and anger. She wondered if the image was her, and each time I tried to show her who it really was, the person who would hold her tight when she herself finally passed through this realm. The day she realized it, she stood before me for so long, I thought she might make herself a living sculpture, frozen in time, and unable to move.

Suddenly, she asked that I be removed so she could take me home, to a new place, different than the one I had been born in. This new home was upstairs in an old house in Milwaukee, one that had sunlight that filled the space and wooden beams that added warmth. That's where I saw him again, my painter. He smiled briefly at me, glancing in my direction with a quick acknowledgment and then turning to continue his work on another canvas.

I saw the other creations his brush had brought to existence, the pain and joy which were a part of them that he lovingly included in each work. They were hung throughout the space, each bowing to me in their own way as the one who came before them. I blessed them, seeing the painter's gentle hand in each creation.

Soon, the painter's wife was back, happily humming a tune while her husband painted. She wrapped me in paper, then cushioned me in a box, and I was on a new journey. There was a couple in Seattle who was getting married, and I would be their wedding gift.

I was unveiled the day after the wedding, and immediately hung in what would be my new home. The painter and his wife had given me to this new couple, along with a collection of teacups that once belonged to her grandmother. My painter straightened my canvas once more and nodded to himself, satisfied.

As they waved goodbye to the young couple, I still felt the painter's longing and his wife's pain, but there was an ease in them as well. I held their former dream in my arms and gave them a new dream to hold, one that could exist in the reality they currently lived in. As I did, I felt their hearts open up to the possibilities of unplanned joy.

At last, my purpose had been fulfilled.

THE END

ABOUT THE AUTHOR

Cherie Burbach spent a decade as a freelance writer, penning articles for places like the *New York Times*, NBC, *Family Circle*, *Christianity Today*, BBC America, and more. While she still writes, she now works full time as an artist.

She is a self-taught artist, painting almost every day with an intention to offer hope and encouragement. She also writes poetry and other works, and feels words and images are closely tied in telling a story of faith and confidence about the future.

For more on Cherie, visit her website, cherieburbach.com.

READER'S DISCUSSION GUIDE

Please note: These discussion questions may contain spoilers!

What is the title's significance to the story? Do most of the people you know live in reality, a hopeful future, or a dreamland of their own making?

Did you identify with Grace's struggle? Why or why not?

The Space Between Dreaming painting helps influence each woman to look at her future differently. How do you feel art helps us look at our lives? Can regular viewing of works of art expand your mind in a way that everyday life cannot?

Did you see yourself in the way Jane handled her relationship with Brad and her career? Why or why not?

When we meet Mrs. Ferch, she is in her eighties and lives a happy, positive life. How might she look if we met her fifty years before? Thirty years before?

Both Grace and Jane experience years of waiting for a certain desired outcome for their lives. Did you find yourself wanting to give either one of them advice? Do you find it is easier to have opinions on a friend's choices rather than making certain decisions for your own life?

9 781737 096269